SUNNY SIDE UP

JENNIFER L. HOLM & MATTHEW HOLM
WITH COLOR BY LARK PIEN

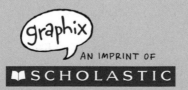

graphix
AN IMPRINT OF
SCHOLASTIC

Library of Congress Control Number: 2014957906

ISBN 978-0-545-74165-1 (hardcover)
ISBN 978-0-545-74166-8 (paperback)

10 9 8 7 6 5 4 3 2 1   15 16 17 18 19

Printed in the U.S.A. 88
First edition, September 2015
Edited by David Levithan
Lettering by Fawn Lau
Color by Lark Pien
Book design by Phil Falco
Creative Director: David Saylor

For Gramps

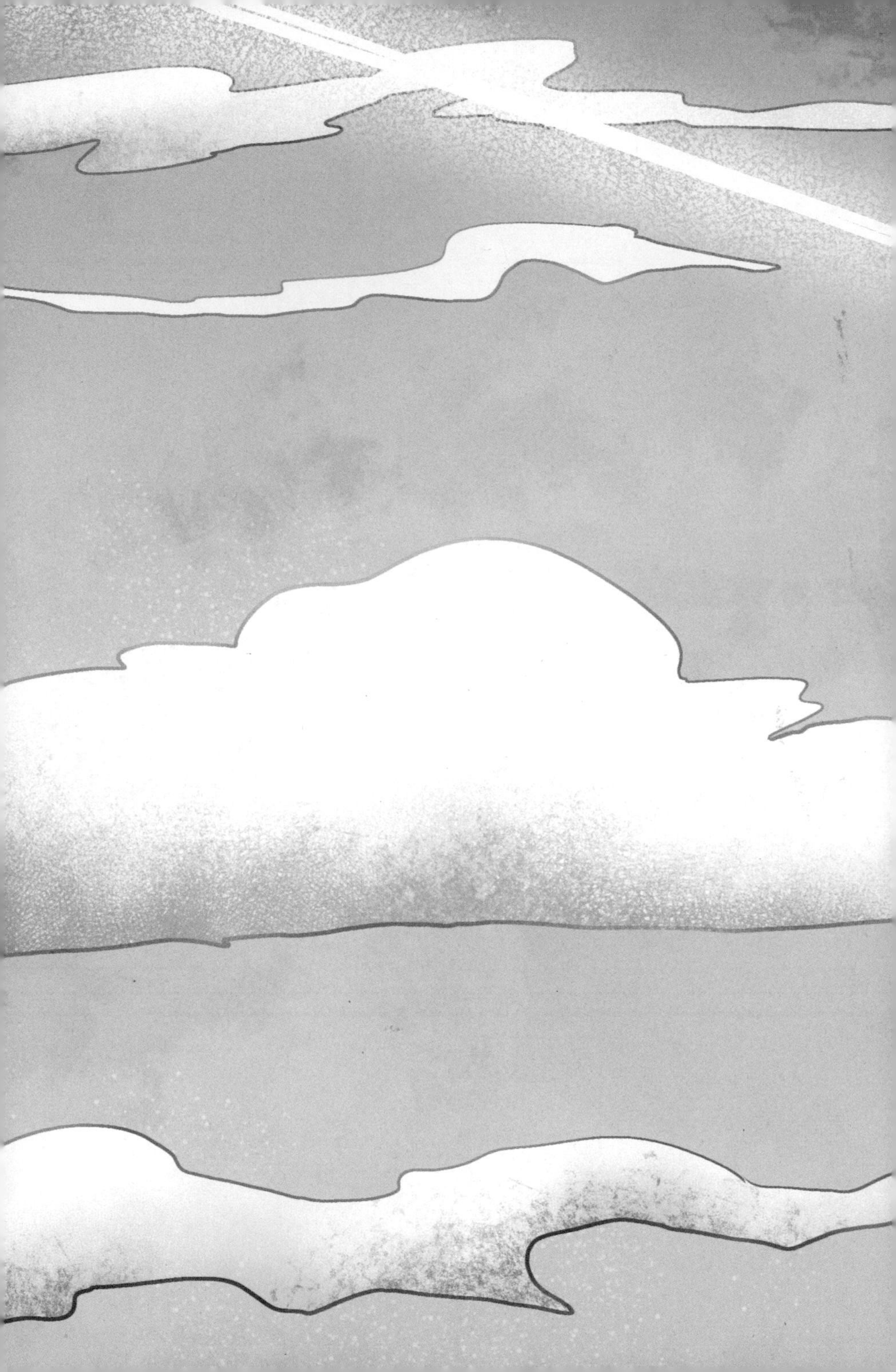

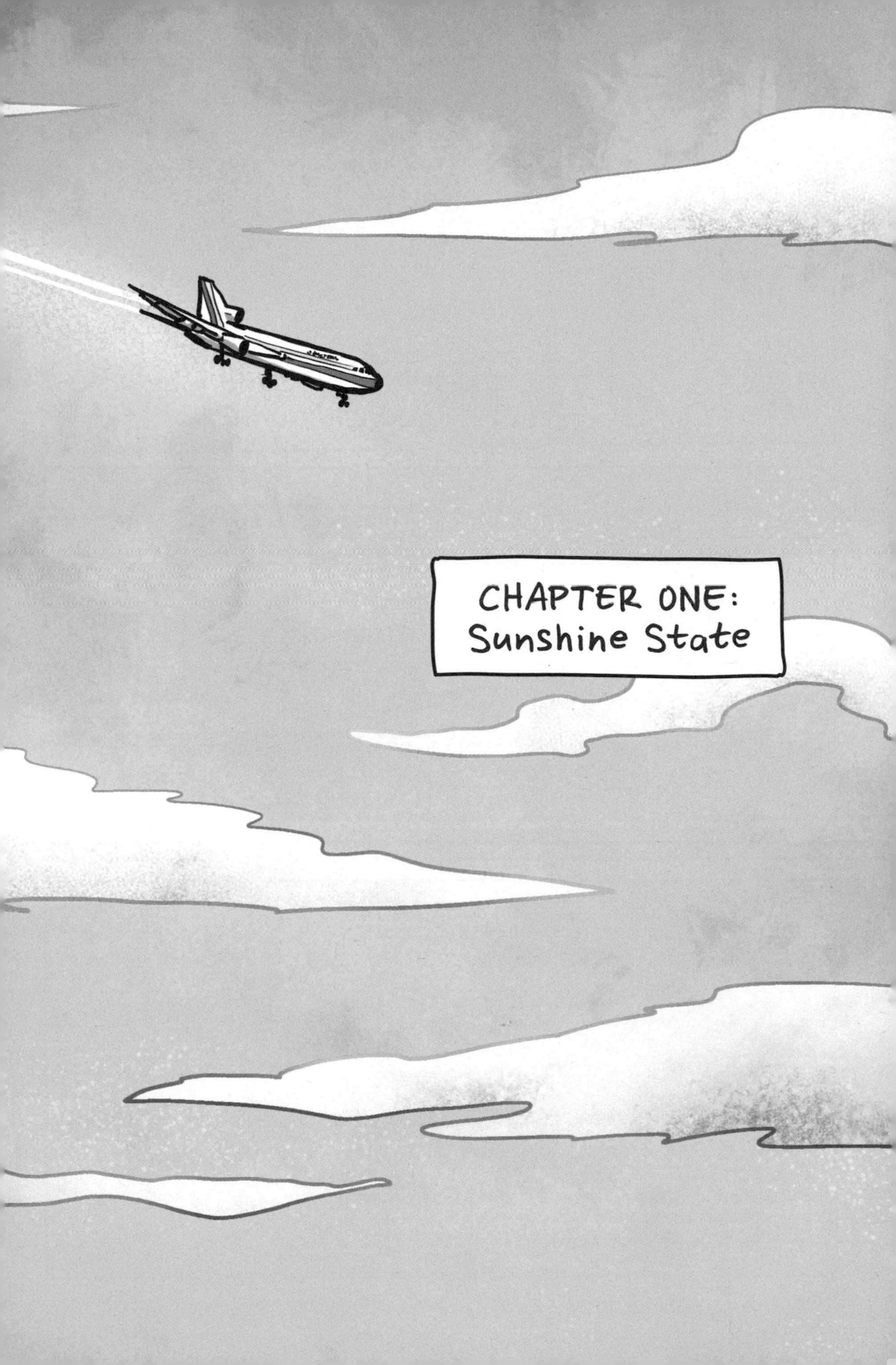
CHAPTER ONE:
Sunshine State

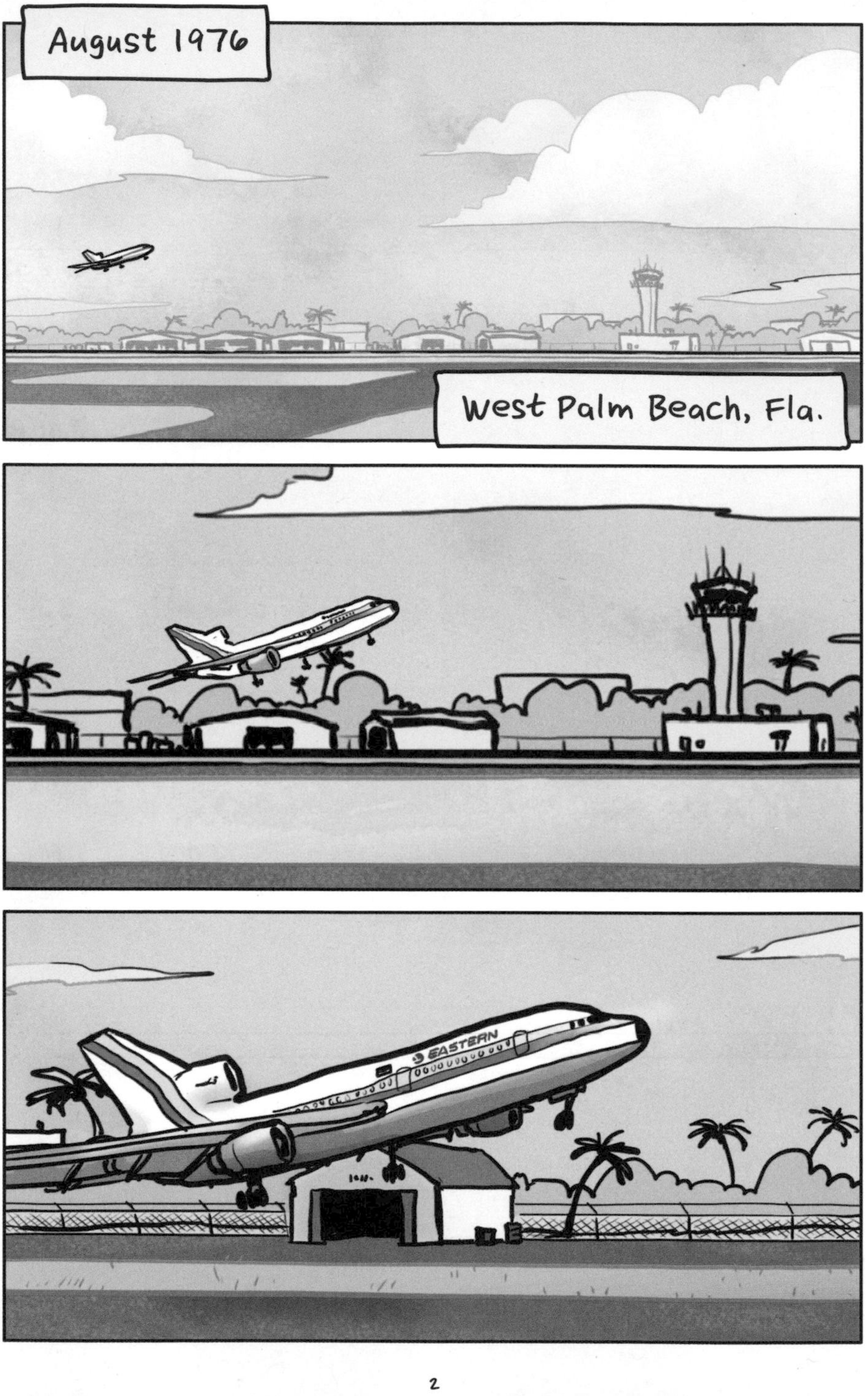
August 1976
West Palm Beach, Fla.
EASTERN

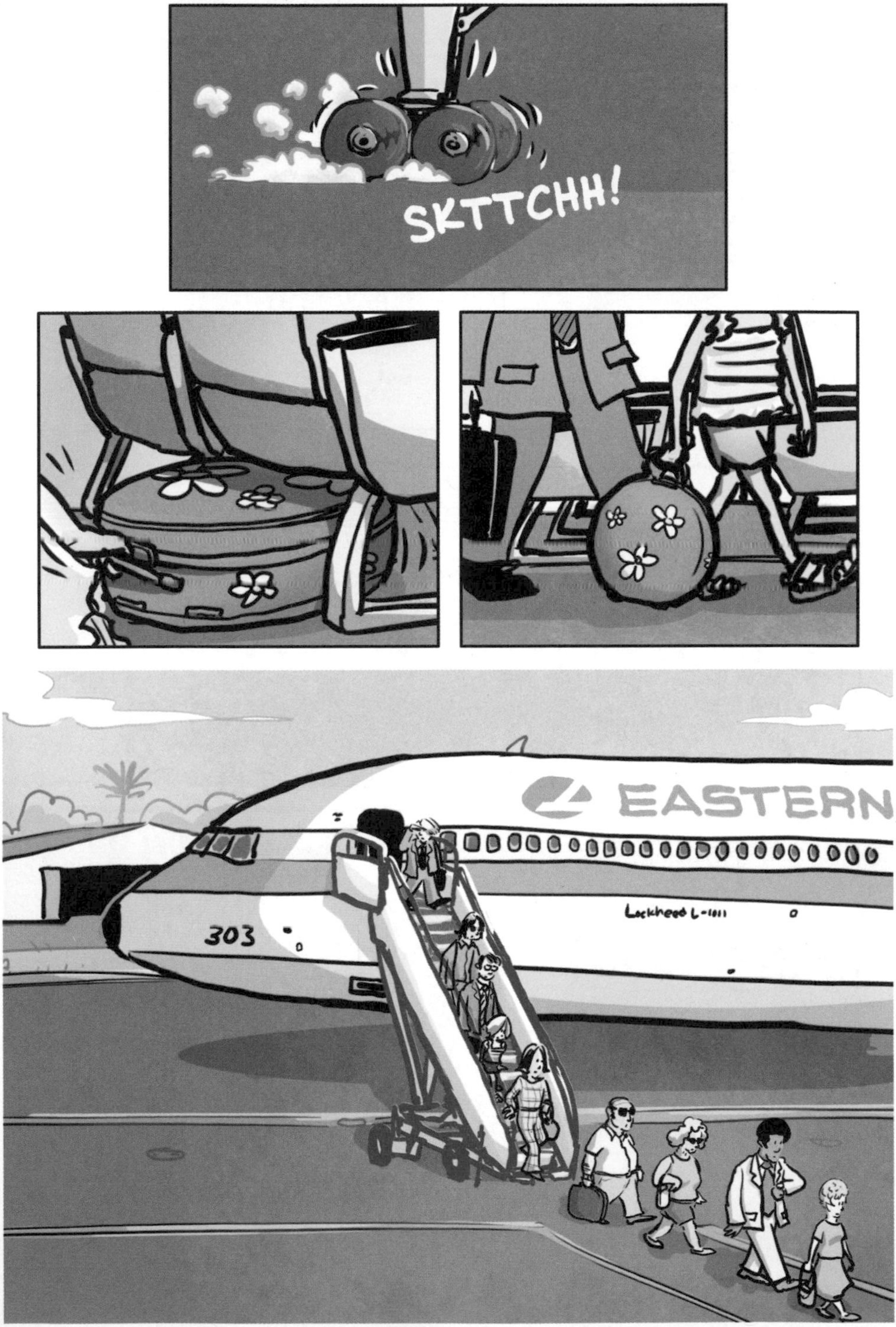
SKTTCHH!
EASTERN
303
Lockheed L-1011

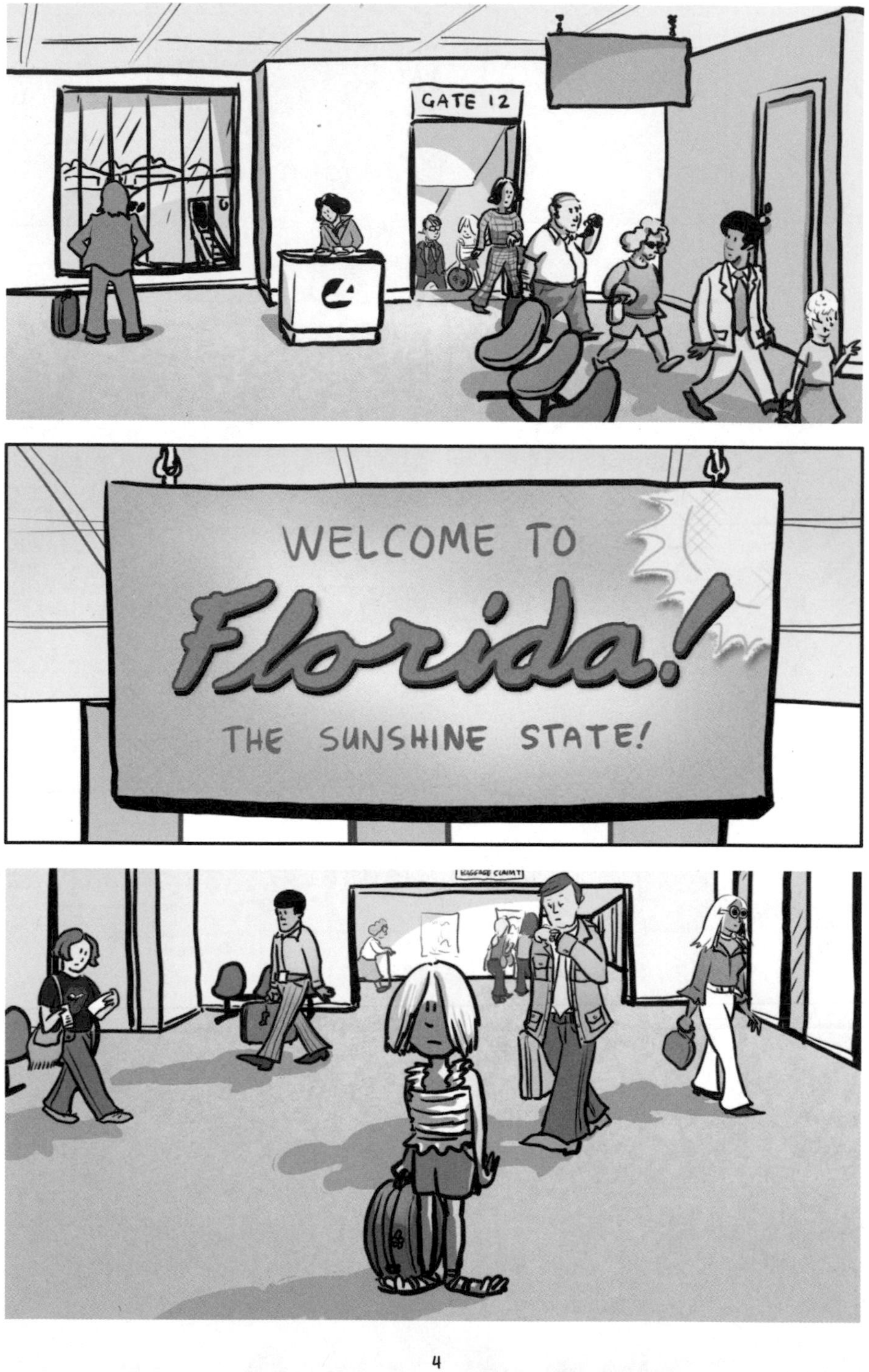
GATE 12
WELCOME TO
Florida!
THE SUNSHINE STATE!
BAGGAGE CLAIM

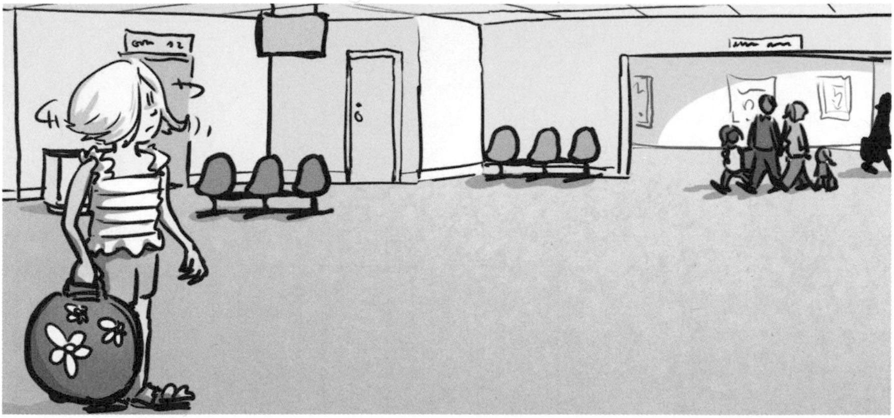

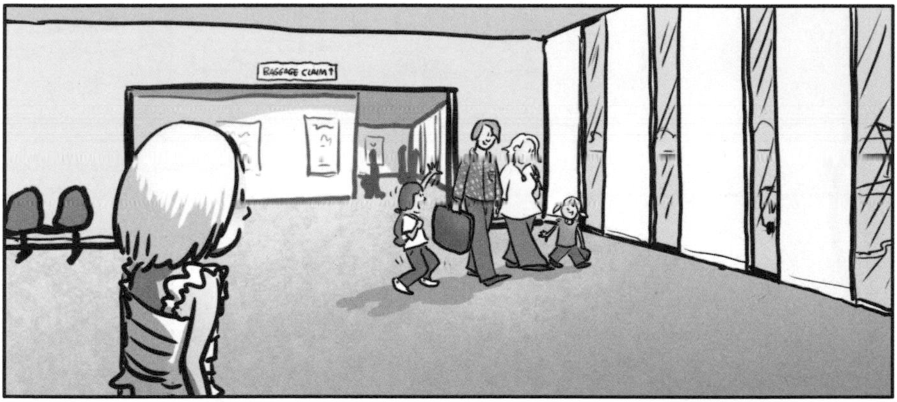
BAGGAGE CLAIM↑

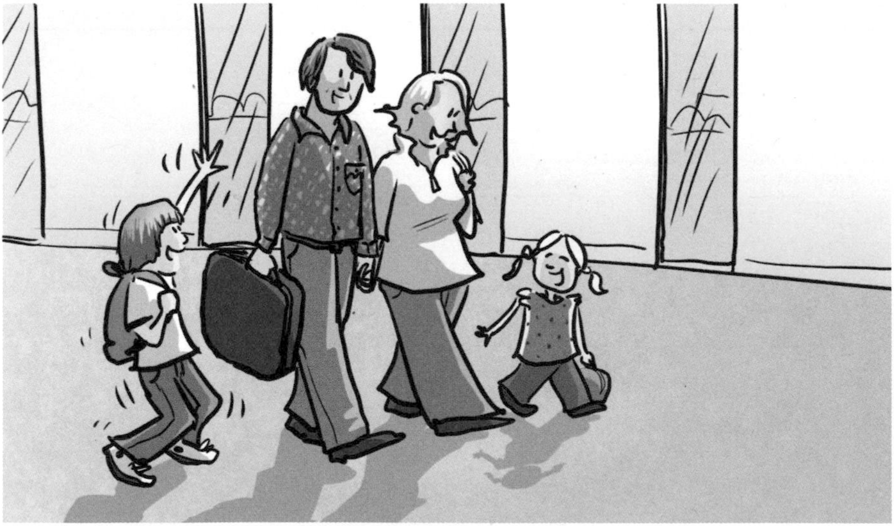

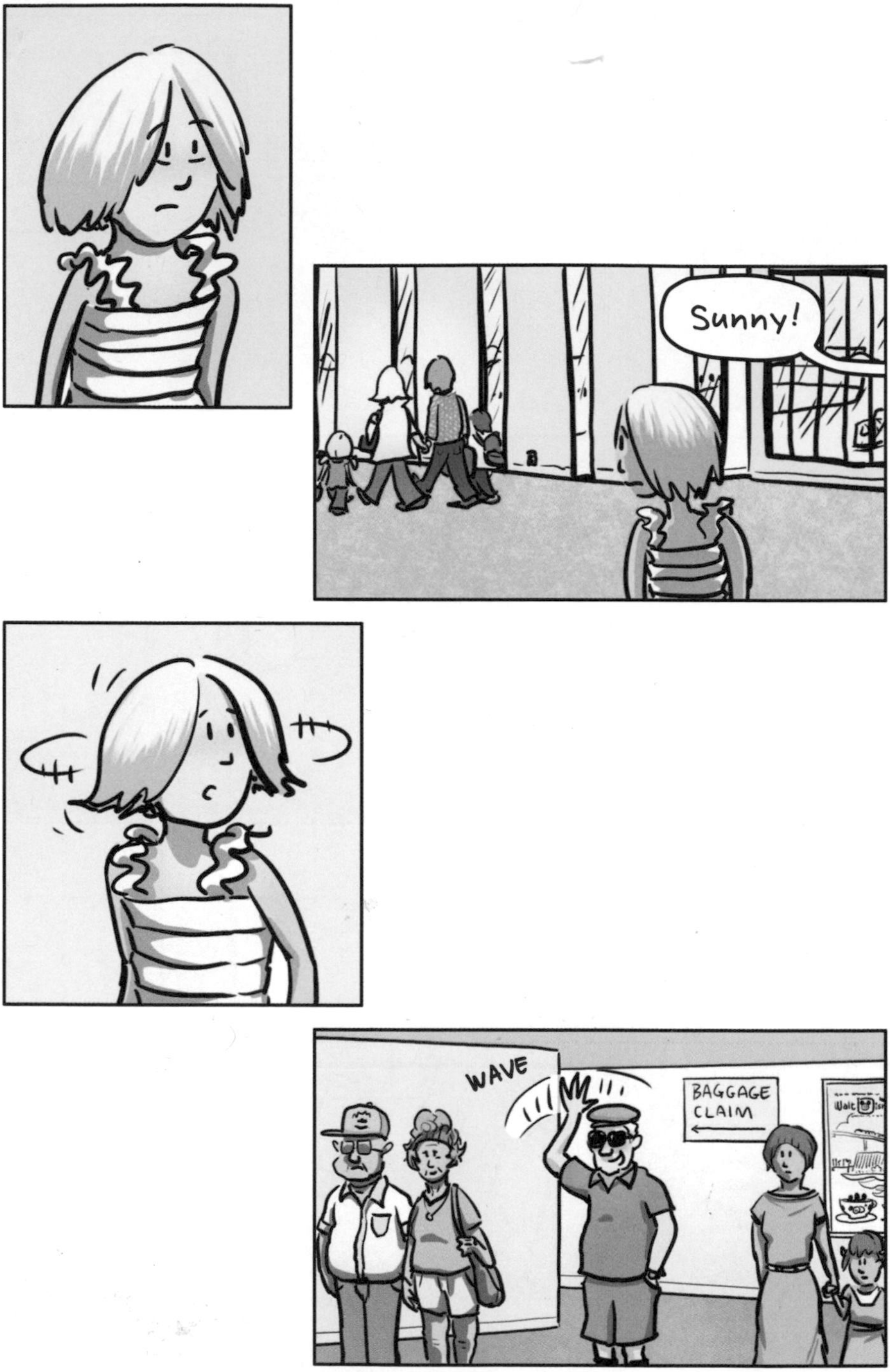
Sunny!
WAVE
BAGGAGE
CLAIM

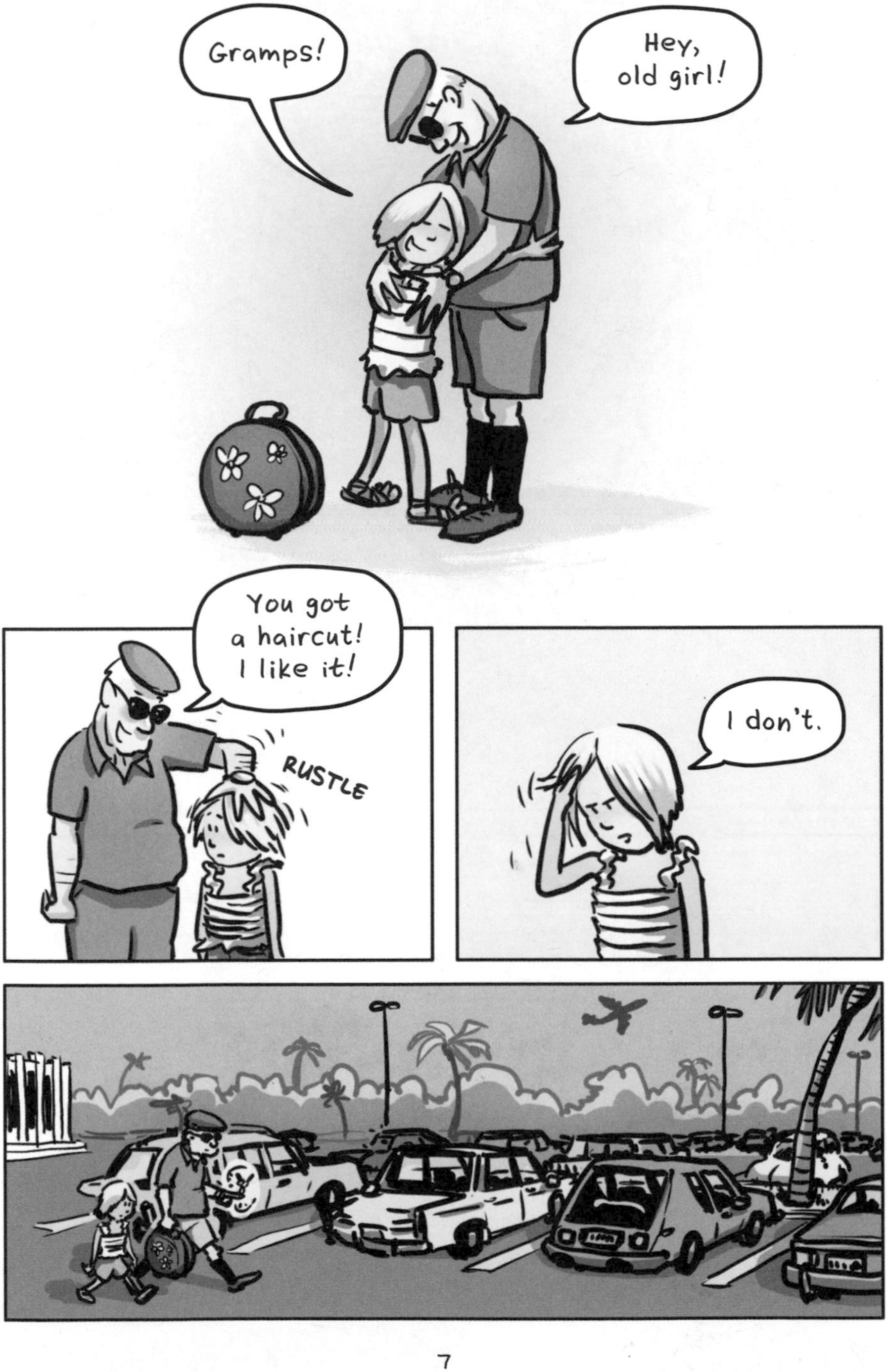
Gramps!
Hey, old girl!
You got a haircut! I like it!
RUSTLE
I don't.

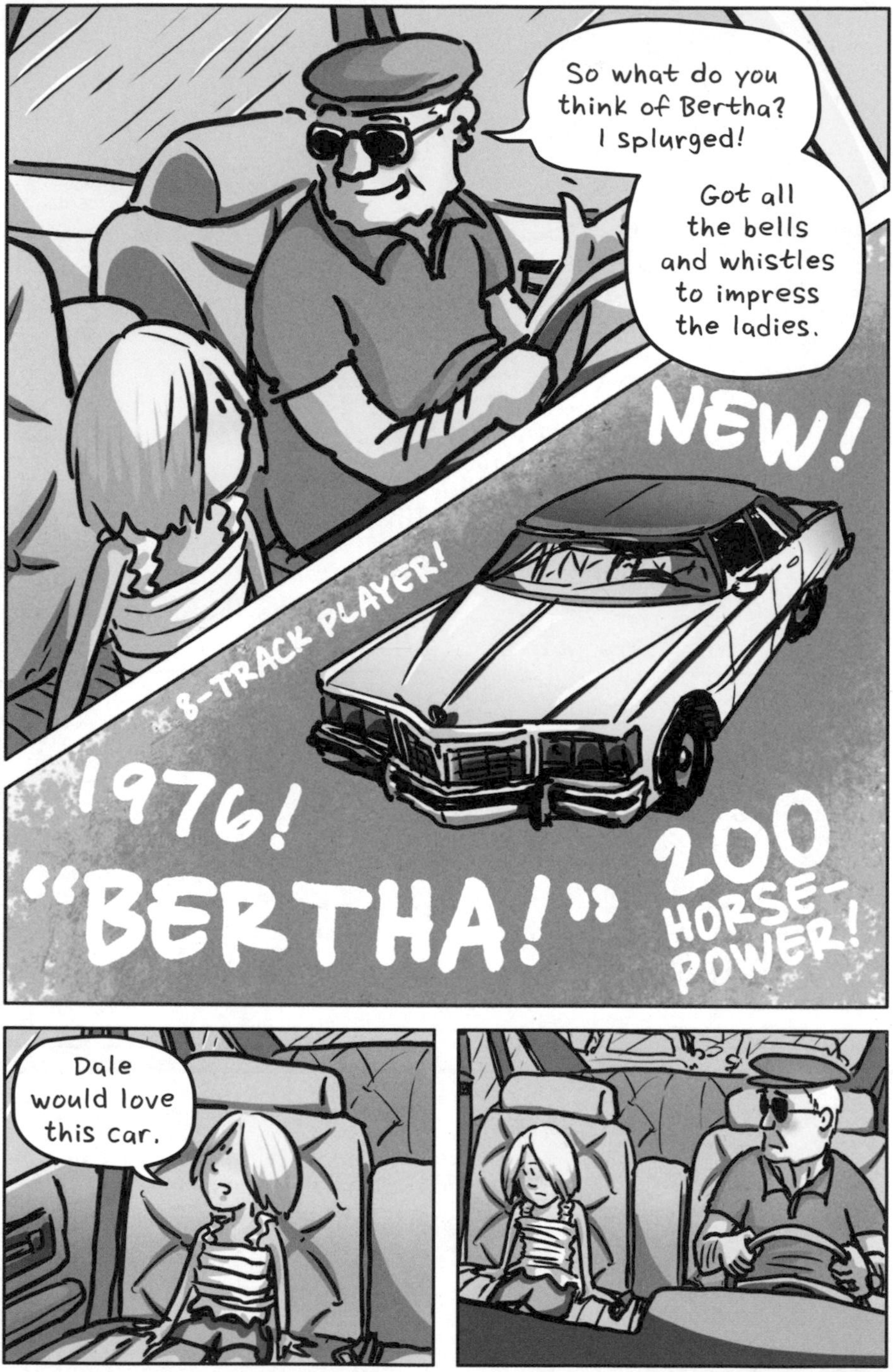
So what do you think of Bertha? I splurged!
Got all the bells and whistles to impress the ladies.
NEW!
8-TRACK PLAYER!
1976!
"BERTHA!"
200 HORSE-POWER!
Dale would love this car.

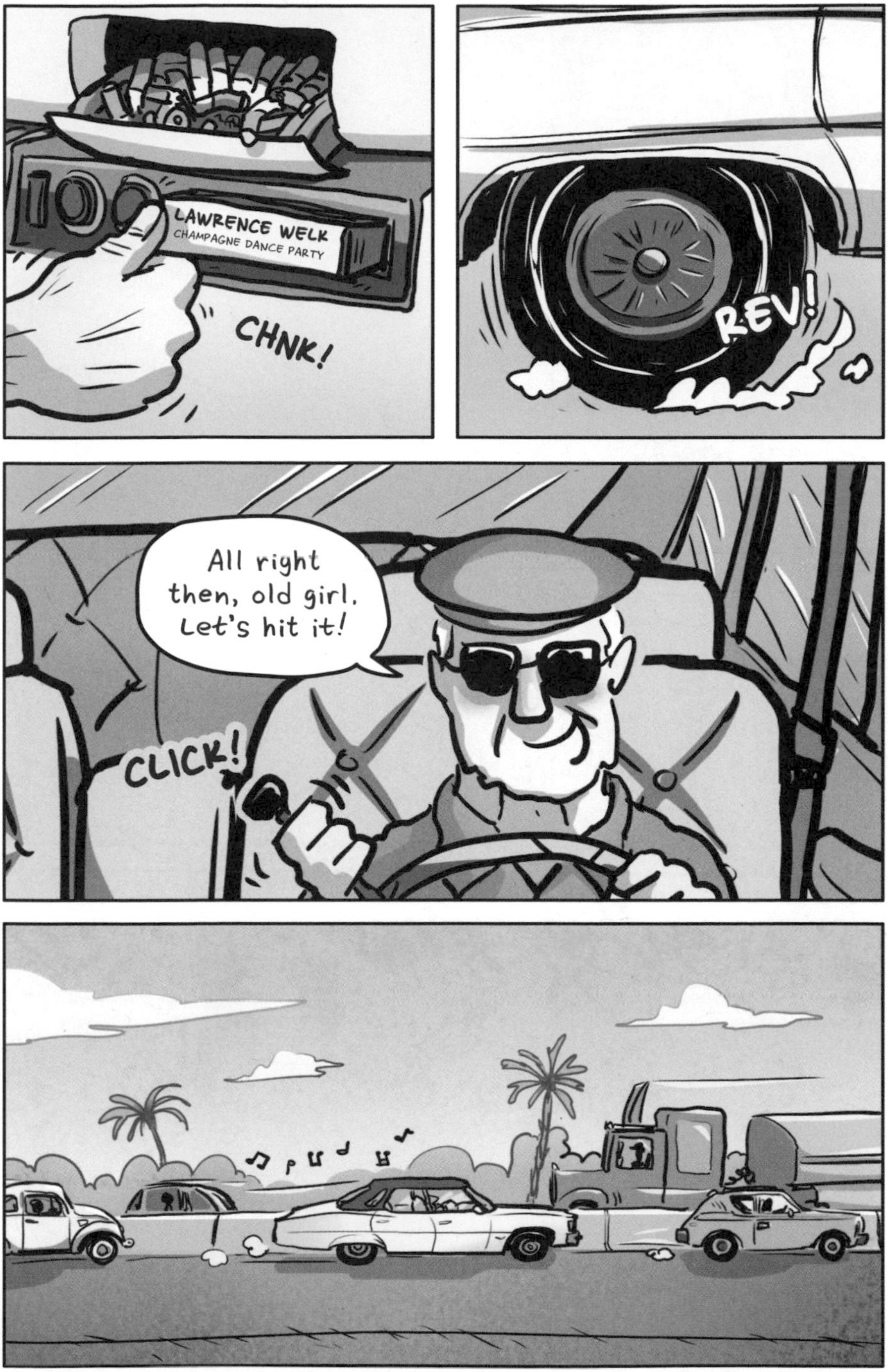
LAWRENCE WELK
CHAMPAGNE DANCE PARTY
CHNK!
REV!
All right then, old girl. Let's hit it!
CLICK!

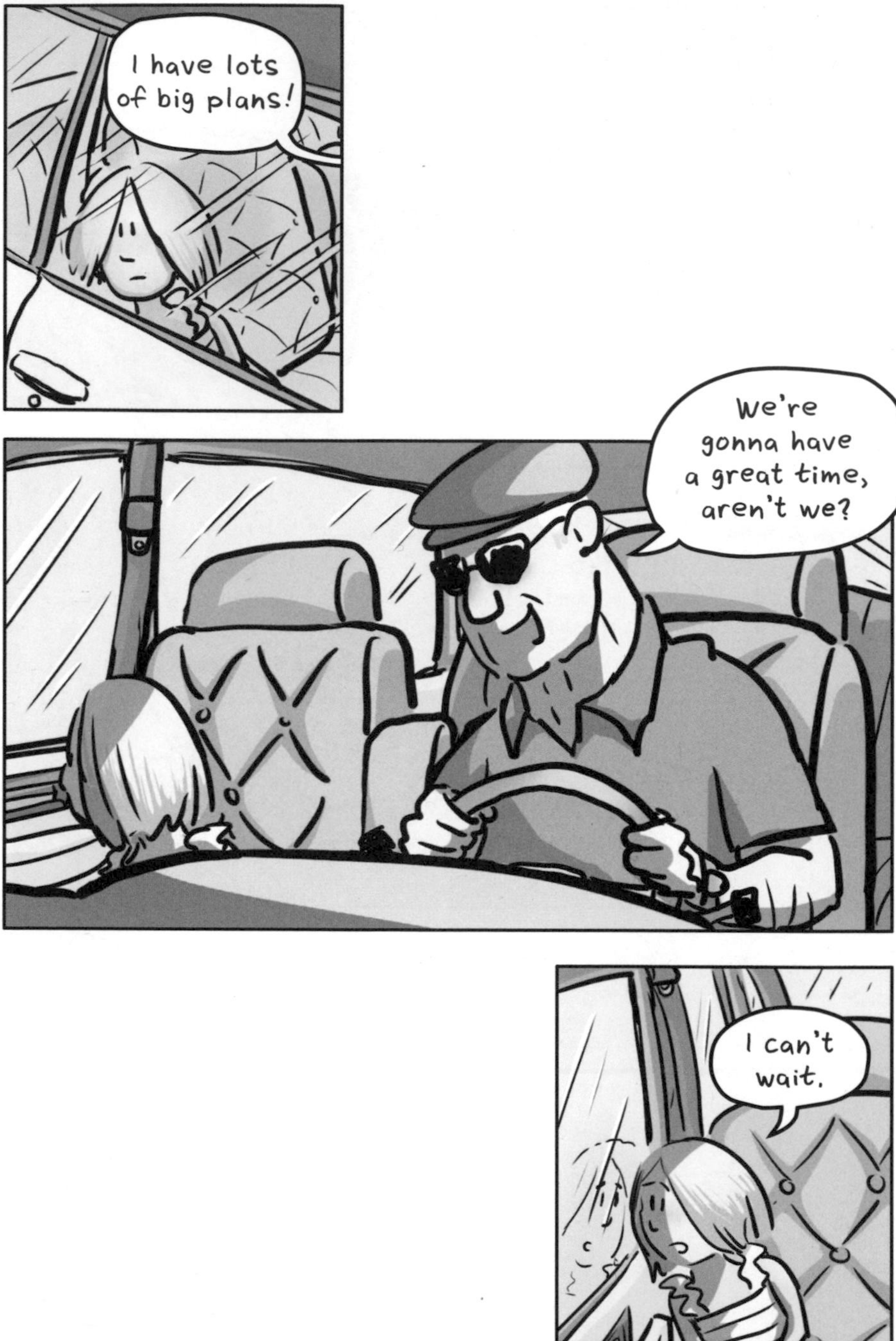
I have lots of big plans!
We're gonna have a great time, aren't we?
I can't wait.

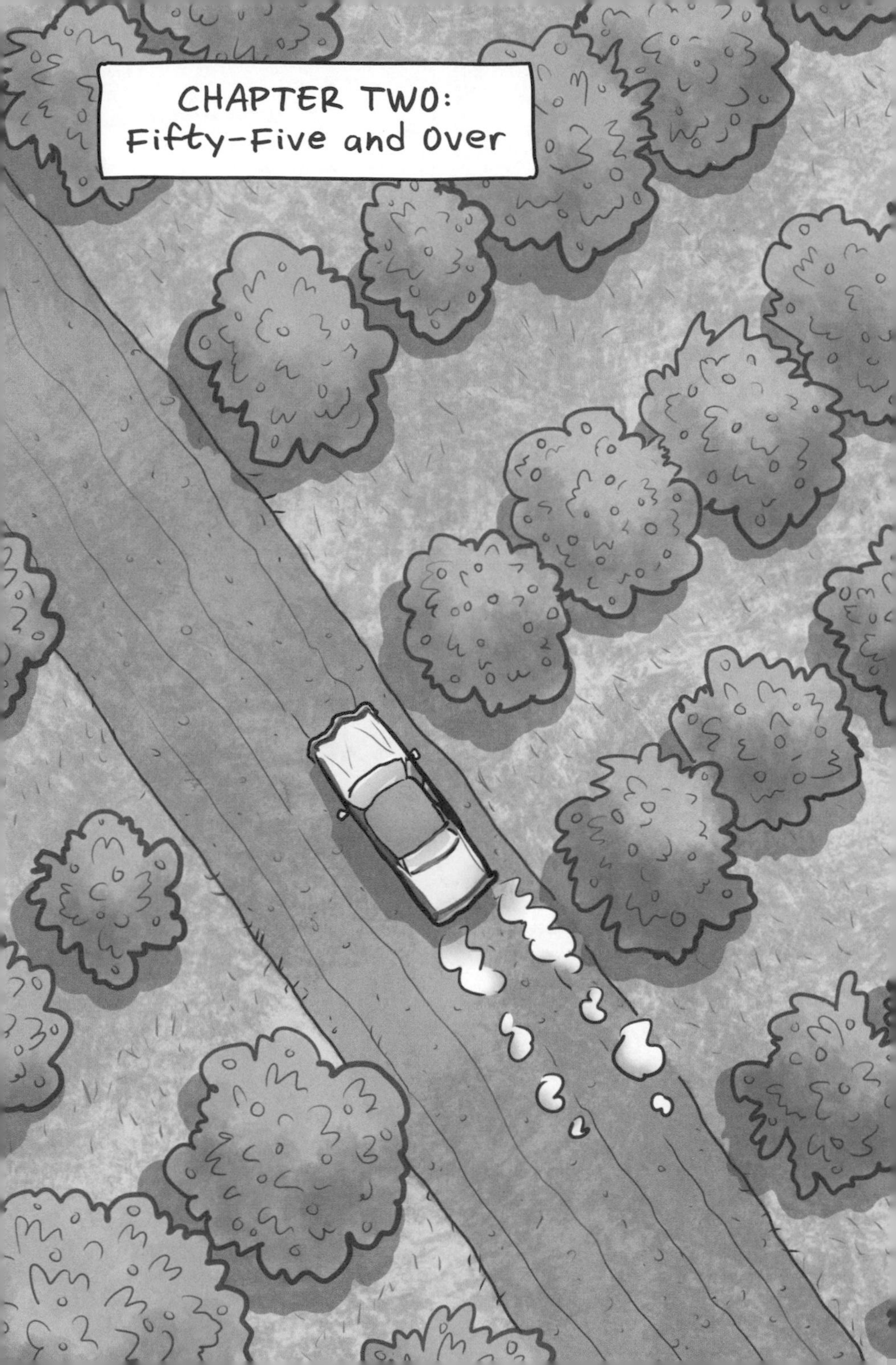
CHAPTER TWO:
Fifty-Five and Over

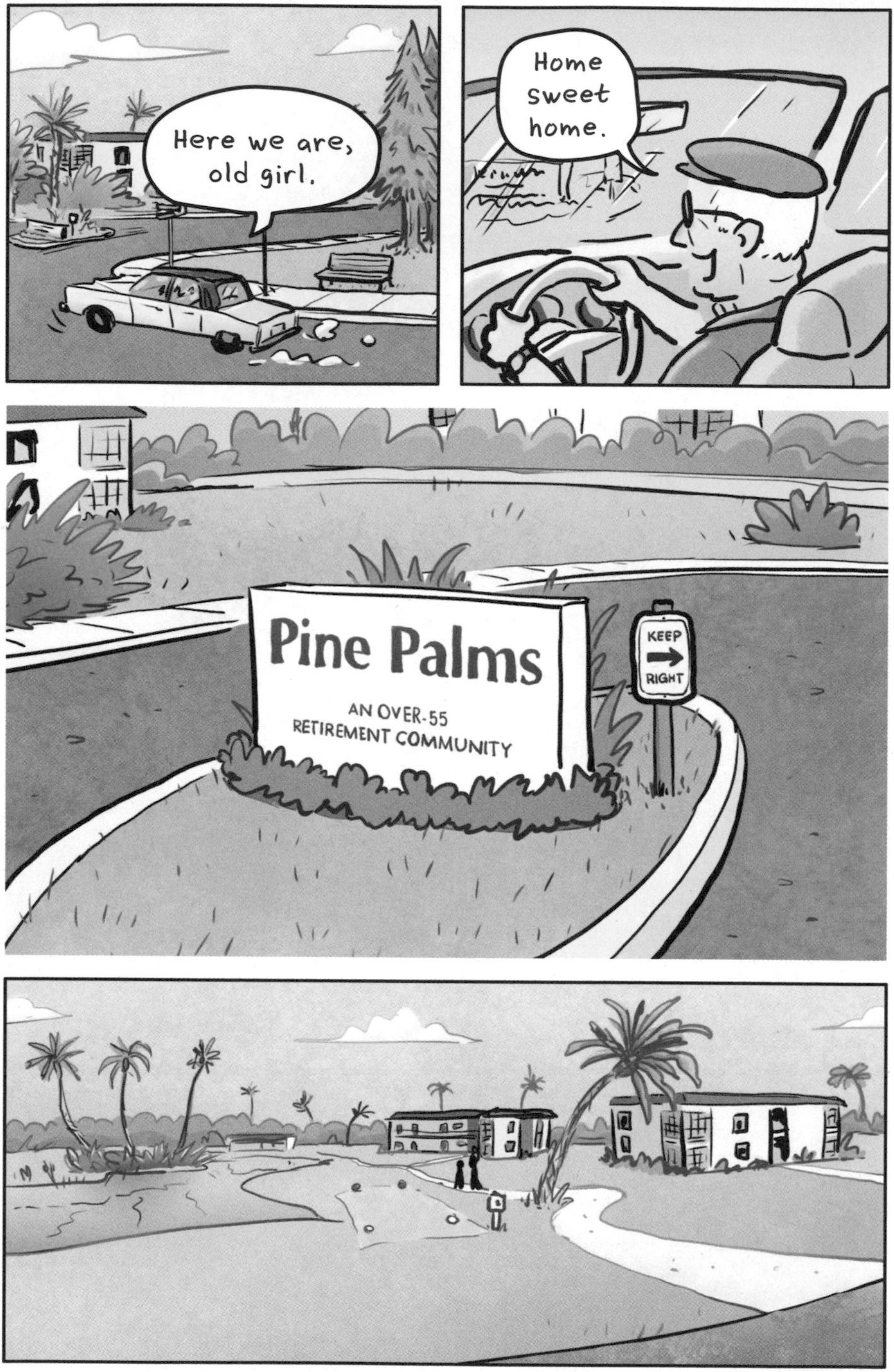
Here we are, old girl.
Home sweet home.
Pine Palms
AN OVER-55 RETIREMENT COMMUNITY
KEEP RIGHT

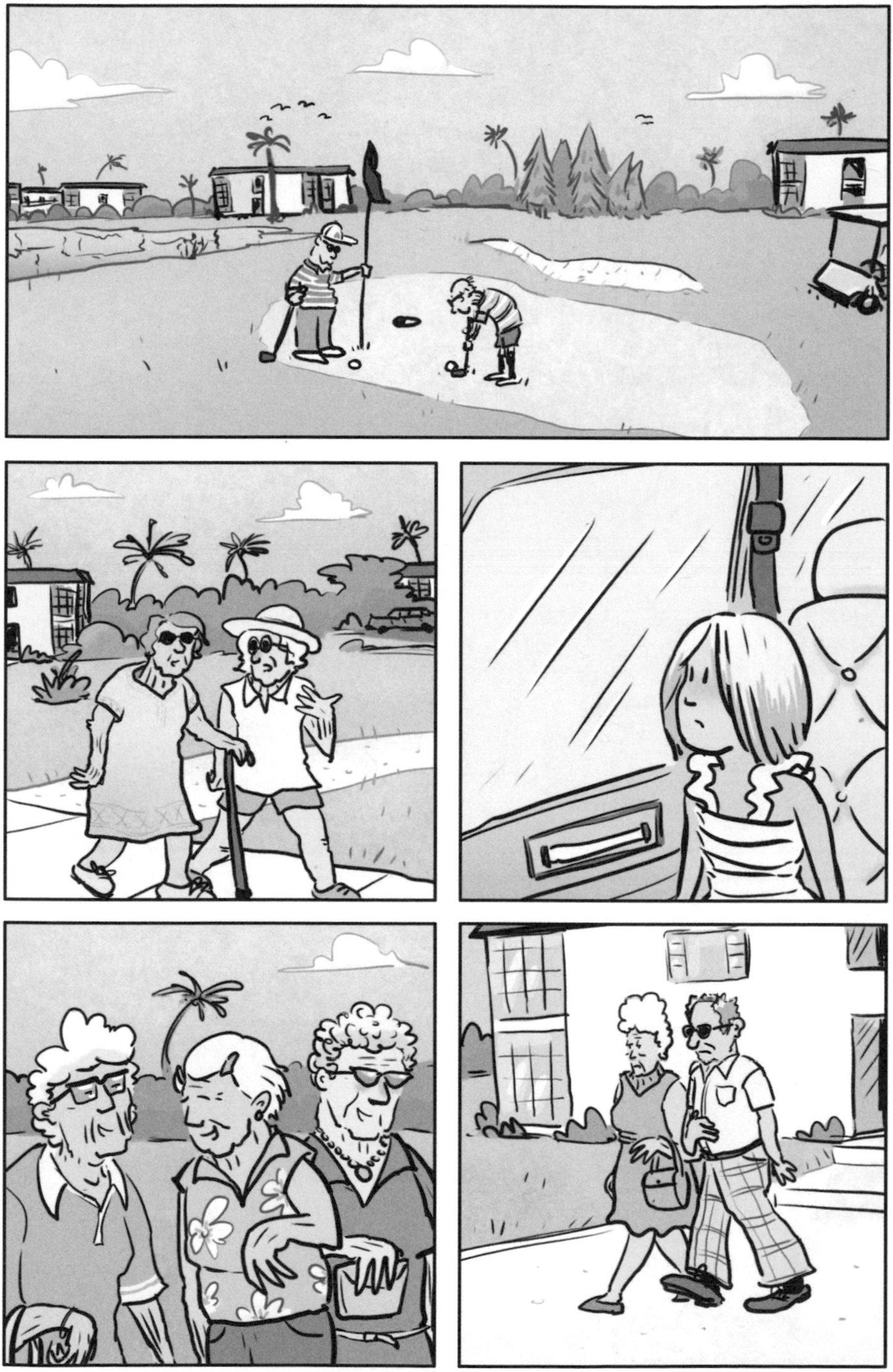

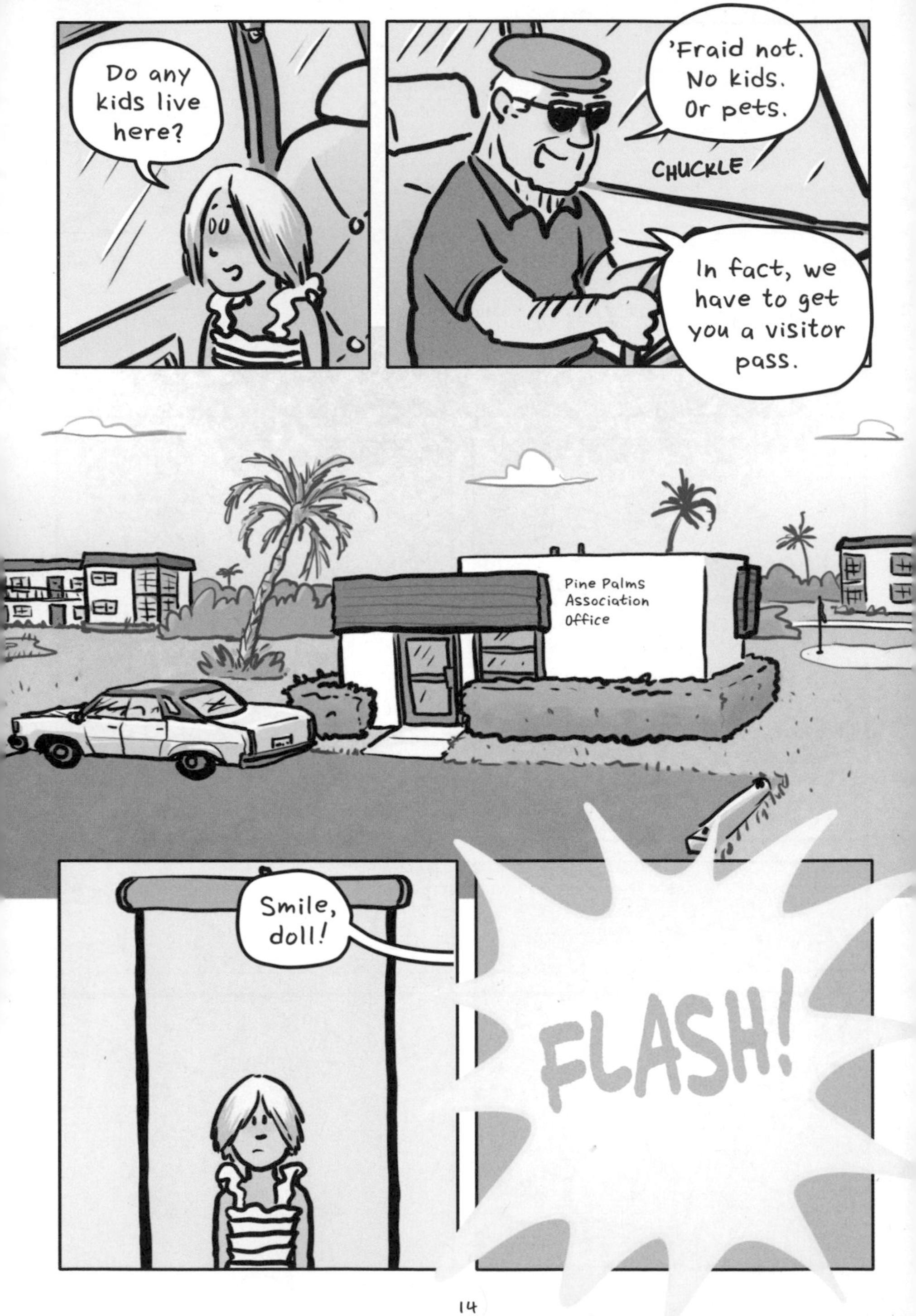

Do any kids live here?
'Fraid not. No kids. Or pets.
CHUCKLE
In fact, we have to get you a visitor pass.
Pine Palms Association Office
Smile, doll!
FLASH!

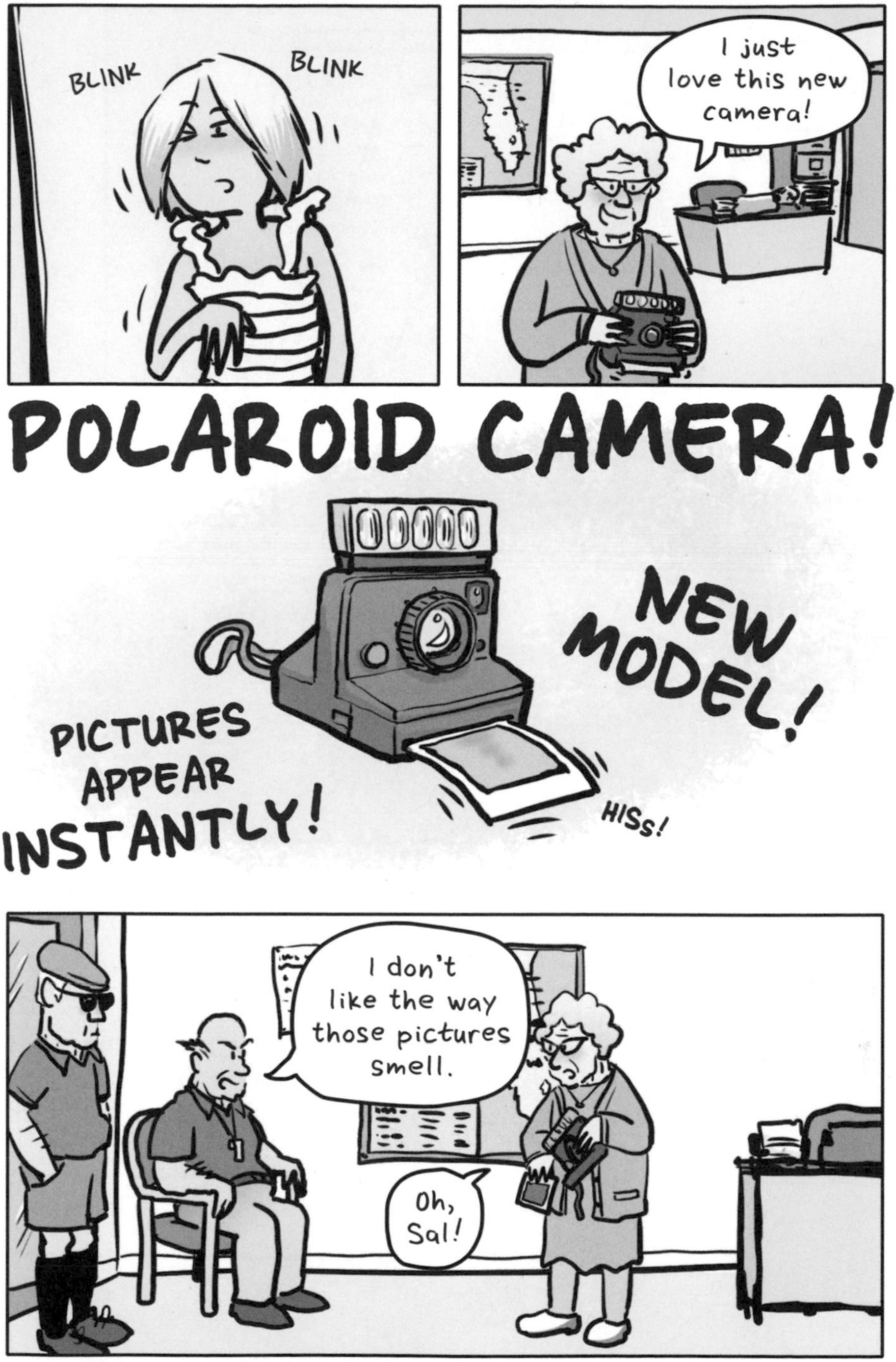
BLINK
BLINK
I just love this new camera!
POLAROID CAMERA!
NEW MODEL!
PICTURES APPEAR INSTANTLY!
HISs!
I don't like the way those pictures smell.
Oh, Sal!

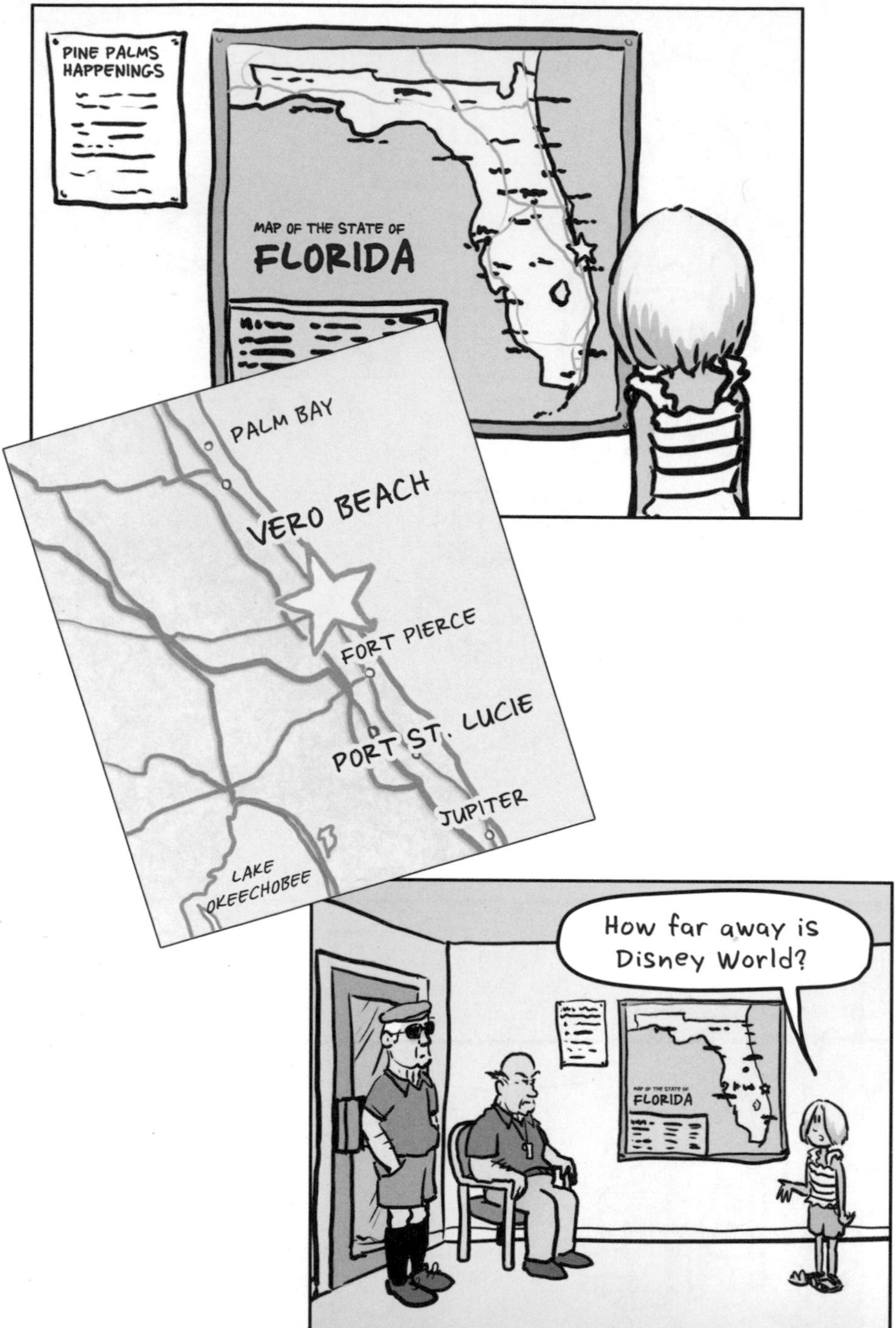
PINE PALMS HAPPENINGS
MAP OF THE STATE OF
FLORIDA
PALM BAY
VERO BEACH
FORT PIERCE
PORT ST. LUCIE
JUPITER
LAKE OKEECHOBEE
How far away is Disney World?
MAP OF THE STATE OF
FLORIDA

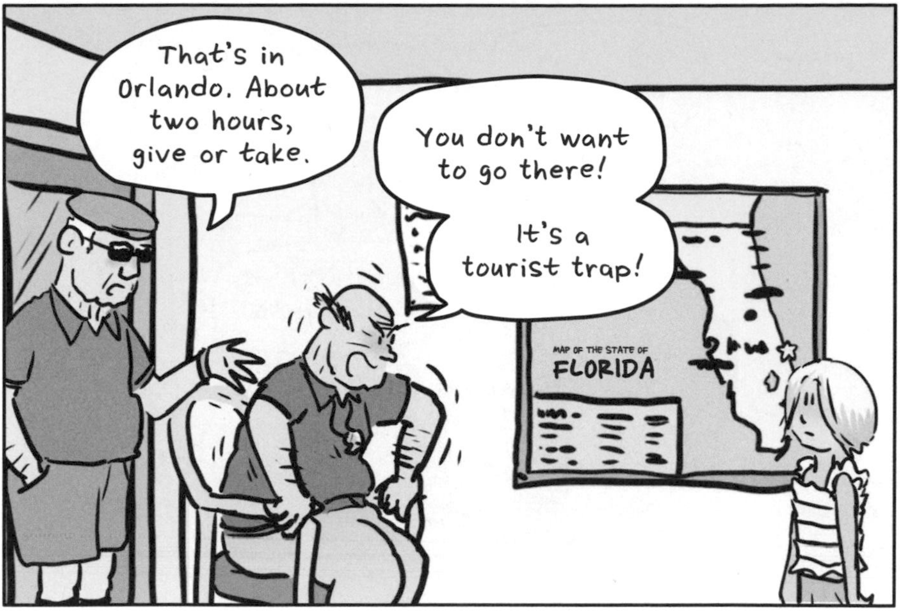
That's in Orlando. About two hours, give or take.
You don't want to go there!
It's a tourist trap!
MAP OF THE STATE OF
FLORIDA

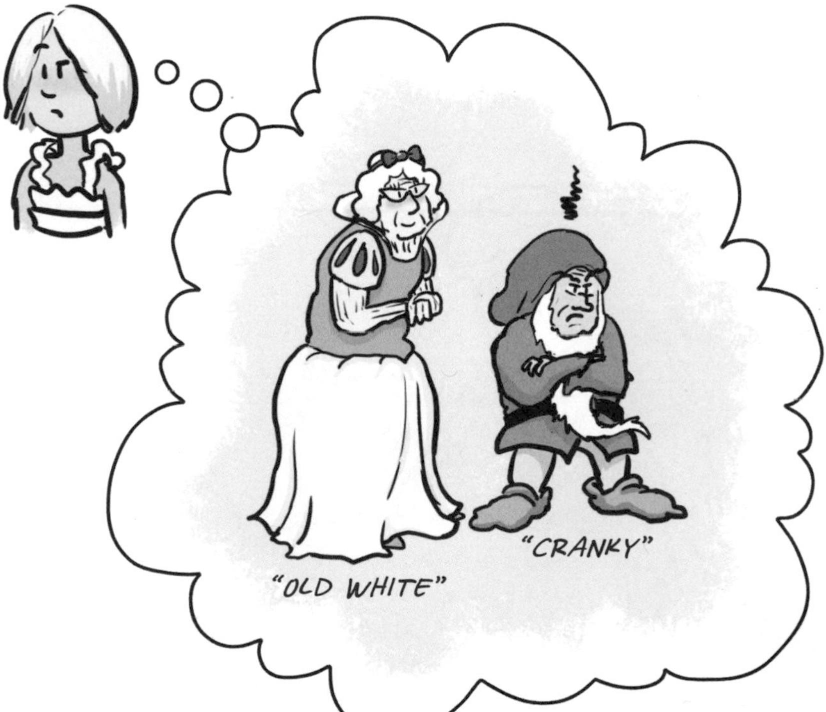
"CRANKY"
"OLD WHITE"

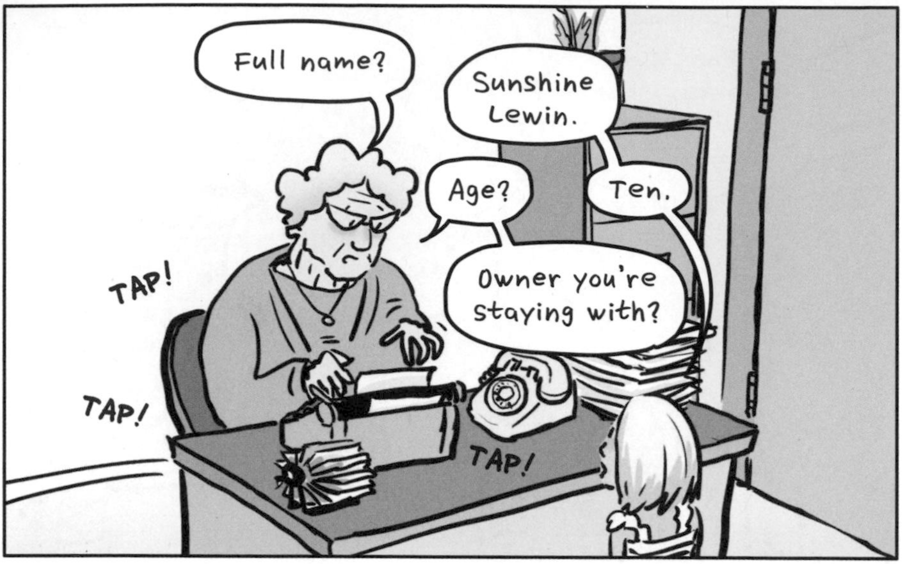
Full name?
Sunshine Lewin.
Age?
Ten.
Owner you're staying with?
TAP!
TAP!
TAP!

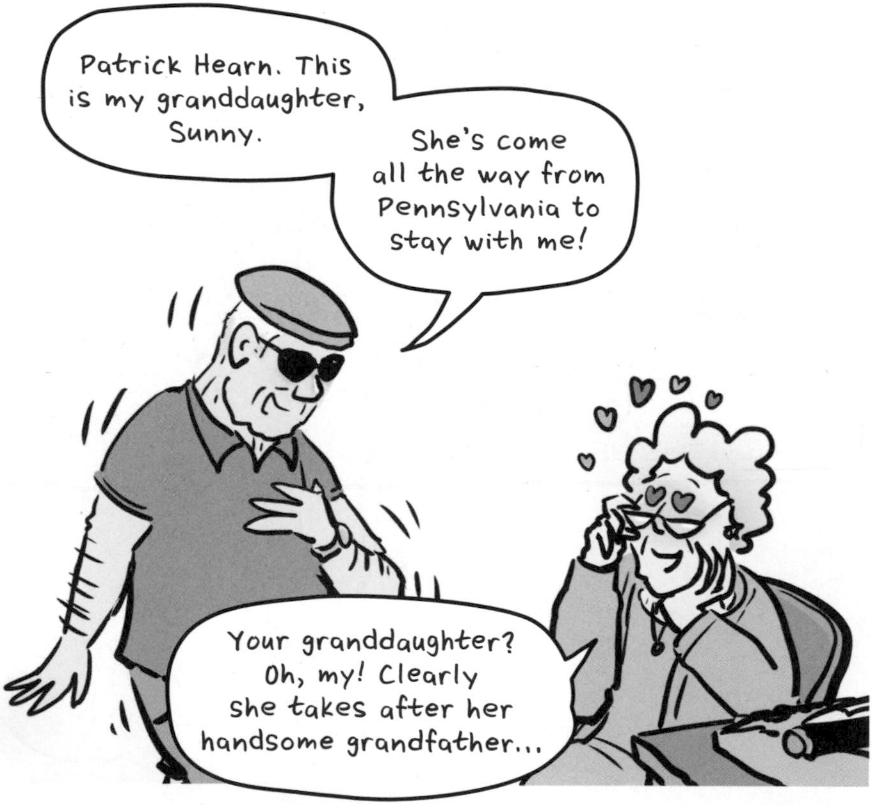
Patrick Hearn. This is my granddaughter, Sunny.
She's come all the way from Pennsylvania to stay with me!
Your granddaughter? Oh, my! Clearly she takes after her handsome grandfather...

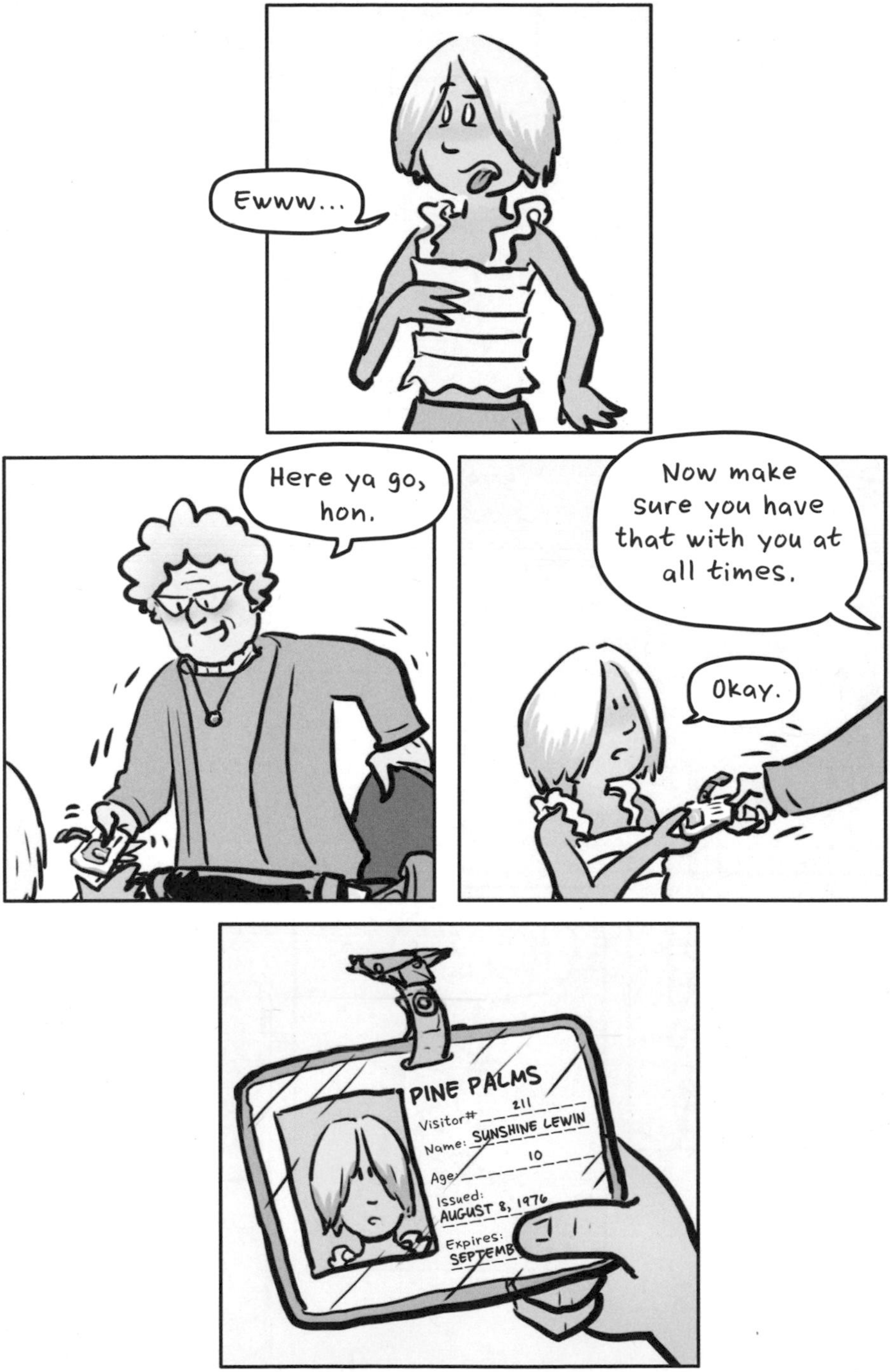
Ewww...
Here ya go, hon.
Now make sure you have that with you at all times.
Okay.
PINE PALMS
Visitor# 211
Name: SUNSHINE LEWIN
Age 10
Issued: AUGUST 8, 1976
Expires: SEPTEMB

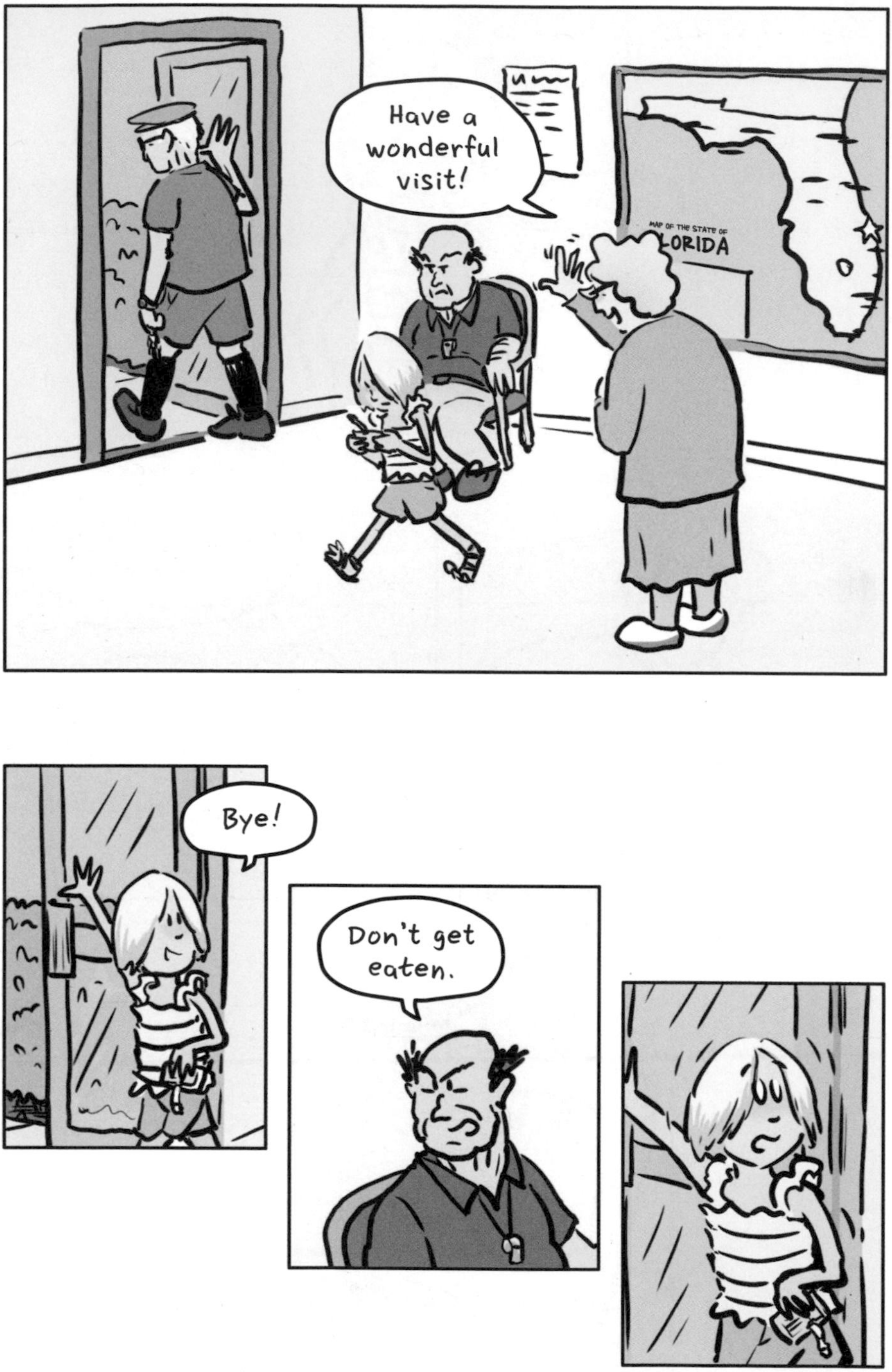
Have a wonderful visit!
MAP OF THE STATE OF
LORIDA
Bye!
Don't get eaten.

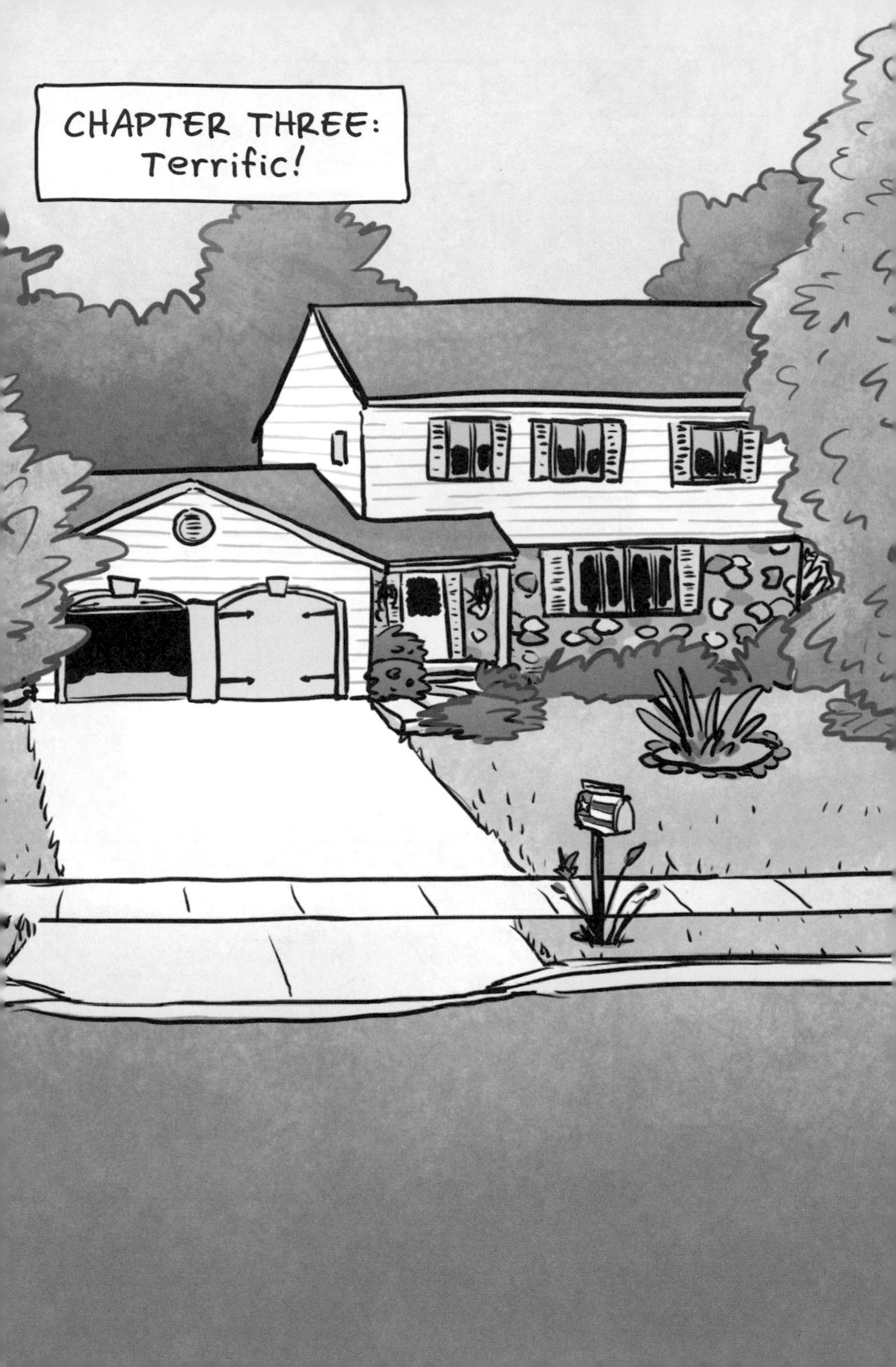
CHAPTER THREE:
Terrific!

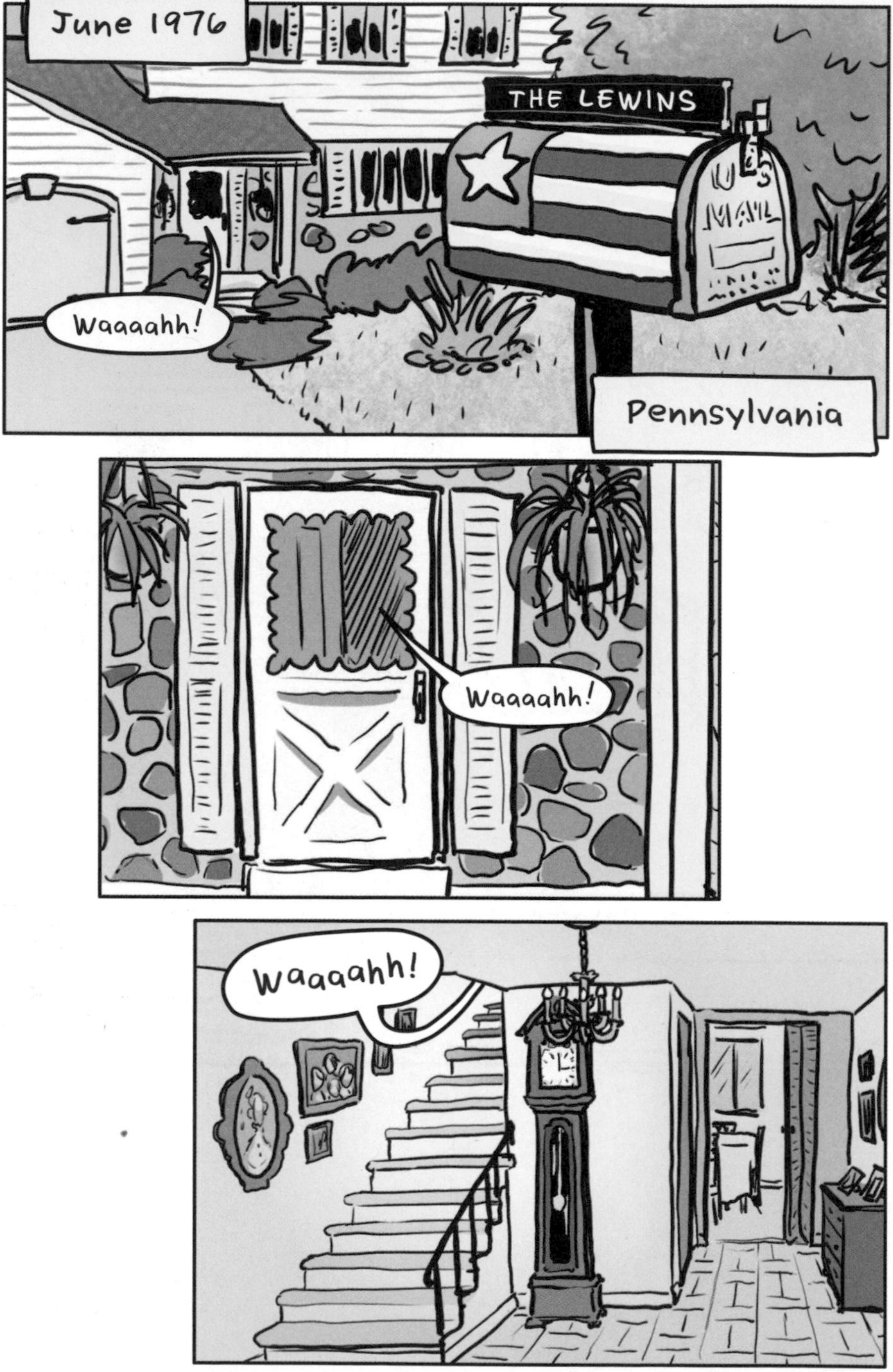
June 1976
THE LEWINS
U.S. MAIL
Waaaahh!
Pennsylvania
Waaaahh!
Waaaahh!

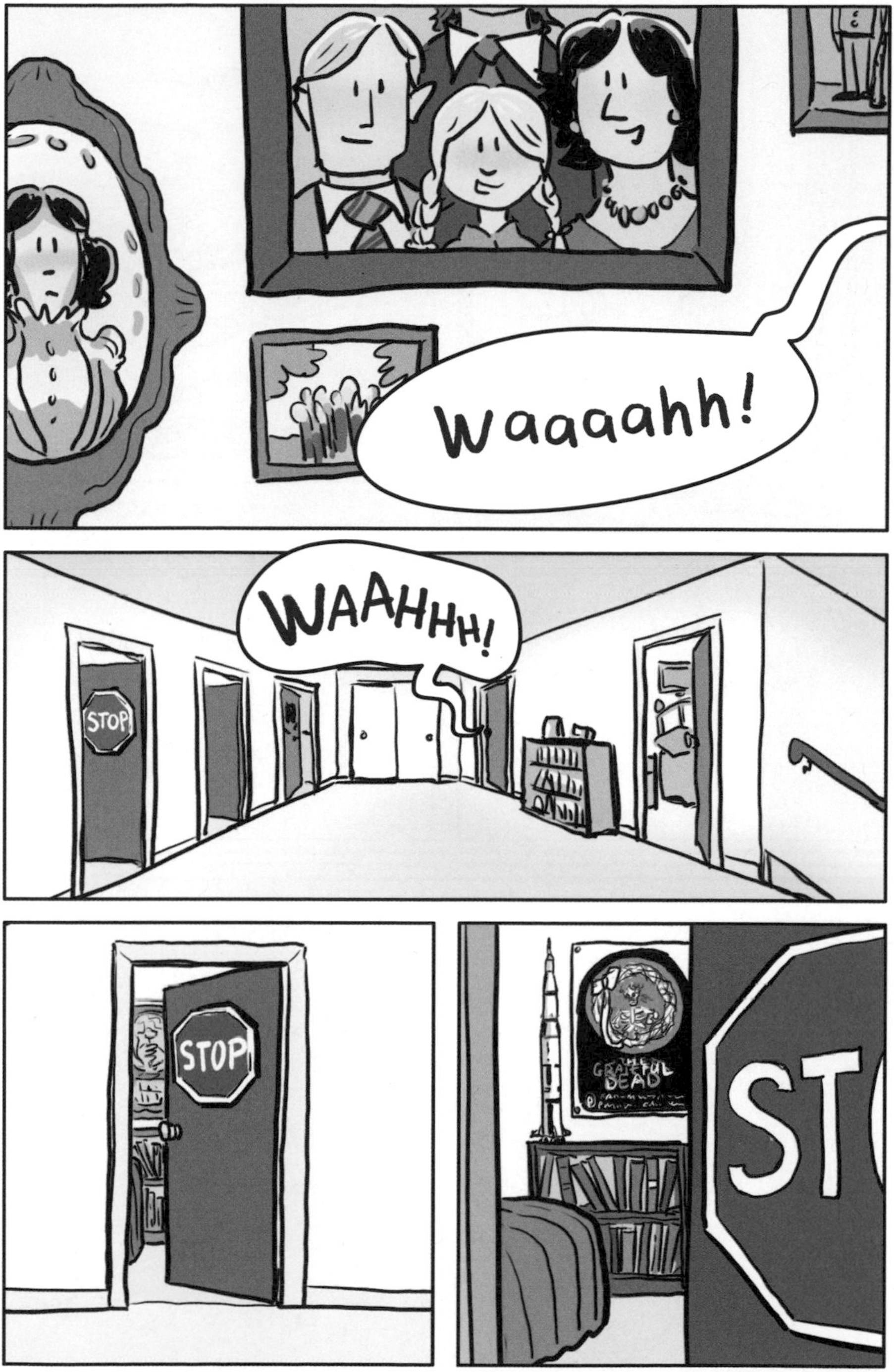
Waaaahh!
WAAHHH!
STOP
STOP
THE GRATEFUL DEAD
ST

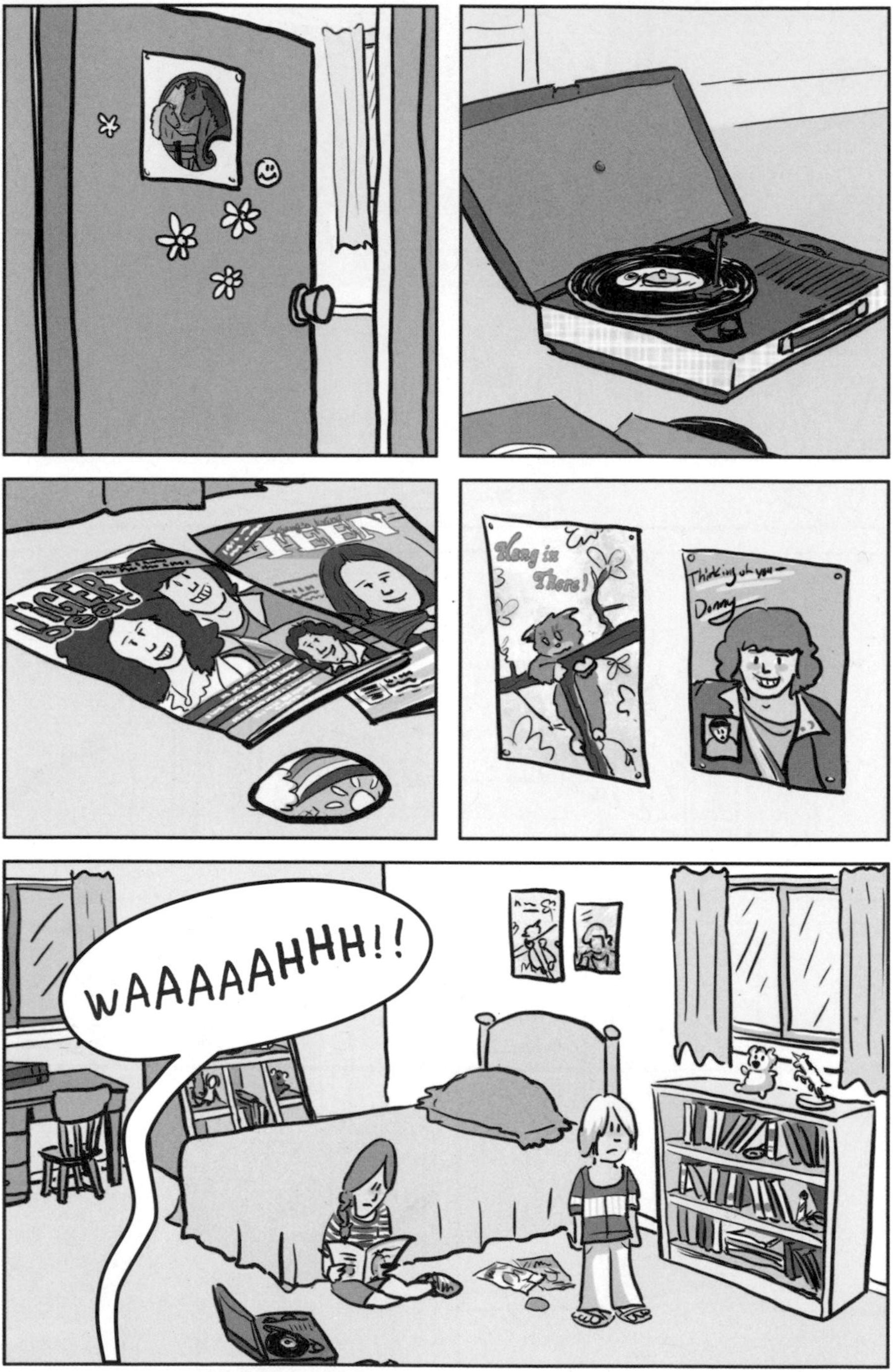
TEEN
Hang in There!
Thinking of you—
Donny
WAAAAAHHH!!

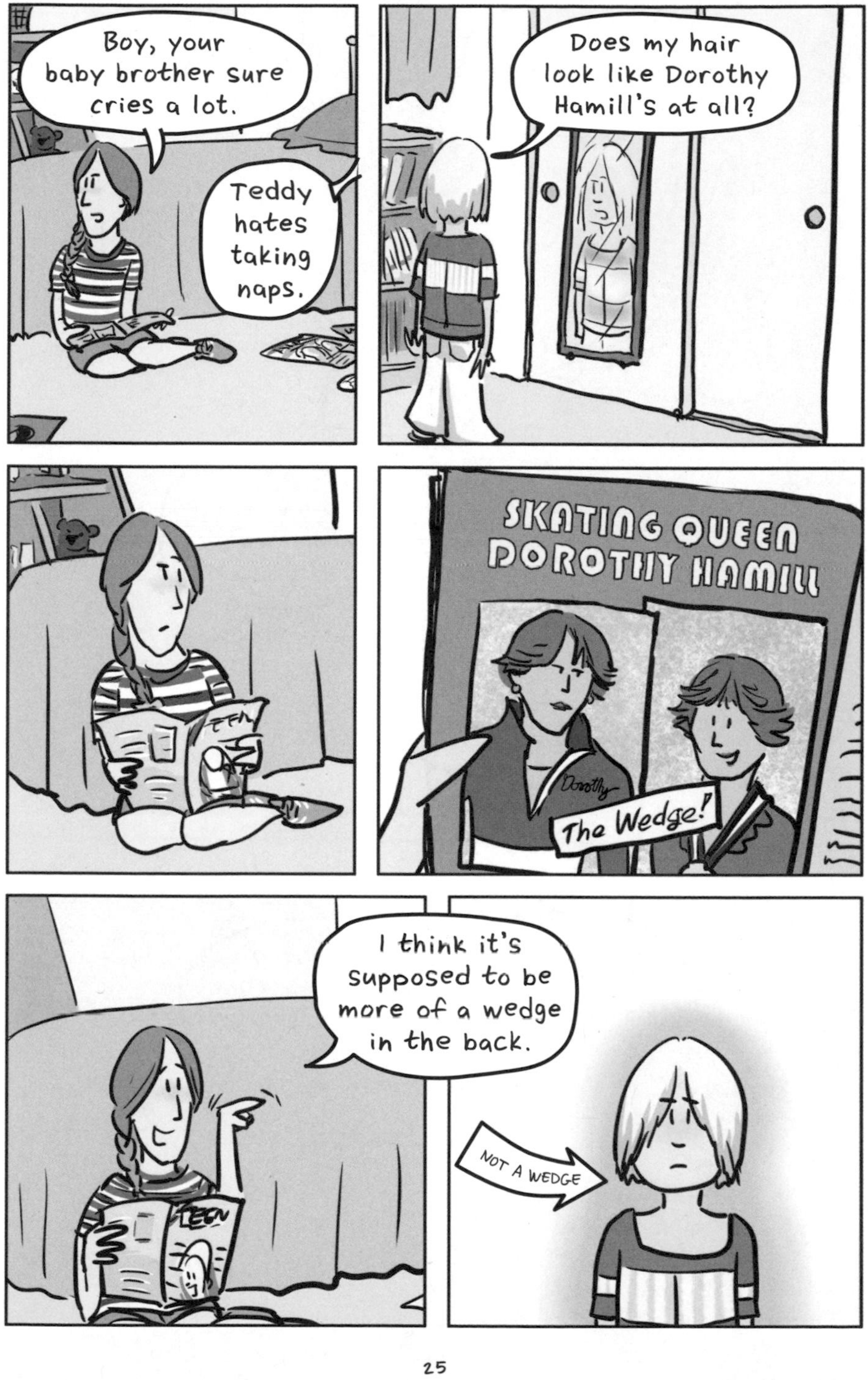
Boy, your baby brother sure cries a lot.
Teddy hates taking naps.
Does my hair look like Dorothy Hamill's at all?
SKATING QUEEN DOROTHY HAMILL
Dorothy
The Wedge!
I think it's supposed to be more of a wedge in the back.
TEEN
NOT A WEDGE

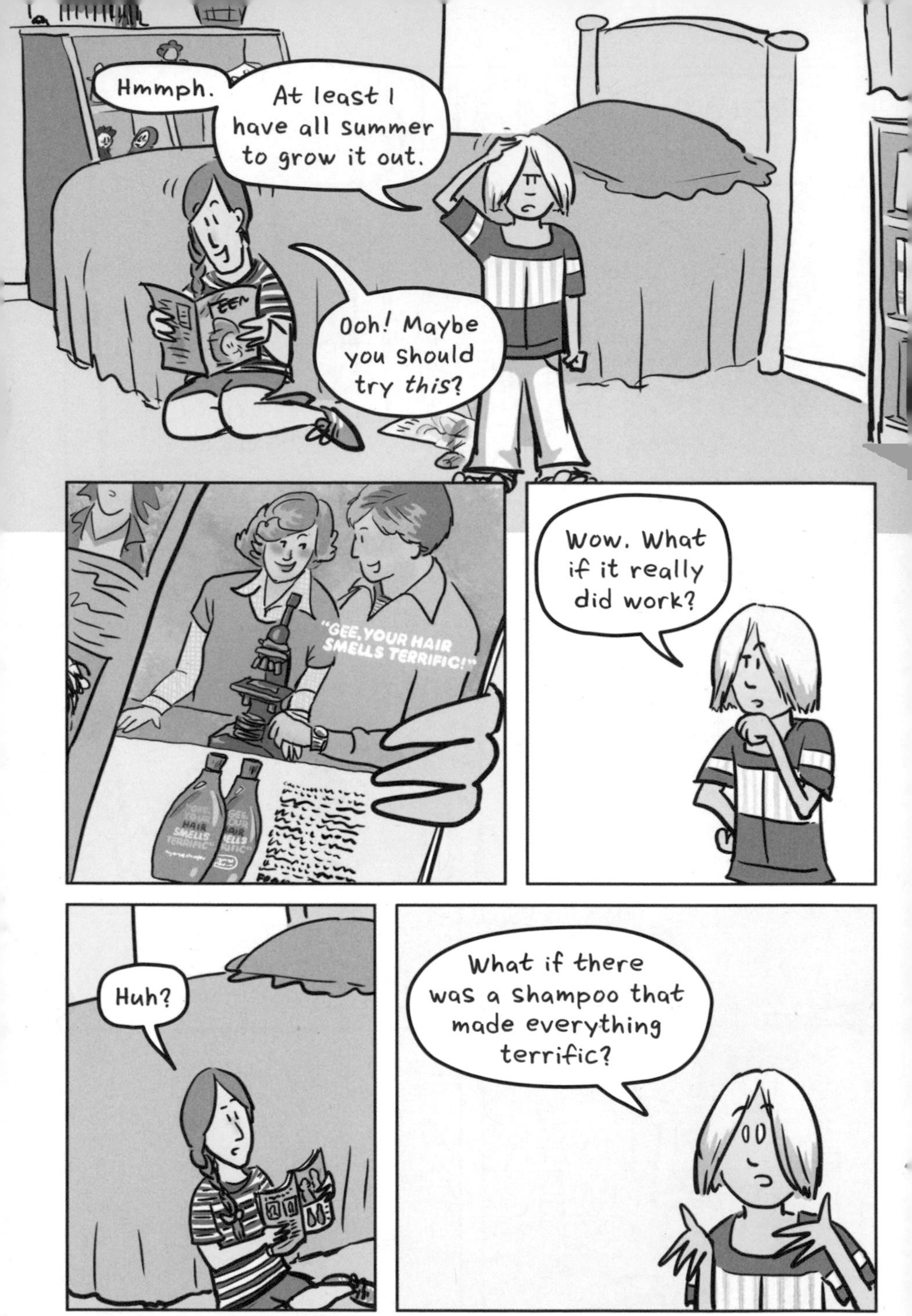
Hmmph.
At least I have all summer to grow it out.
Ooh! Maybe you should try *this*?
"GEE, YOUR HAIR SMELLS TERRIFIC!"
Wow. What if it really did work?
Huh?
What if there was a shampoo that made everything terrific?

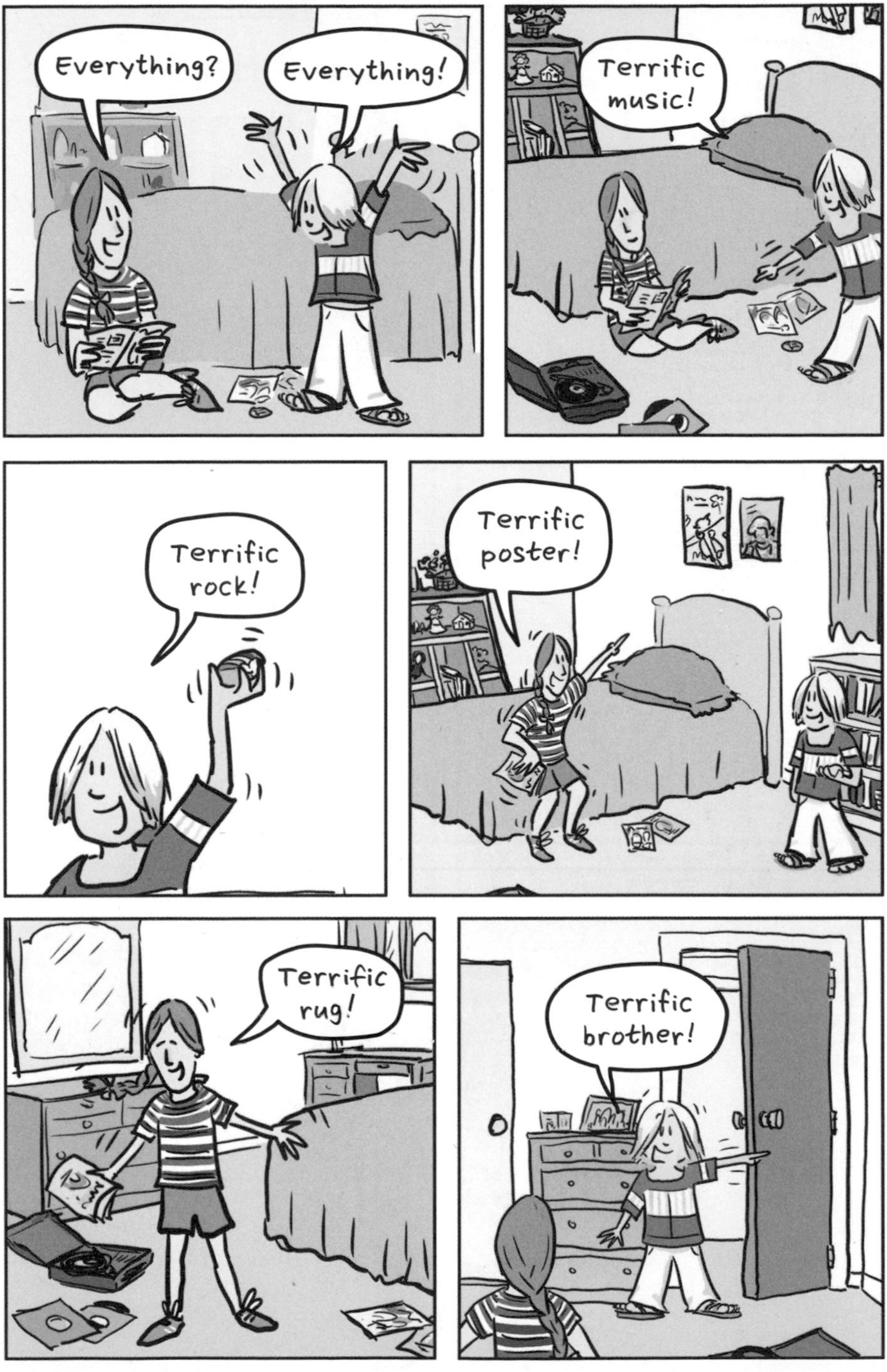
Everything?
Everything!
Terrific music!
Terrific rock!
Terrific poster!
Terrific rug!
Terrific brother!

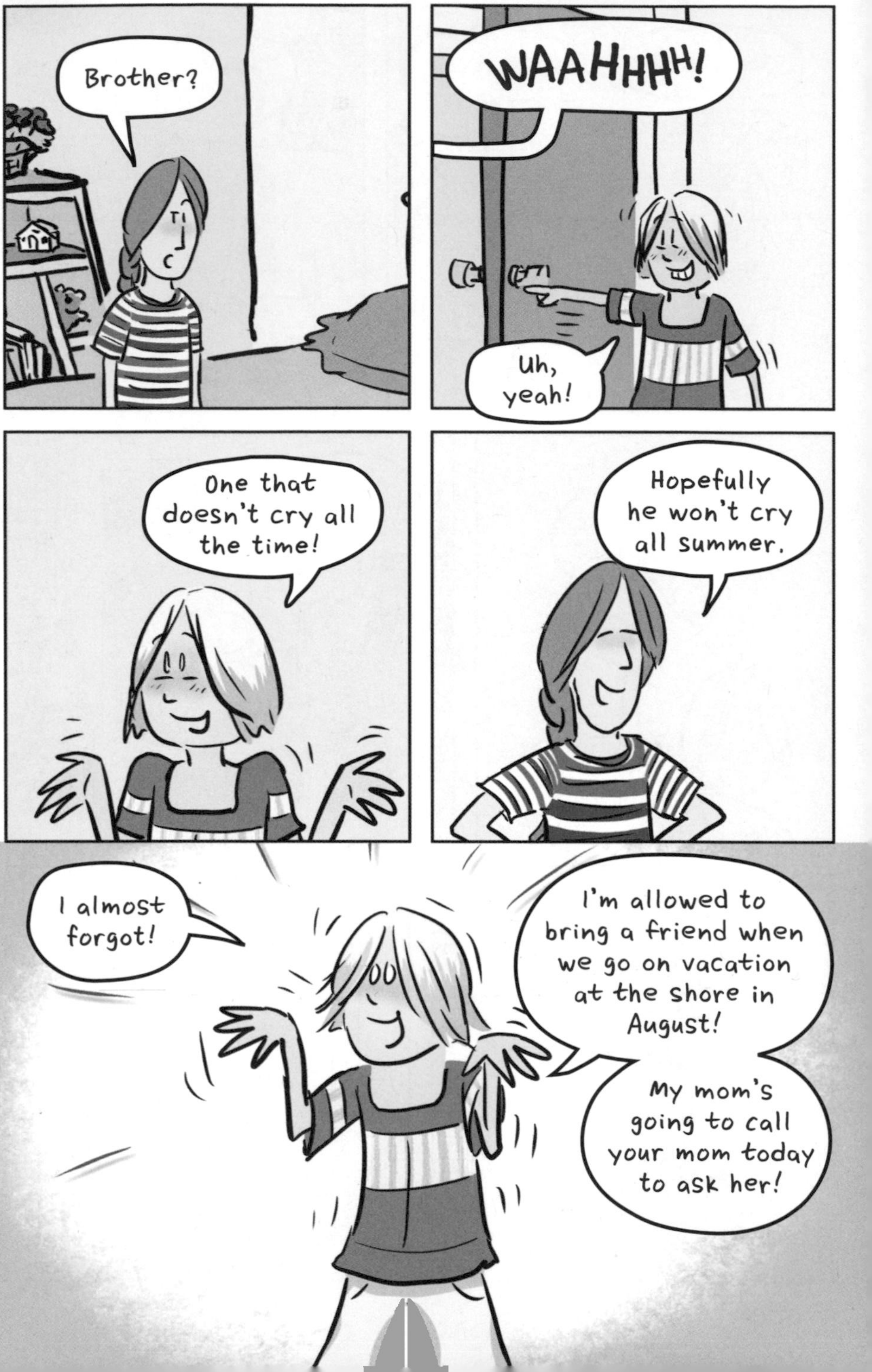
Brother?
WAAHHHH!
Uh, yeah!
One that doesn't cry all the time!
Hopefully he won't cry all summer.
I almost forgot!
I'm allowed to bring a friend when we go on vacation at the shore in August!
My mom's going to call your mom today to ask her!

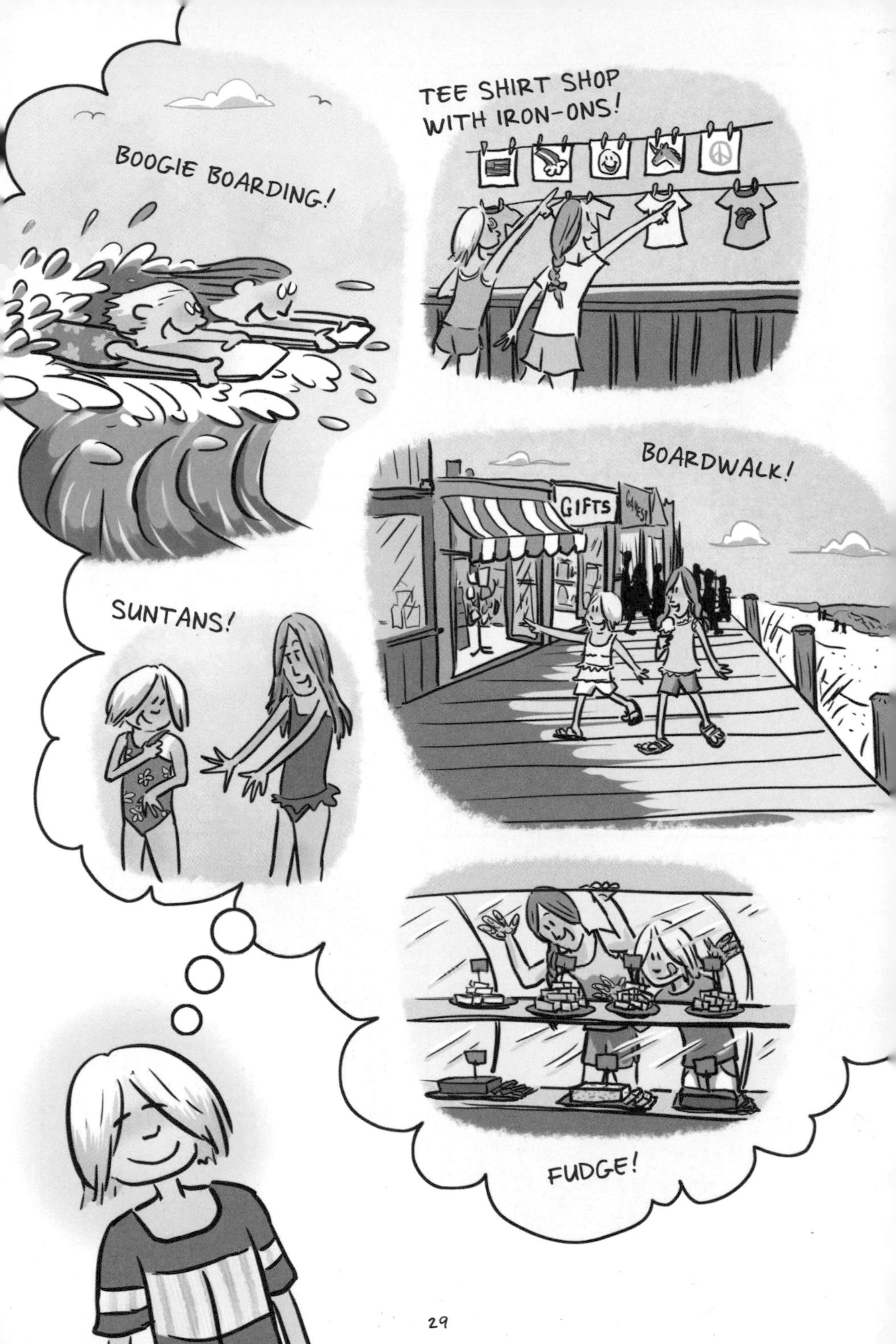
BOOGIE BOARDING!
TEE SHIRT SHOP WITH IRON-ONS!
BOARDWALK!
GIFTS
GAMES!
SUNTANS!
FUDGE!

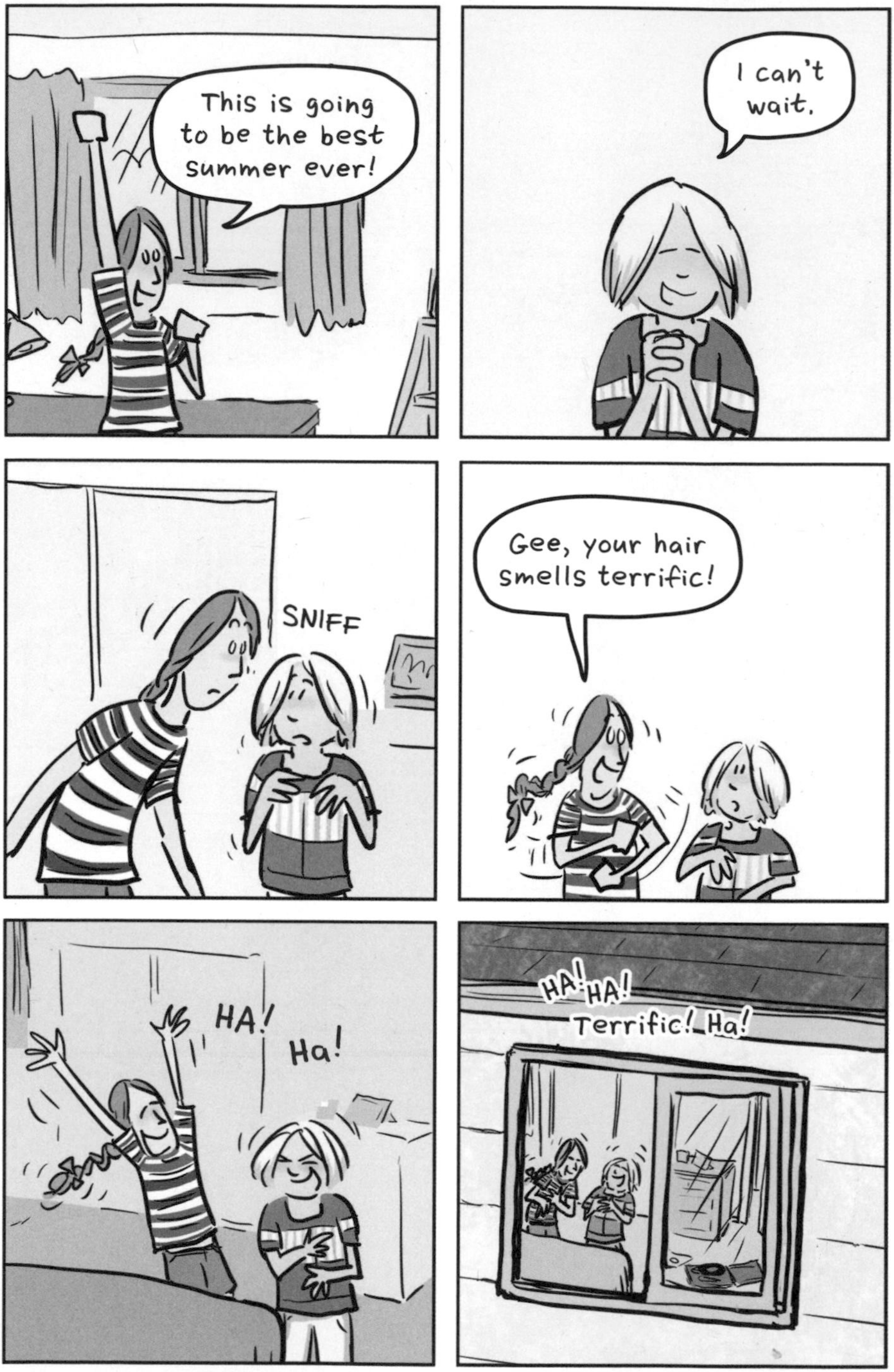
This is going to be the best summer ever!
I can't wait.
SNIFF
Gee, your hair smells terrific!
HA!
Ha!
HA! HA!
Terrific! Ha!

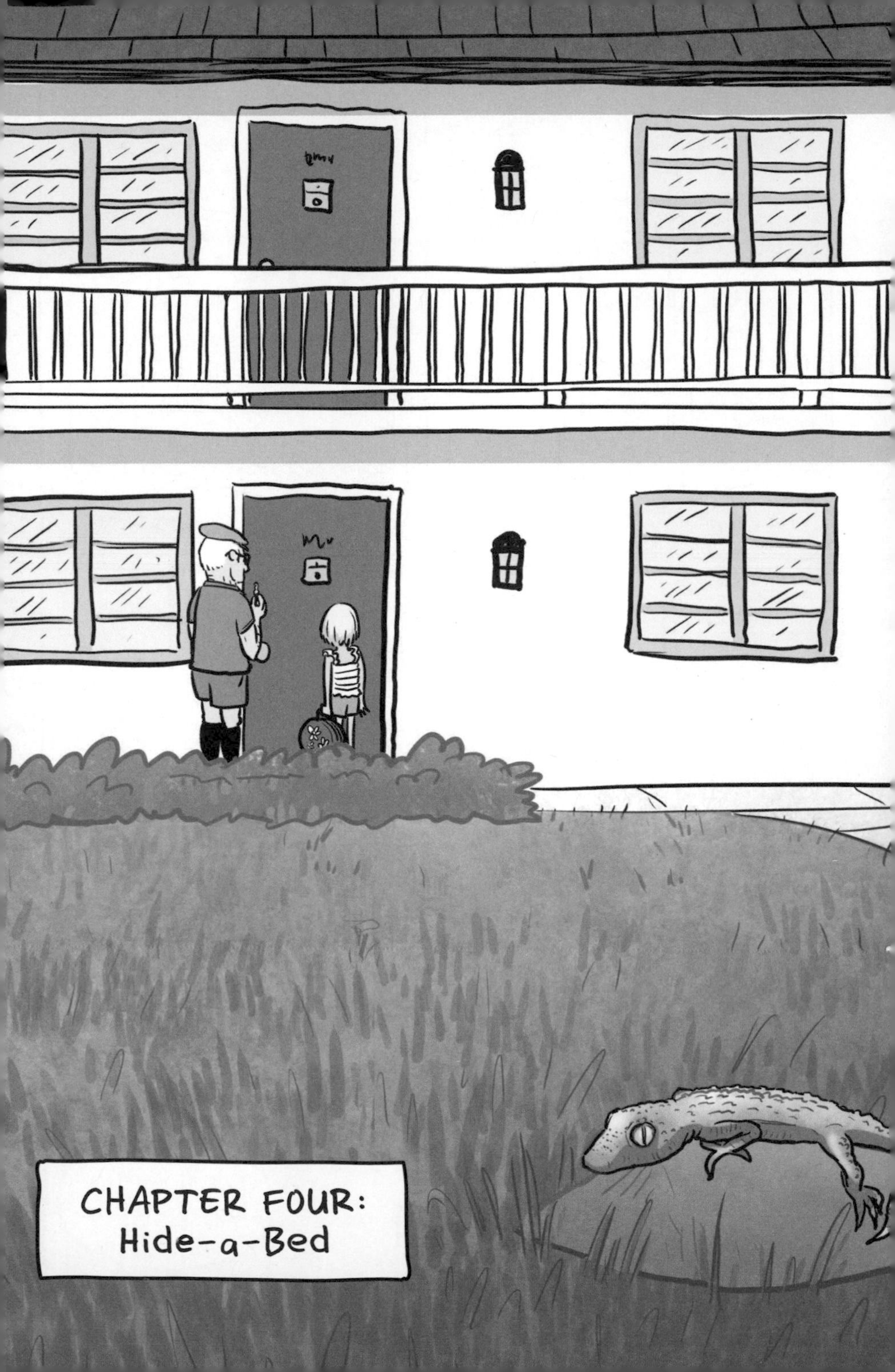
CHAPTER FOUR:
Hide-a-Bed

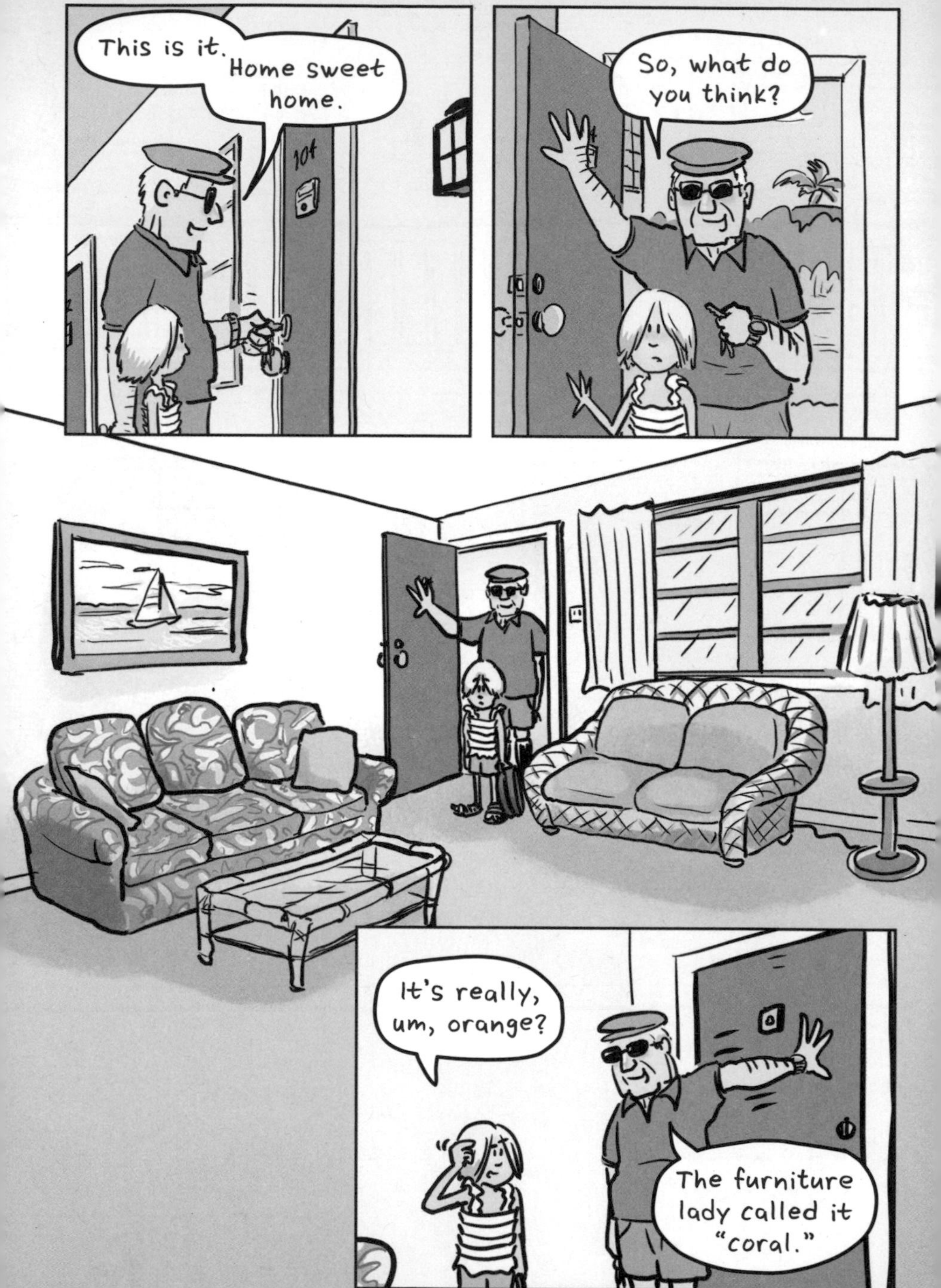
This is it.
Home sweet home.
104
So, what do you think?
It's really, um, orange?
The furniture lady called it "coral."

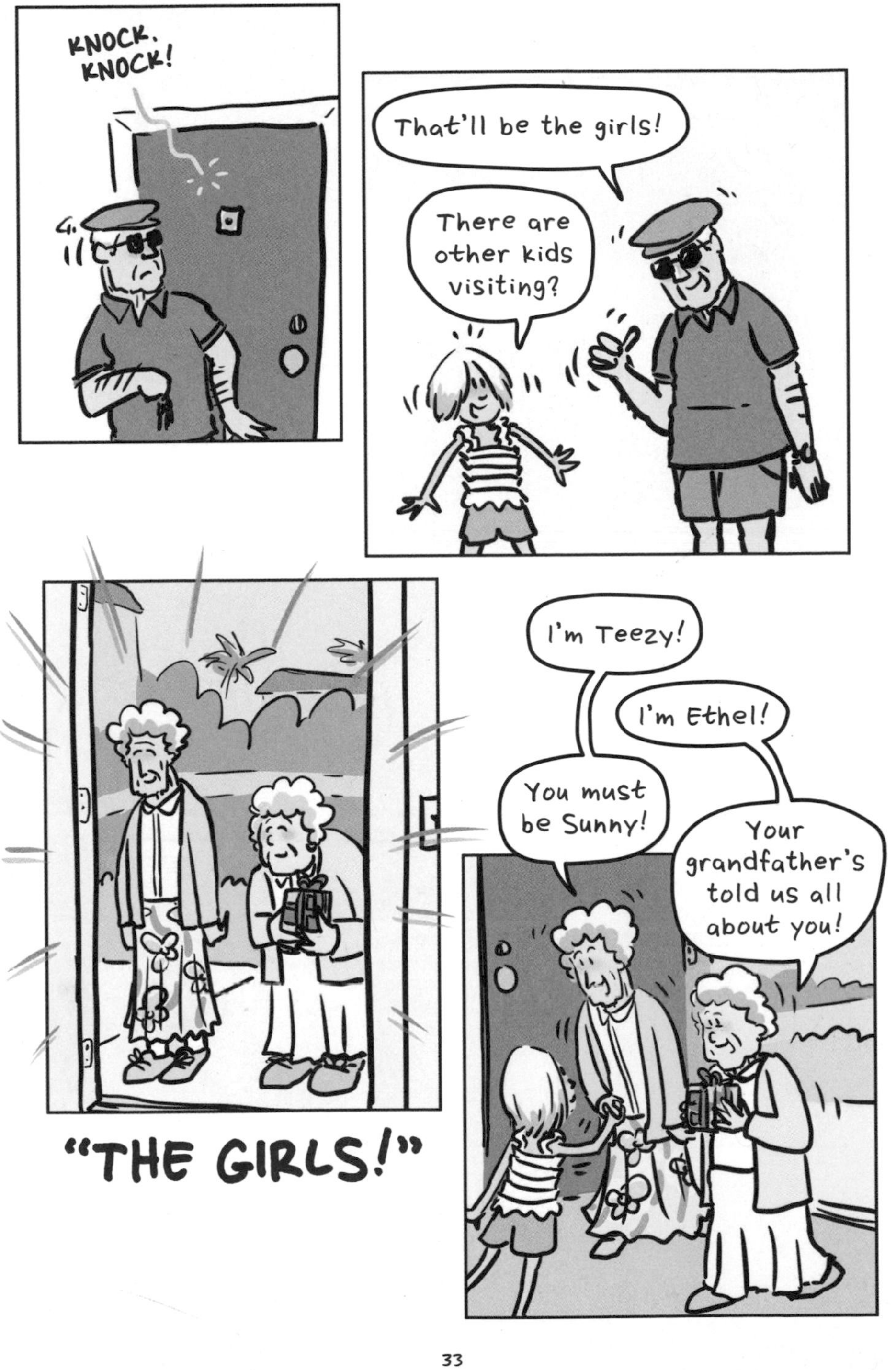
KNOCK. KNOCK!
That'll be the girls!
There are other kids visiting?
I'm Teezy!
I'm Ethel!
You must be Sunny!
Your grandfather's told us all about you!
"THE GIRLS!"

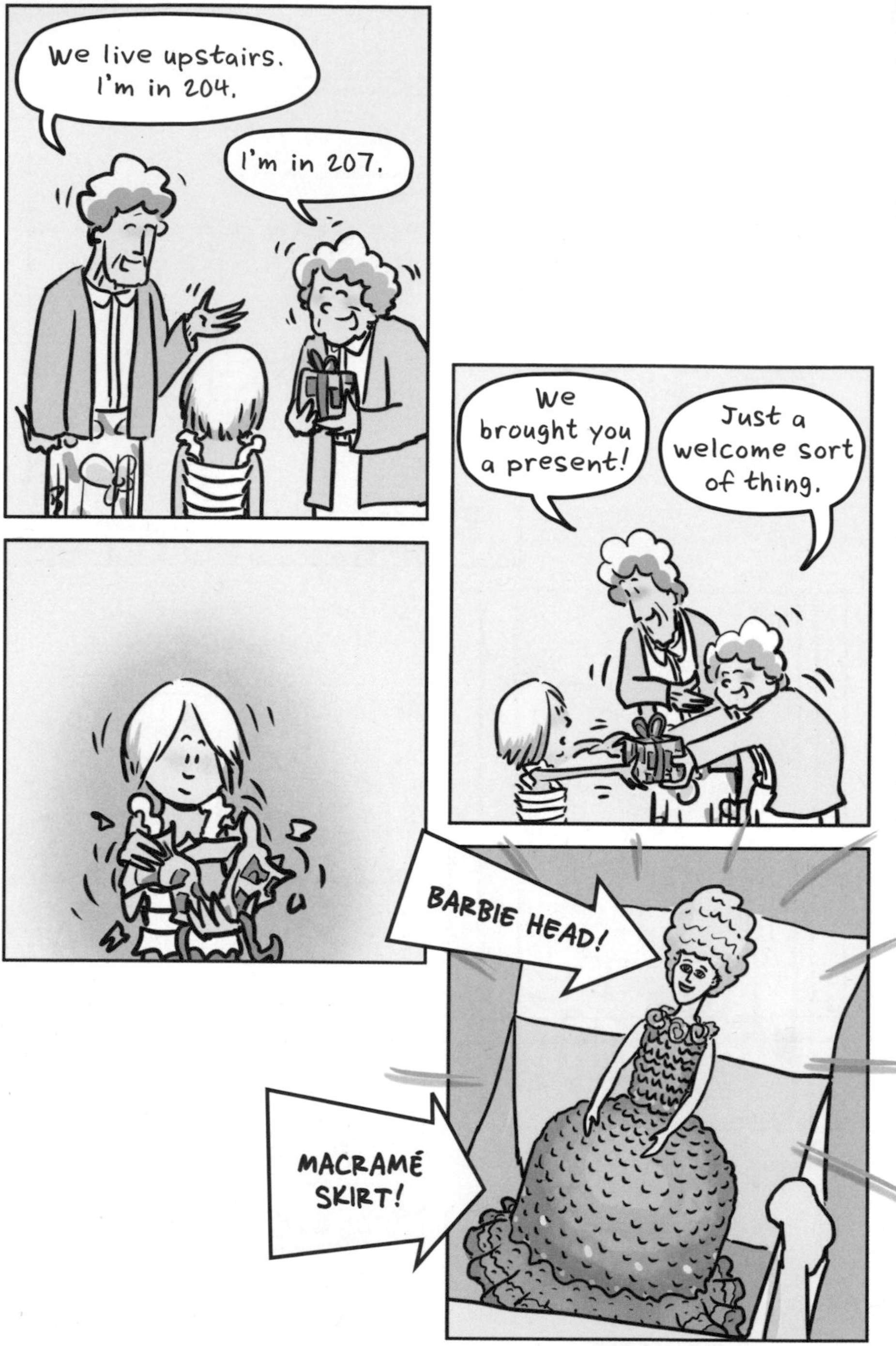
We live upstairs. I'm in 204.
I'm in 207.
We brought you a present!
Just a welcome sort of thing.
BARBIE HEAD!
MACRAMÉ SKIRT!

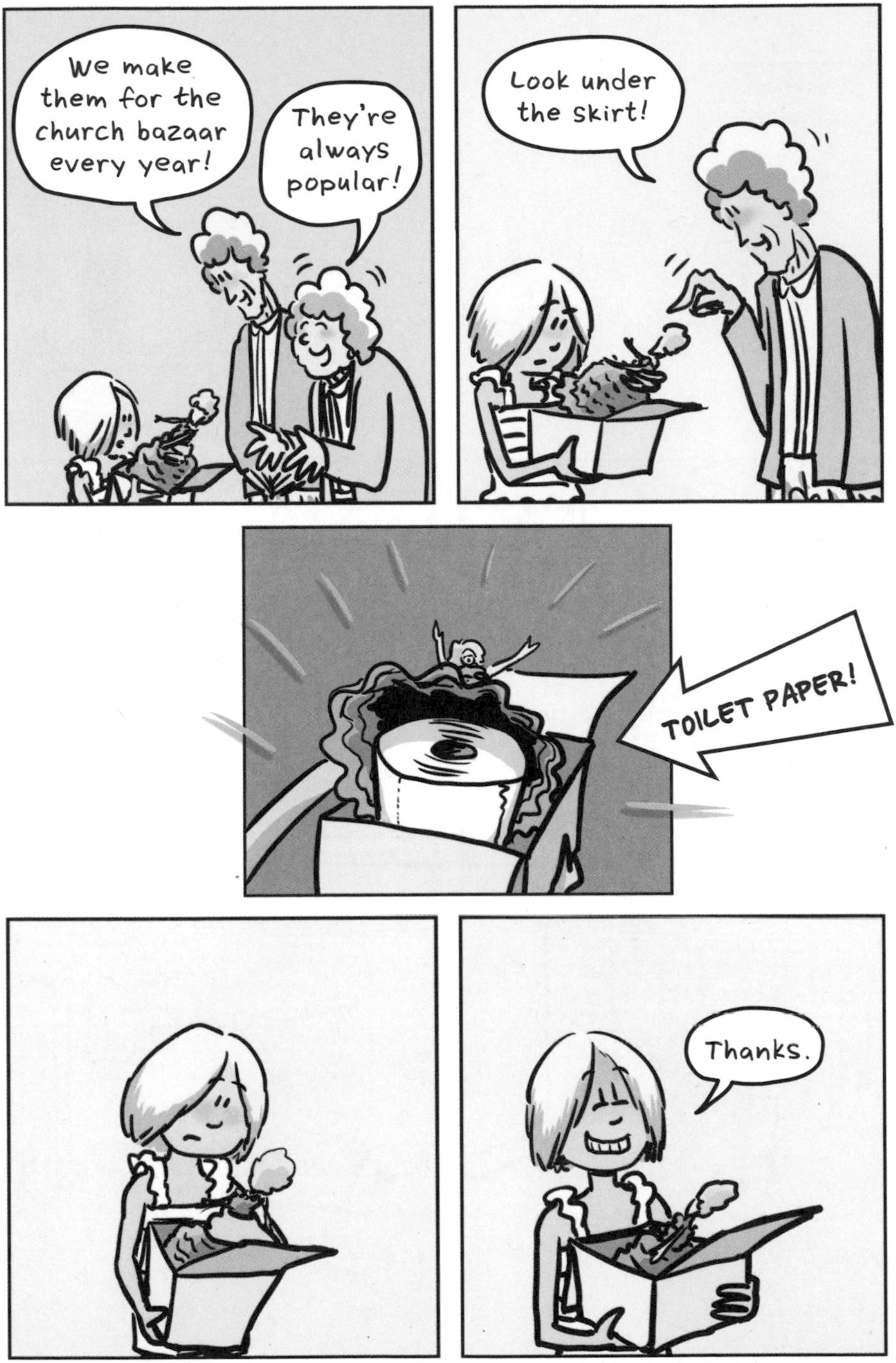
We make them for the church bazaar every year!
They're always popular!
Look under the skirt!
TOILET PAPER!
Thanks.

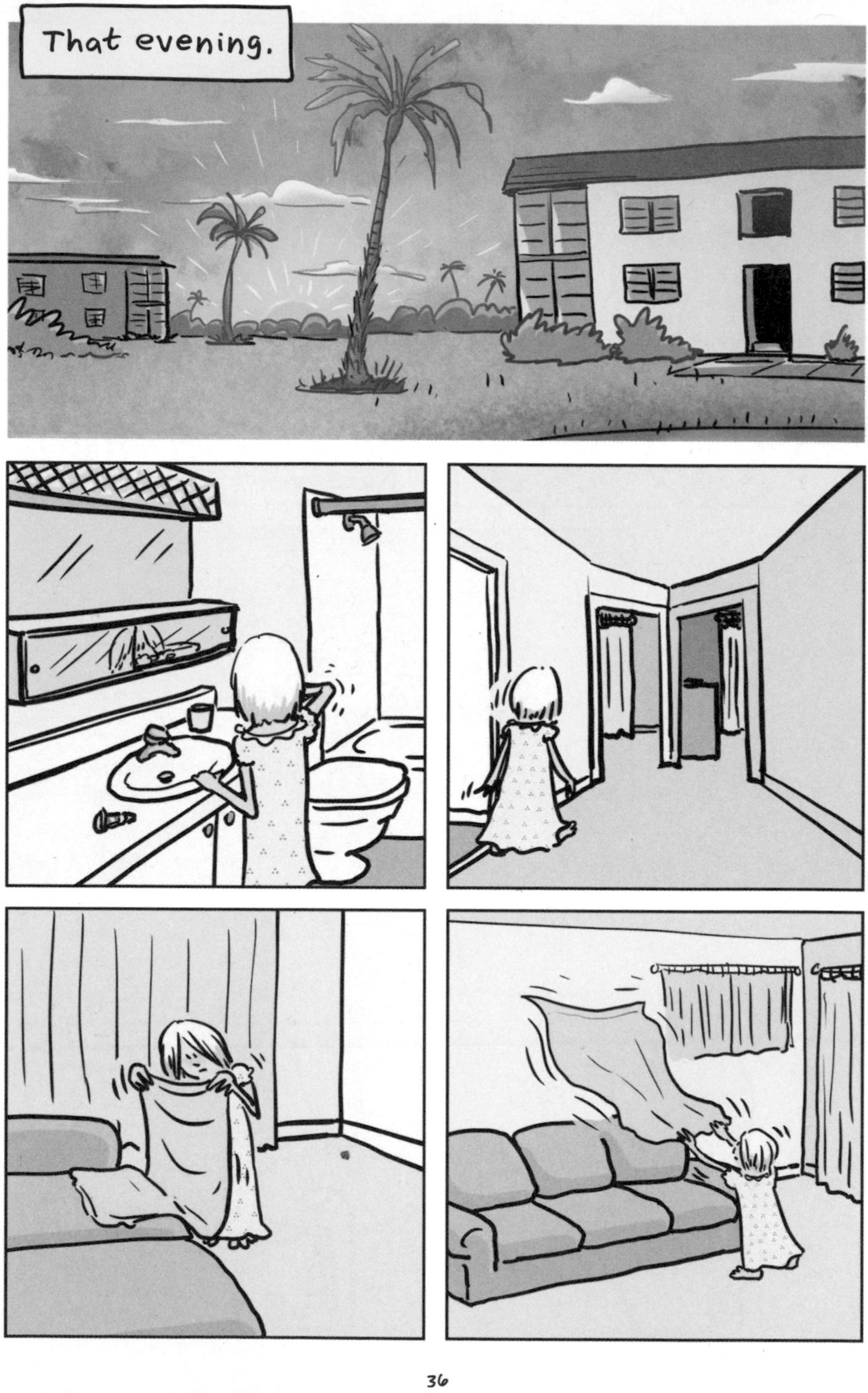
That evening.

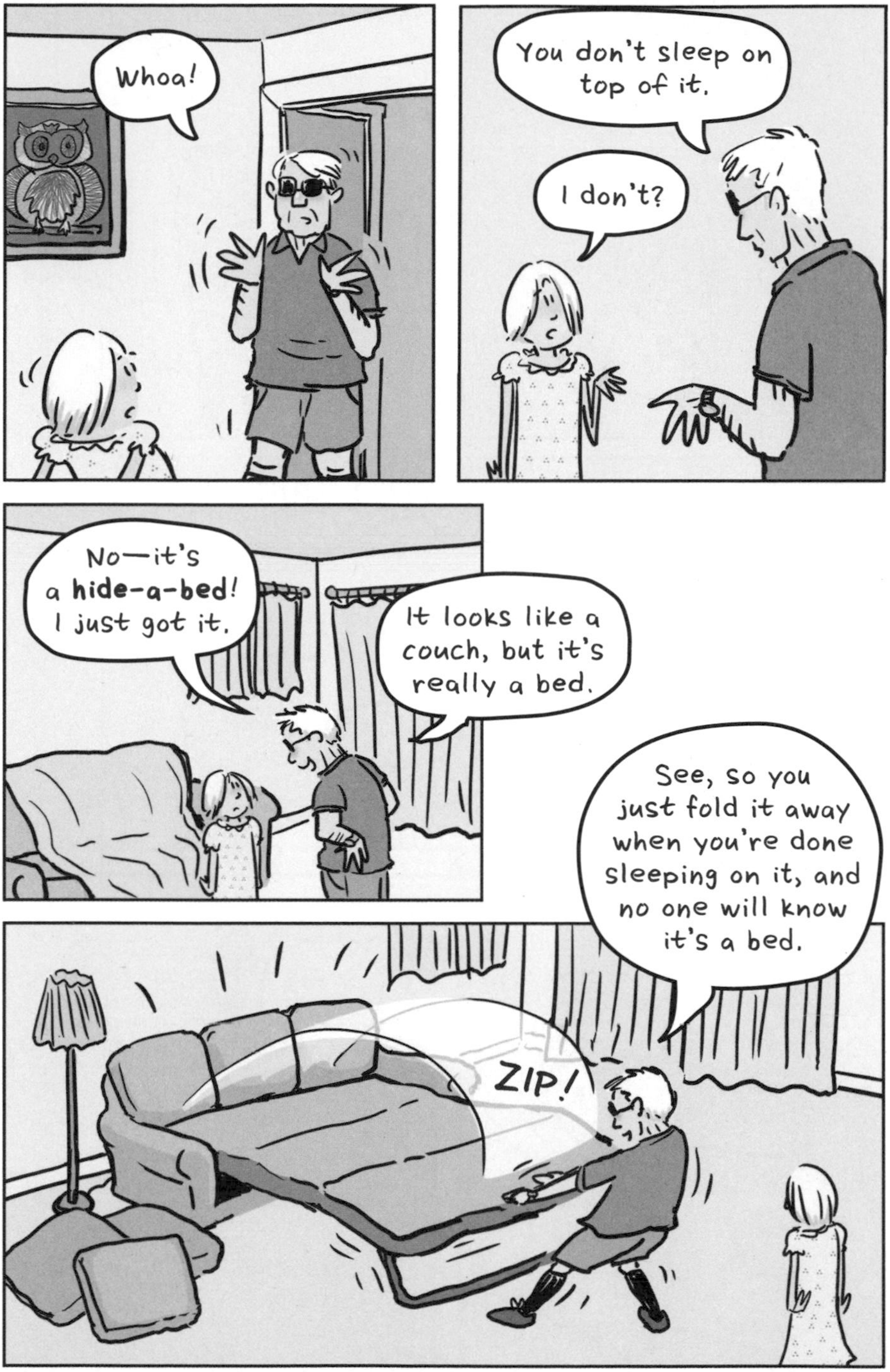
Whoa!
You don't sleep on top of it.
I don't?
No—it's a **hide-a-bed**! I just got it.
It looks like a couch, but it's really a bed.
See, so you just fold it away when you're done sleeping on it, and no one will know it's a bed.
ZIP!

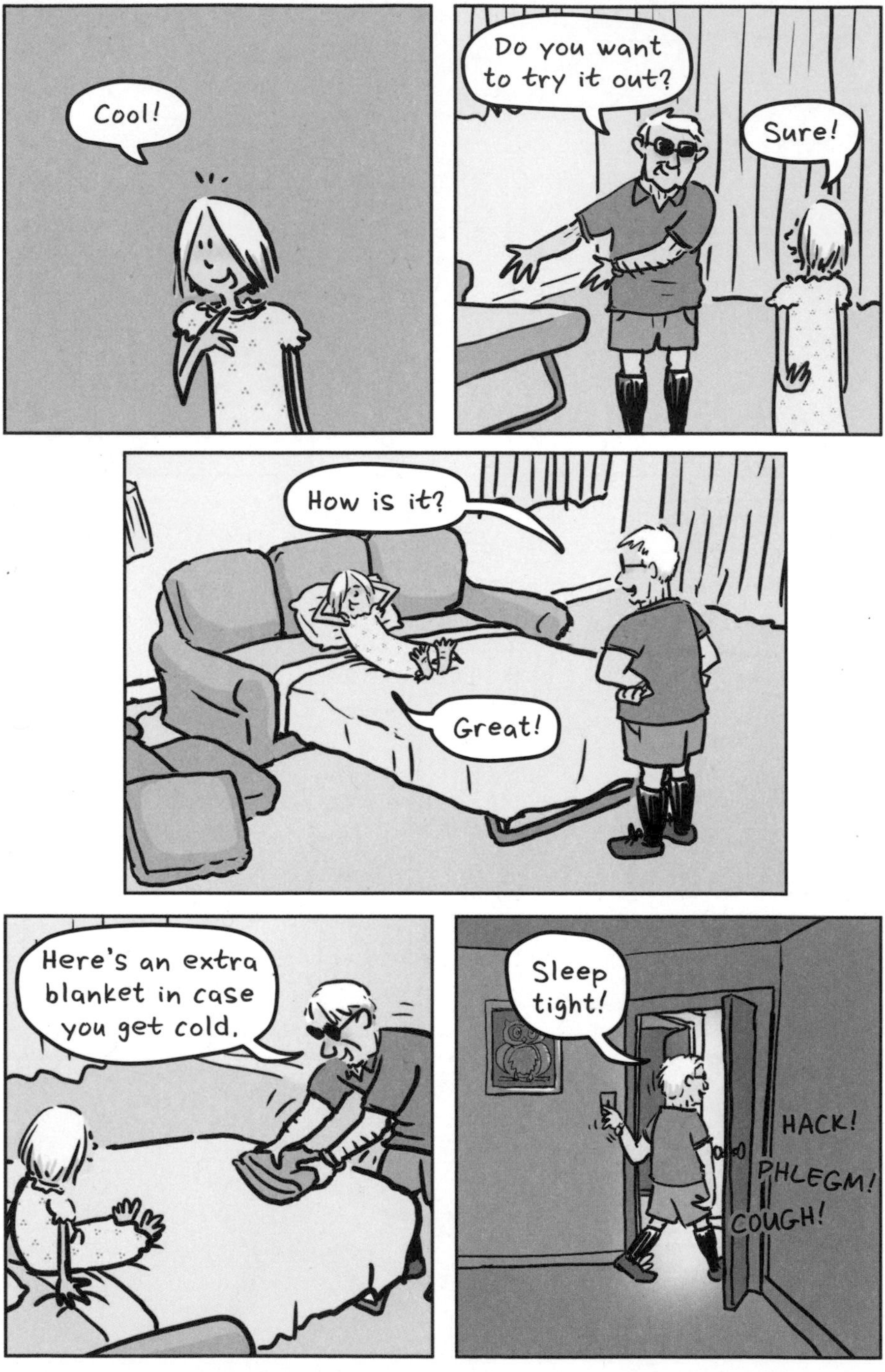
Cool!
Do you want to try it out?
Sure!
How is it?
Great!
Here's an extra blanket in case you get cold.
Sleep tight!
HACK!
PHLEGM!
COUGH!

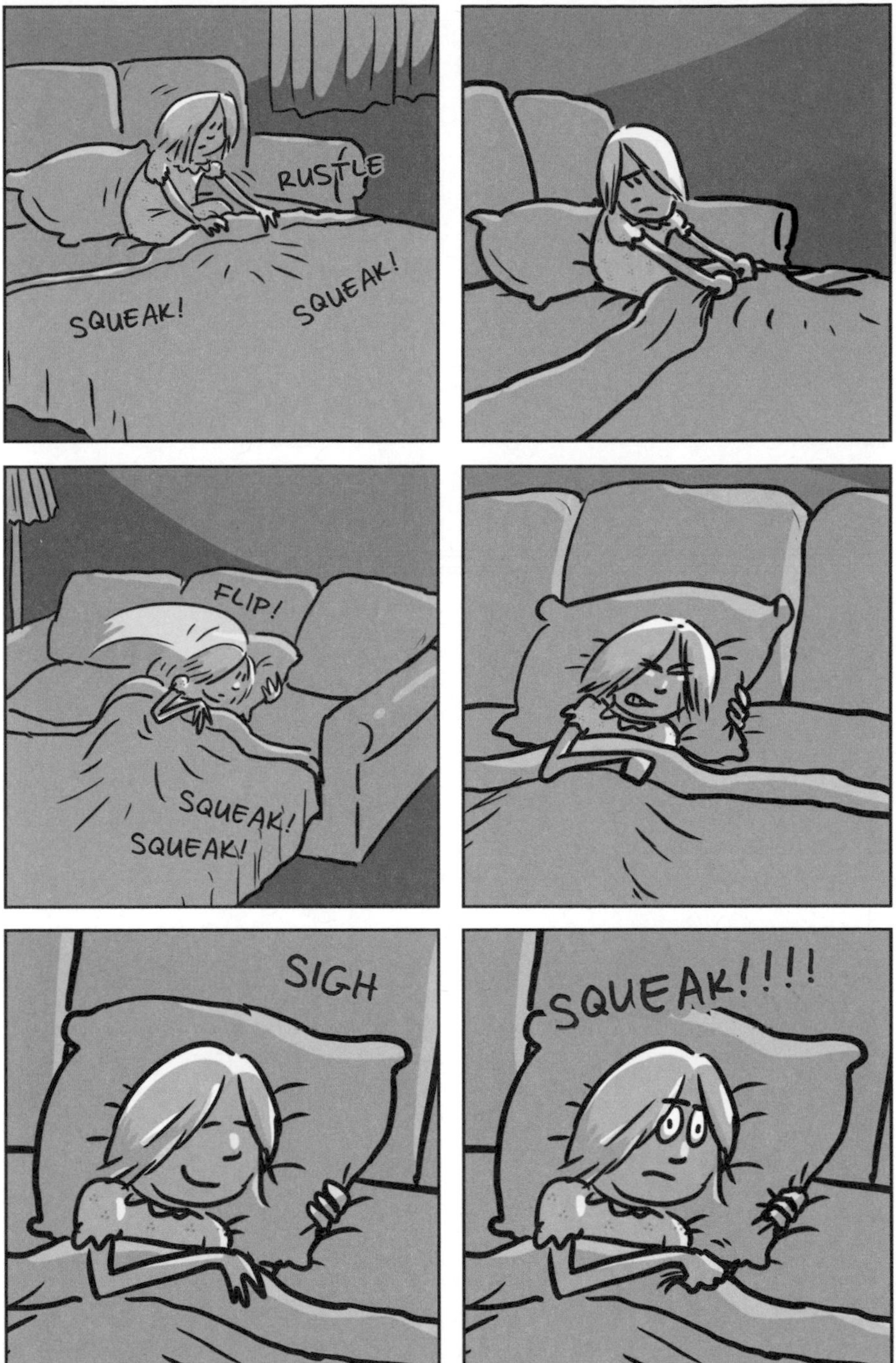
RUSTLE
SQUEAK!
SQUEAK!
FLIP!
SQUEAK!
SQUEAK!
SIGH
SQUEAK!!!!

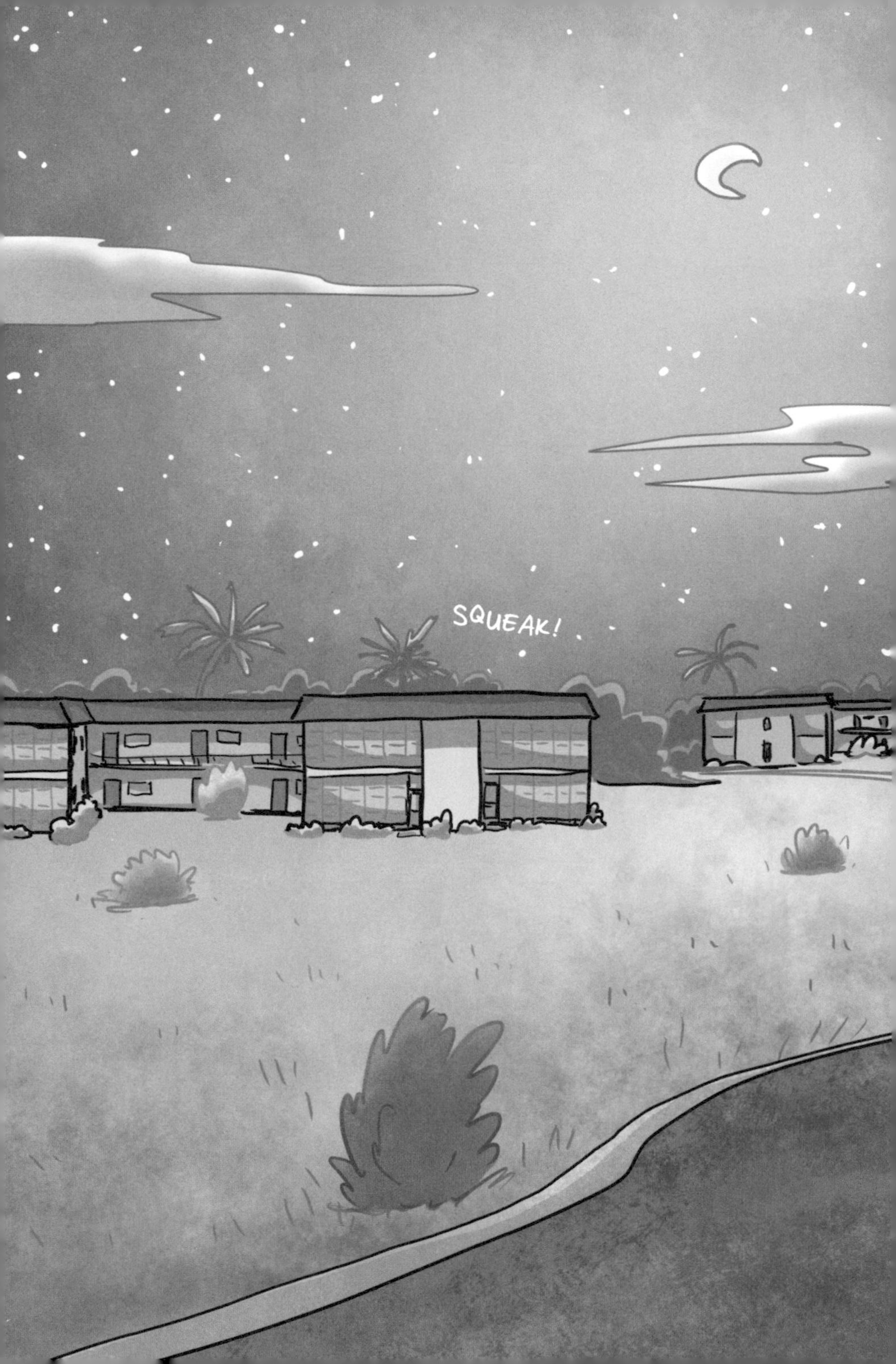
SQUEAK!

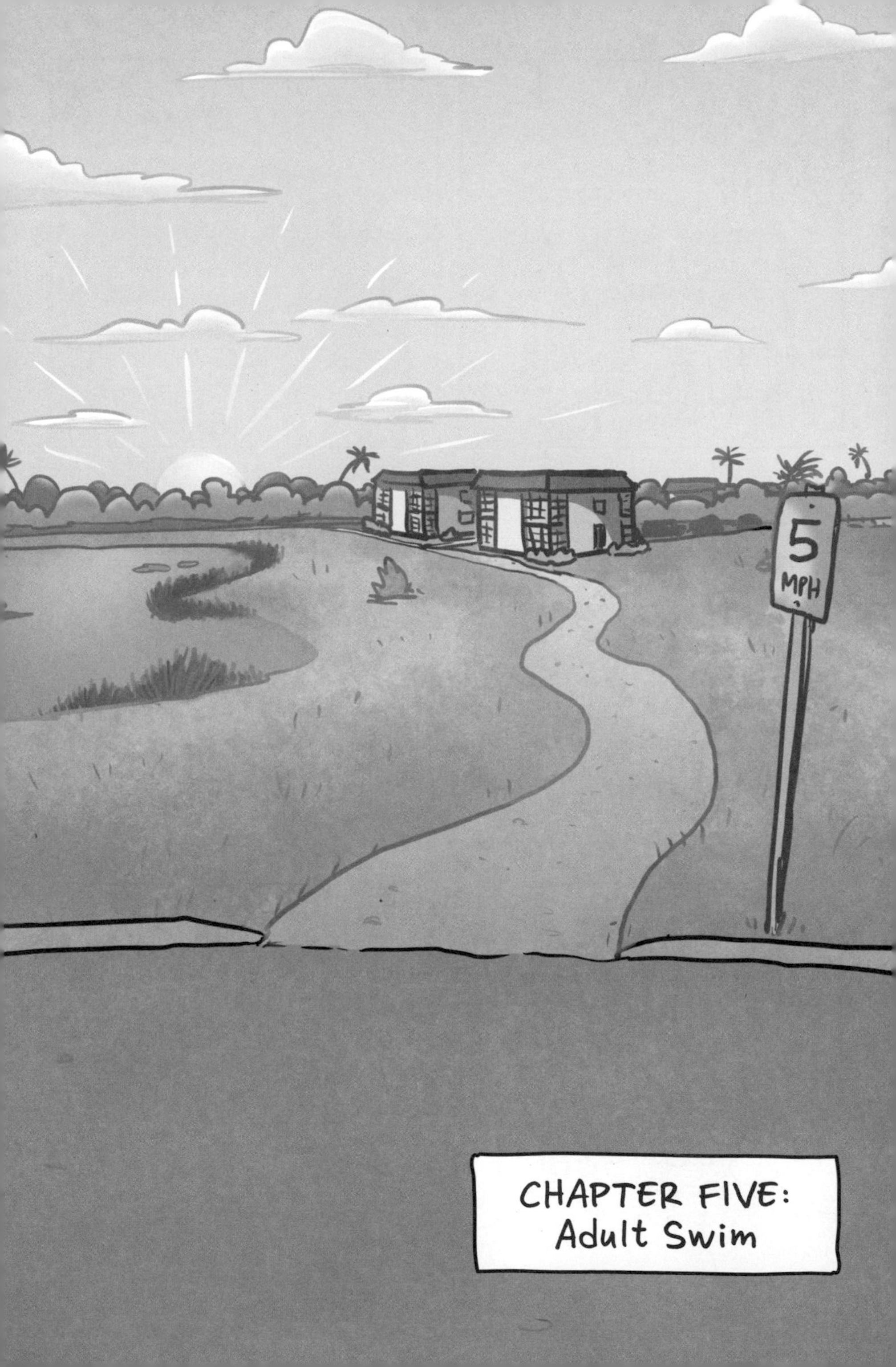
5
MPH
CHAPTER FIVE:
Adult Swim

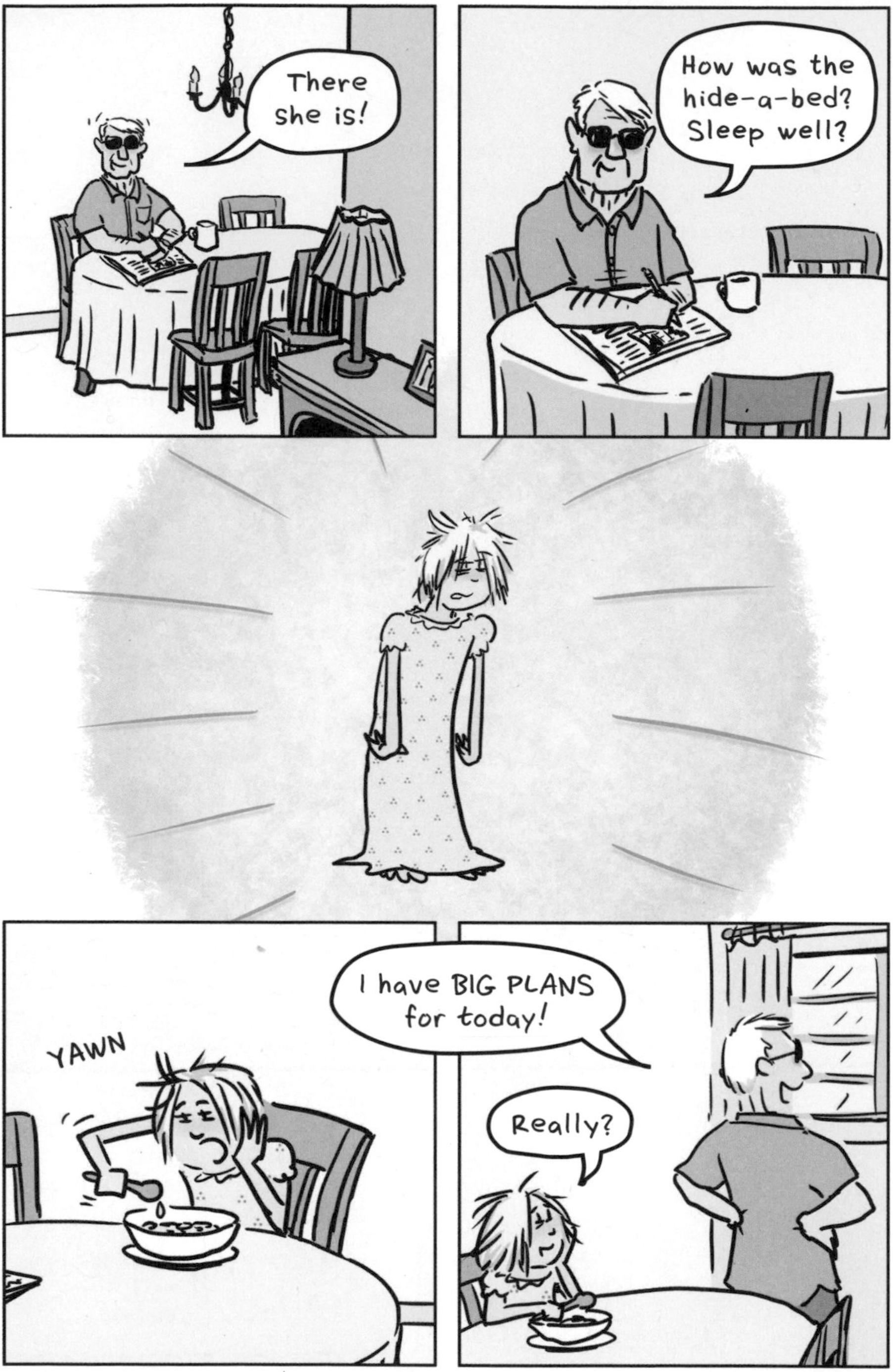

There she is!
How was the hide-a-bed? Sleep well?
YAWN
I have BIG PLANS for today!
Really?

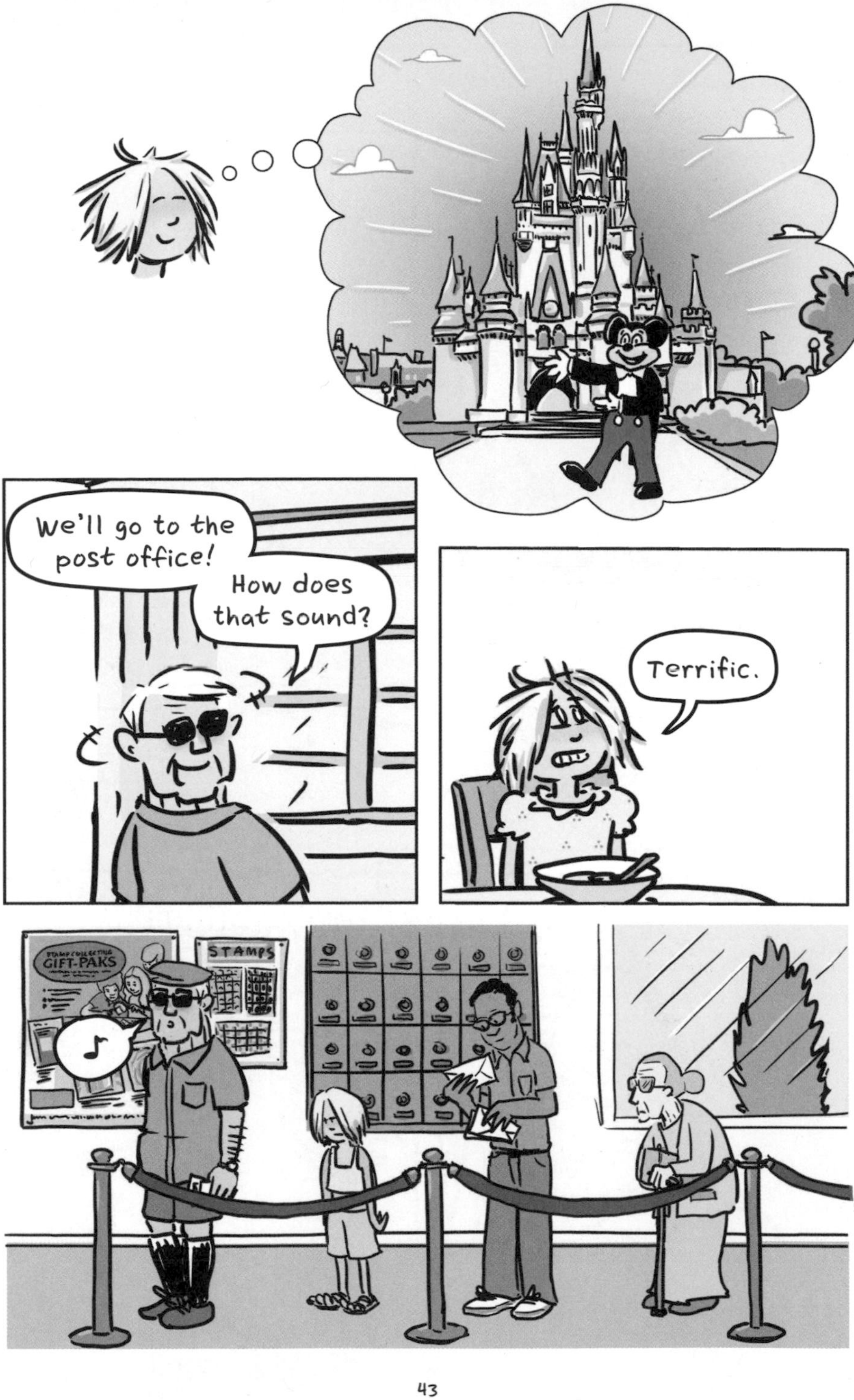
We'll go to the post office!
How does that sound?
Terrific.
GIFT-PAKS
STAMPS

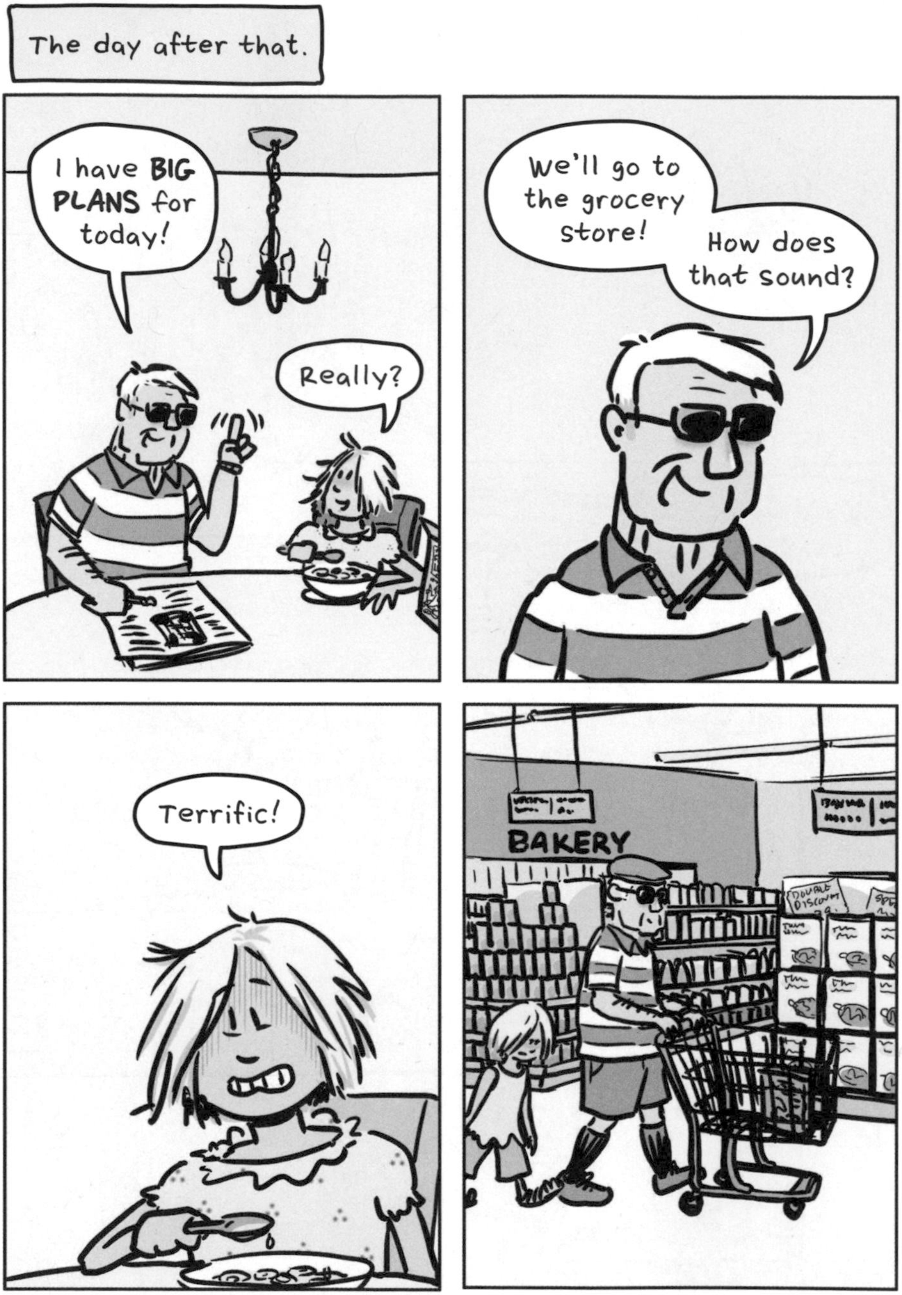
The day after that.
I have BIG PLANS for today!
Really?
We'll go to the grocery store!
How does that sound?
Terrific!
BAKERY
DOUBLE DISCOUNT

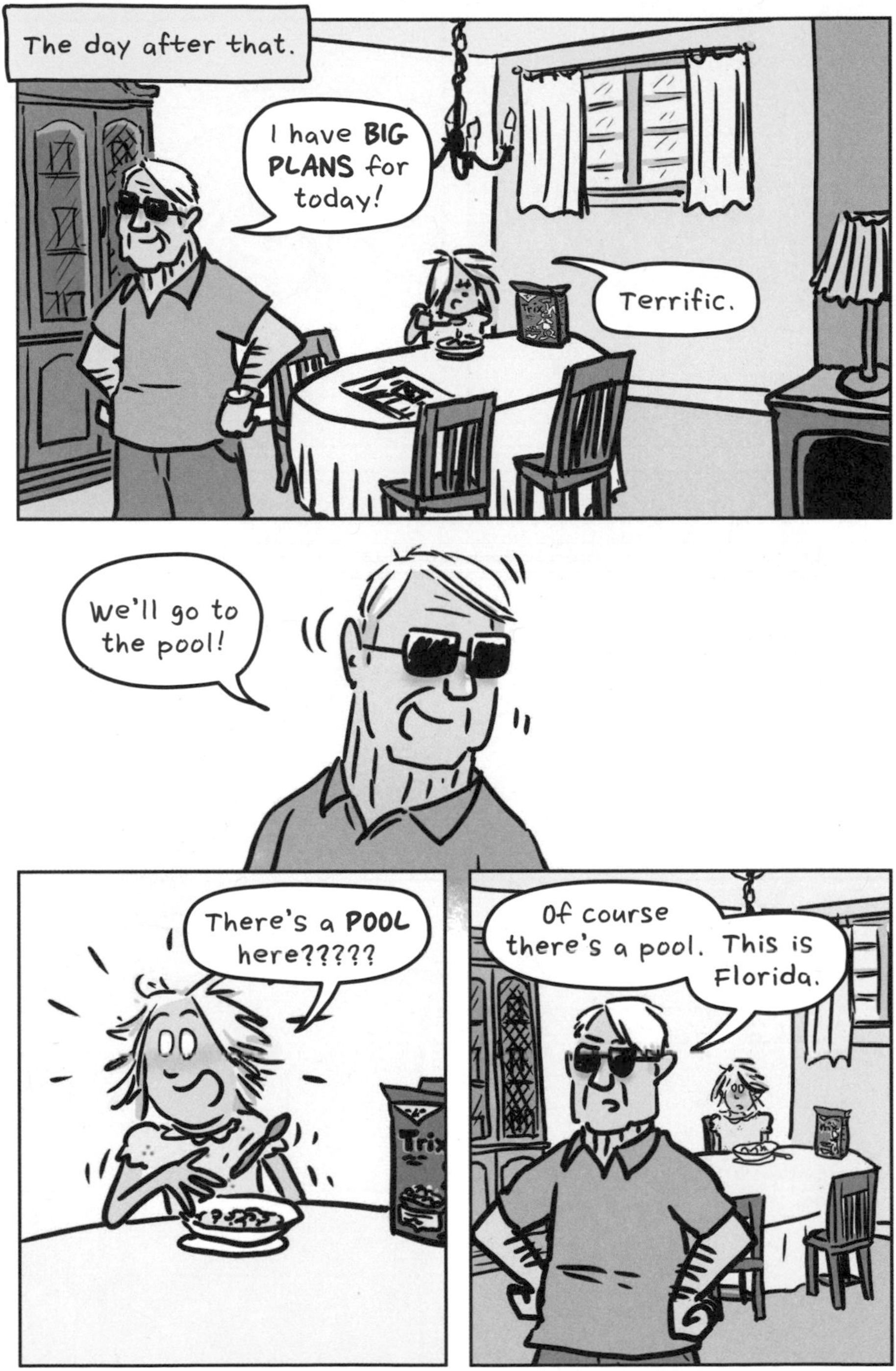

The day after that.
I have BIG PLANS for today!
Terrific.
We'll go to the pool!
There's a POOL here?????
Of course there's a pool. This is Florida.

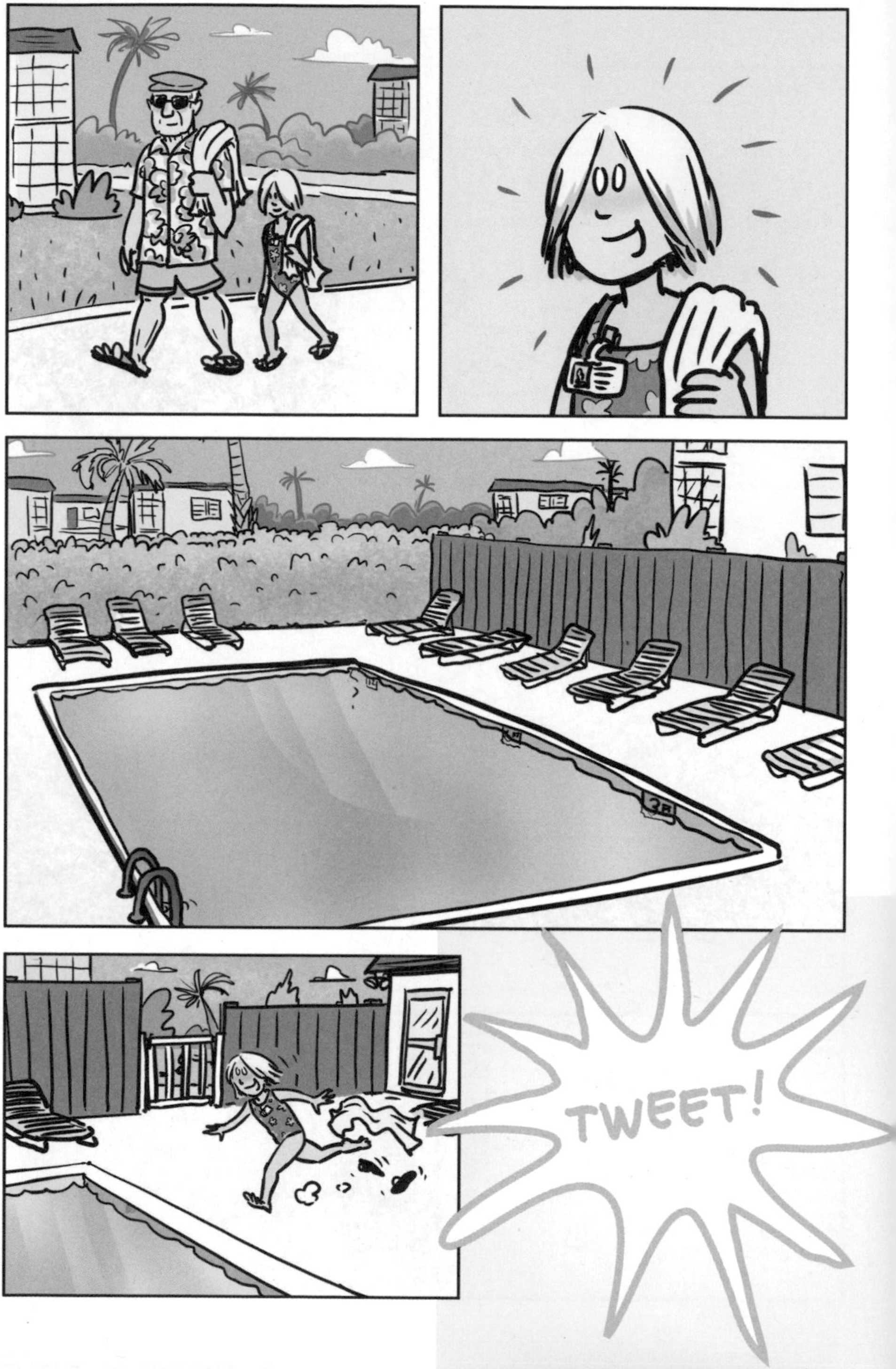
TWEET!

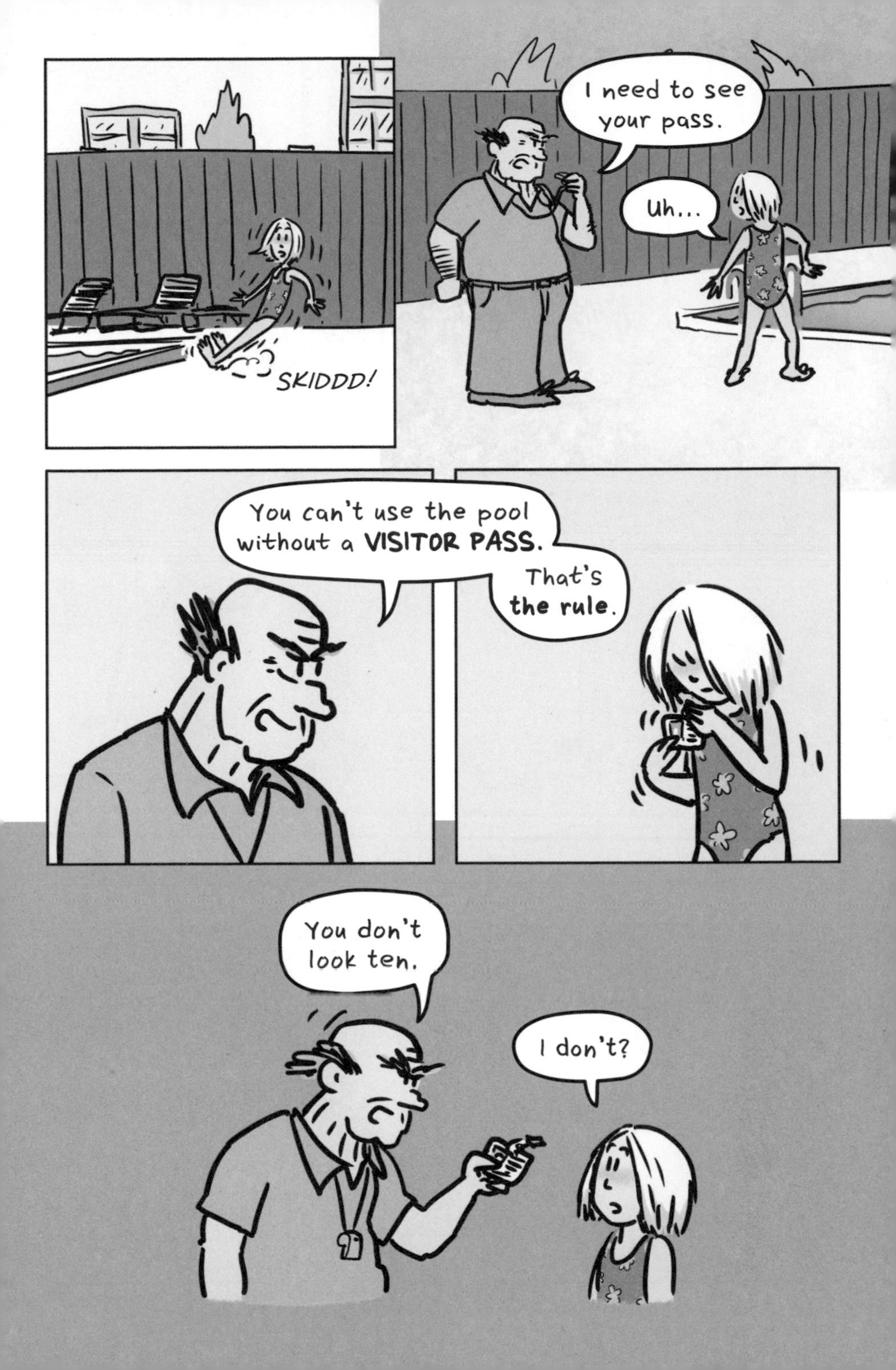
SKIDDD!
I need to see your pass.
Uh...
You can't use the pool without a **VISITOR PASS.**
That's **the rule.**
You don't look ten.
I don't?

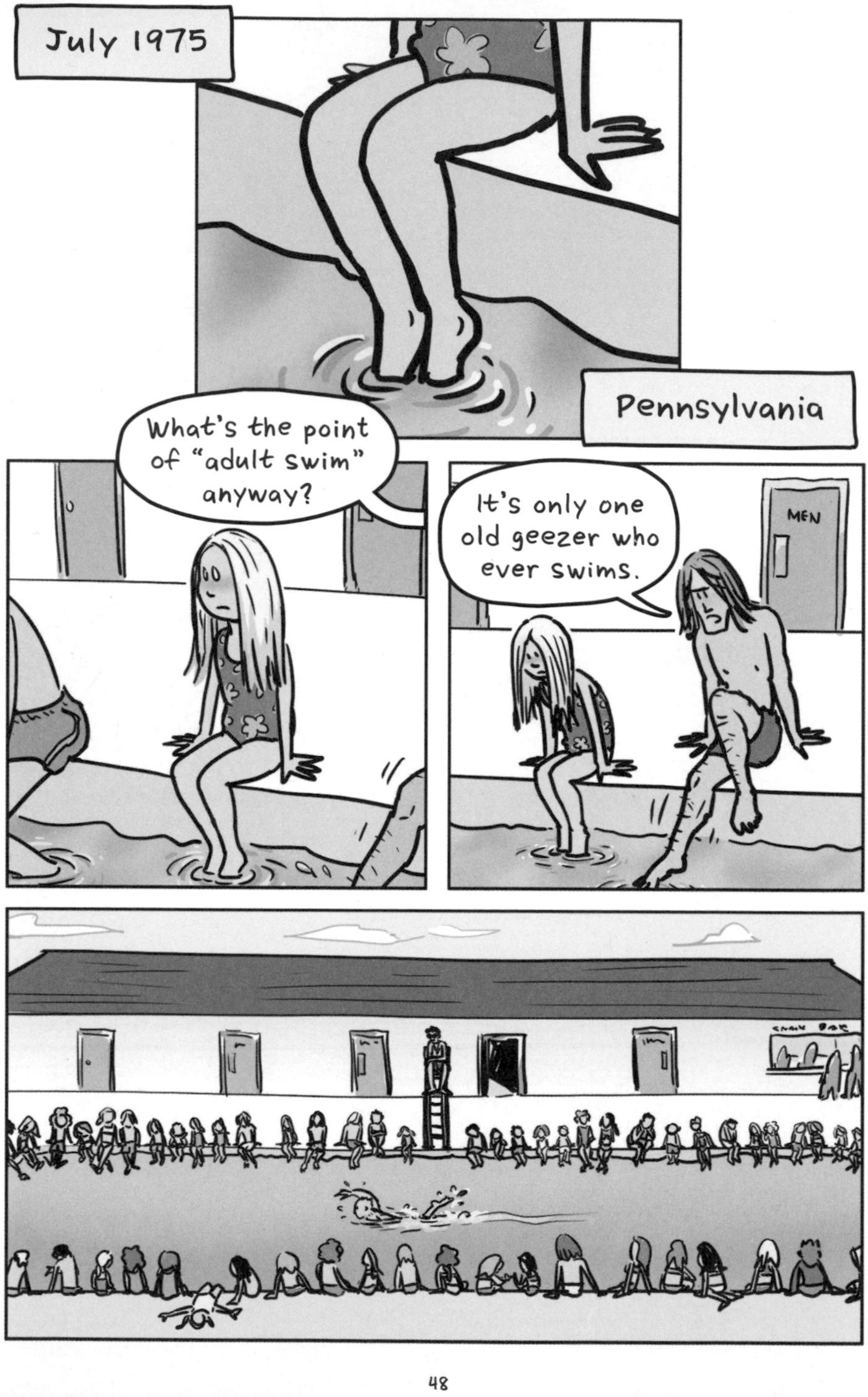
July 1975
Pennsylvania
What's the point of "adult swim" anyway?
It's only one old geezer who ever swims.
MEN

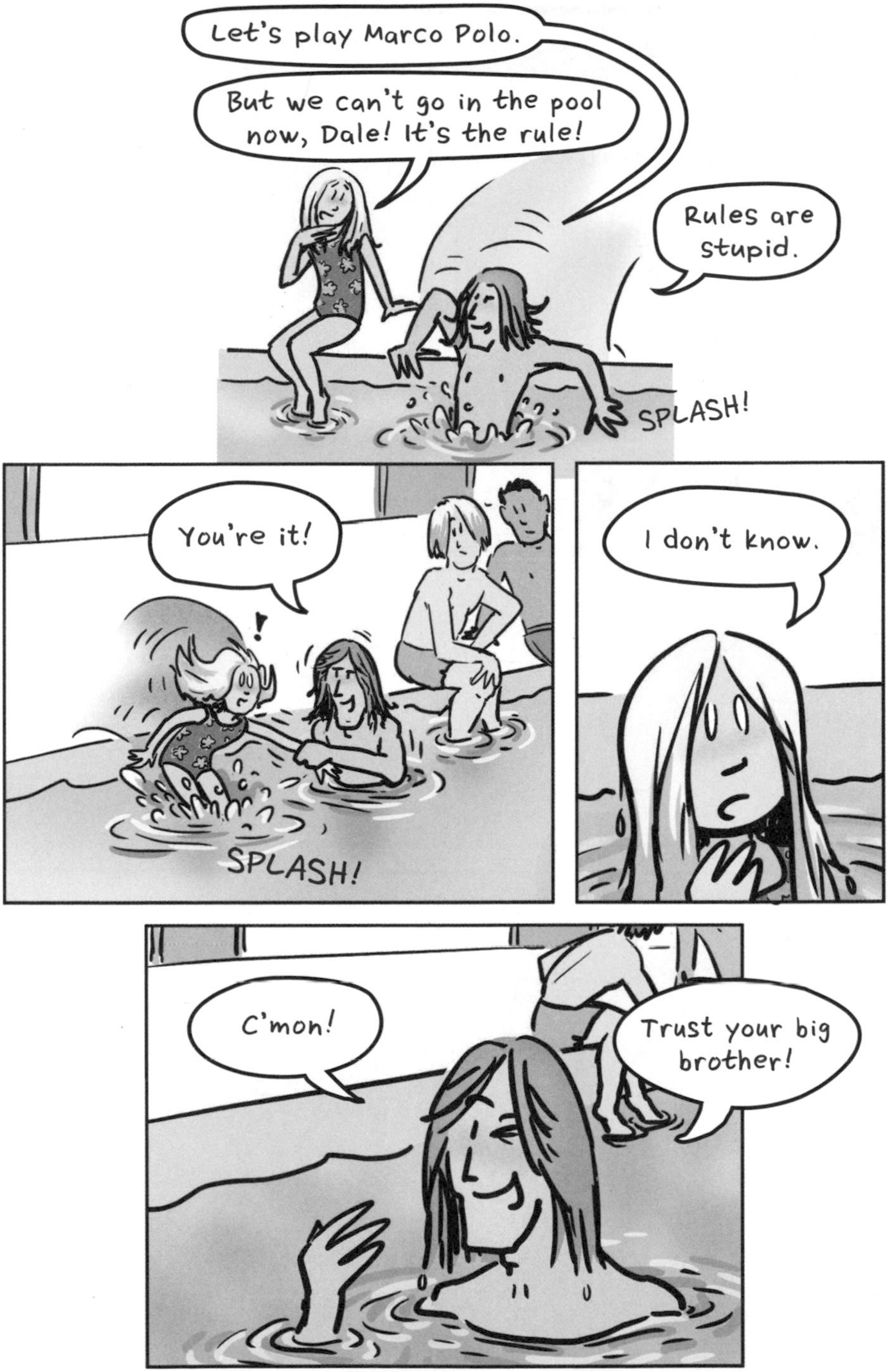
Let's play Marco Polo.
But we can't go in the pool now, Dale! It's the rule!
Rules are stupid.
SPLASH!
You're it!
SPLASH!
I don't know.
C'mon!
Trust your big brother!

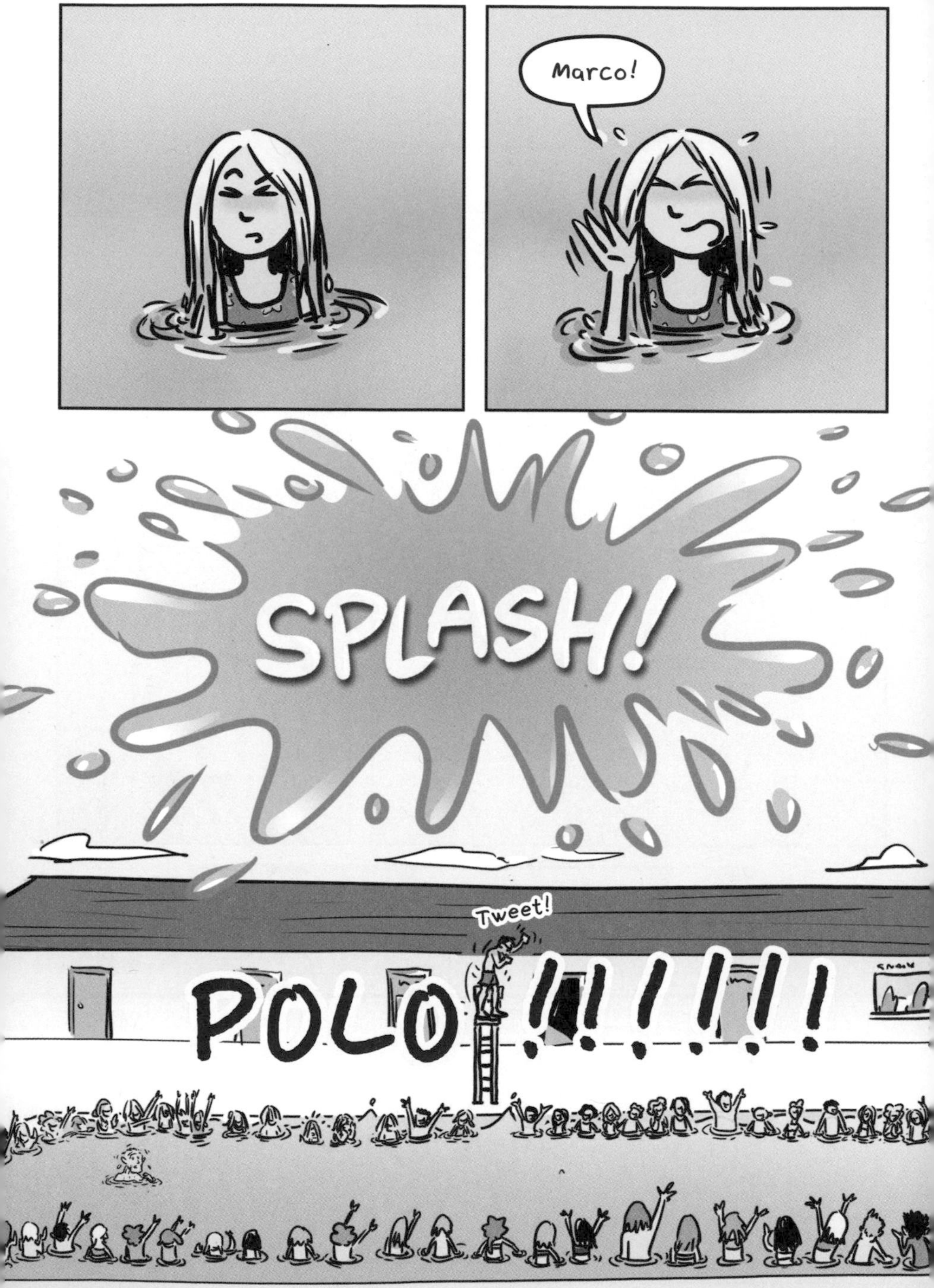
Marco!
SPLASH!
Tweet!
POLO!!!!!!

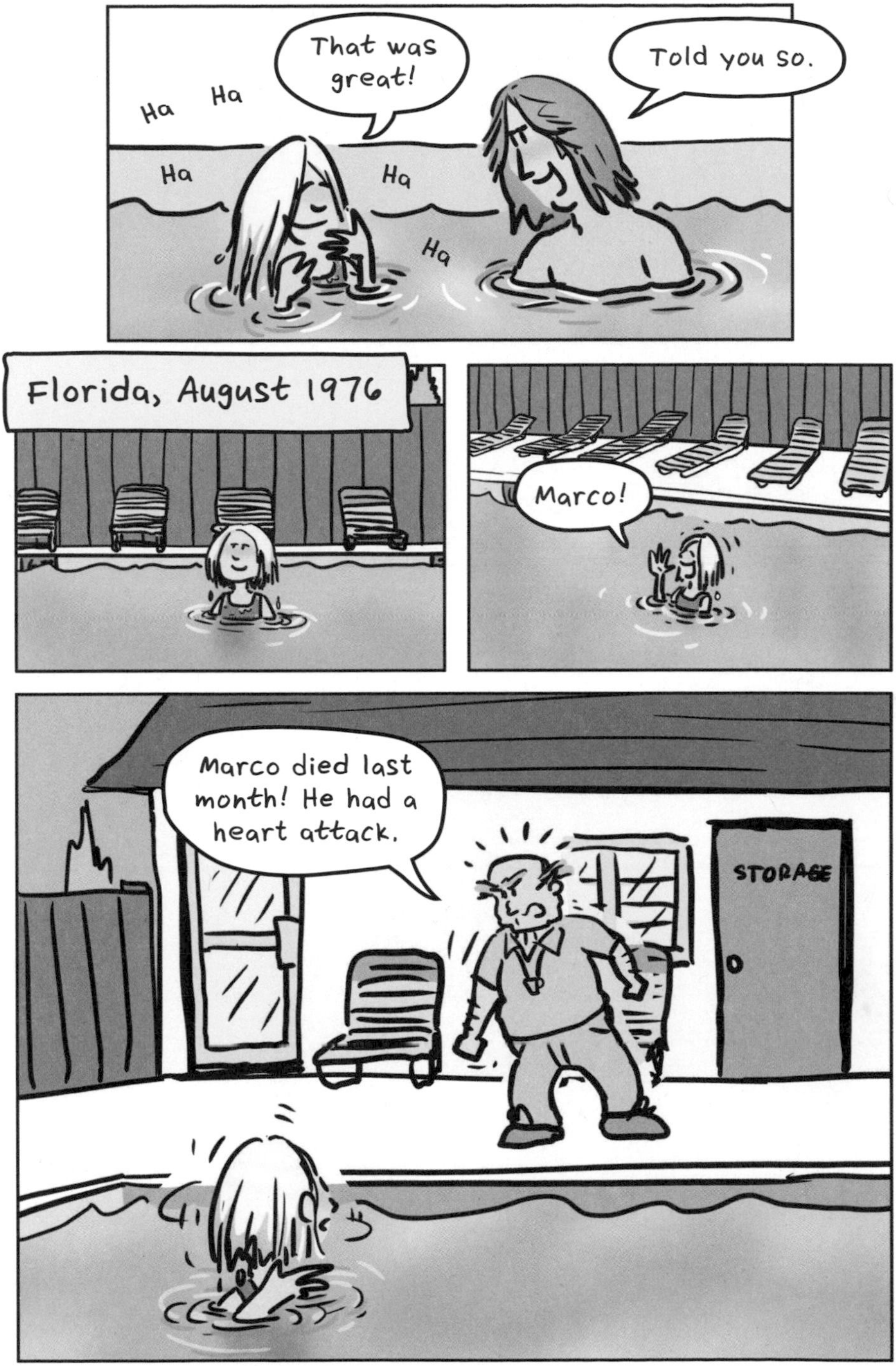
Ha Ha
That was great!
Told you so.
Ha
Ha
Ha
Florida, August 1976
Marco!
Marco died last month! He had a heart attack.
STORAGE

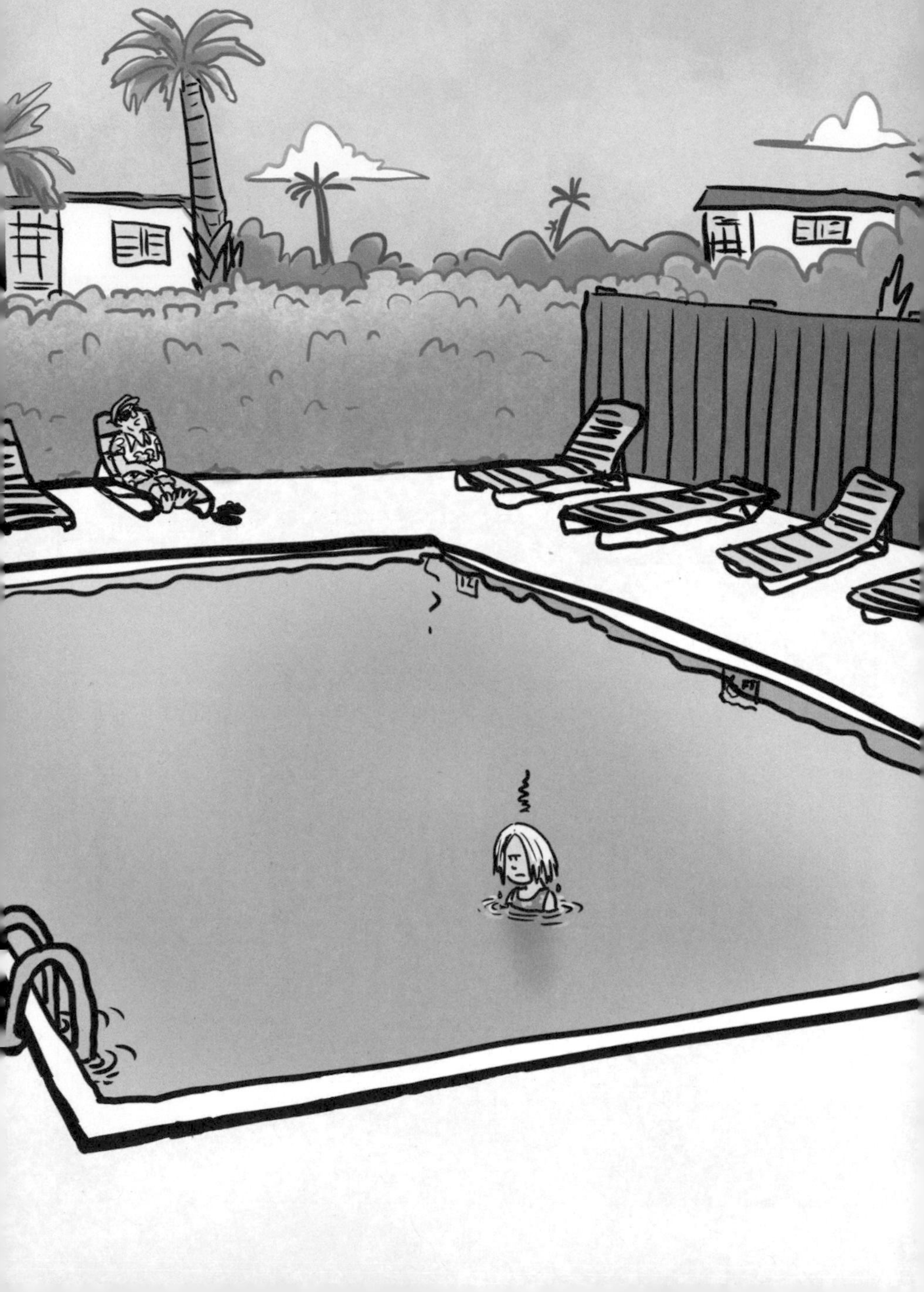

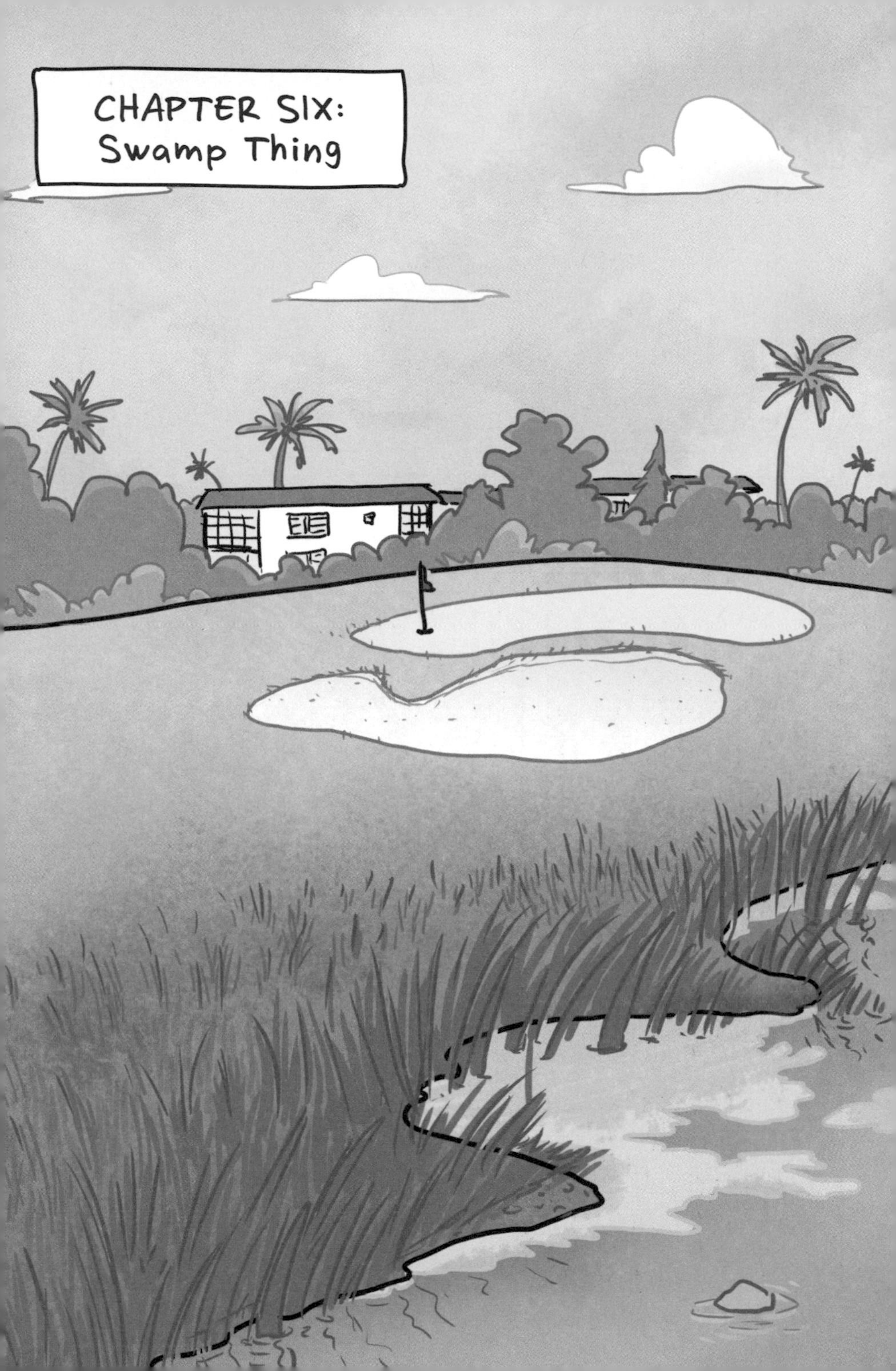
CHAPTER SIX:
Swamp Thing

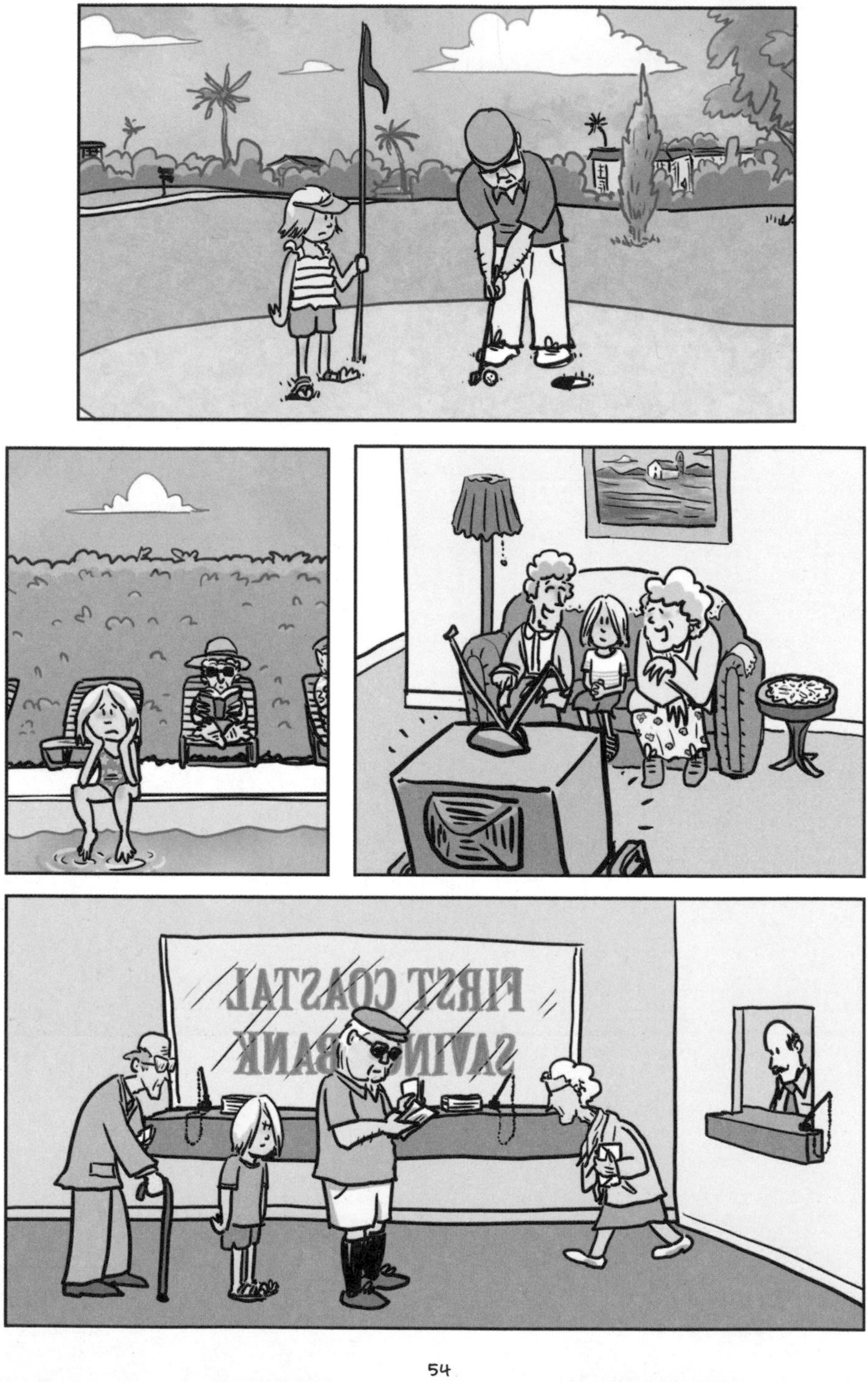
FIRST COASTAL
SAVIN BANK

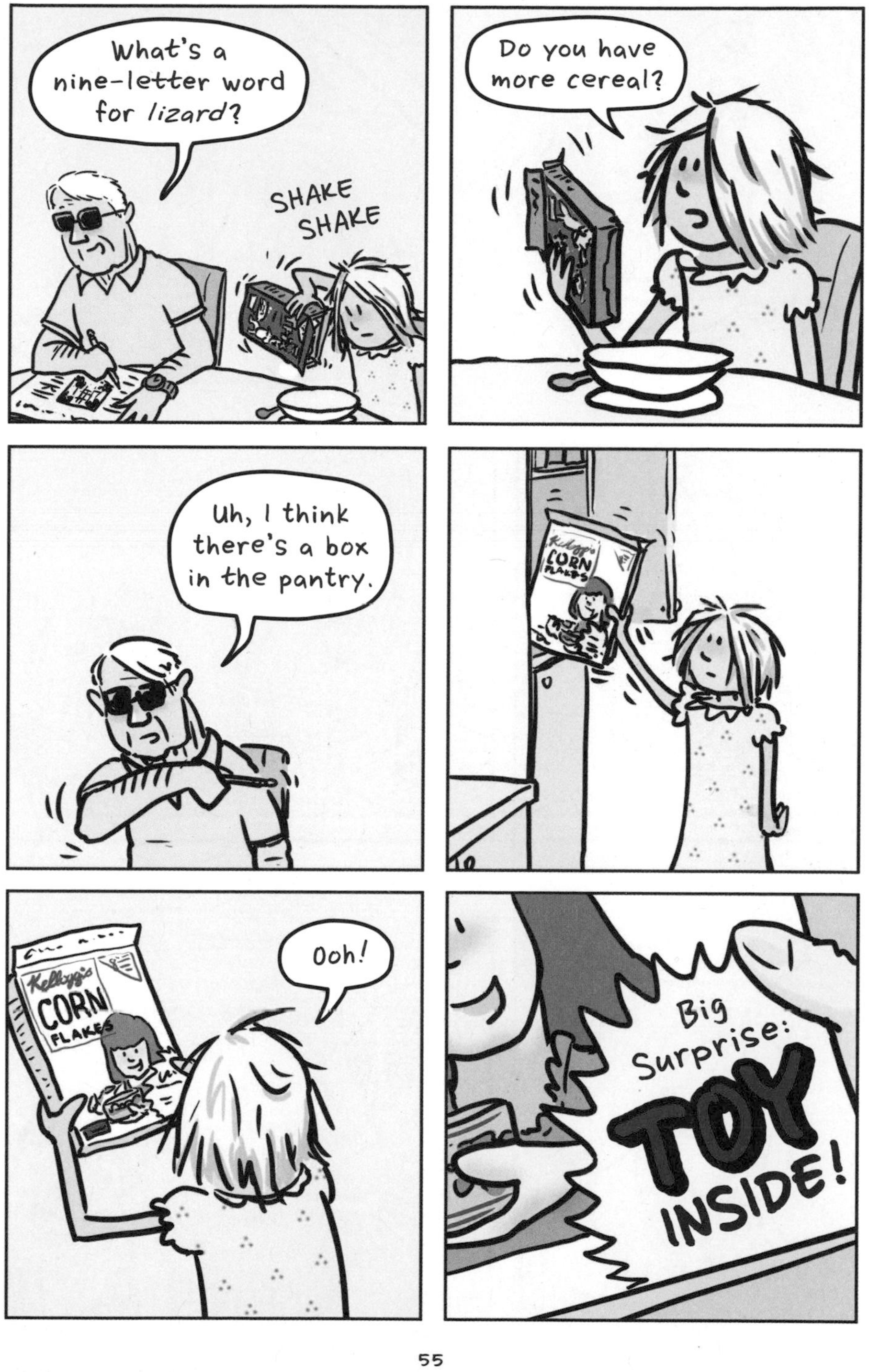

What's a nine-letter word for *lizard*?
SHAKE SHAKE
Do you have more cereal?
Uh, I think there's a box in the pantry.
Kellogg's CORN FLAKES
Ooh!
Big Surprise: TOY INSIDE!

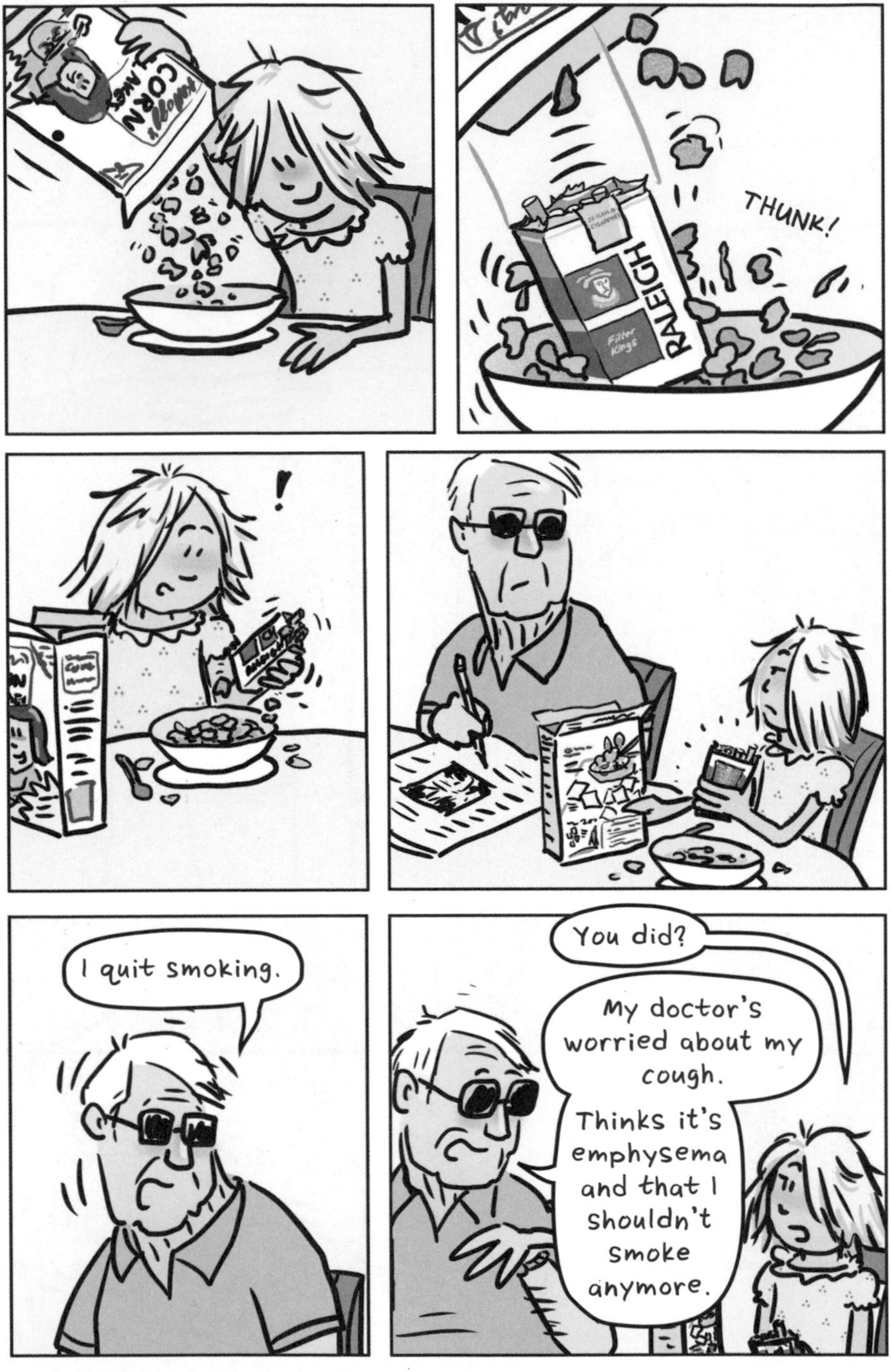
CORN FLAKES
RALEIGH
Filter Kings
THUNK!
!
I quit smoking.
You did?
My doctor's worried about my cough.
Thinks it's emphysema and that I shouldn't smoke anymore.

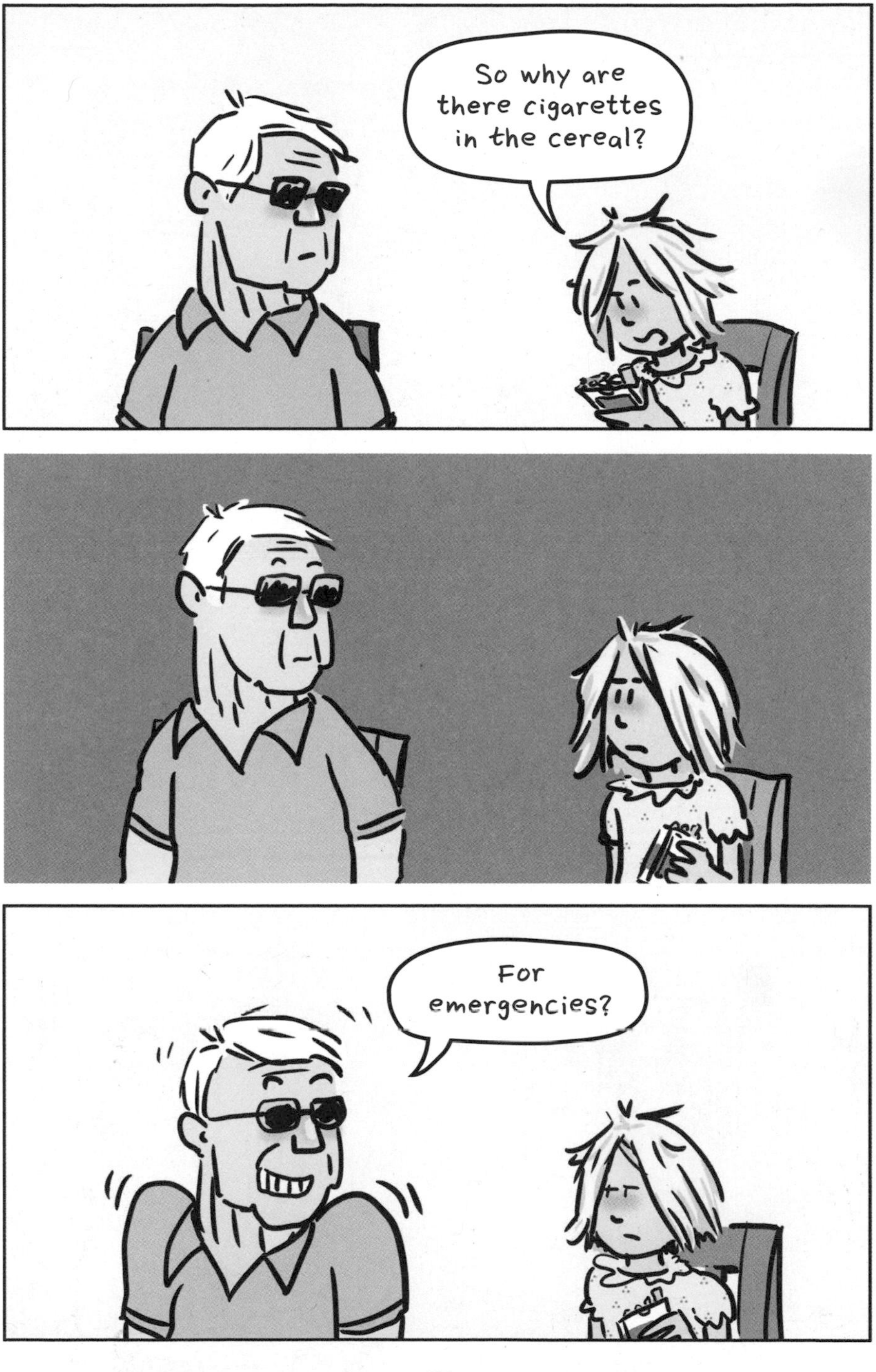
So why are there cigarettes in the cereal?
For emergencies?

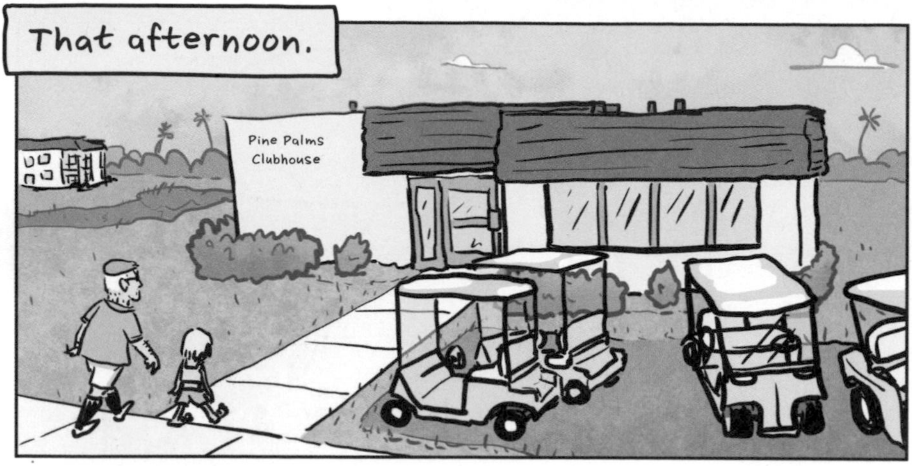
That afternoon.
Pine Palms
Clubhouse

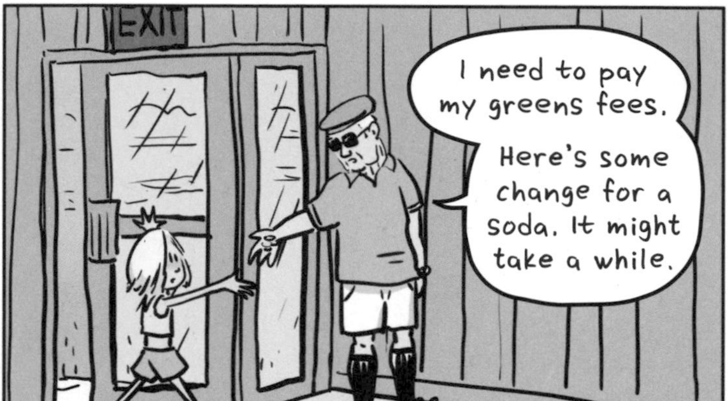
EXIT
I need to pay my greens fees.
Here's some change for a soda. It might take a while.

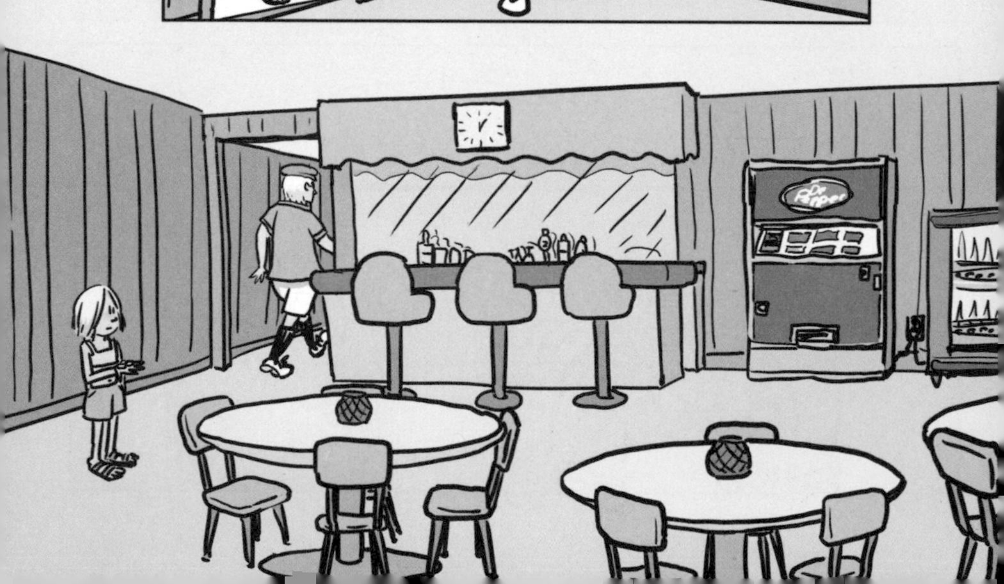
Dr Pepper

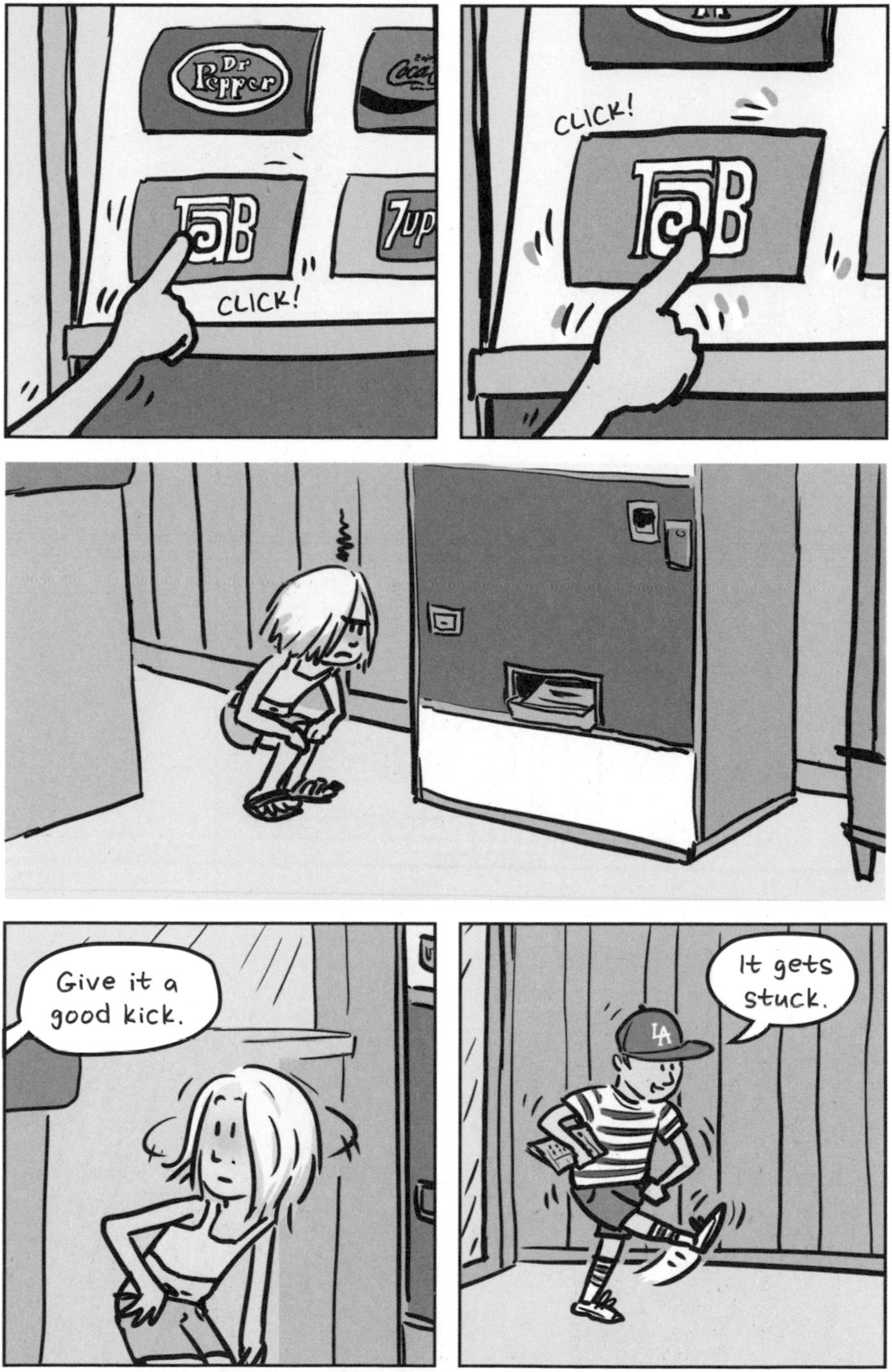
Dr Pepper
Coca-Cola
TaB
7up
CLICK!
CLICK!
TaB
Give it a good kick.
It gets stuck.
LA

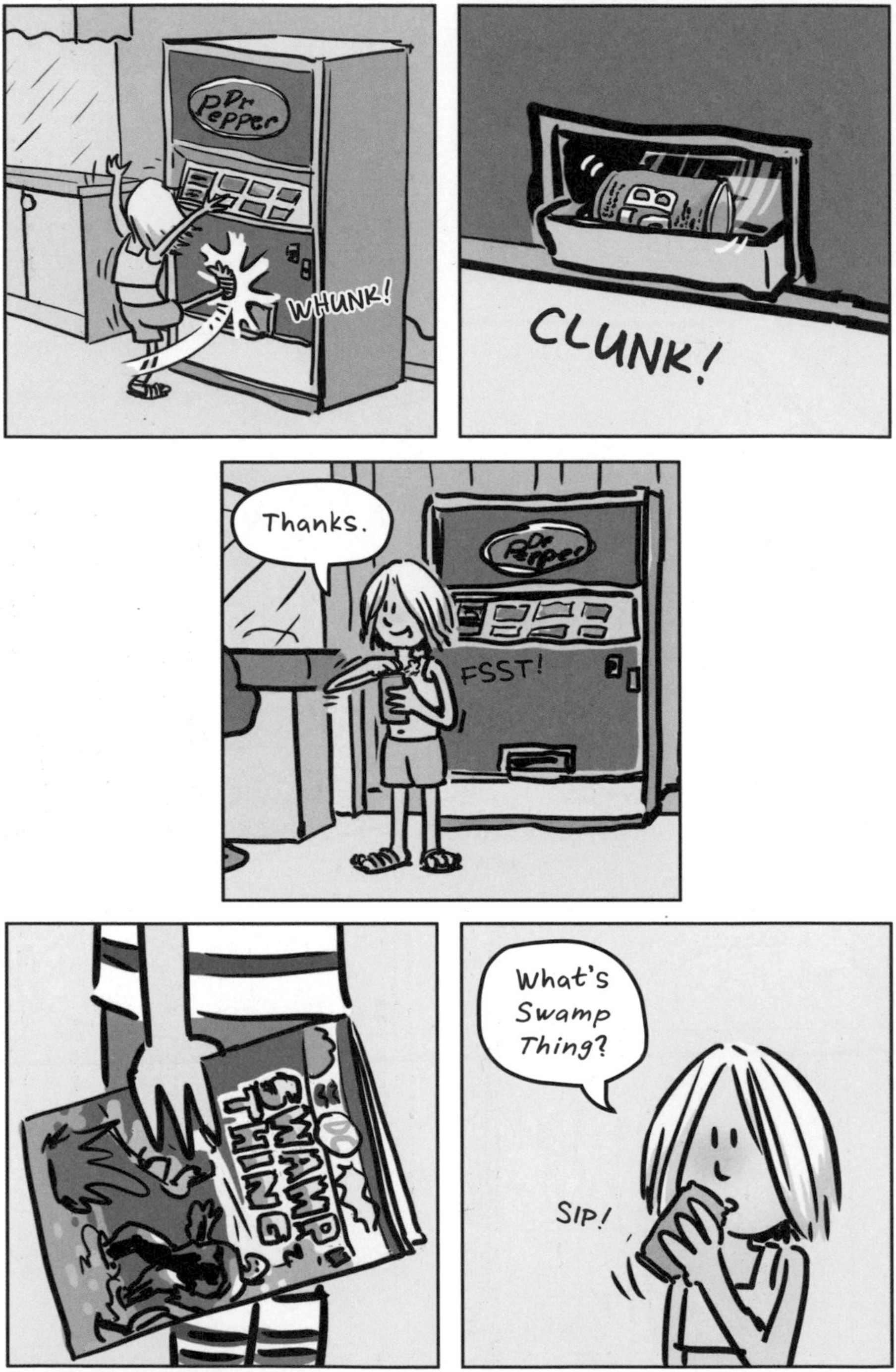
Dr Pepper
WHUNK!
CLUNK!
Thanks.
Dr Pepper
FSST!
DC
SWAMP THING
What's Swamp Thing?
SIP!

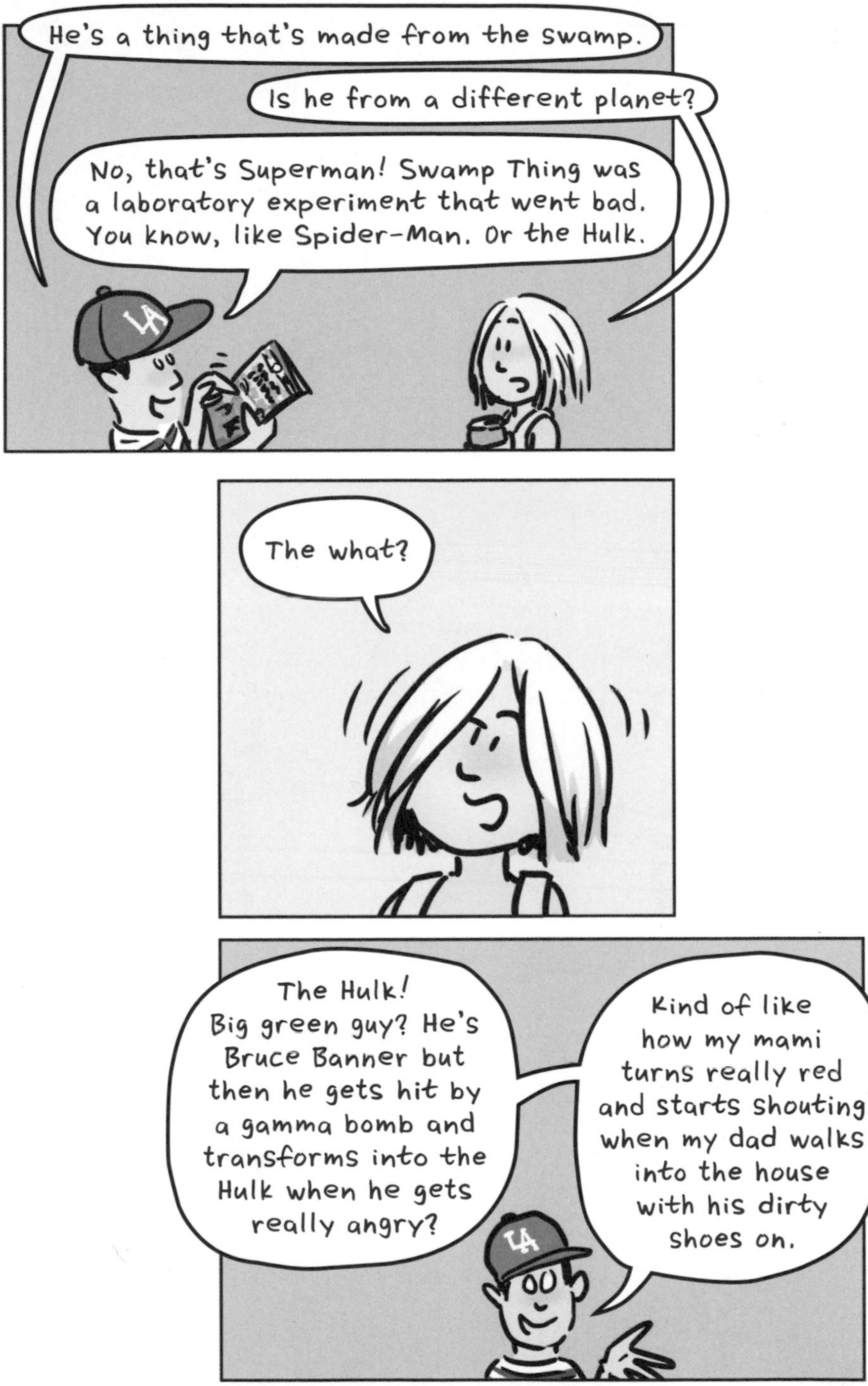
He's a thing that's made from the swamp.
Is he from a different planet?
No, that's Superman! Swamp Thing was a laboratory experiment that went bad. You know, like Spider-Man. Or the Hulk.
The what?
The Hulk! Big green guy? He's Bruce Banner but then he gets hit by a gamma bomb and transforms into the Hulk when he gets really angry?
Kind of like how my mami turns really red and starts shouting when my dad walks into the house with his dirty shoes on.

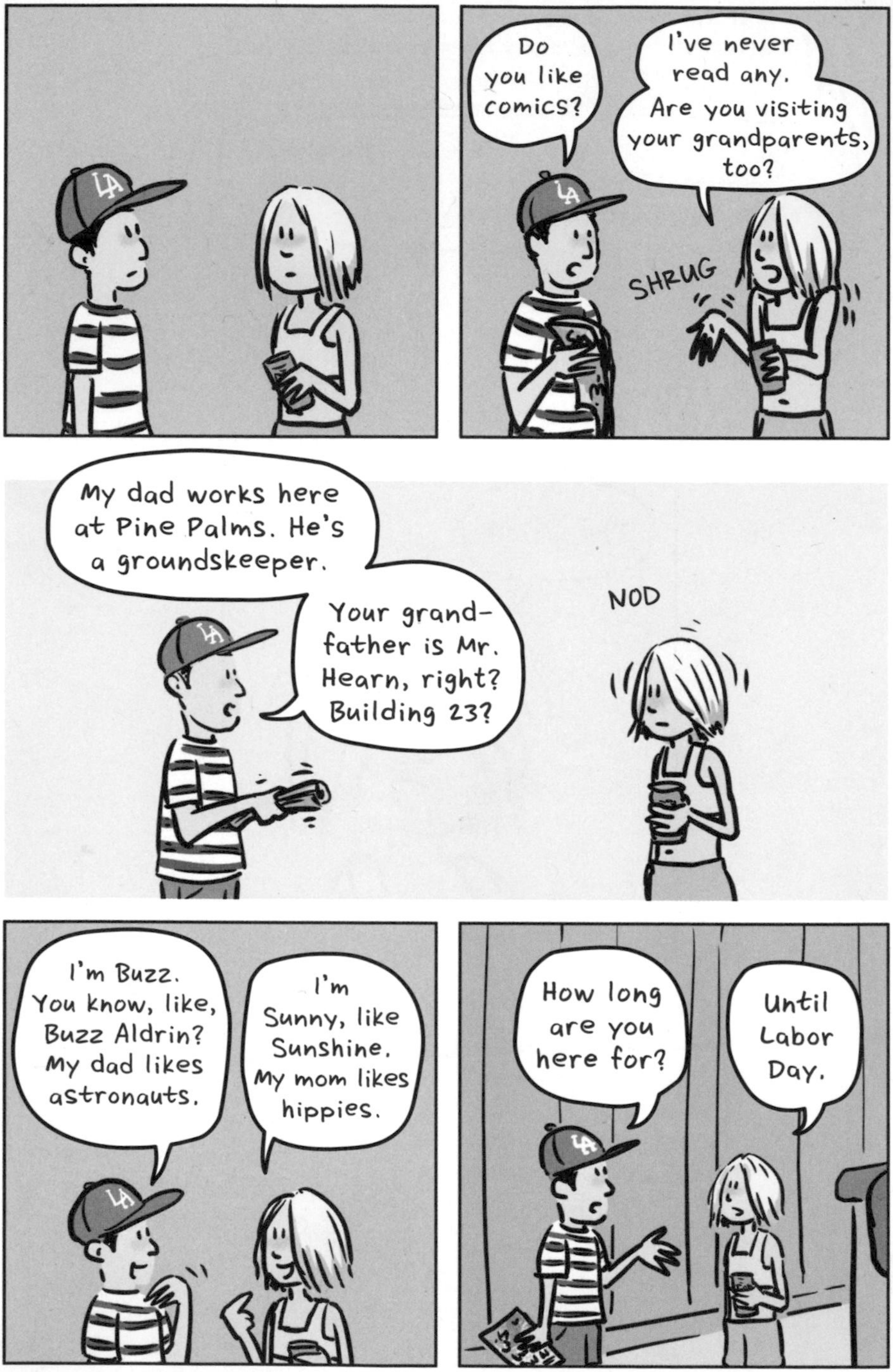
Do you like comics?
I've never read any. Are you visiting your grandparents, too?
SHRUG
My dad works here at Pine Palms. He's a groundskeeper.
Your grandfather is Mr. Hearn, right? Building 23?
NOD
I'm Buzz. You know, like, Buzz Aldrin? My dad likes astronauts.
I'm Sunny, like Sunshine. My mom likes hippies.
How long are you here for?
Until Labor Day.

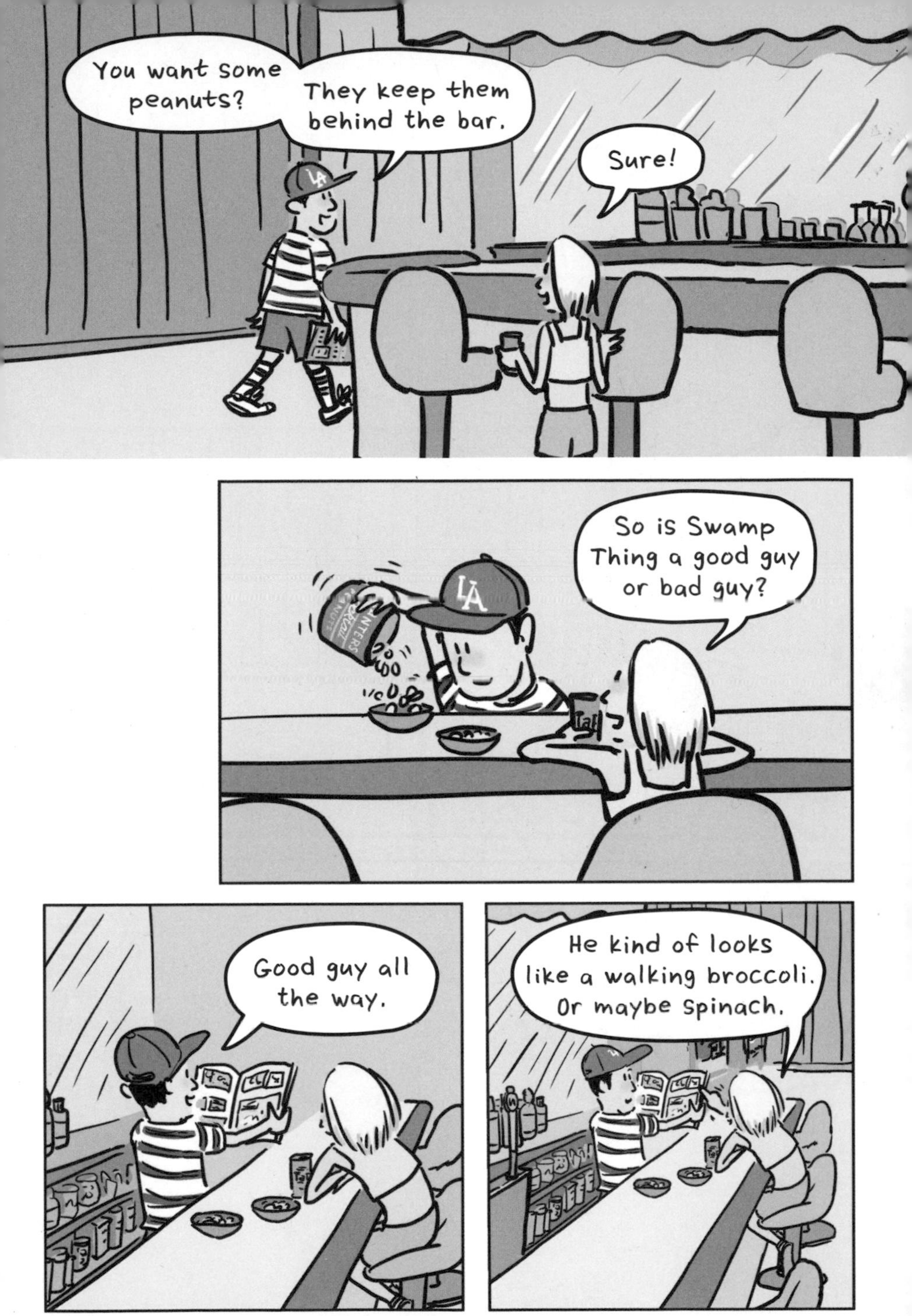
You want some peanuts?
They keep them behind the bar.
Sure!
So is Swamp Thing a good guy or bad guy?
Good guy all the way.
He kind of looks like a walking broccoli. Or maybe spinach.

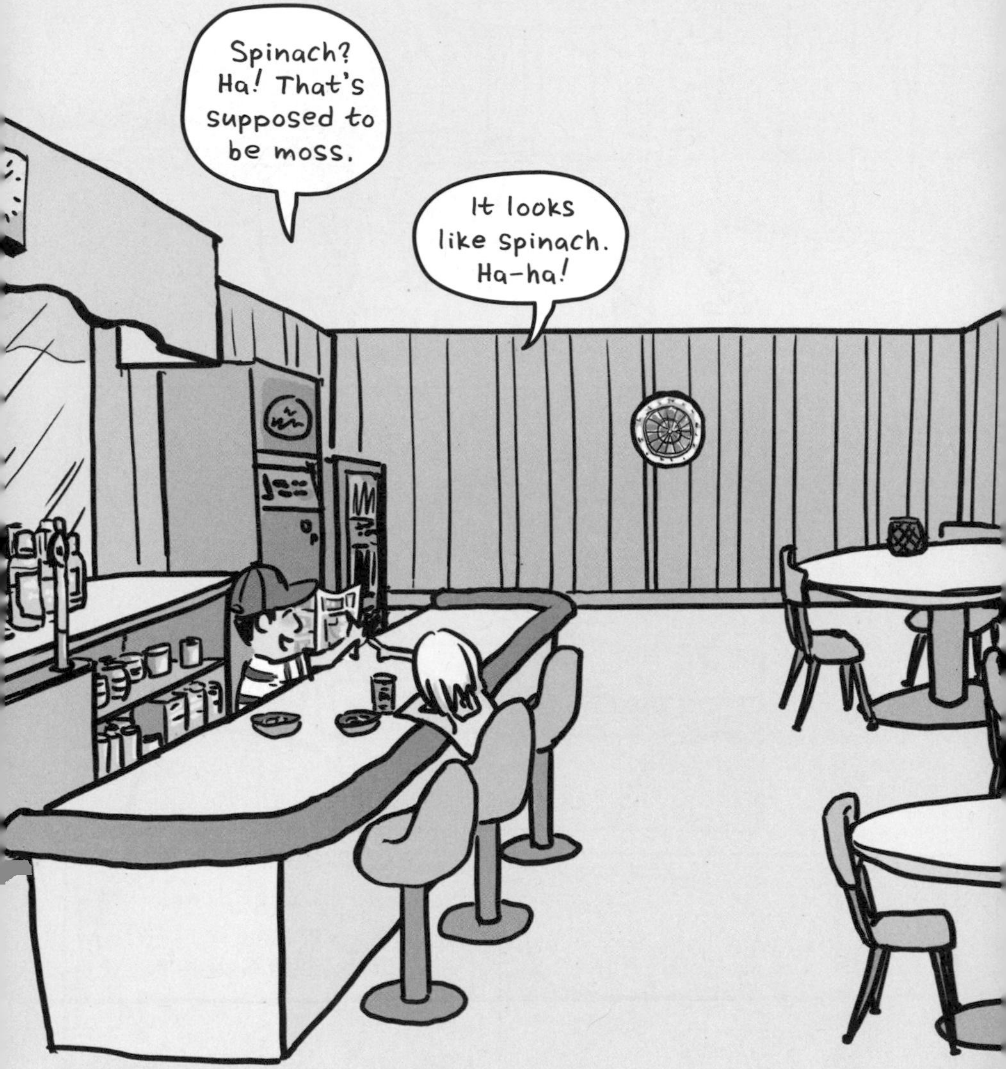
Spinach? Ha! That's supposed to be moss.
It looks like spinach. Ha-ha!

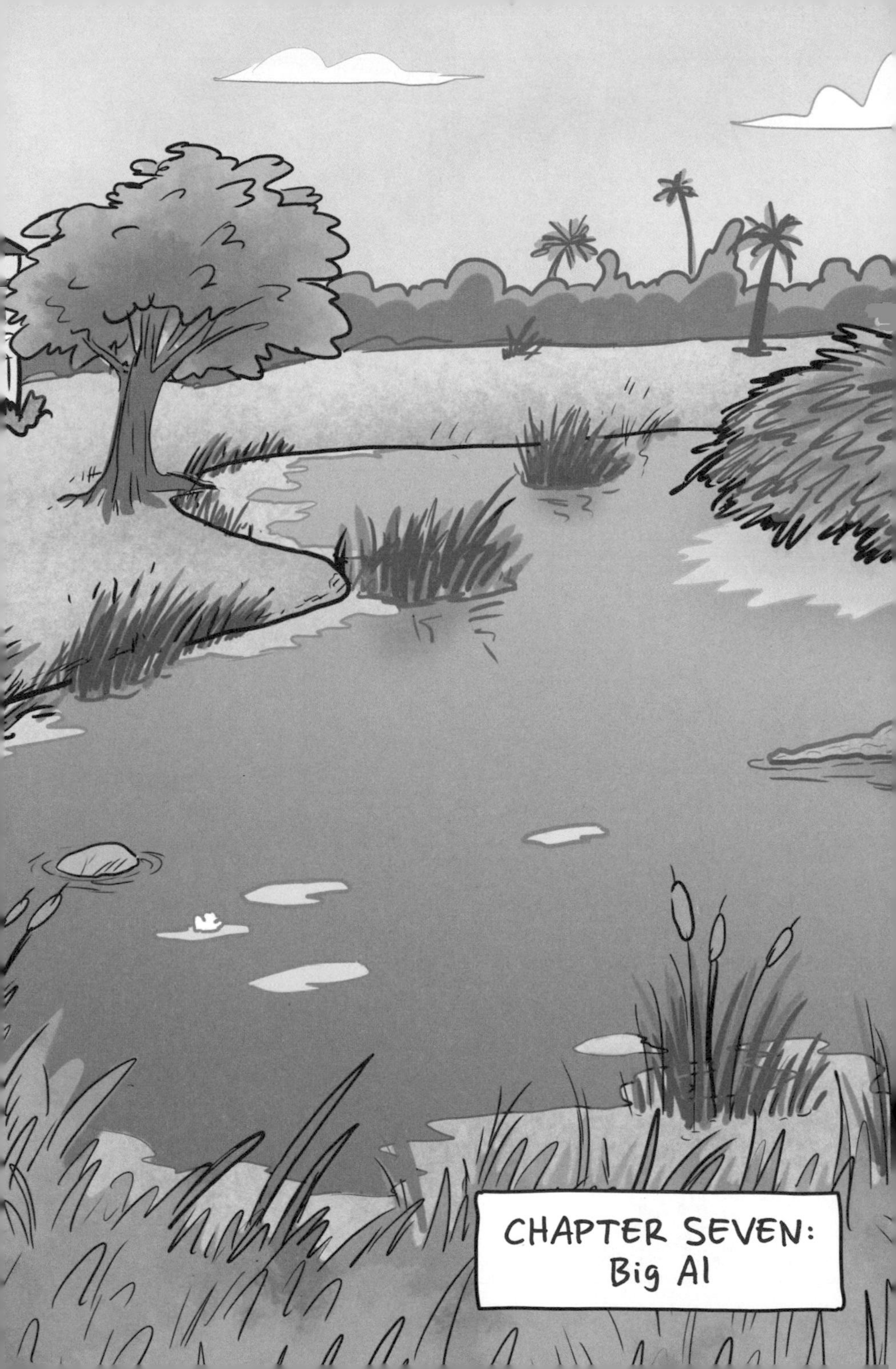
CHAPTER SEVEN:
Big Al

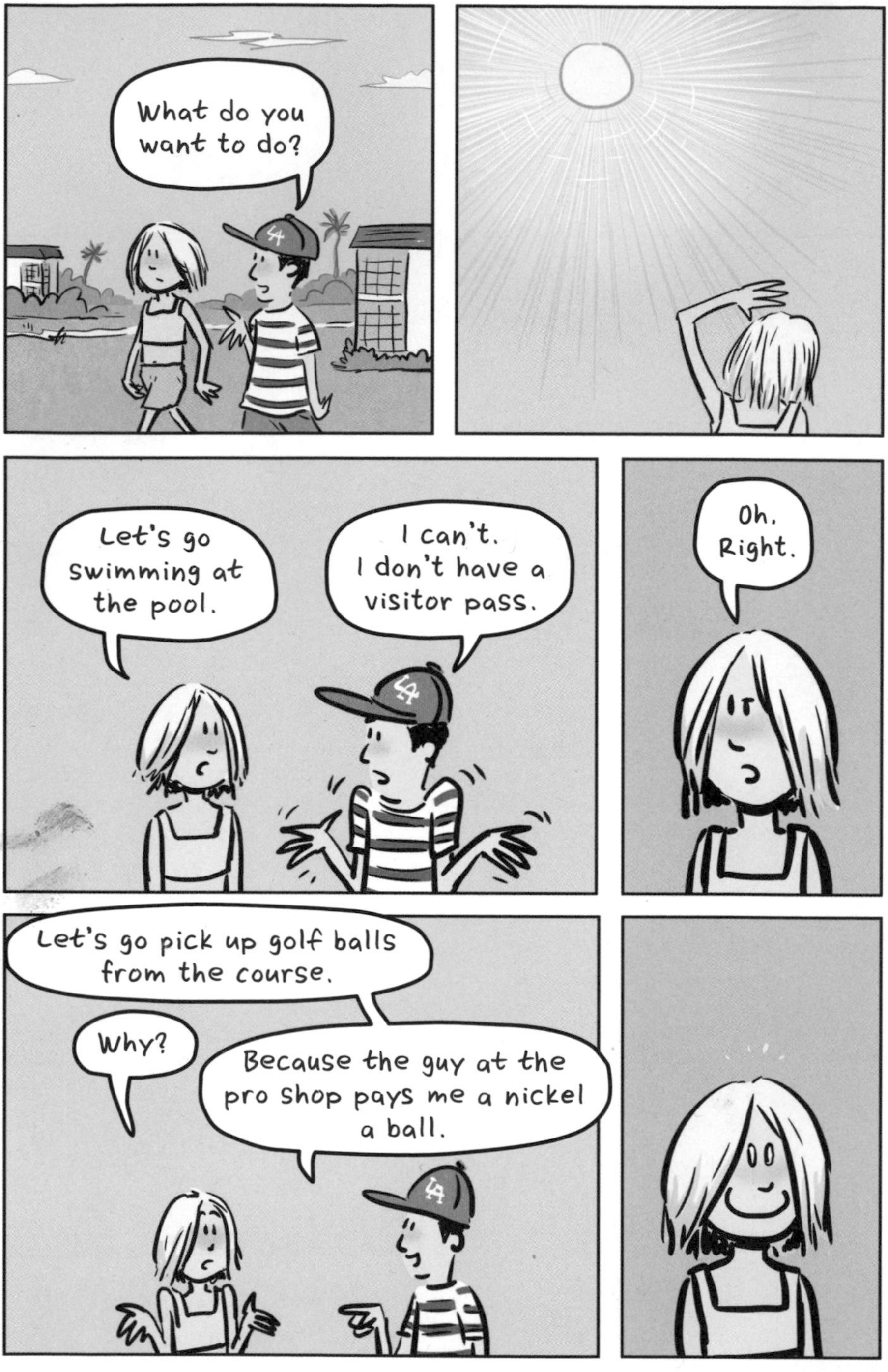
What do you want to do?
Let's go swimming at the pool.
I can't. I don't have a visitor pass.
Oh. Right.
Let's go pick up golf balls from the course.
Why?
Because the guy at the pro shop pays me a nickel a ball.

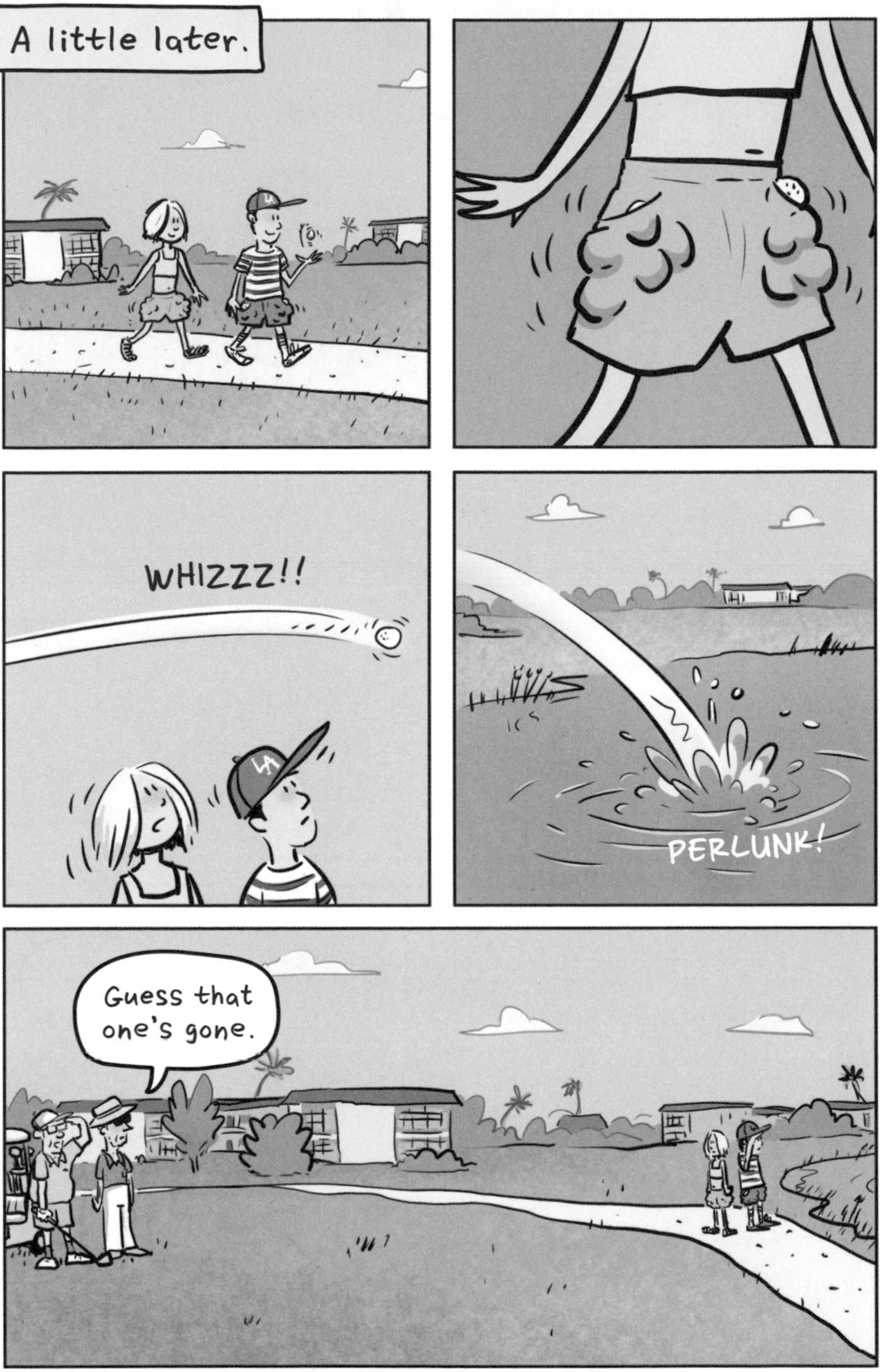
A little later.
WHIZZZ!!
PERLUNK!
Guess that one's gone.

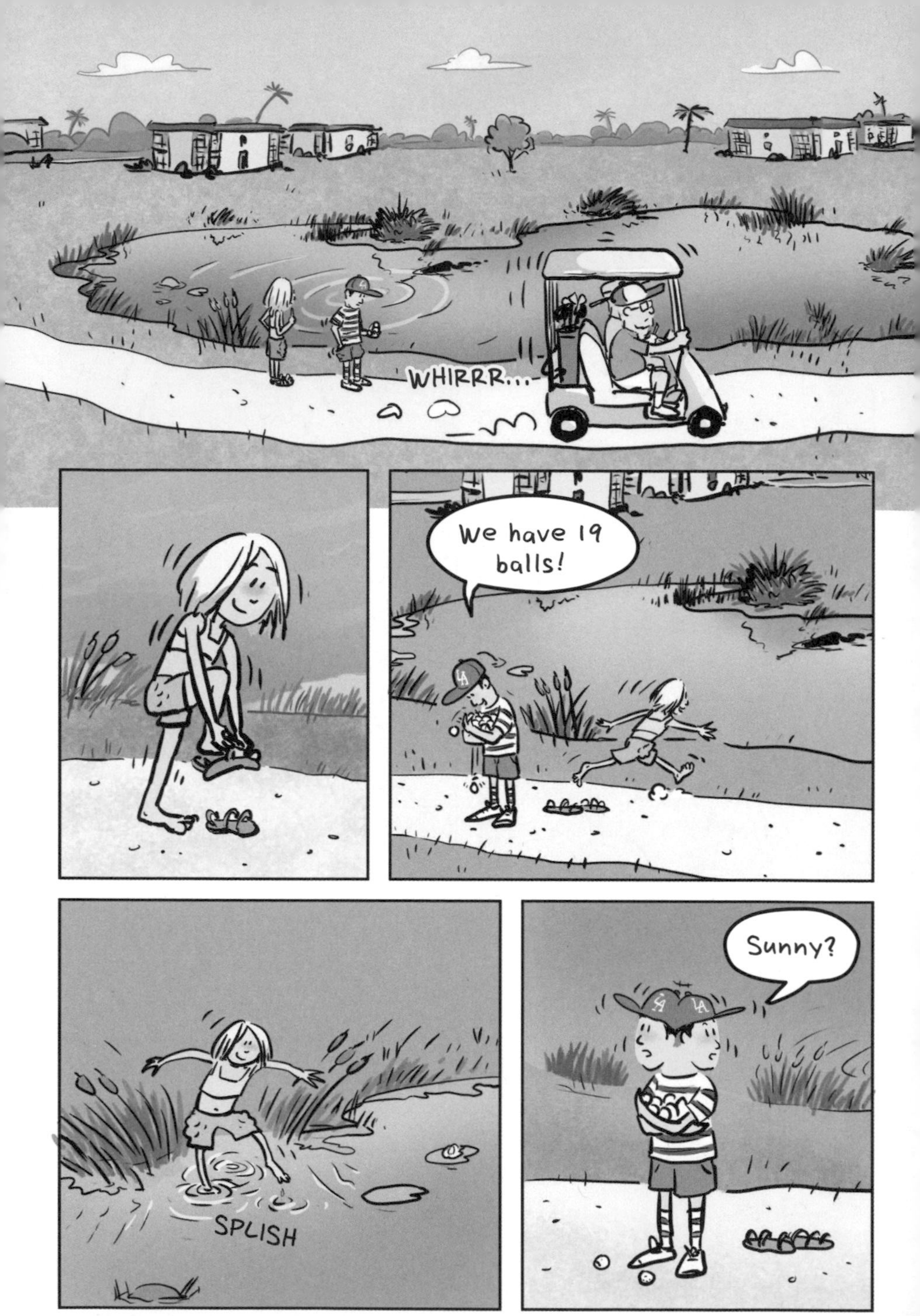

WHIRRR...
We have 19 balls!
SPLISH
Sunny?

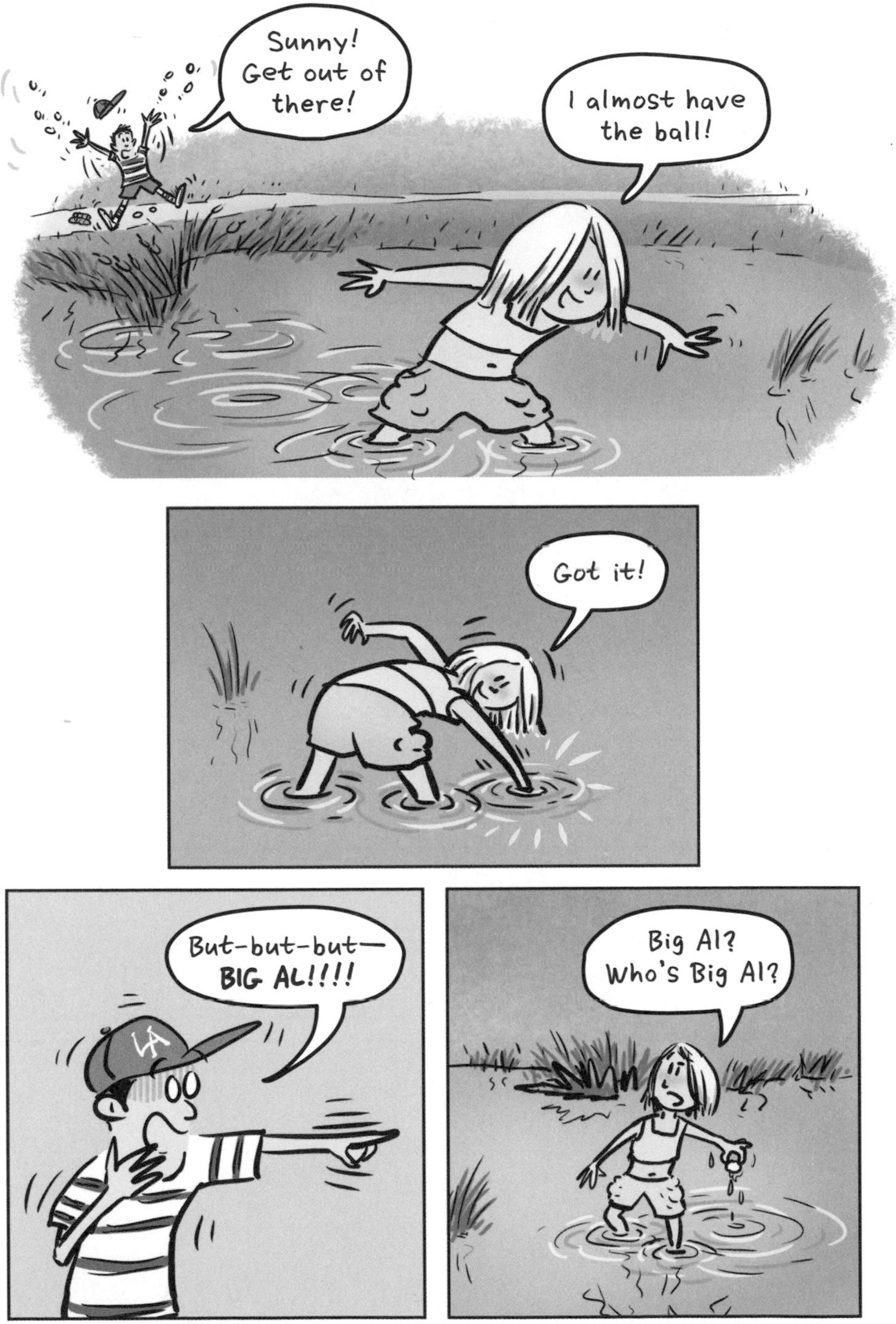
Sunny! Get out of there!
I almost have the ball!
Got it!
But-but-but—**BIG AL!!!!**
Big Al? Who's Big Al?

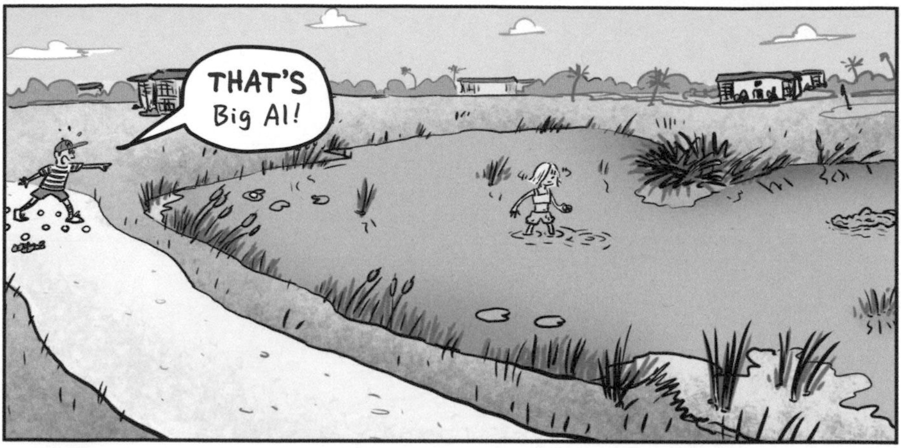
THAT'S
Big Al!

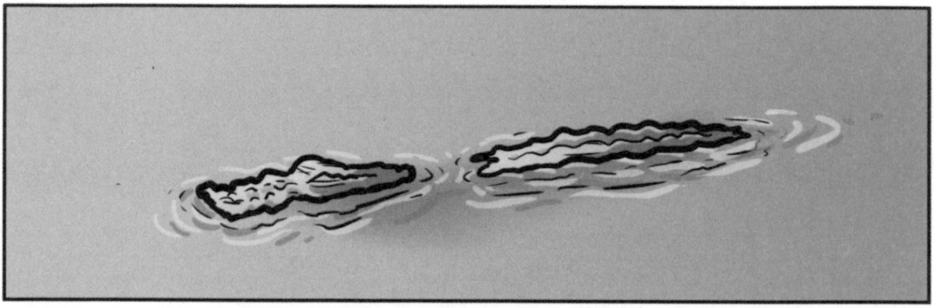

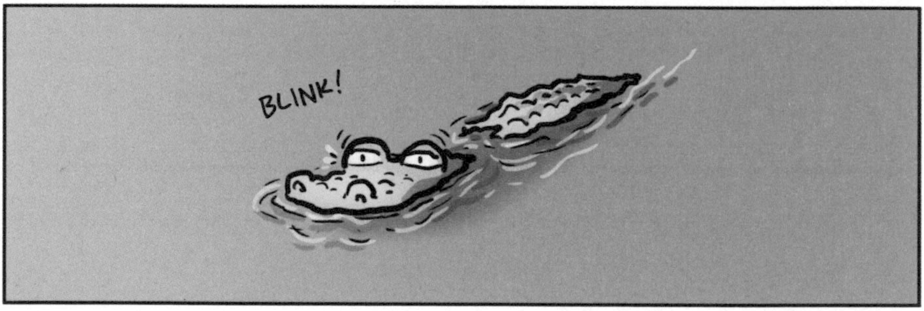
BLINK!

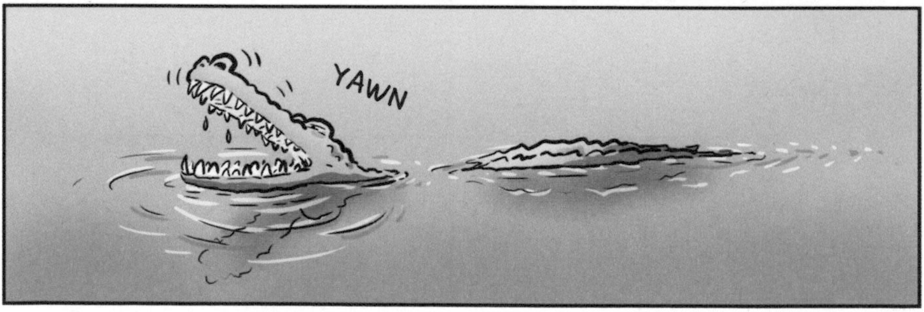
YAWN

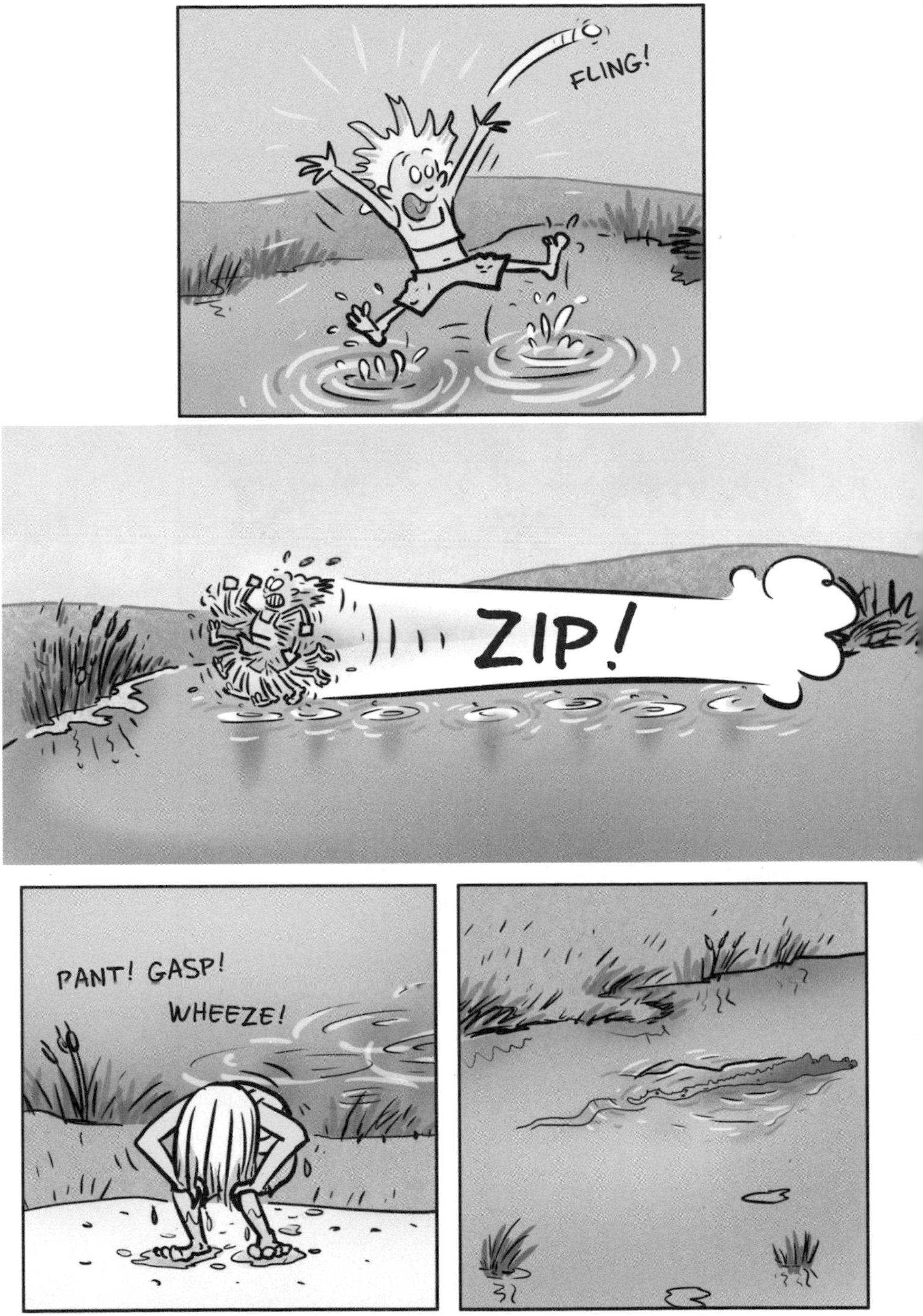
FLING!
ZIP!
PANT! GASP!
WHEEZE!

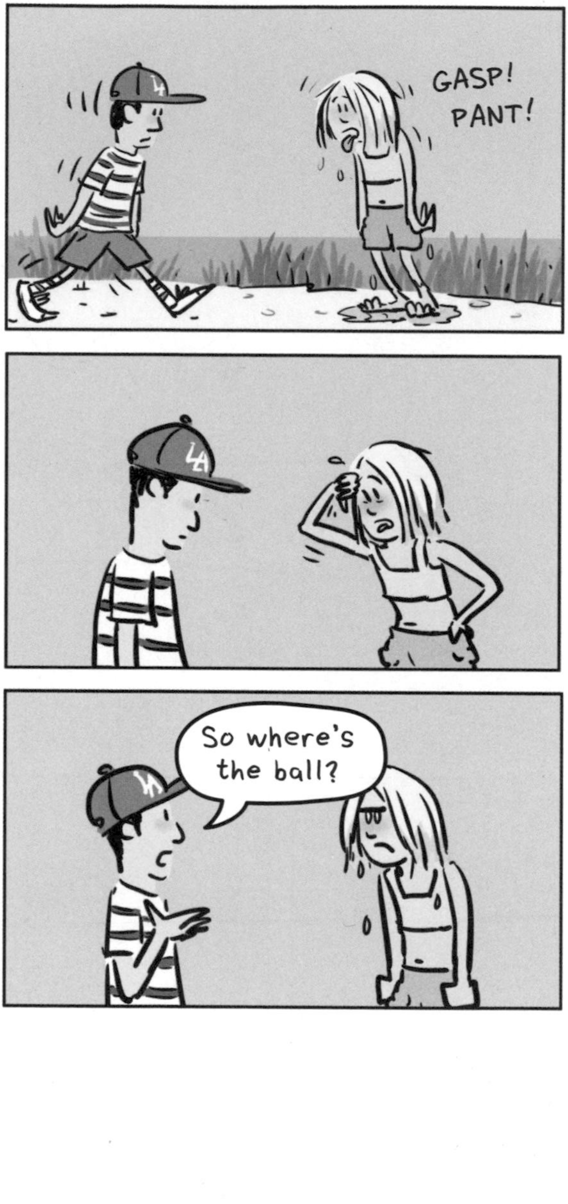
GASP!
PANT!
So where's the ball?

CHAPTER EIGHT:
Spinner Rack

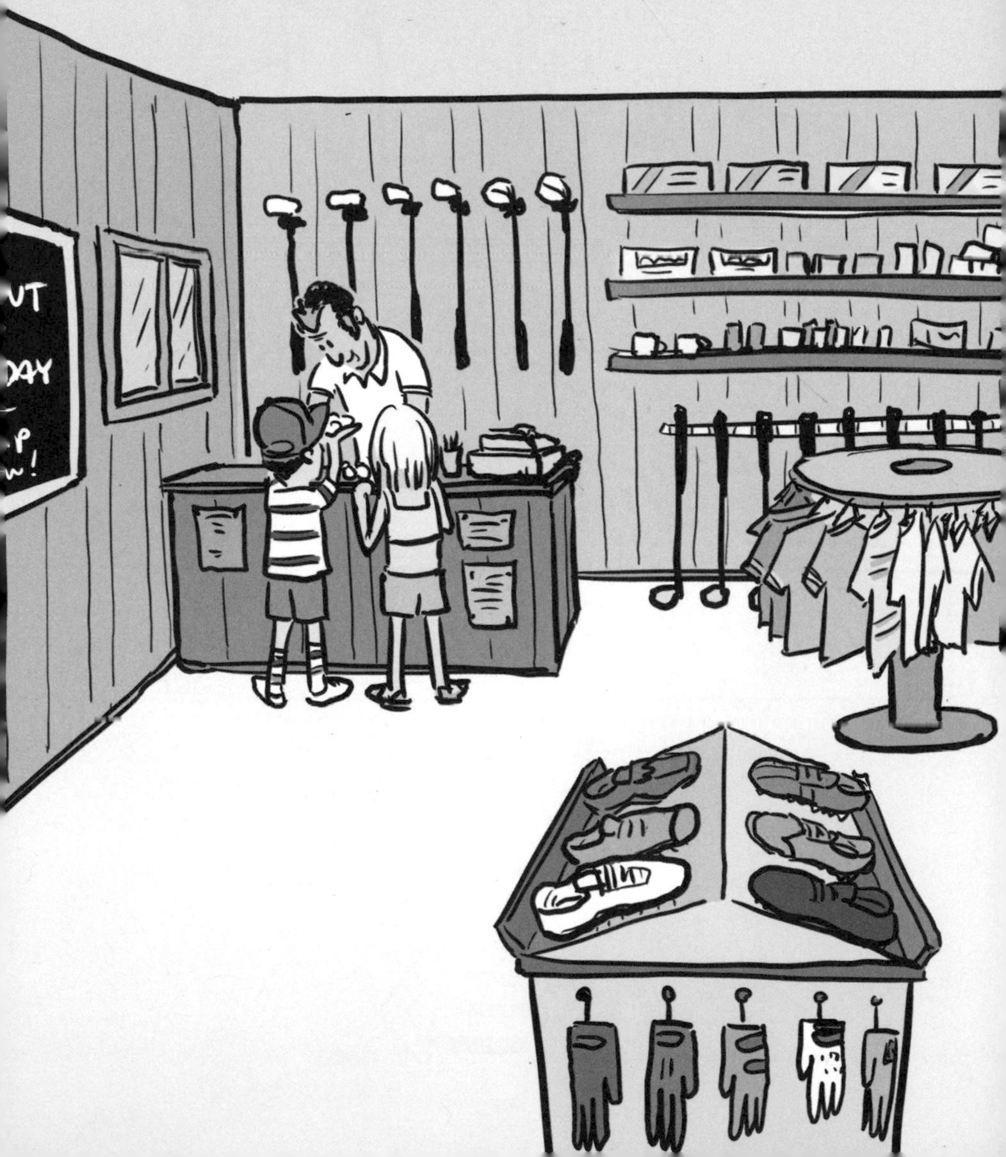

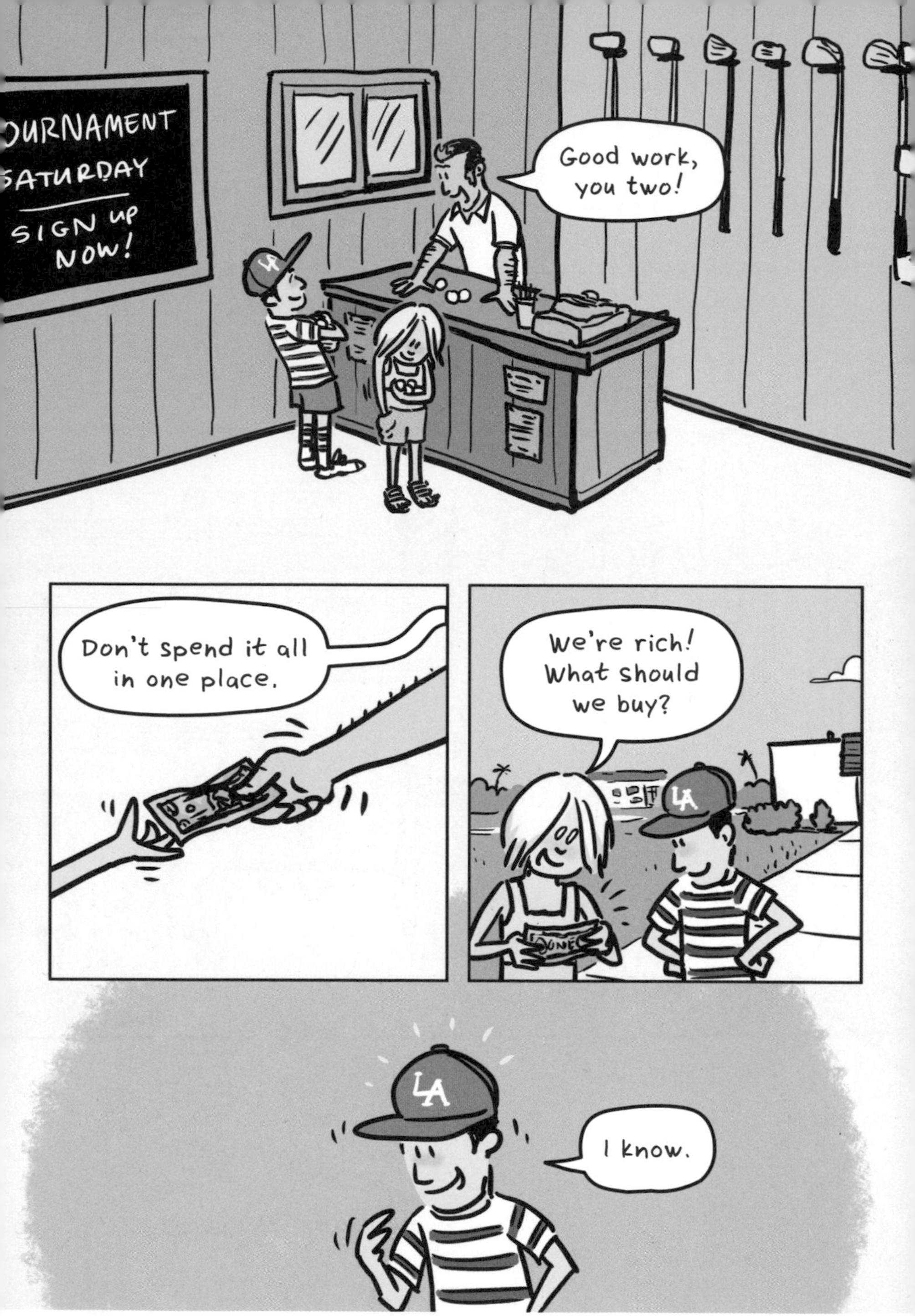
OURNAMENT
SATURDAY
SIGN UP NOW!
Good work, you two!
Don't spend it all in one place.
We're rich! What should we buy?
I know.

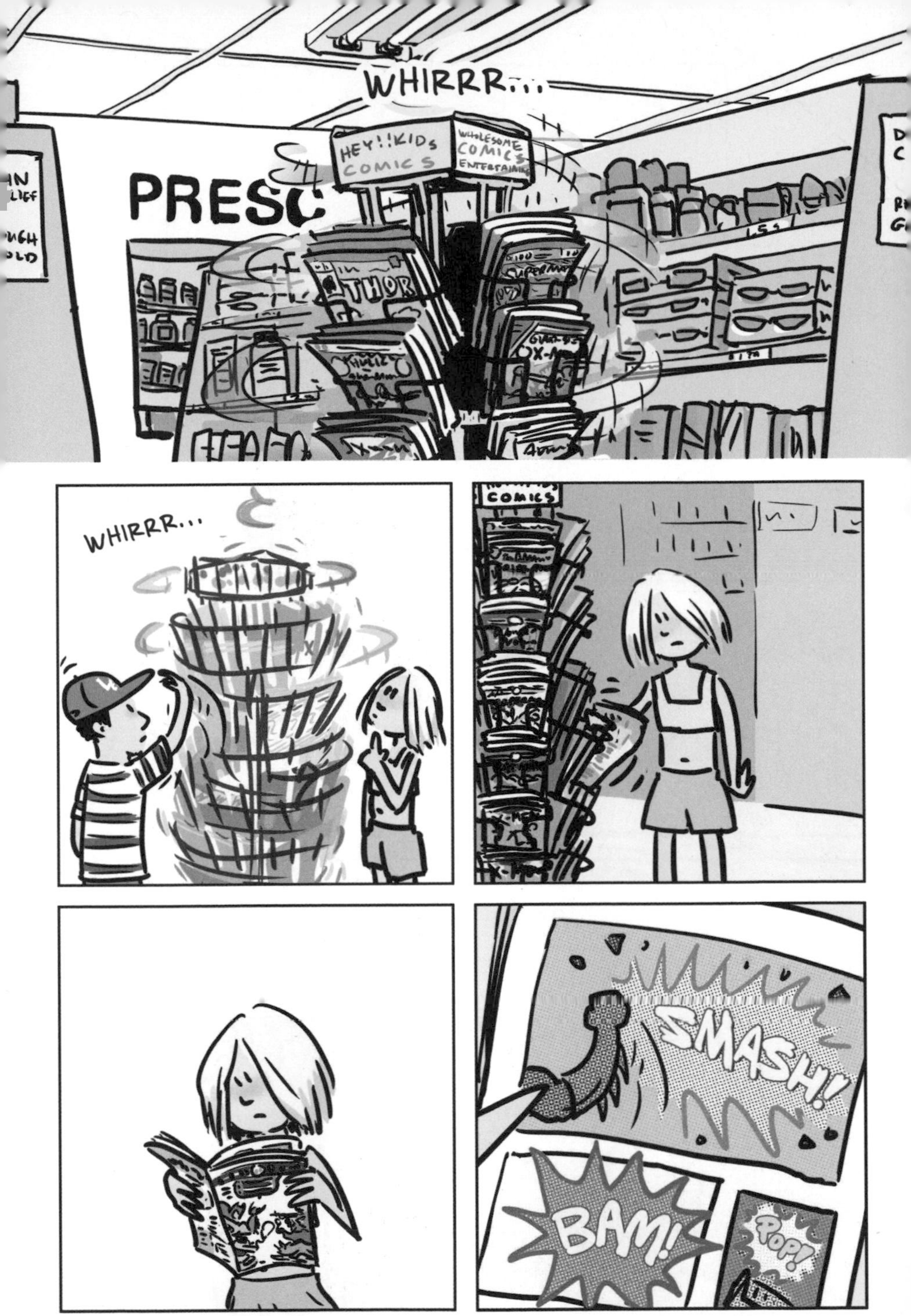
WHIRRR...
HEY!!KIDS COMICS
WHOLESOME COMICS
PRESC
THOR
WHIRRR...
COMICS
SMASH!
BAM!
POP!

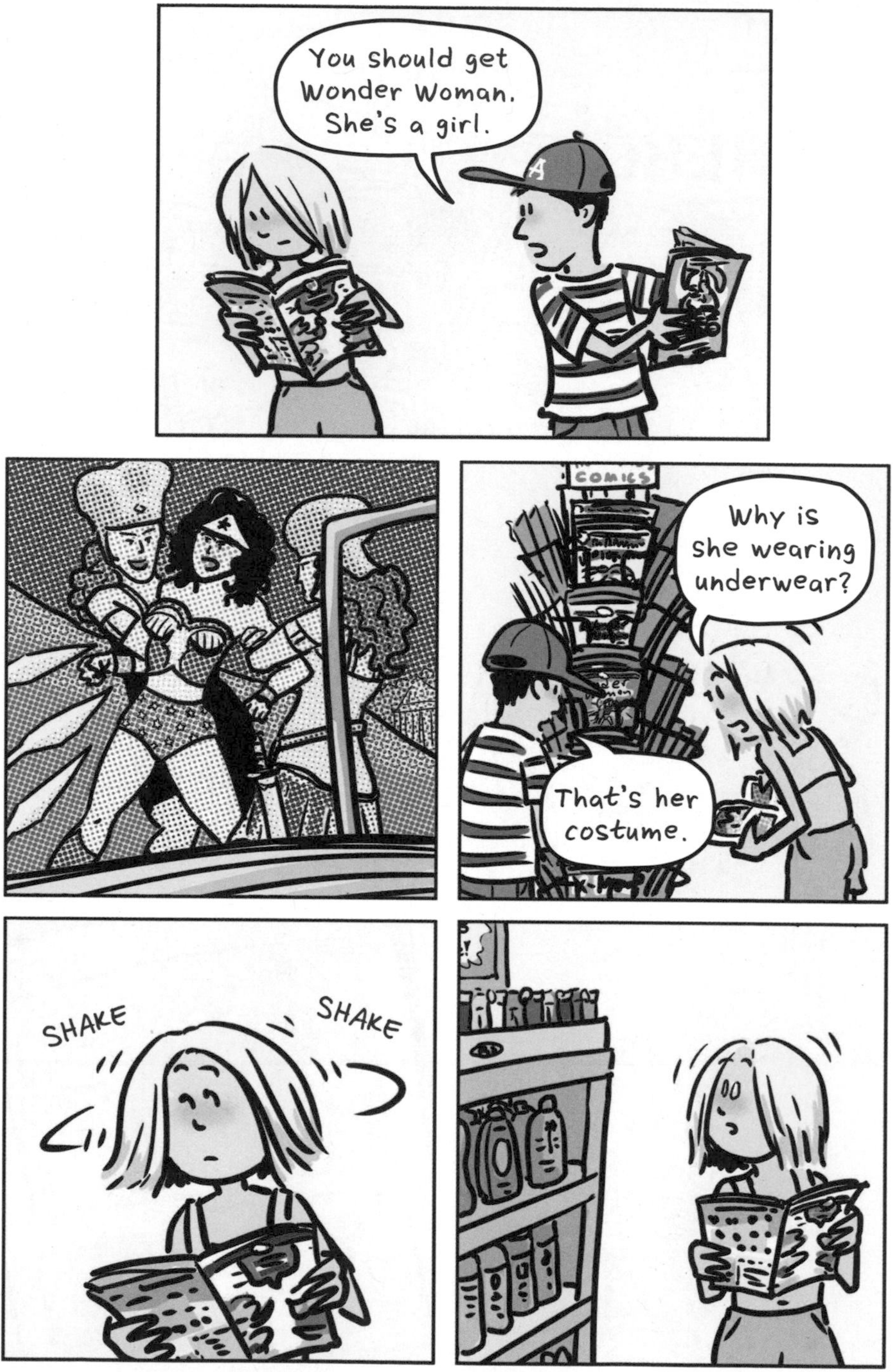
You should get Wonder Woman. She's a girl.
COMICS
Why is she wearing underwear?
That's her costume.
SHAKE
SHAKE

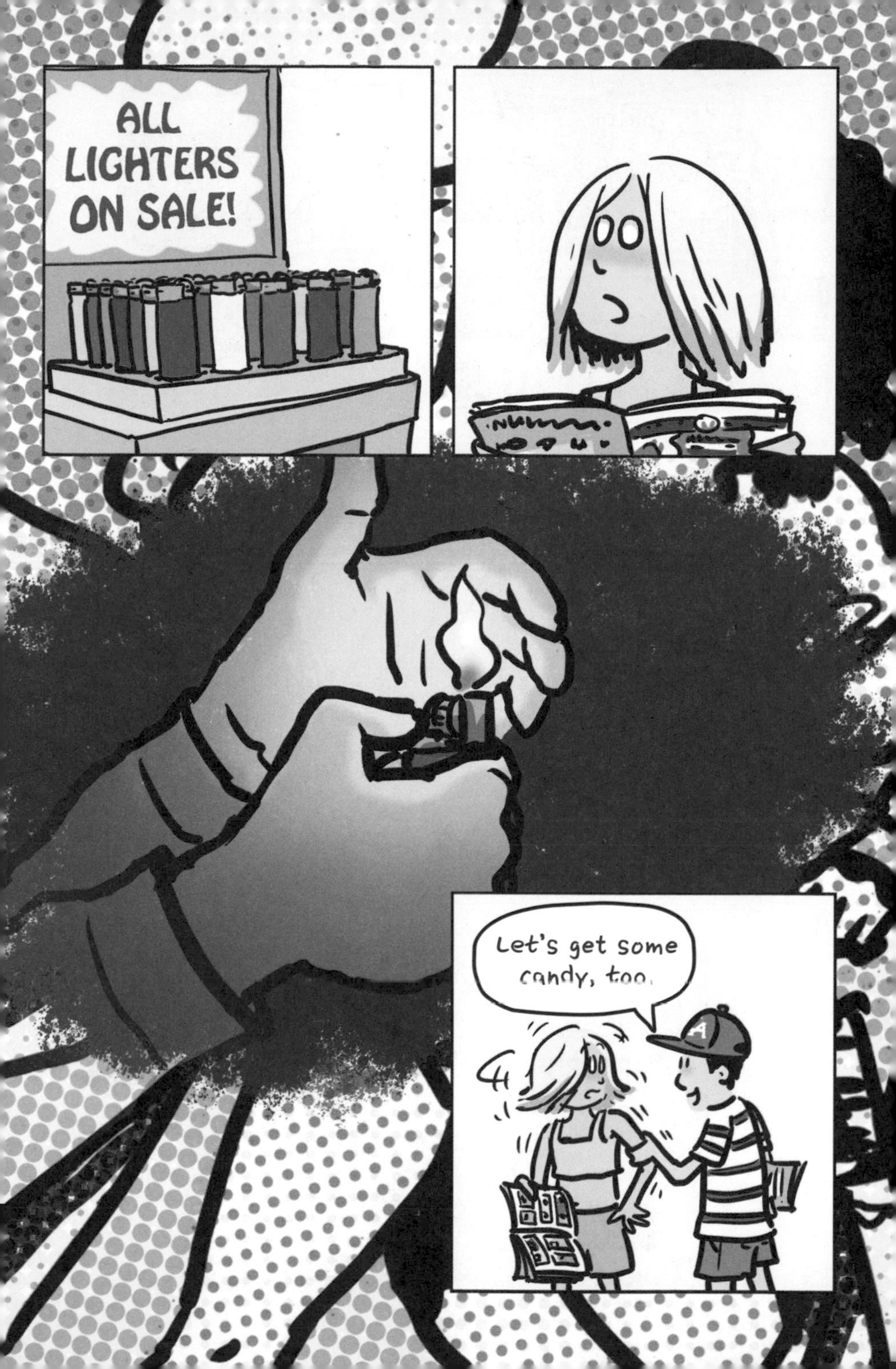
ALL LIGHTERS ON SALE!
Let's get some candy, too.

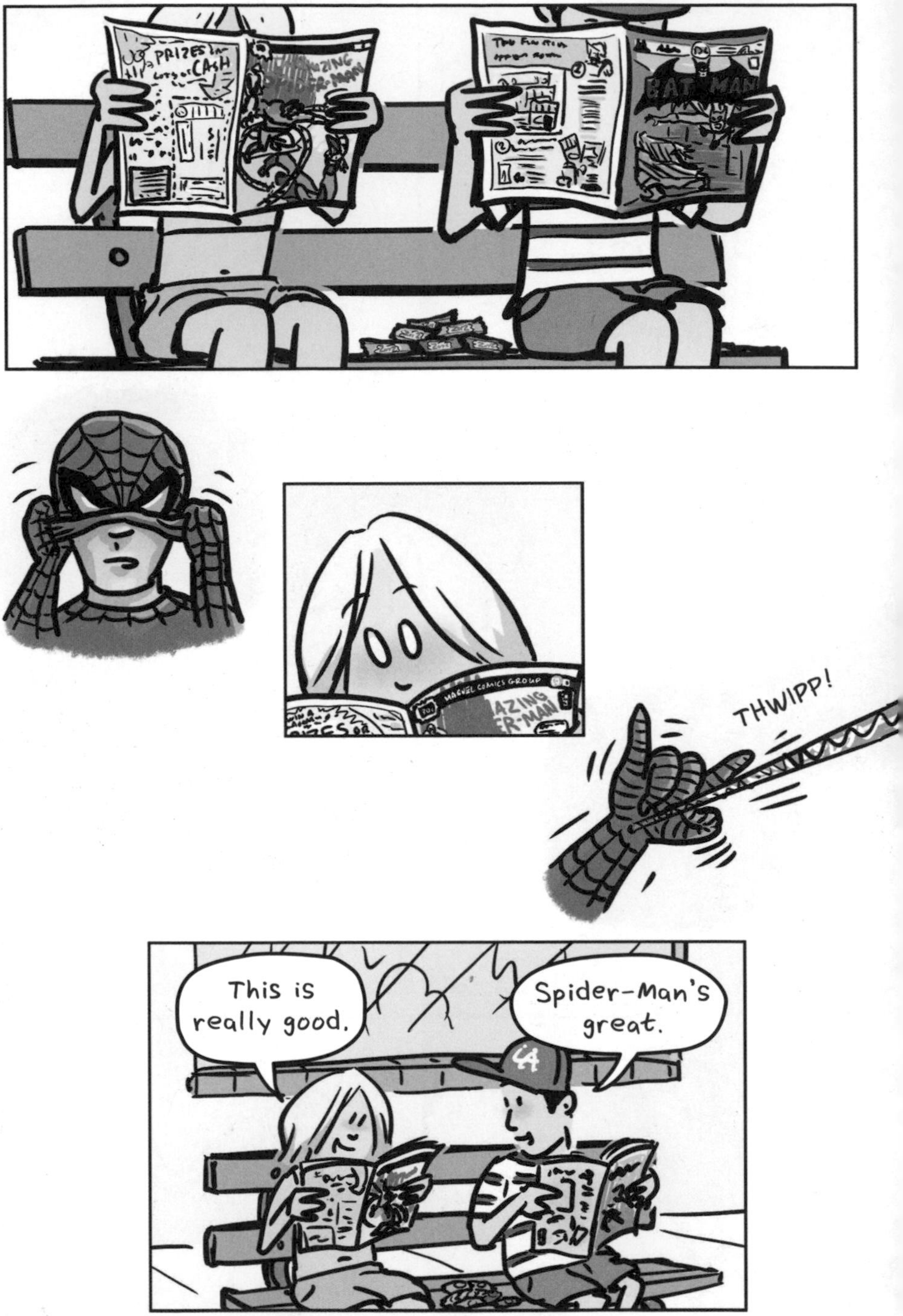
PRIZES
CASH
BATMAN
MARVEL COMICS GROUP
AZING
ER-MAN
THWIPP!
This is really good.
Spider-Man's great.

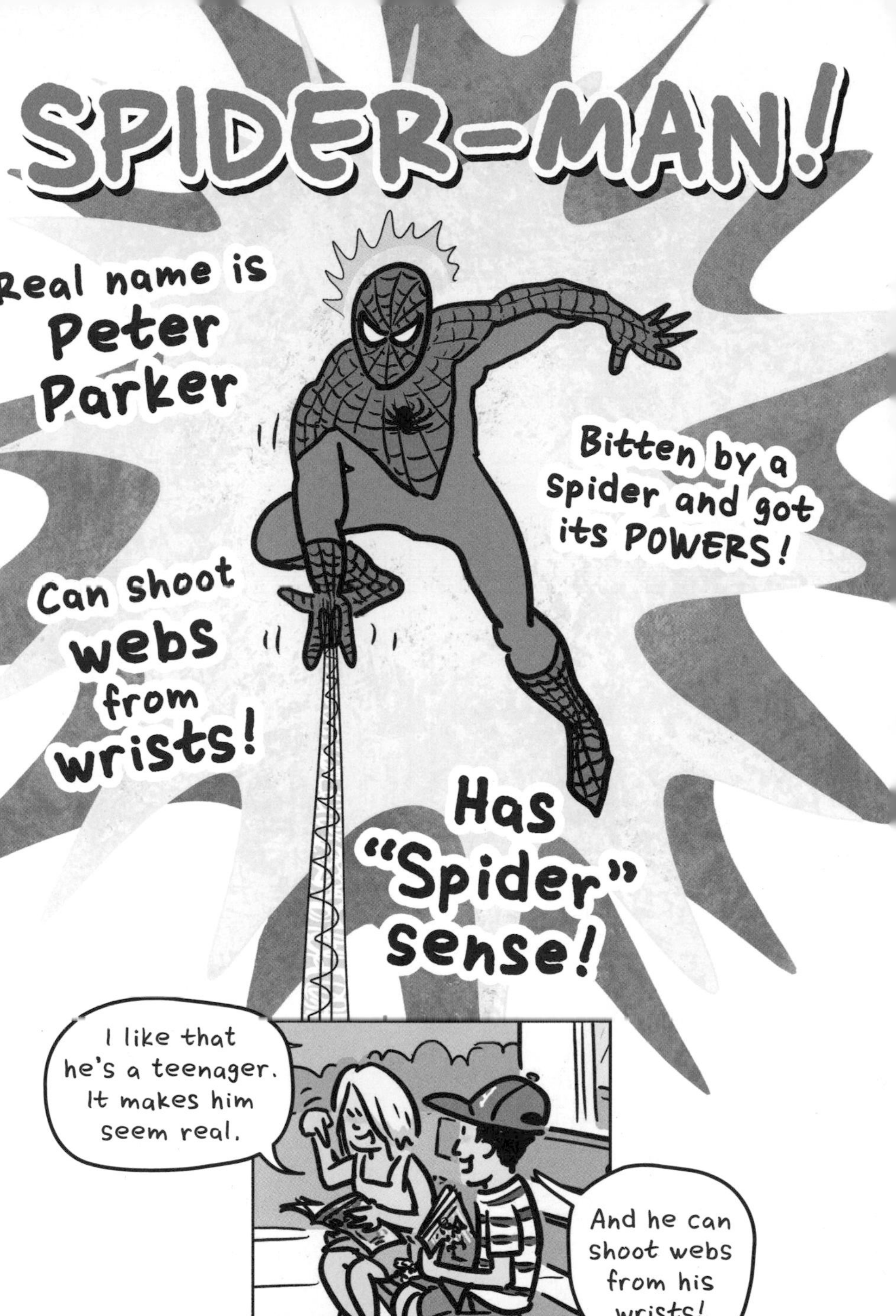
SPIDER-MAN!
Real name is Peter Parker
Bitten by a spider and got its POWERS!
Can shoot webs from wrists!
Has "Spider" sense!
I like that he's a teenager. It makes him seem real.
And he can shoot webs from his wrists!

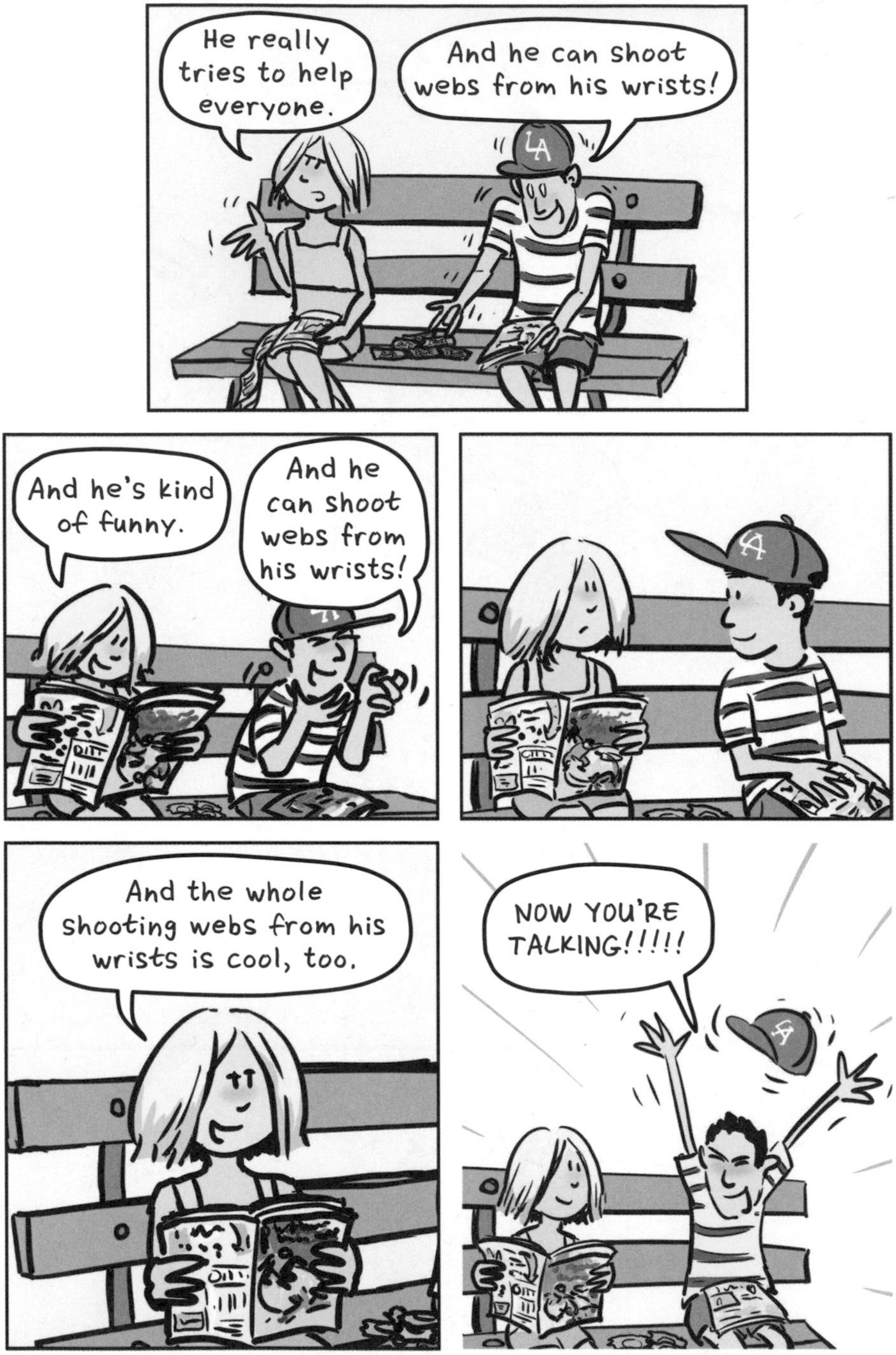
He really tries to help everyone.
And he can shoot webs from his wrists!
And he's kind of funny.
And he can shoot webs from his wrists!
And the whole shooting webs from his wrists is cool, too.
NOW YOU'RE TALKING!!!!!

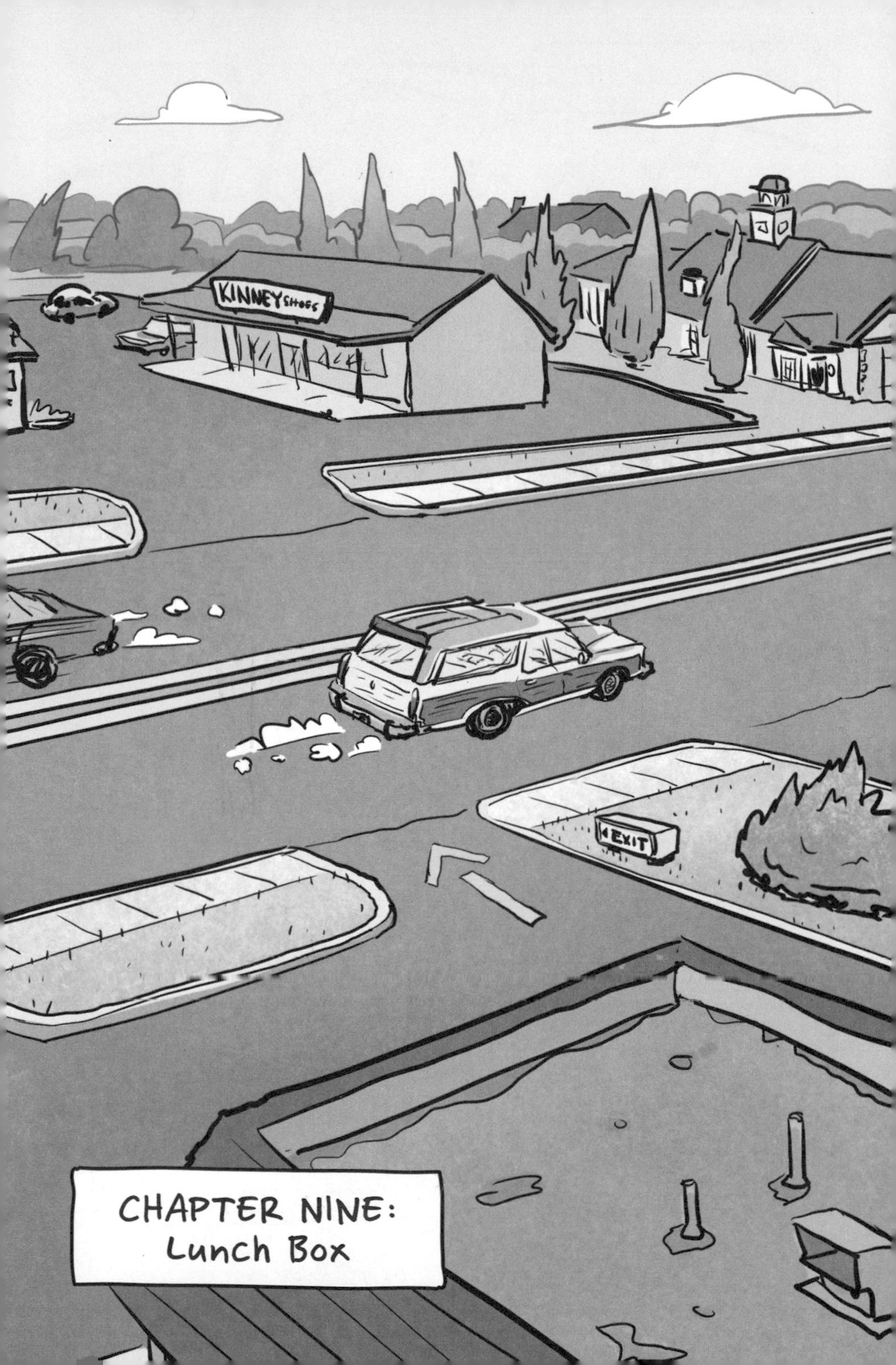
KINNEY SHOES
EXIT
CHAPTER NINE:
Lunch Box

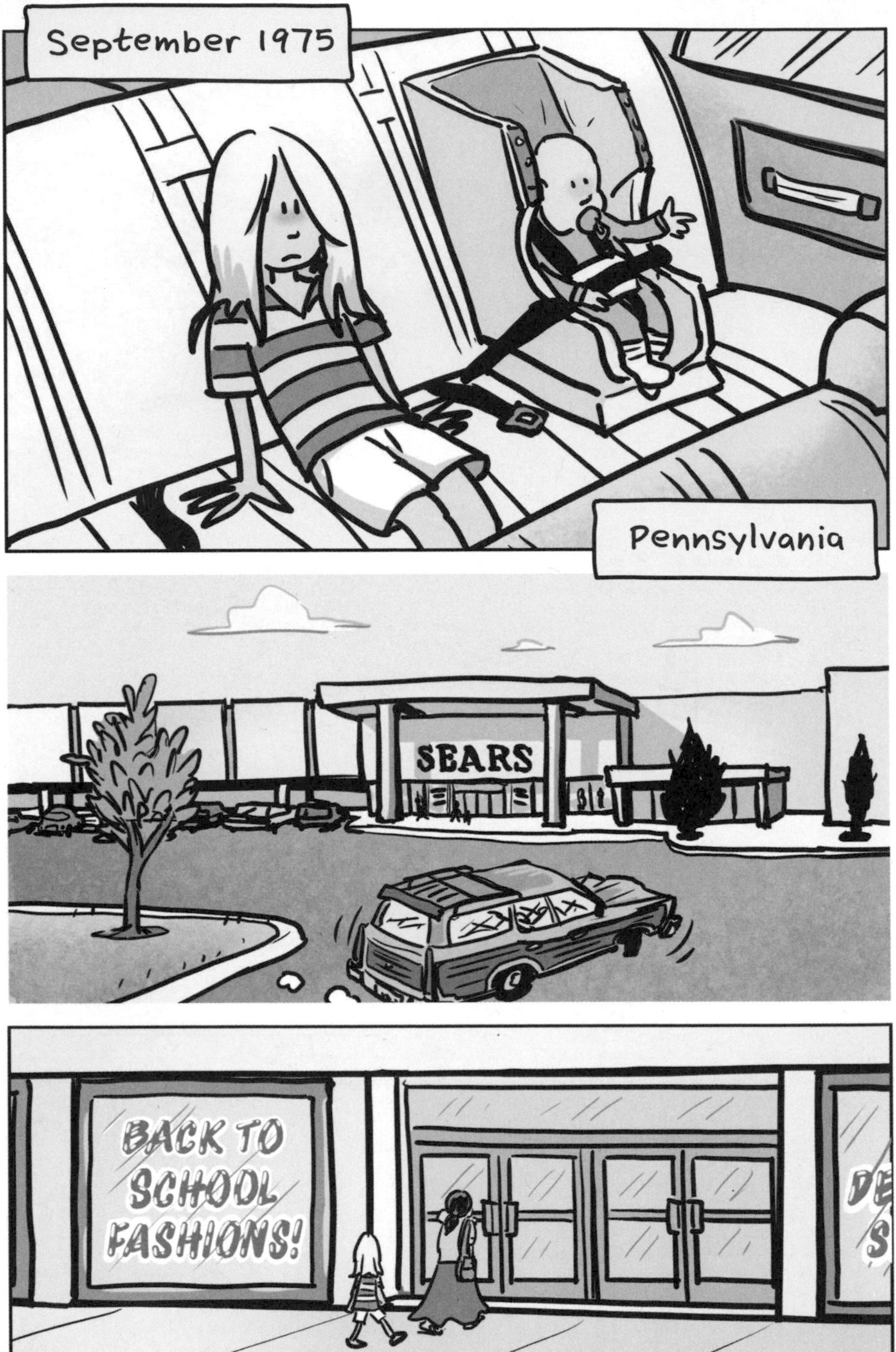
September 1975
Pennsylvania
SEARS
BACK TO SCHOOL FASHIONS!

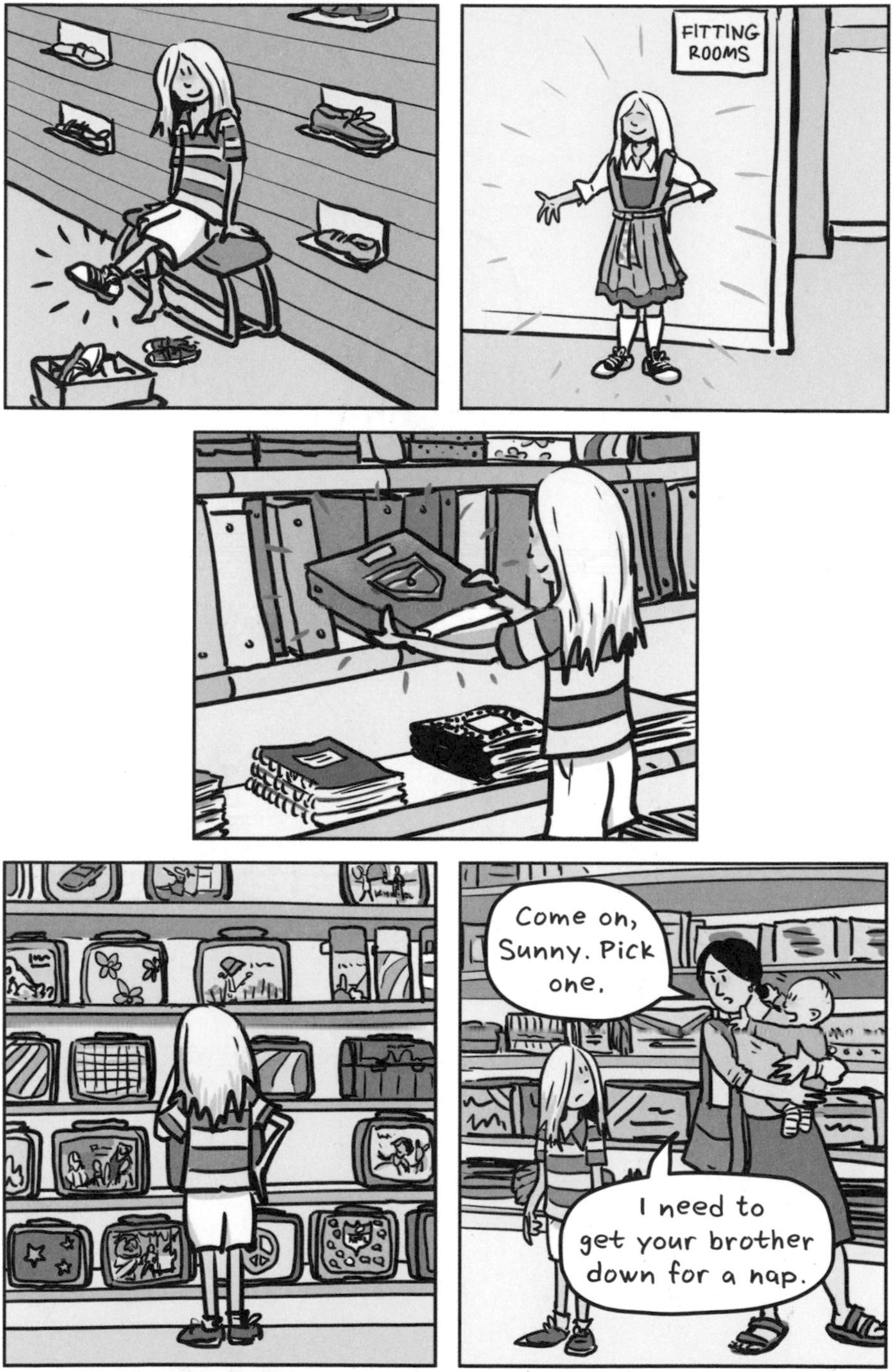
FITTING ROOMS
Come on, Sunny. Pick one.
I need to get your brother down for a nap.

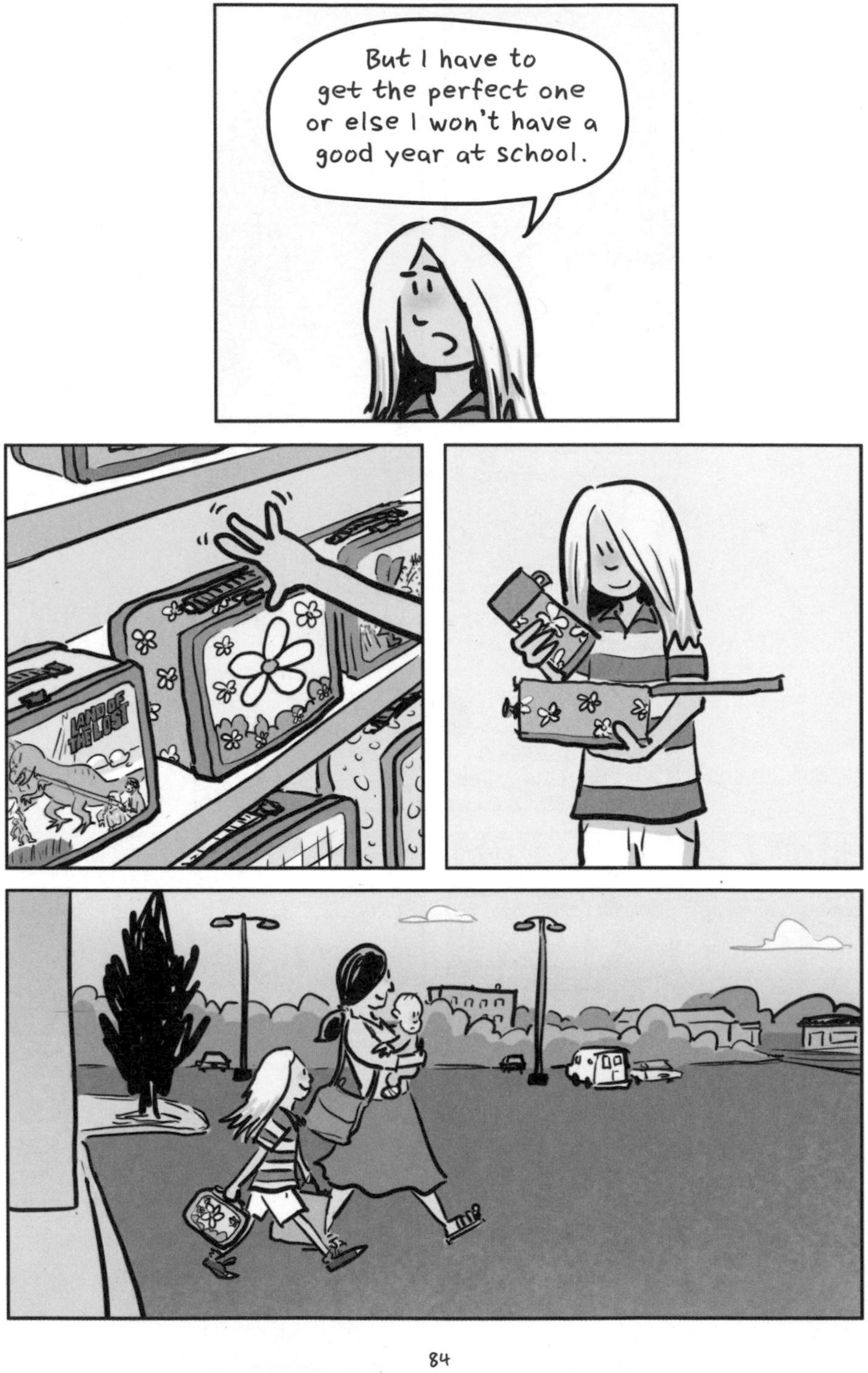
But I have to get the perfect one or else I won't have a good year at school.
LAND OF THE LOST

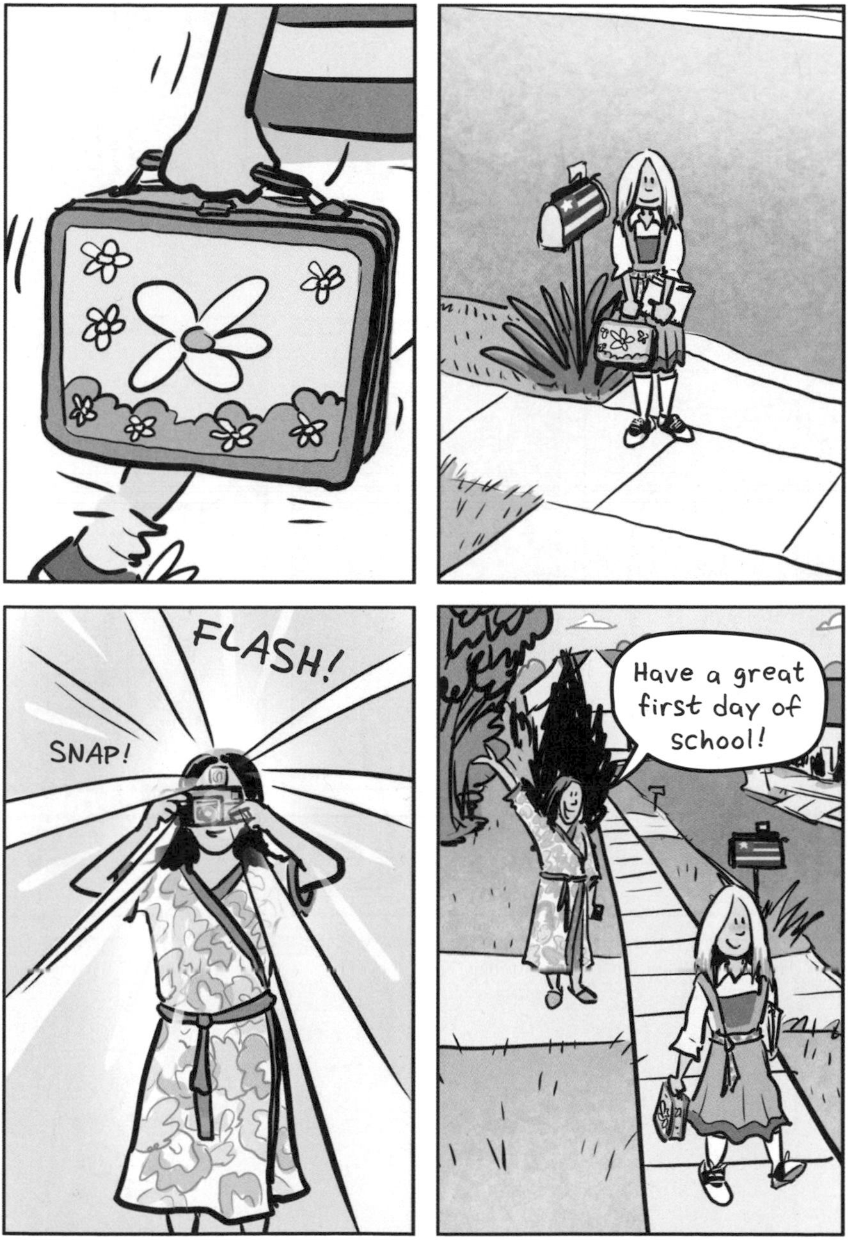
FLASH!
SNAP!
Have a great first day of school!

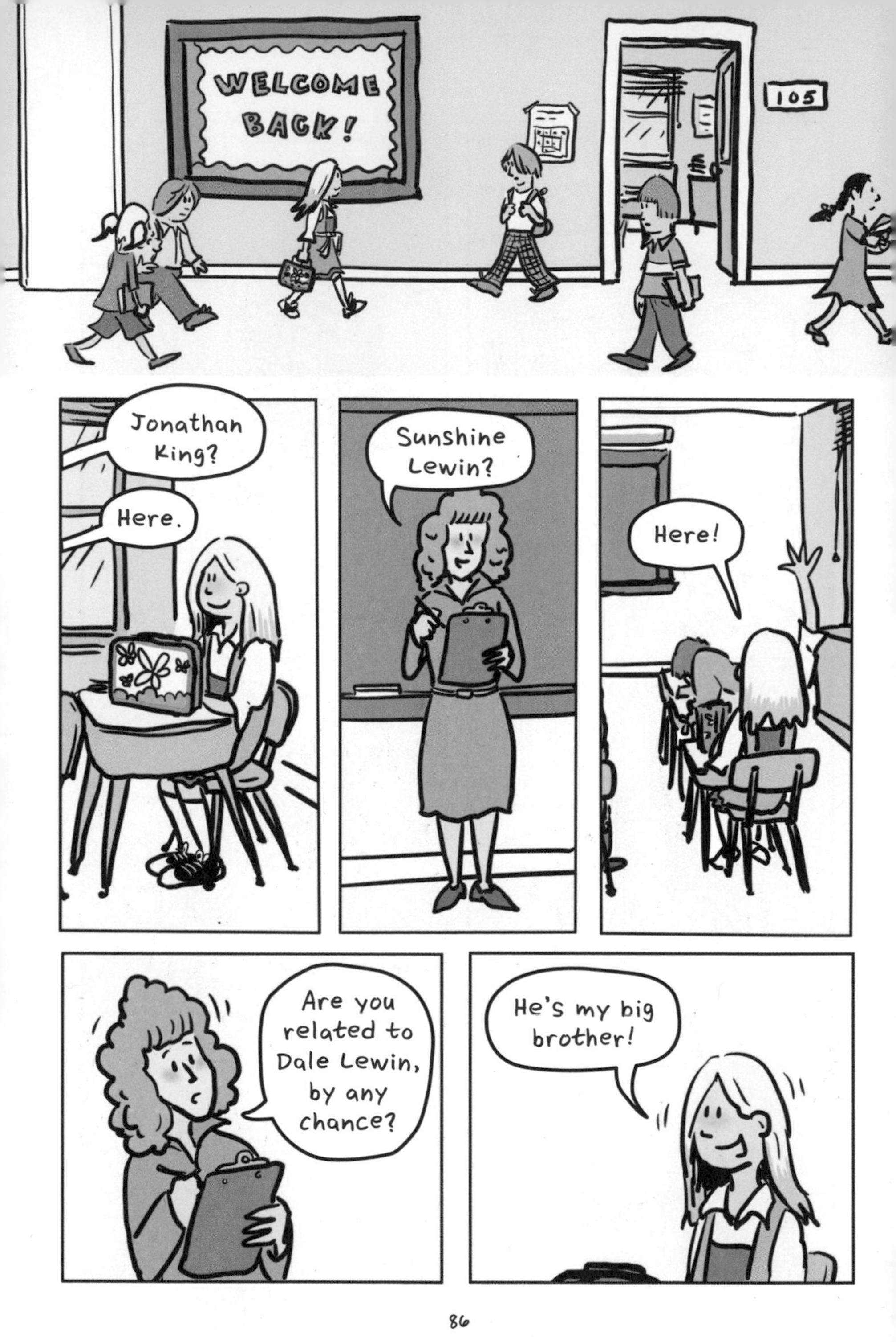
WELCOME BACK!
105
Jonathan King?
Here.
Sunshine Lewin?
Here!
Are you related to Dale Lewin, by any chance?
He's my big brother!

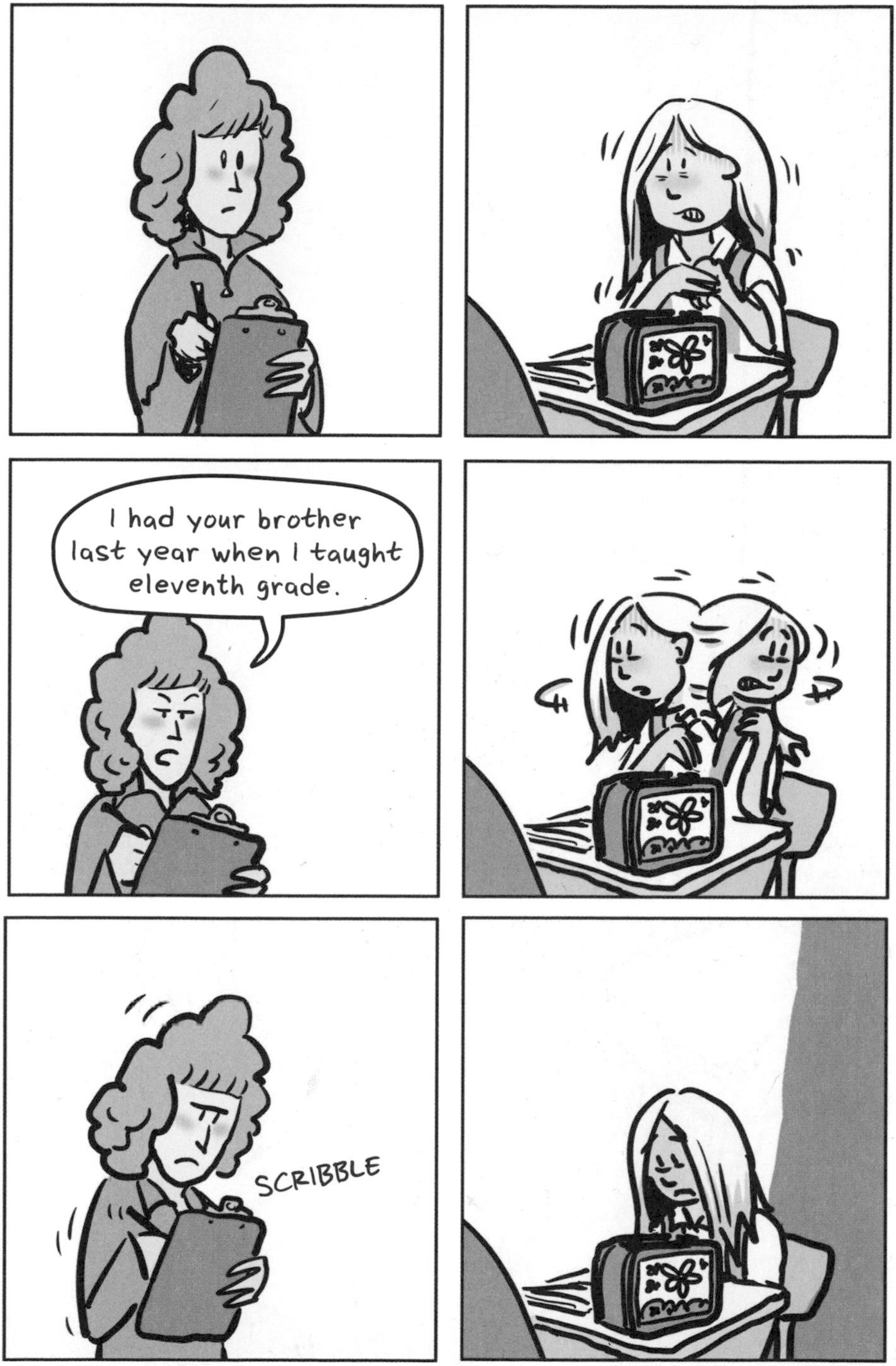
I had your brother last year when I taught eleventh grade.
SCRIBBLE

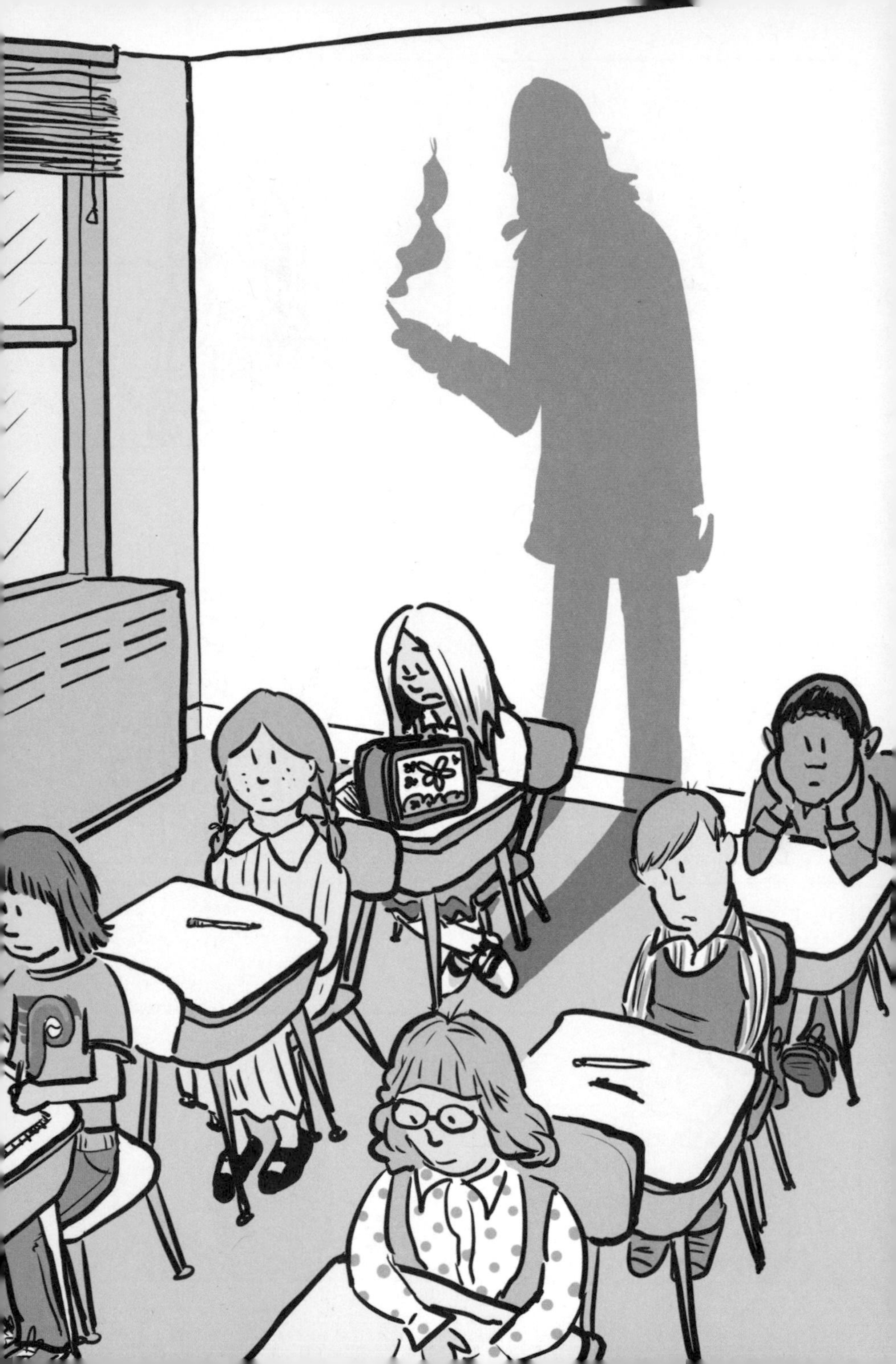

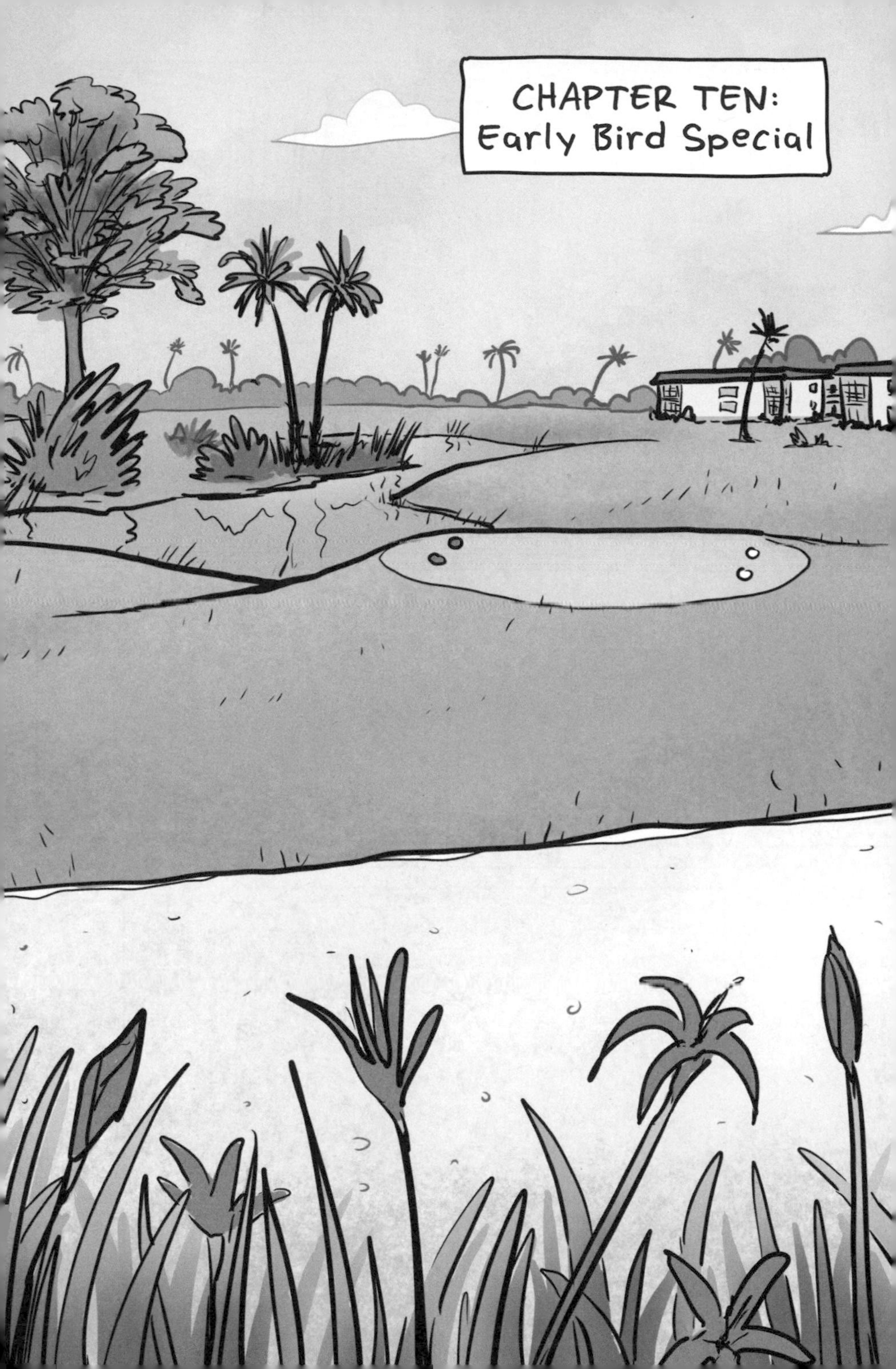
CHAPTER TEN:
Early Bird Special

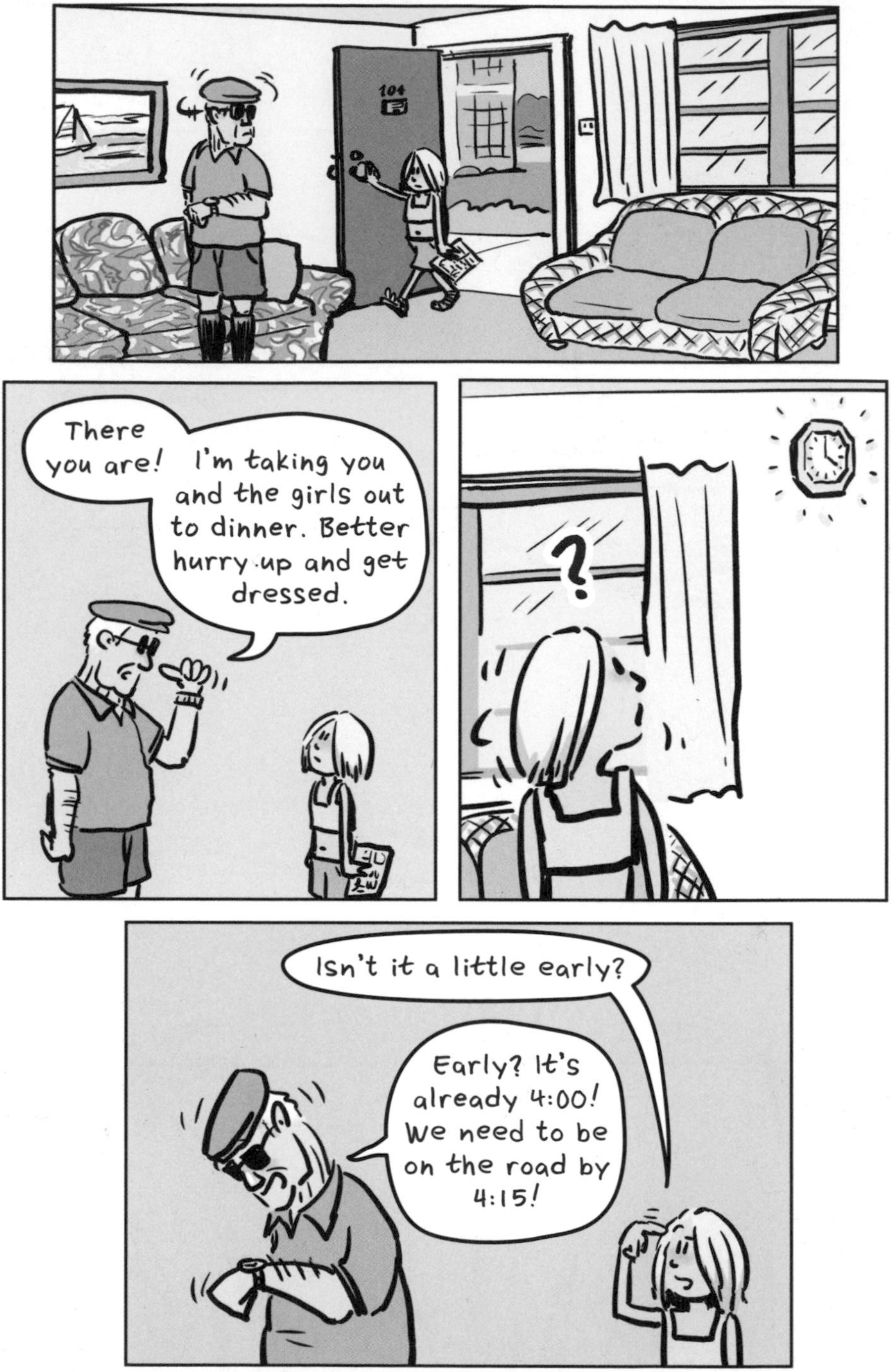
104
There you are! I'm taking you and the girls out to dinner. Better hurry up and get dressed.
?
Isn't it a little early?
Early? It's already 4:00! We need to be on the road by 4:15!

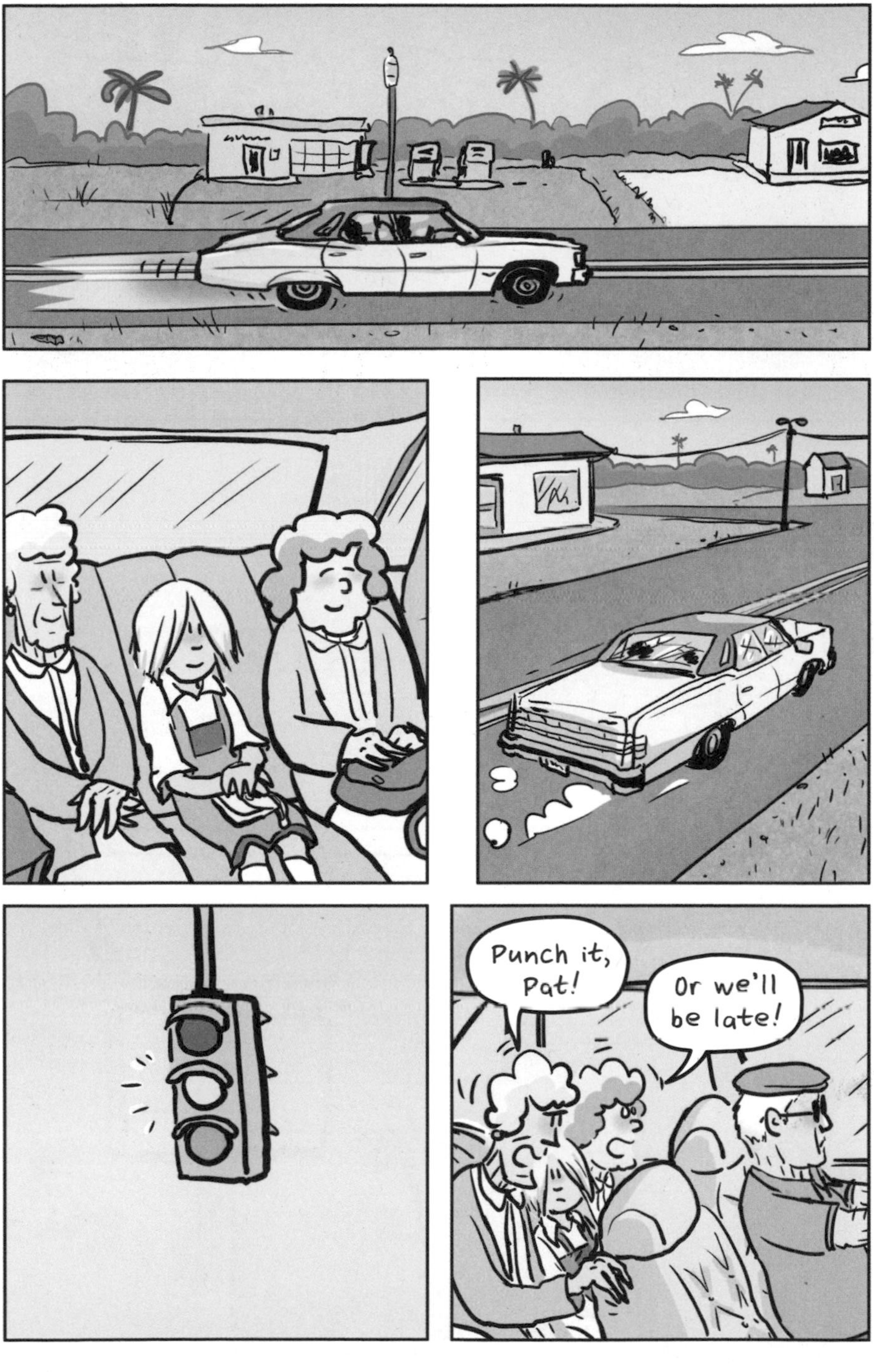
Punch it, Pat!
Or we'll be late!

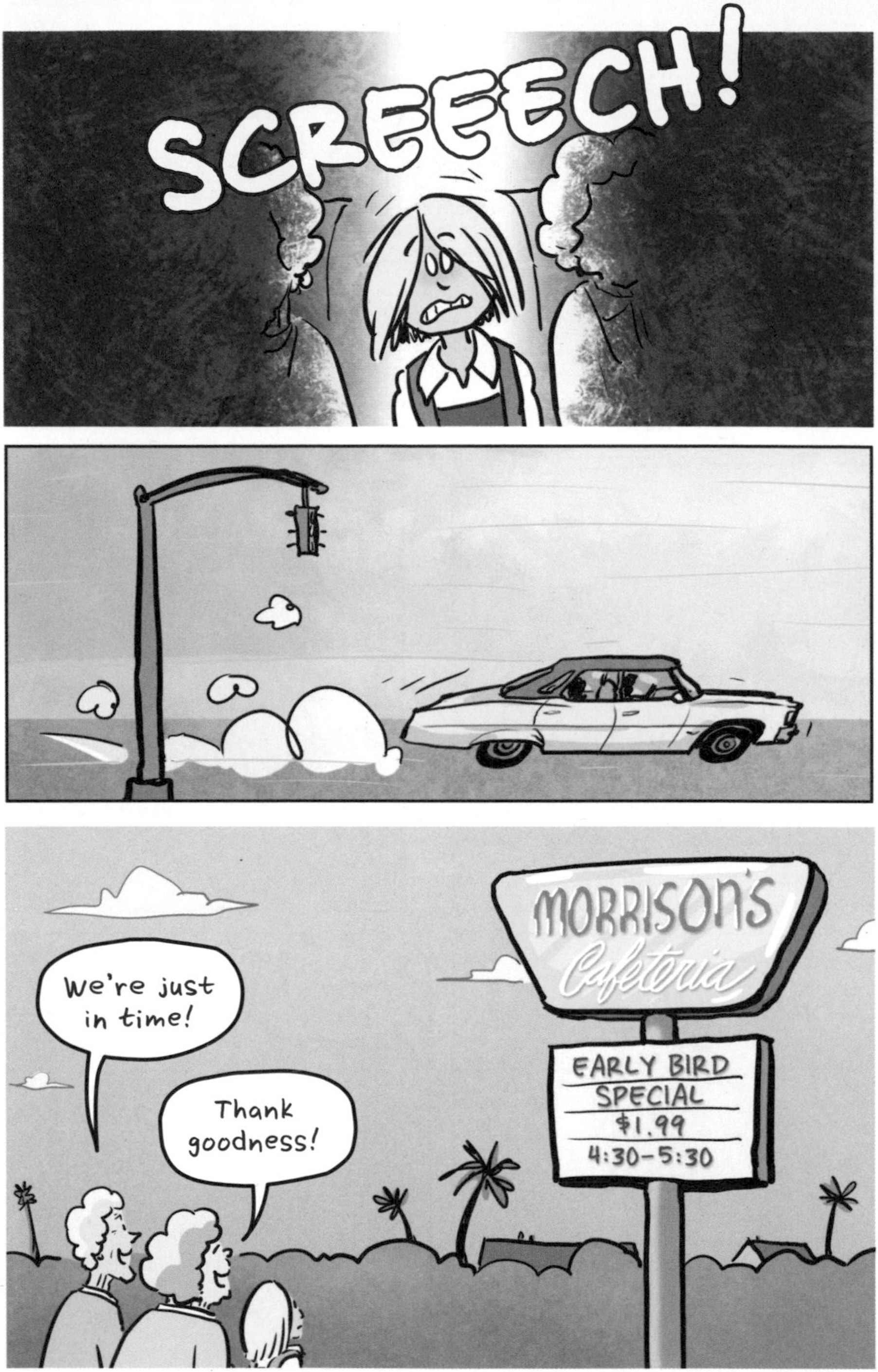
SCREEECH!
We're just in time!
Thank goodness!
MORRISON'S
Cafeteria
EARLY BIRD
SPECIAL
$1.99
4:30–5:30

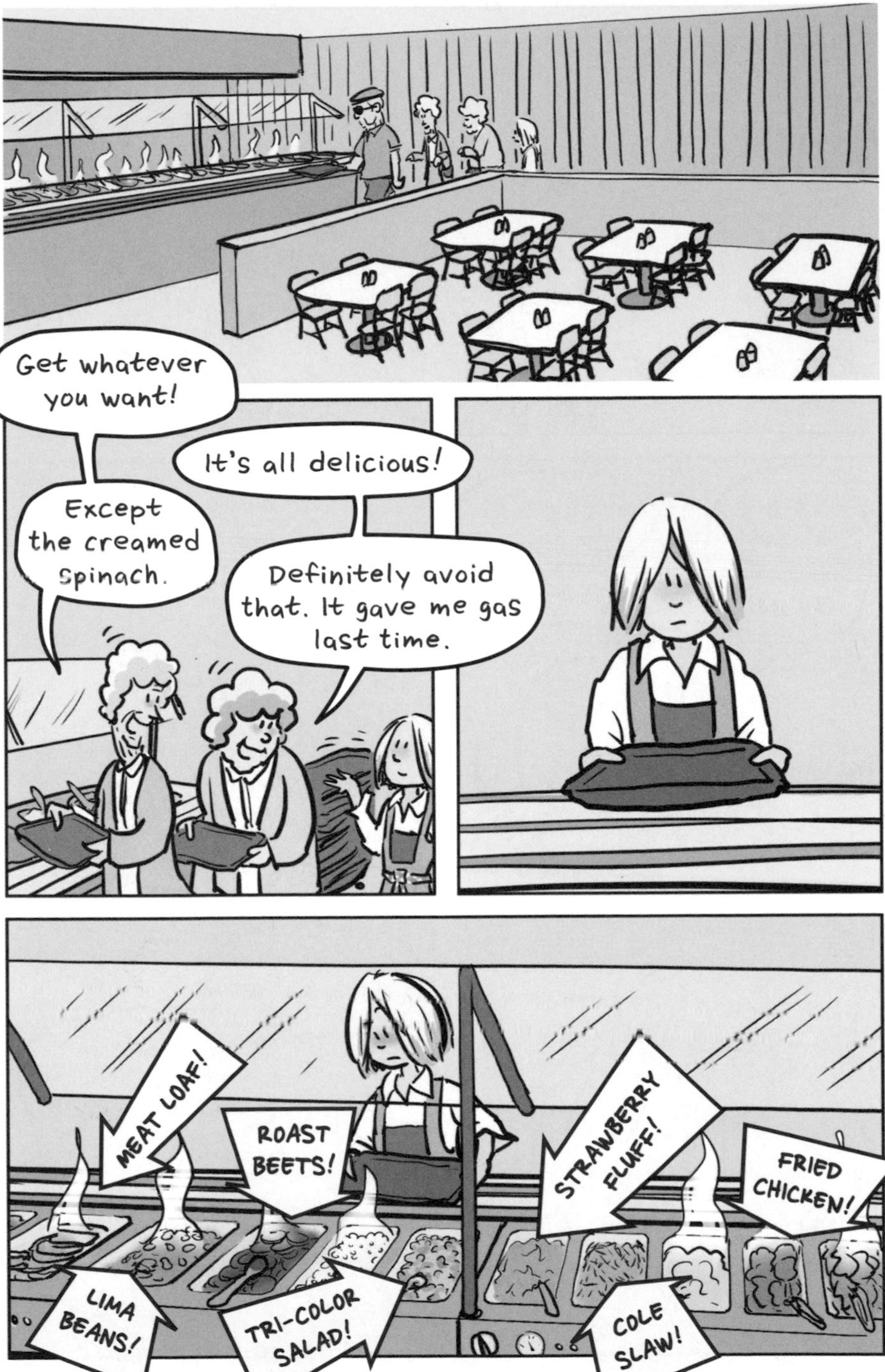
Get whatever you want!
It's all delicious!
Except the creamed spinach.
Definitely avoid that. It gave me gas last time.
MEAT LOAF!
ROAST BEETS!
STRAWBERRY FLUFF!
FRIED CHICKEN!
LIMA BEANS!
TRI-COLOR SALAD!
COLE SLAW!

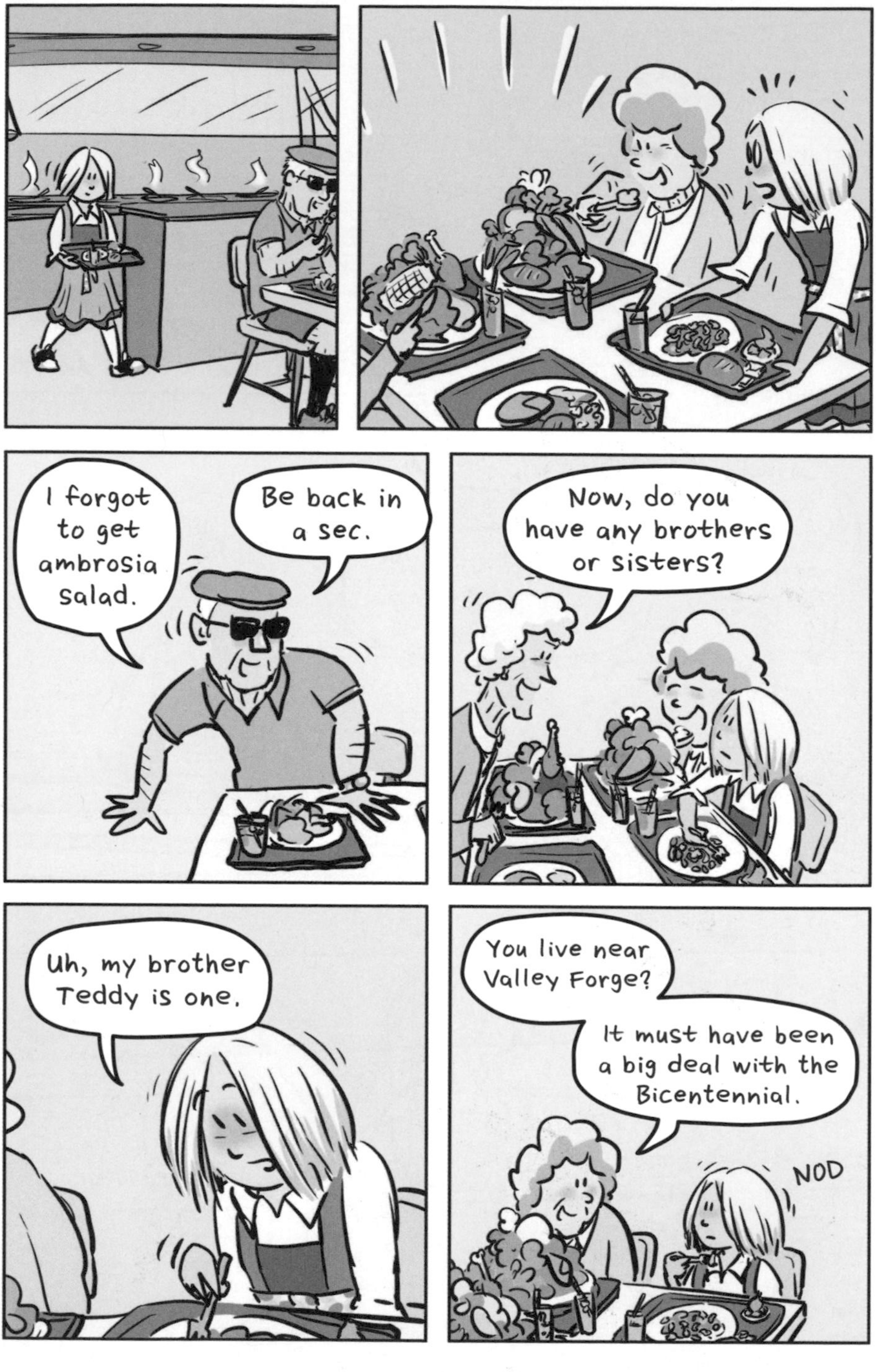
I forgot to get ambrosia salad.
Be back in a sec.
Now, do you have any brothers or sisters?
Uh, my brother Teddy is one.
You live near Valley Forge?
It must have been a big deal with the Bicentennial.
NOD

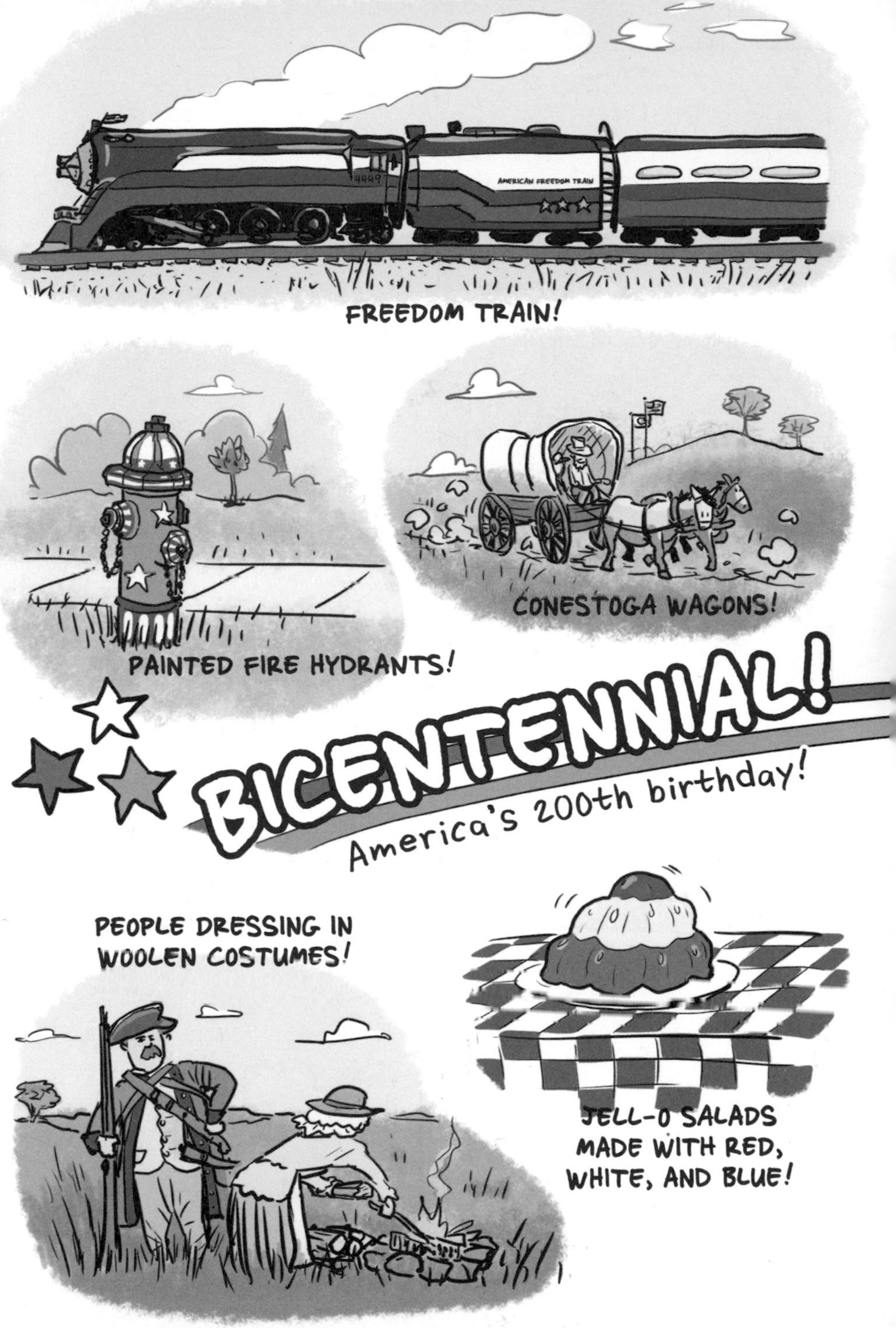
4449
AMERICAN FREEDOM TRAIN
FREEDOM TRAIN!
PAINTED FIRE HYDRANTS!
CONESTOGA WAGONS!
BICENTENNIAL!
America's 200th birthday!
PEOPLE DRESSING IN WOOLEN COSTUMES!
JELL-O SALADS MADE WITH RED, WHITE, AND BLUE!

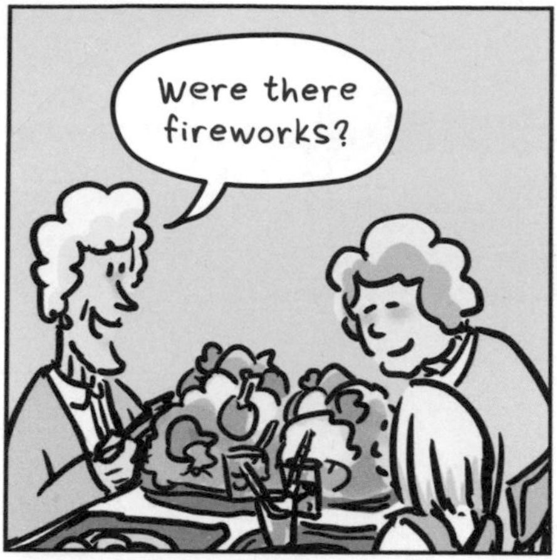
Were there fireworks?

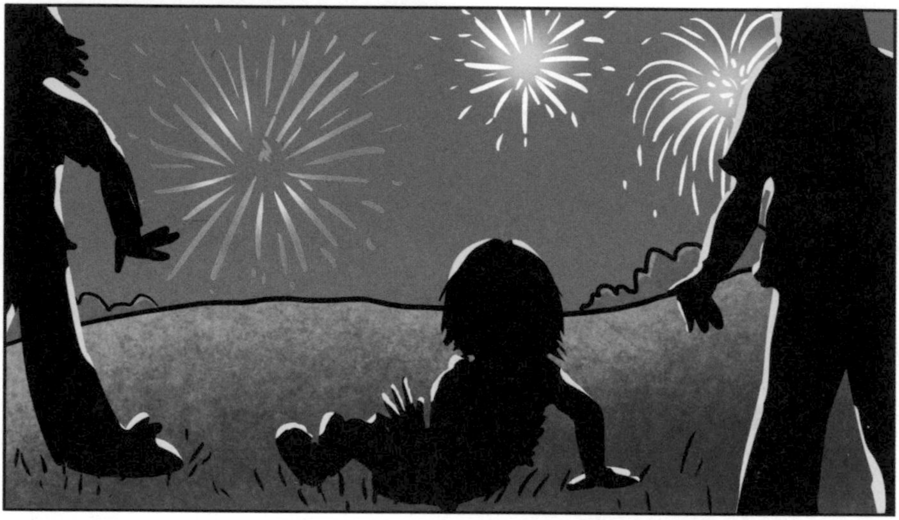

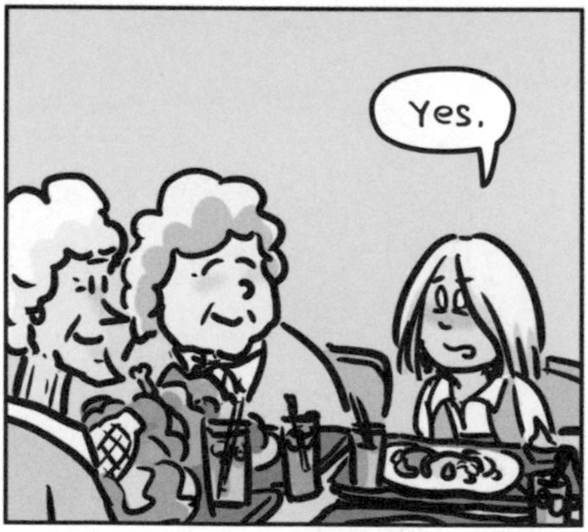
Yes.

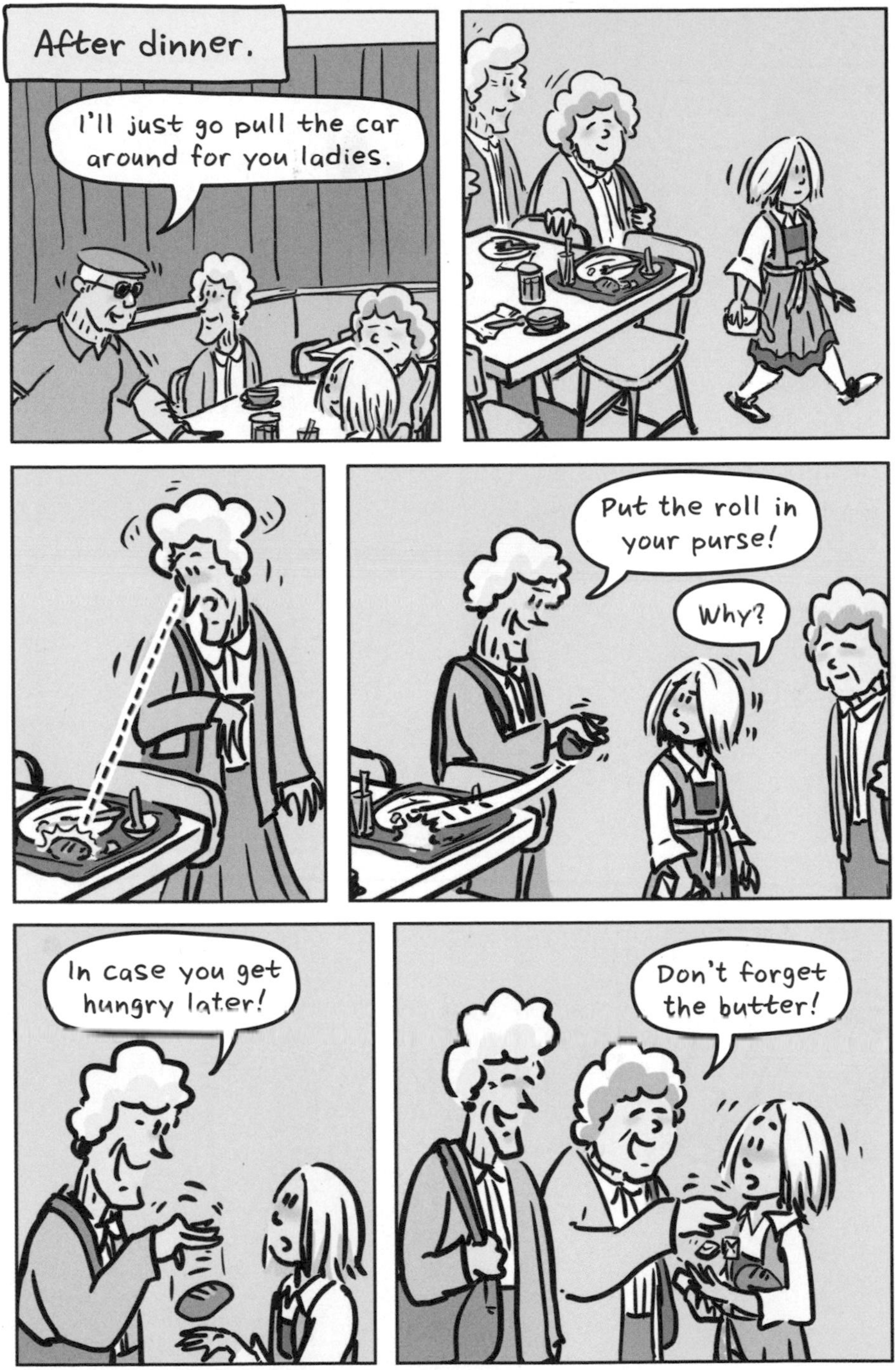
After dinner.
I'll just go pull the car around for you ladies.
Put the roll in your purse!
Why?
In case you get hungry later!
Don't forget the butter!

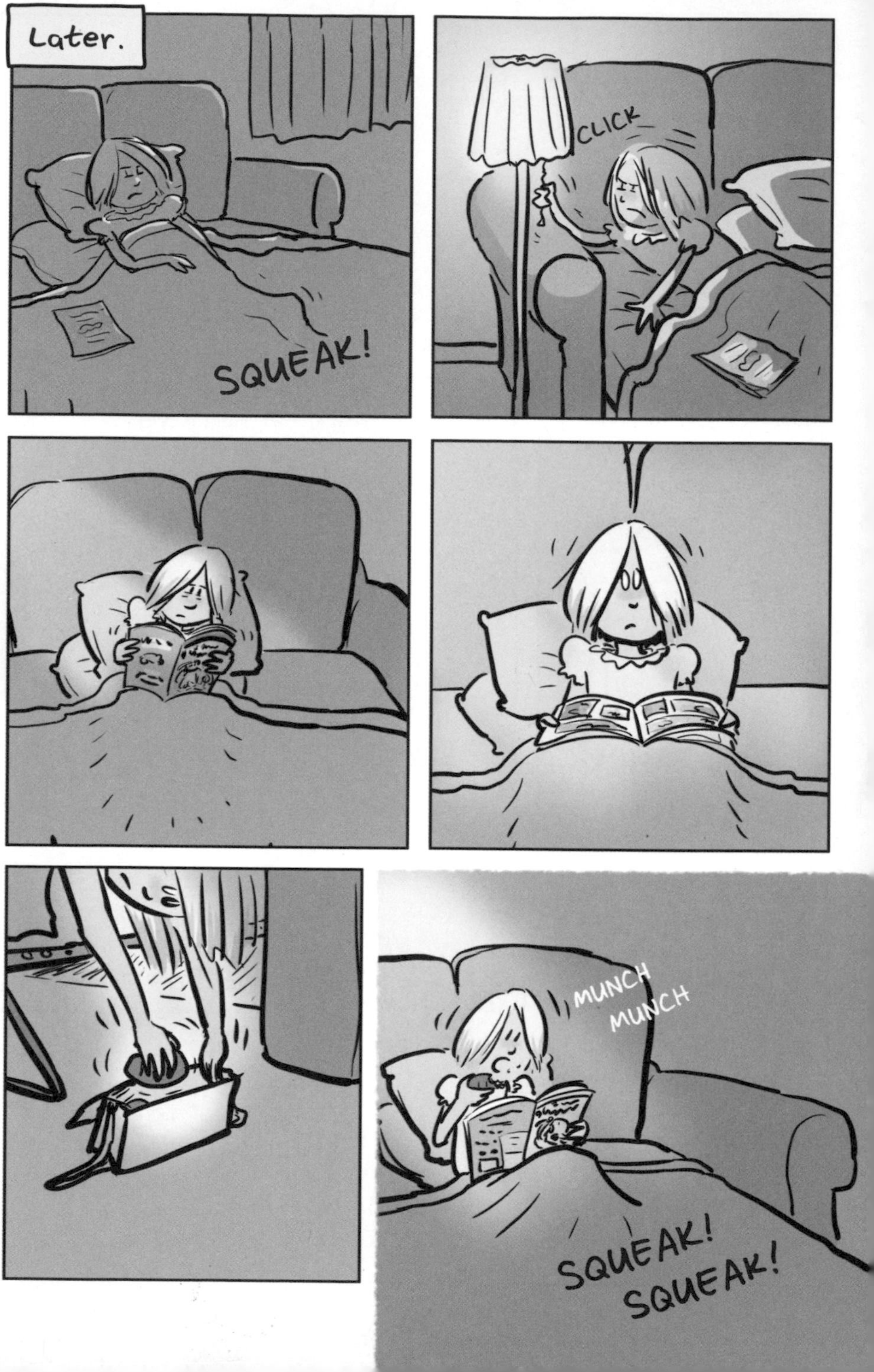
Later.
SQUEAK!
CLICK
MUNCH
MUNCH
SQUEAK!
SQUEAK!

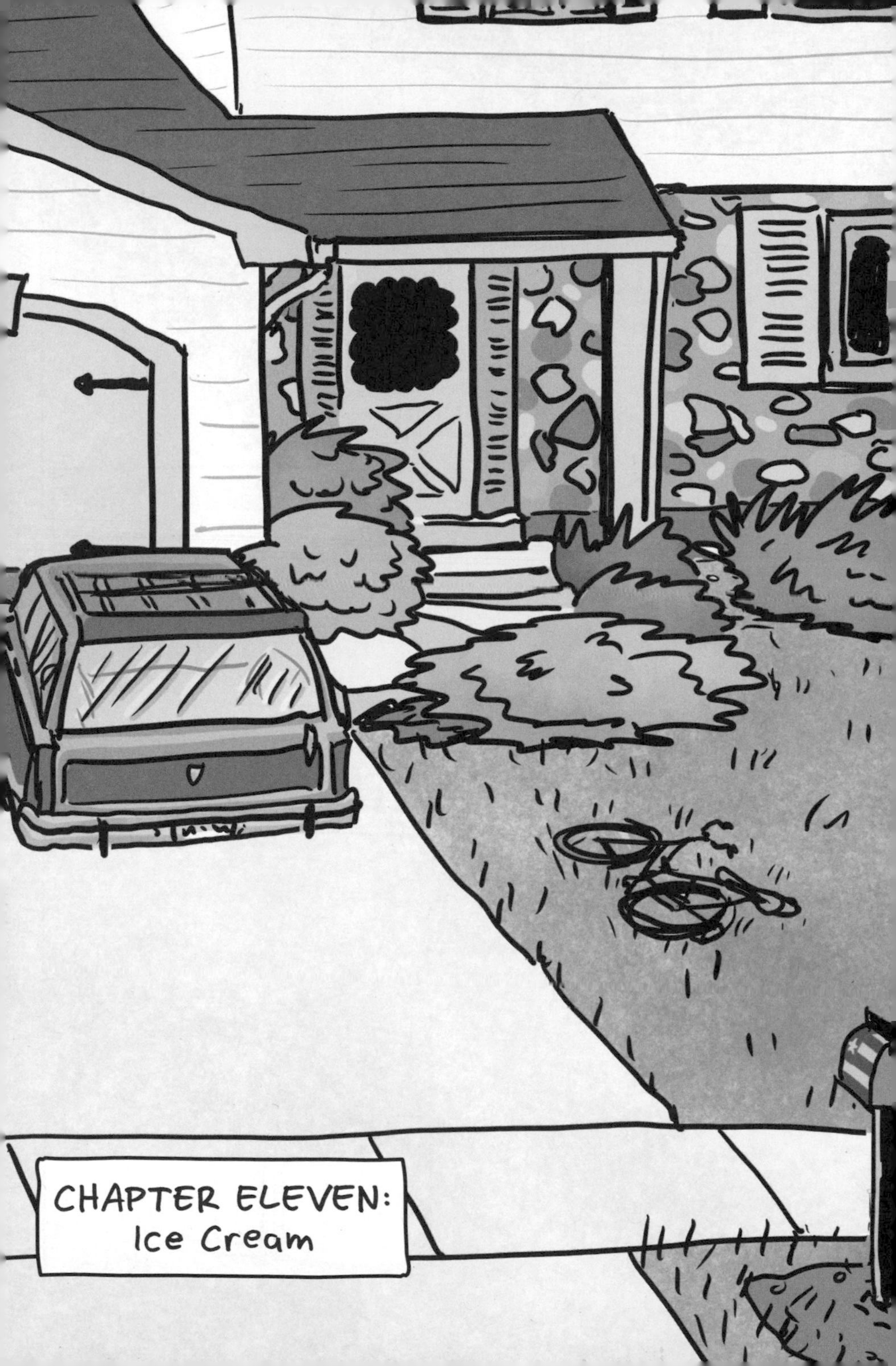
CHAPTER ELEVEN:
Ice Cream

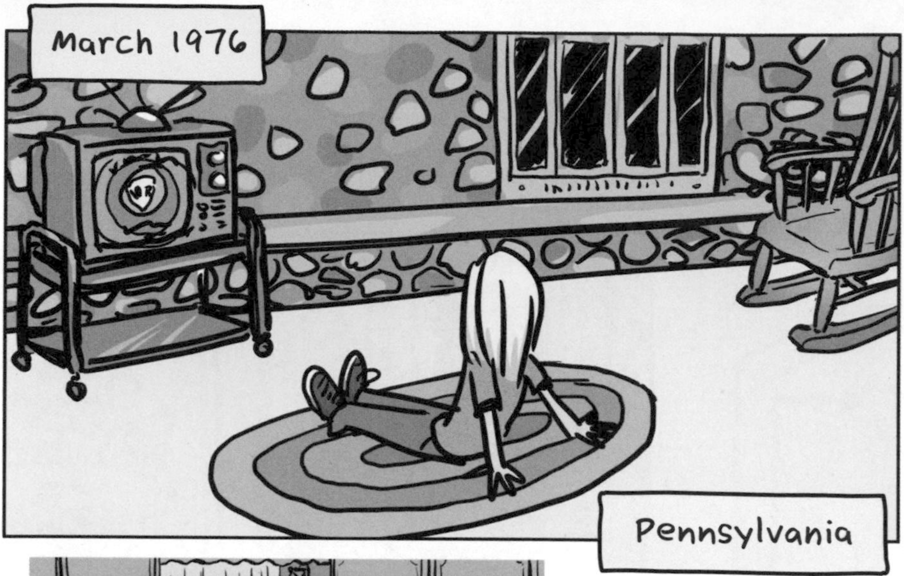
March 1976
Pennsylvania

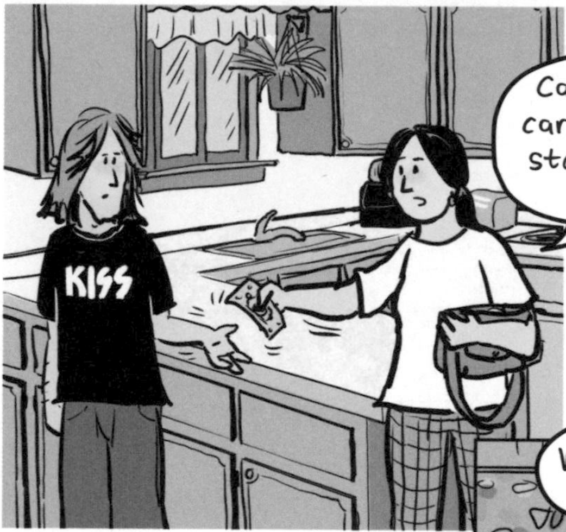
Can you take my car and run to the store and pick up some milk?
KISS

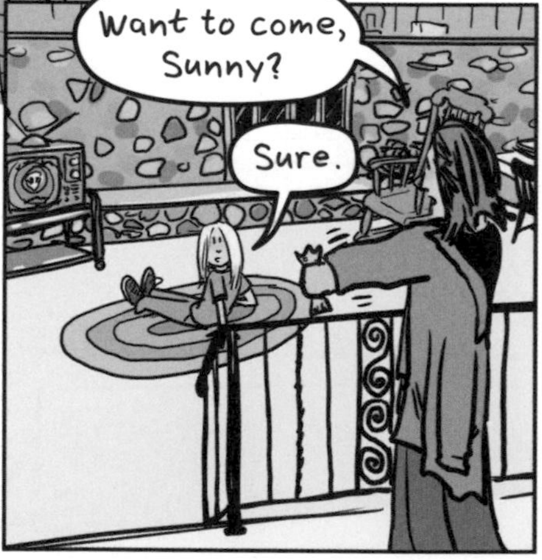
Want to come, Sunny?
Sure.

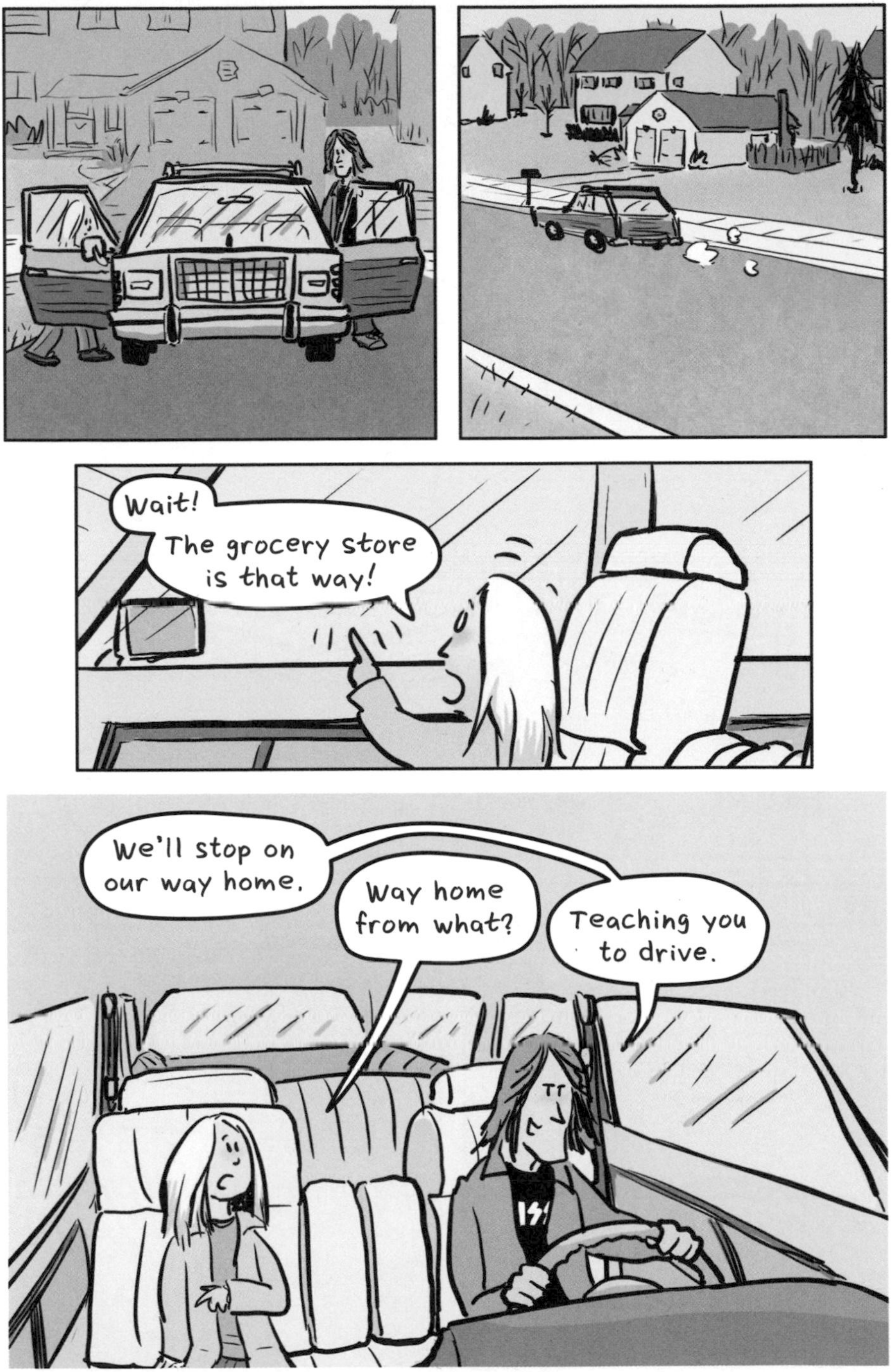
Wait!
The grocery store is that way!
We'll stop on our way home.
Way home from what?
Teaching you to drive.

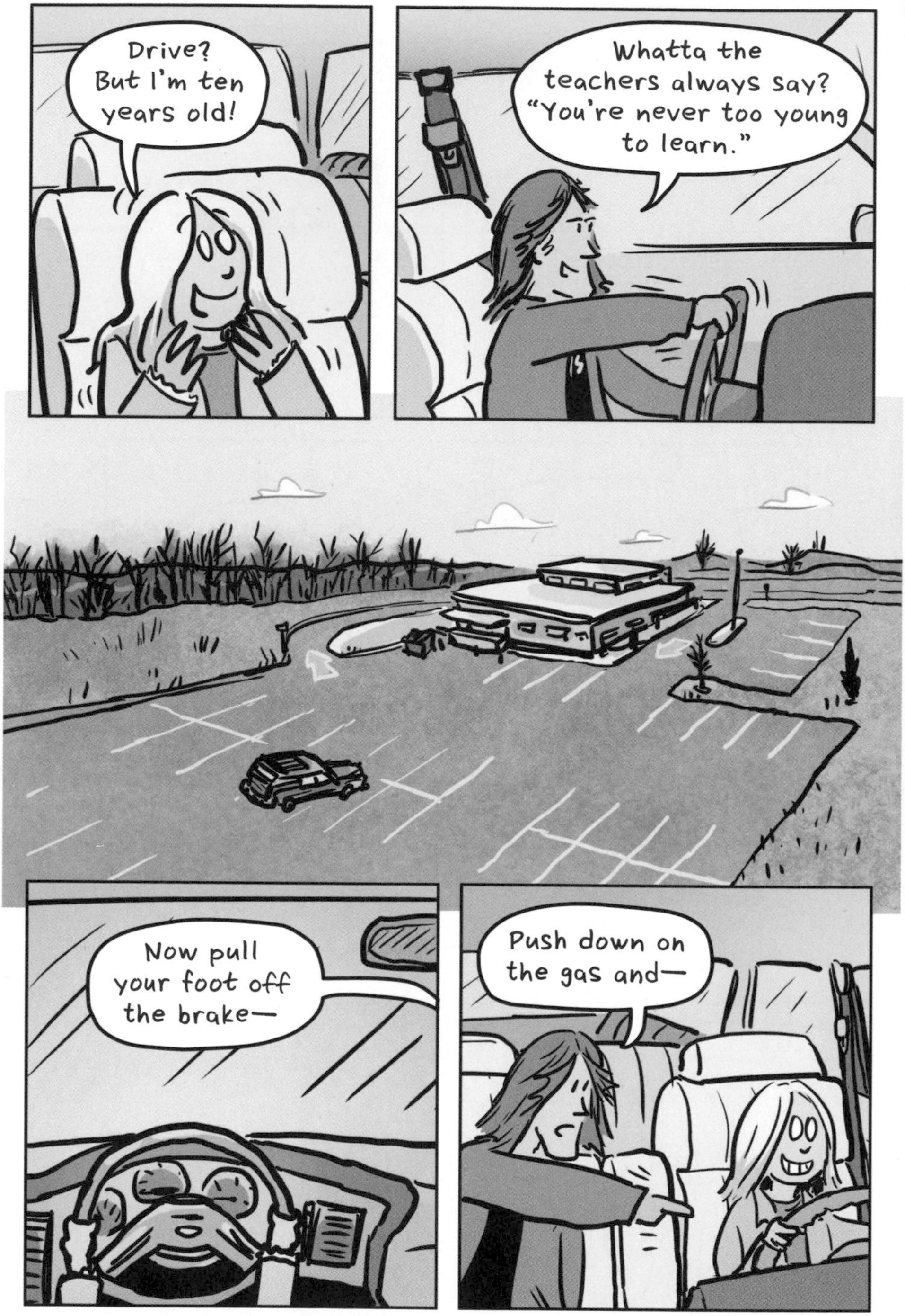
Drive? But I'm ten years old!
Whatta the teachers always say? "You're never too young to learn."
Now pull your foot off the brake—
Push down on the gas and—

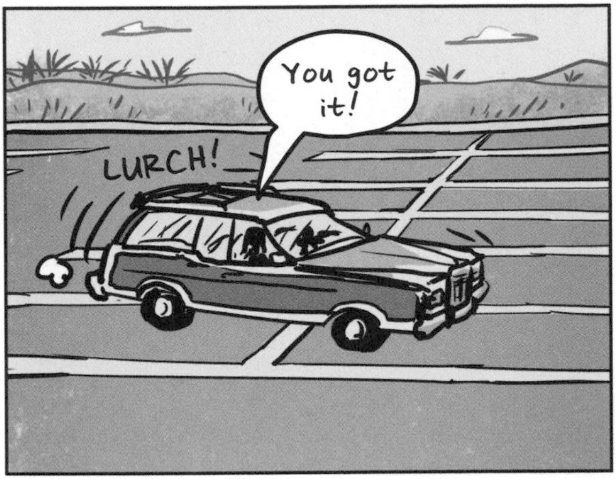
You got it!
LURCH!

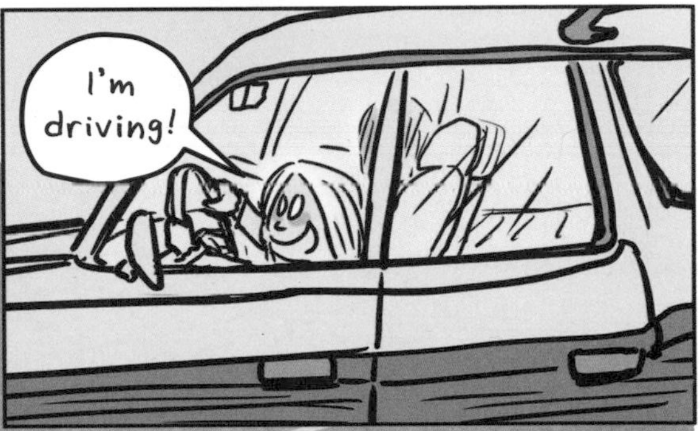
I'm driving!

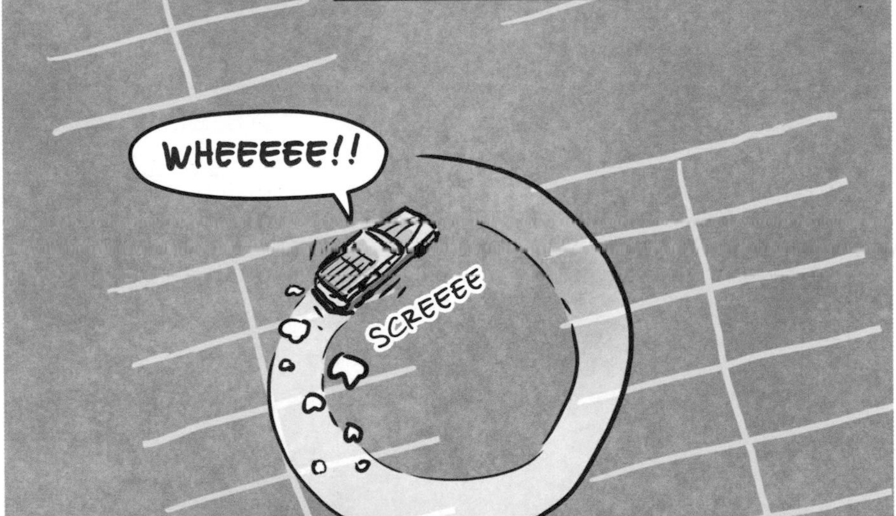
WHEEEEEE!!
SCREEEEE

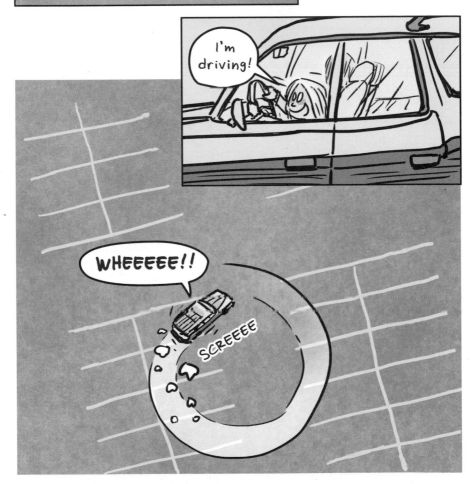

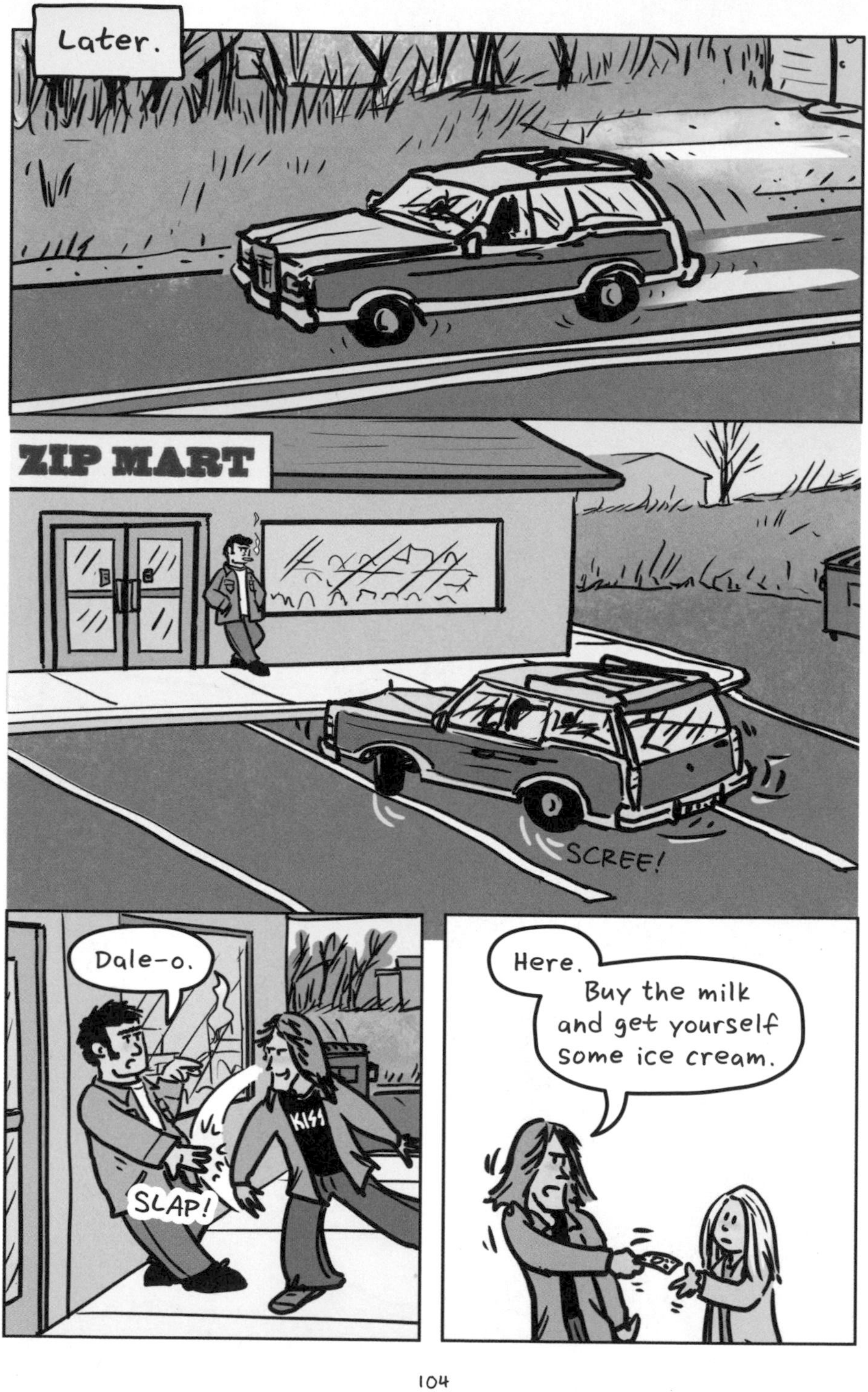
Later.
ZIP MART
SCREE!
Dale-o.
KISS
SLAP!
Here.
Buy the milk and get yourself some ice cream.

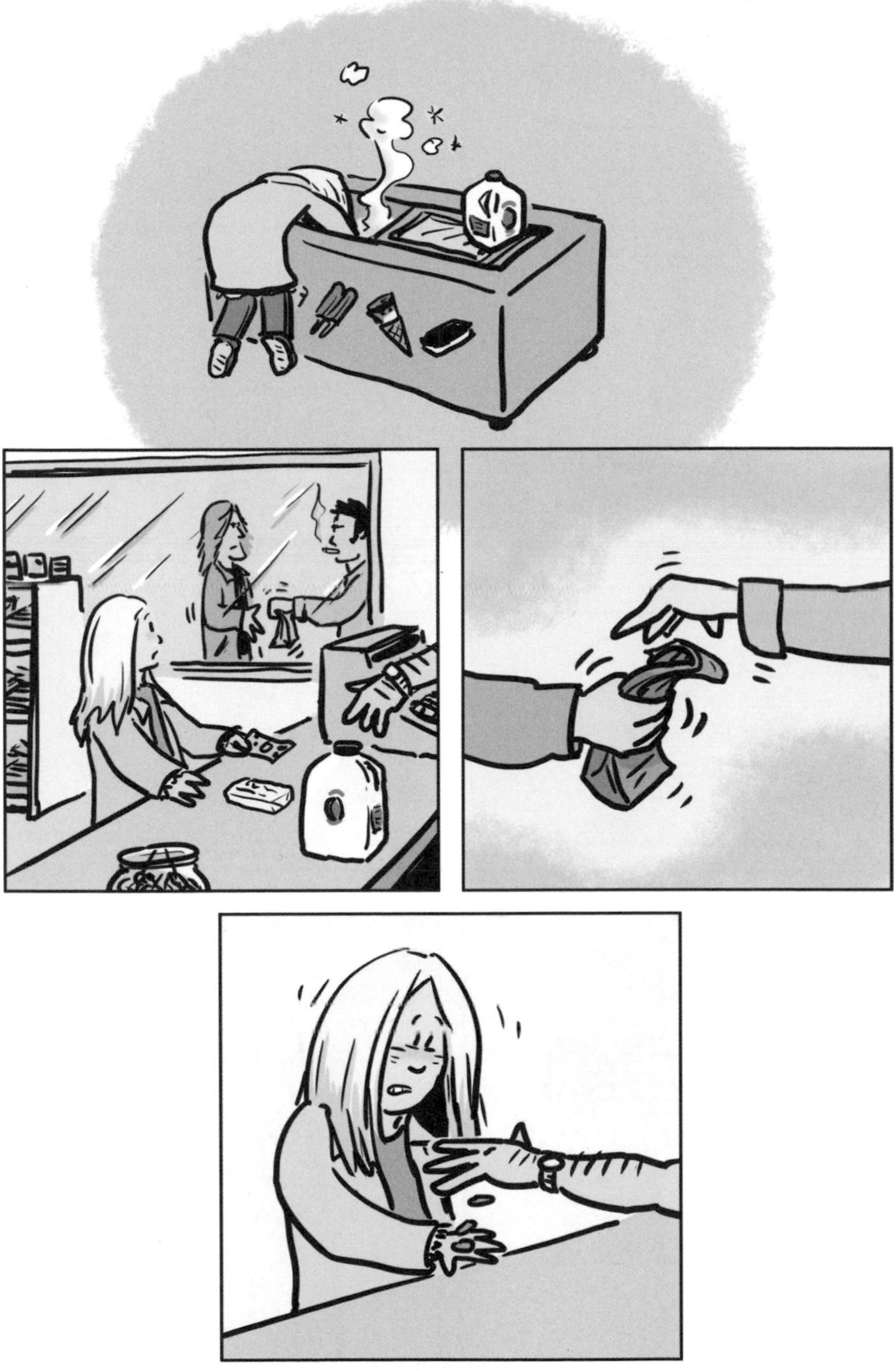

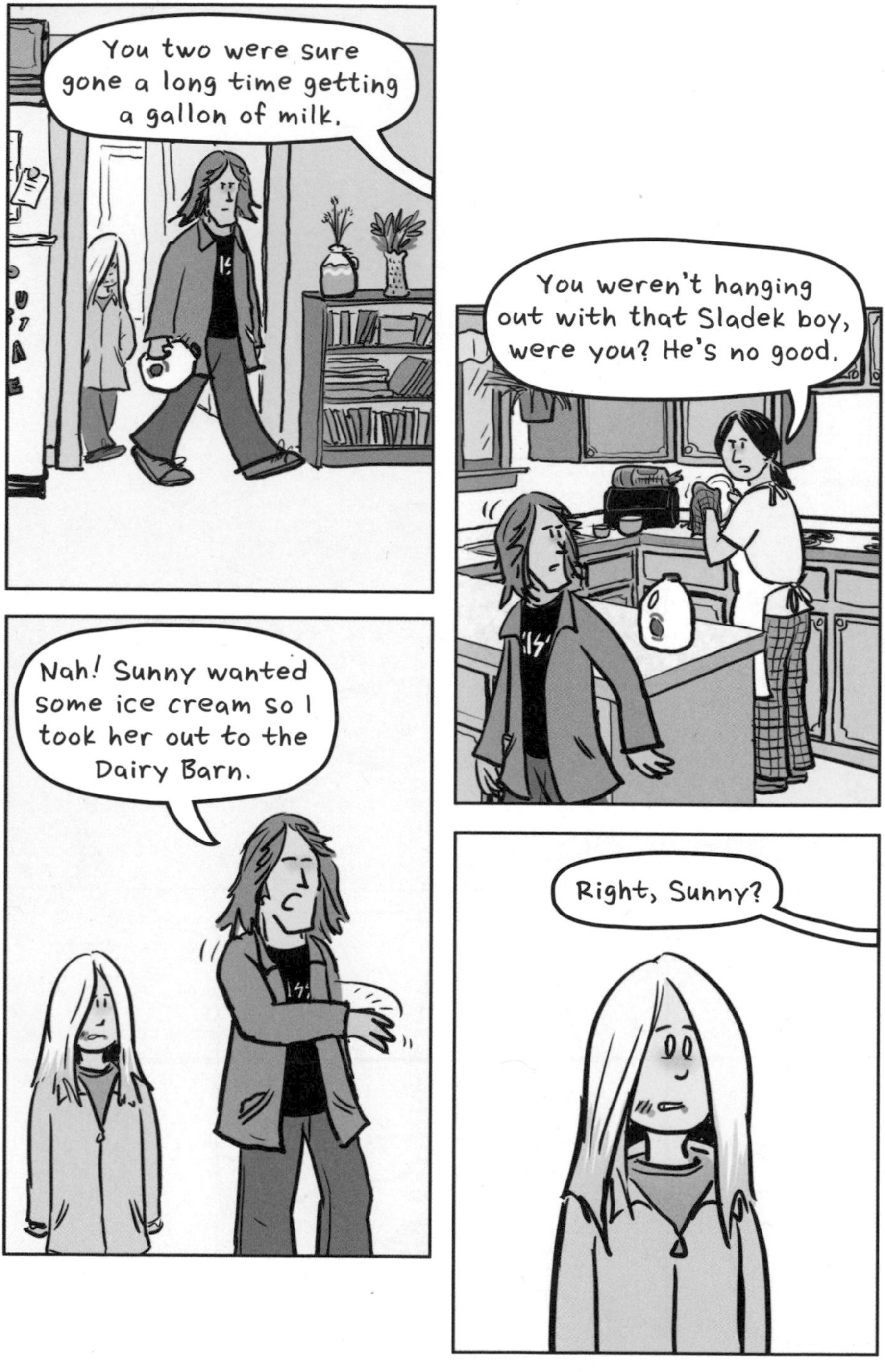
You two were sure gone a long time getting a gallon of milk.
You weren't hanging out with that Sladek boy, were you? He's no good.
Nah! Sunny wanted some ice cream so I took her out to the Dairy Barn.
Right, Sunny?

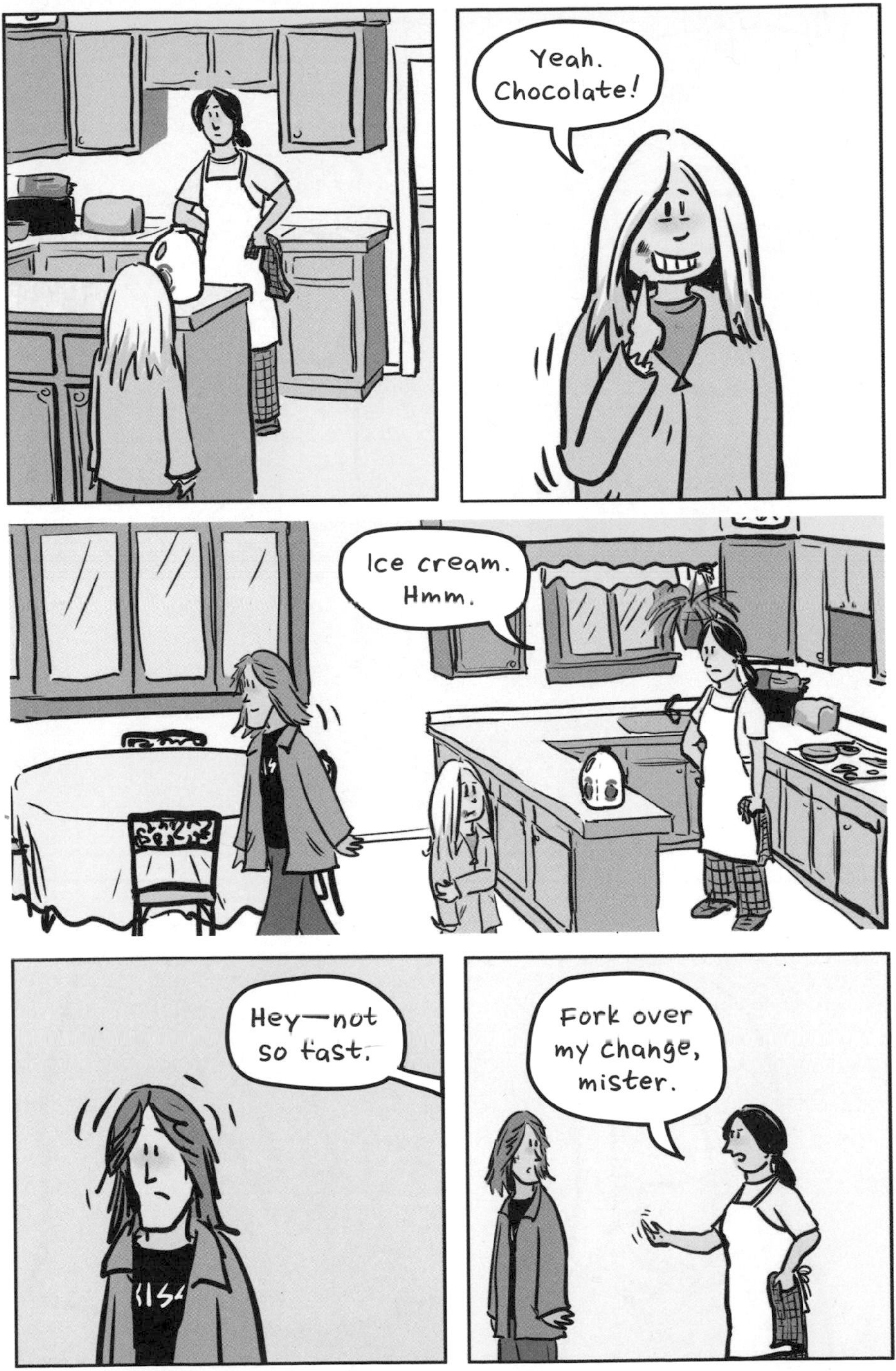
Yeah. Chocolate!
Ice cream. Hmm.
Hey—not so fast.
Fork over my change, mister.

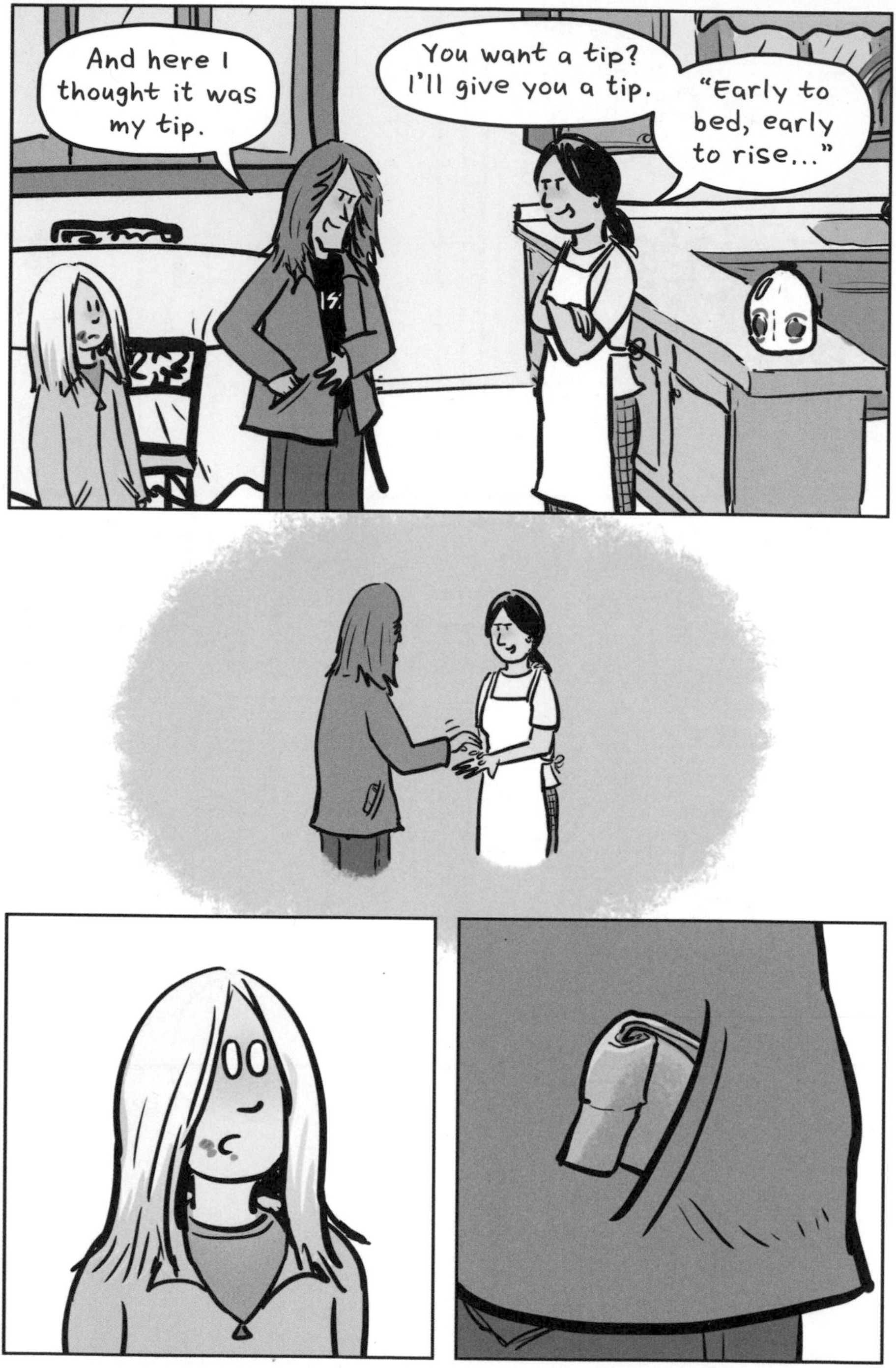

And here I thought it was my tip.
You want a tip? I'll give you a tip.
"Early to bed, early to rise..."

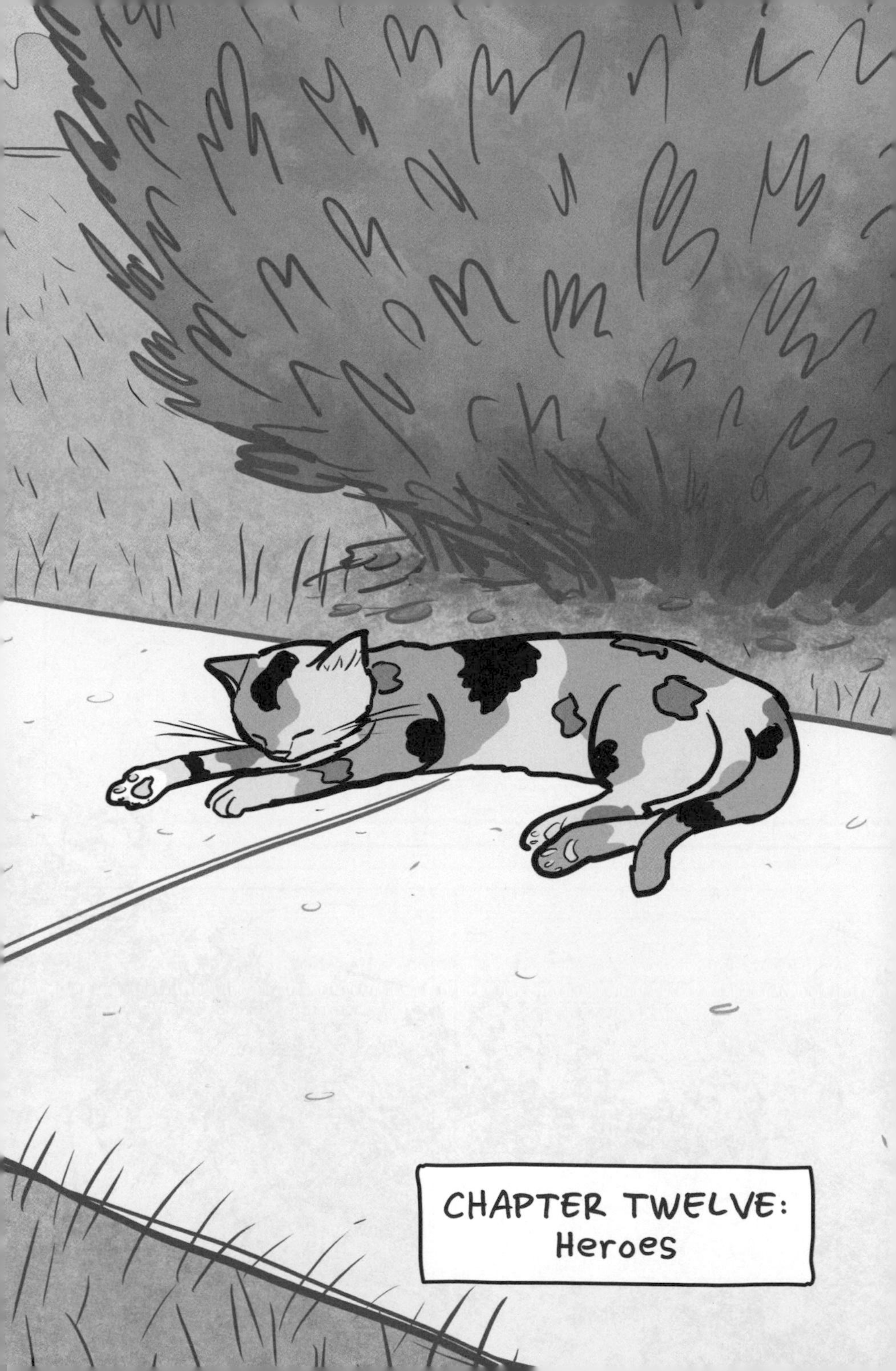
CHAPTER TWELVE:
Heroes

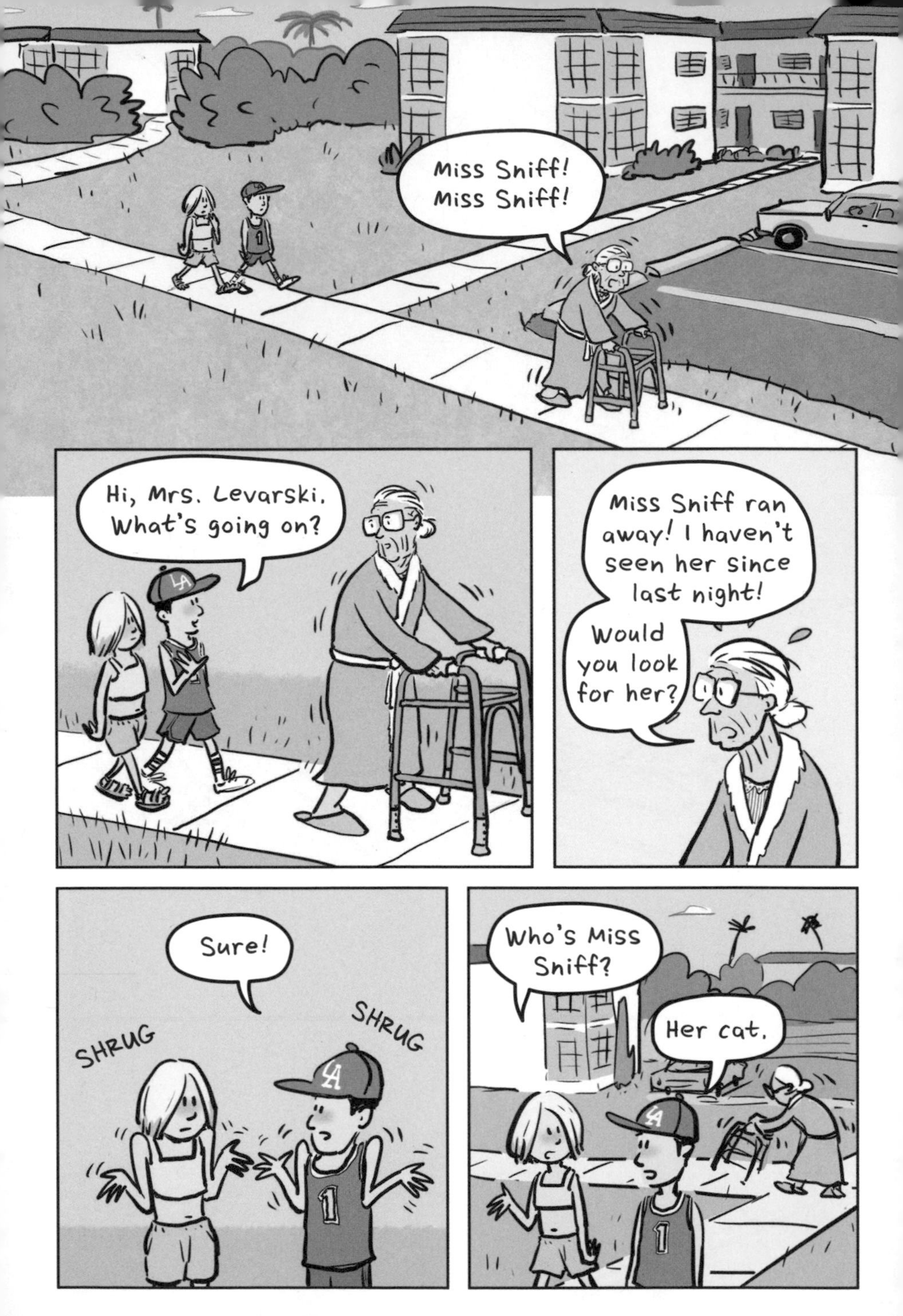
Miss Sniff!
Miss Sniff!
Hi, Mrs. Levarski. What's going on?
Miss Sniff ran away! I haven't seen her since last night!
Would you look for her?
Sure!
SHRUG
SHRUG
Who's Miss Sniff?
Her cat.

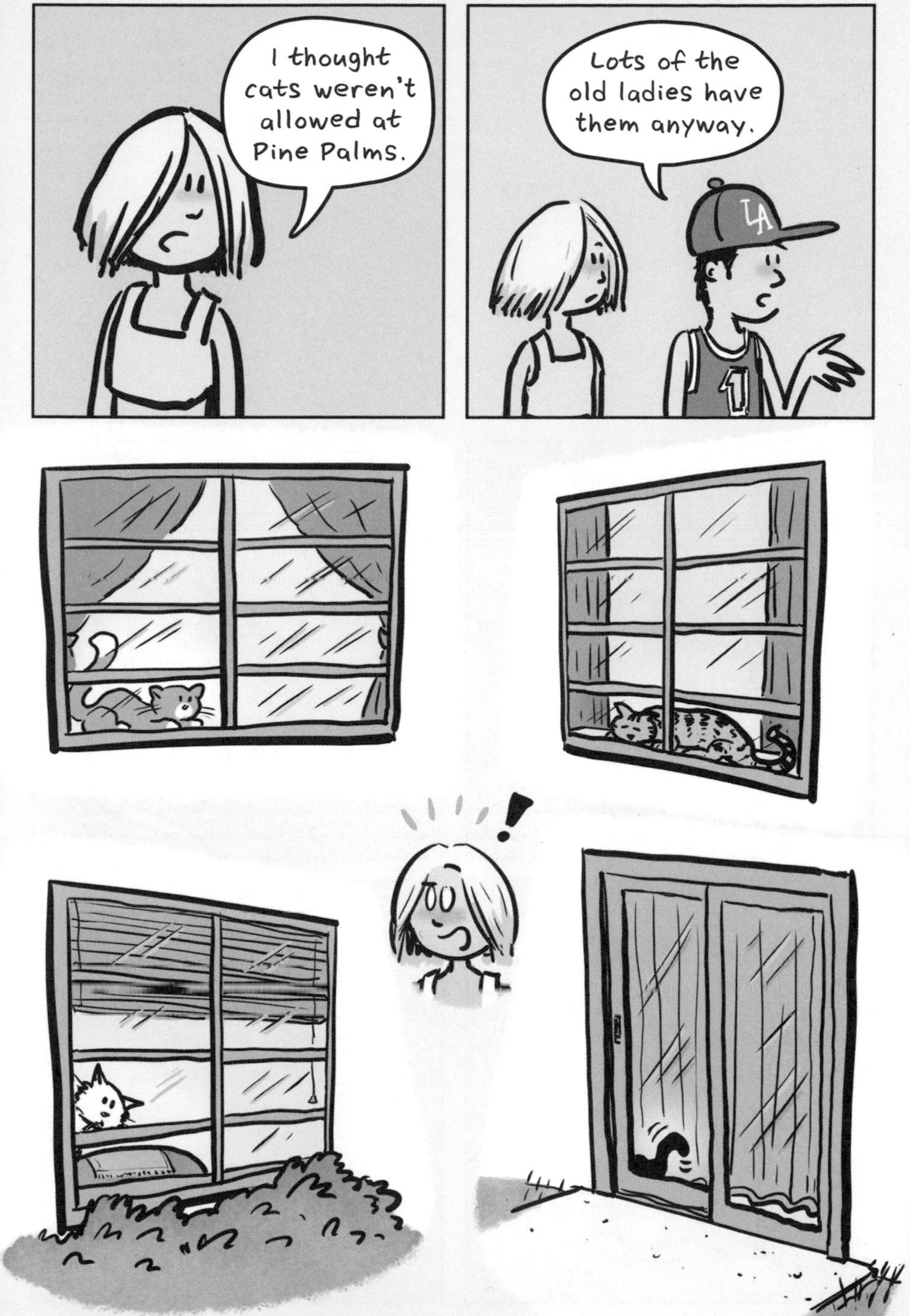
I thought cats weren't allowed at Pine Palms.
Lots of the old ladies have them anyway.
LA
!

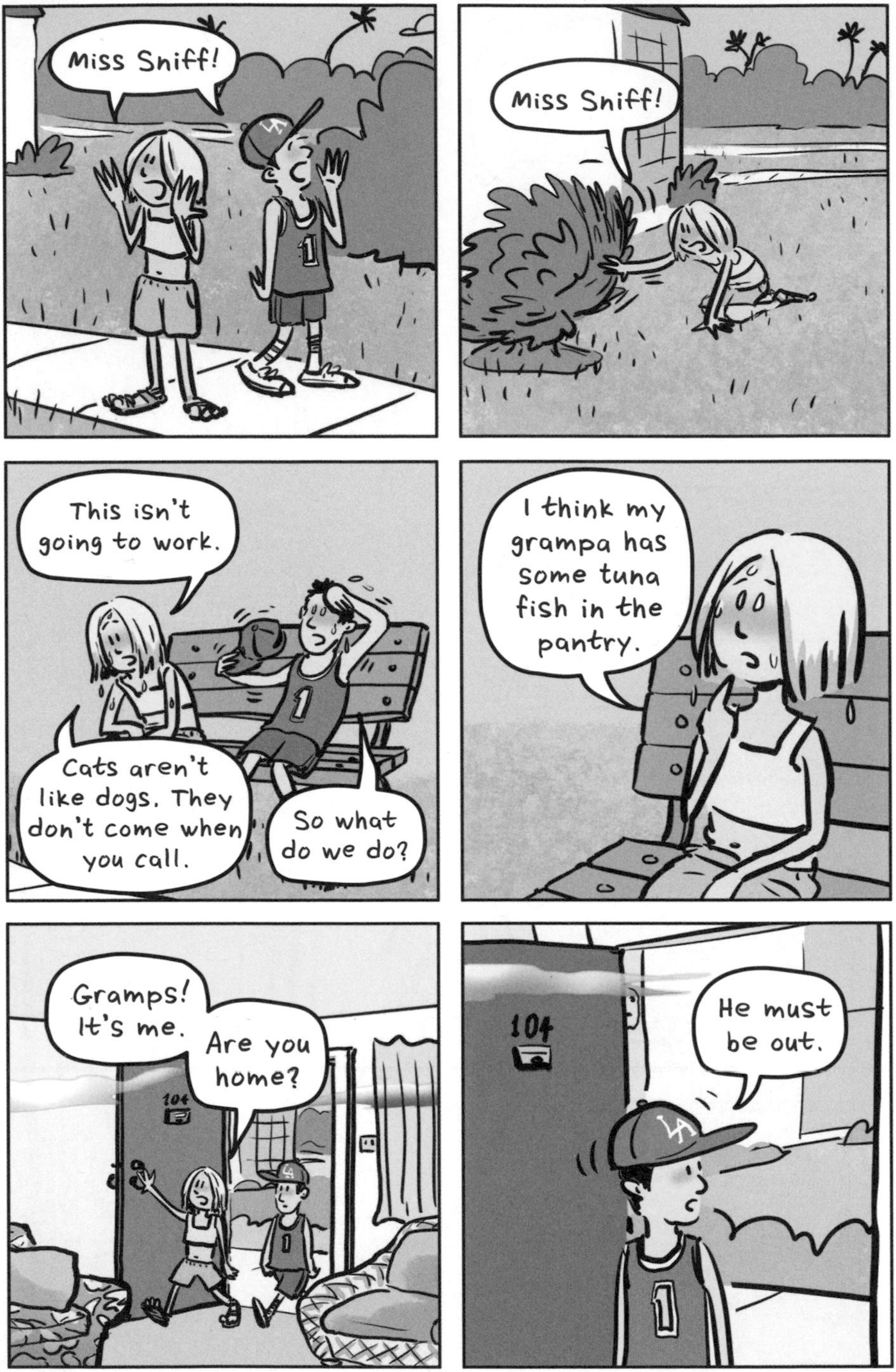
Miss Sniff!
Miss Sniff!
This isn't going to work.
Cats aren't like dogs. They don't come when you call.
So what do we do?
I think my grampa has some tuna fish in the pantry.
Gramps! It's me.
Are you home?
104
104
He must be out.

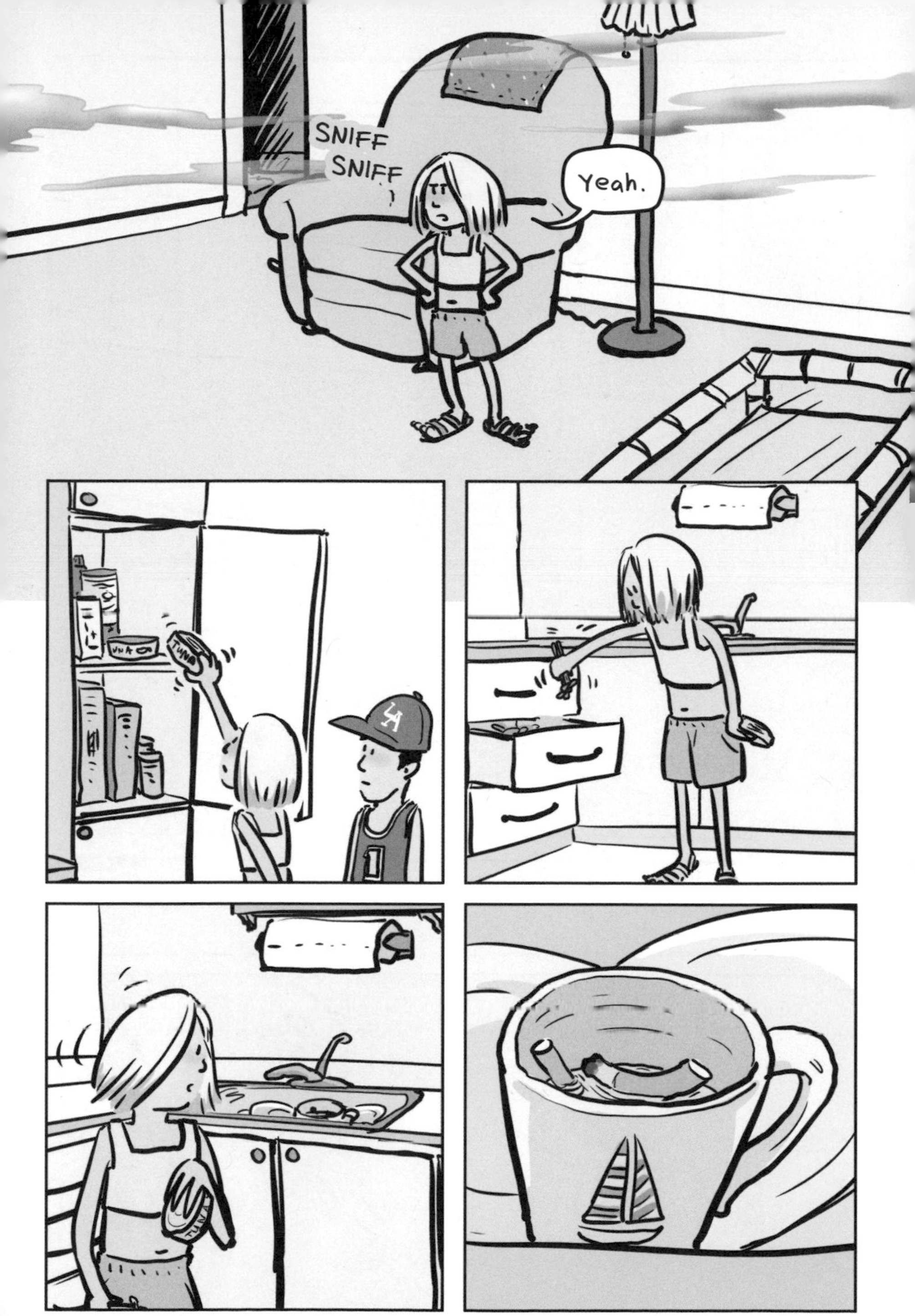
SNIFF
SNIFF
Yeah.
TUNA
TUNA

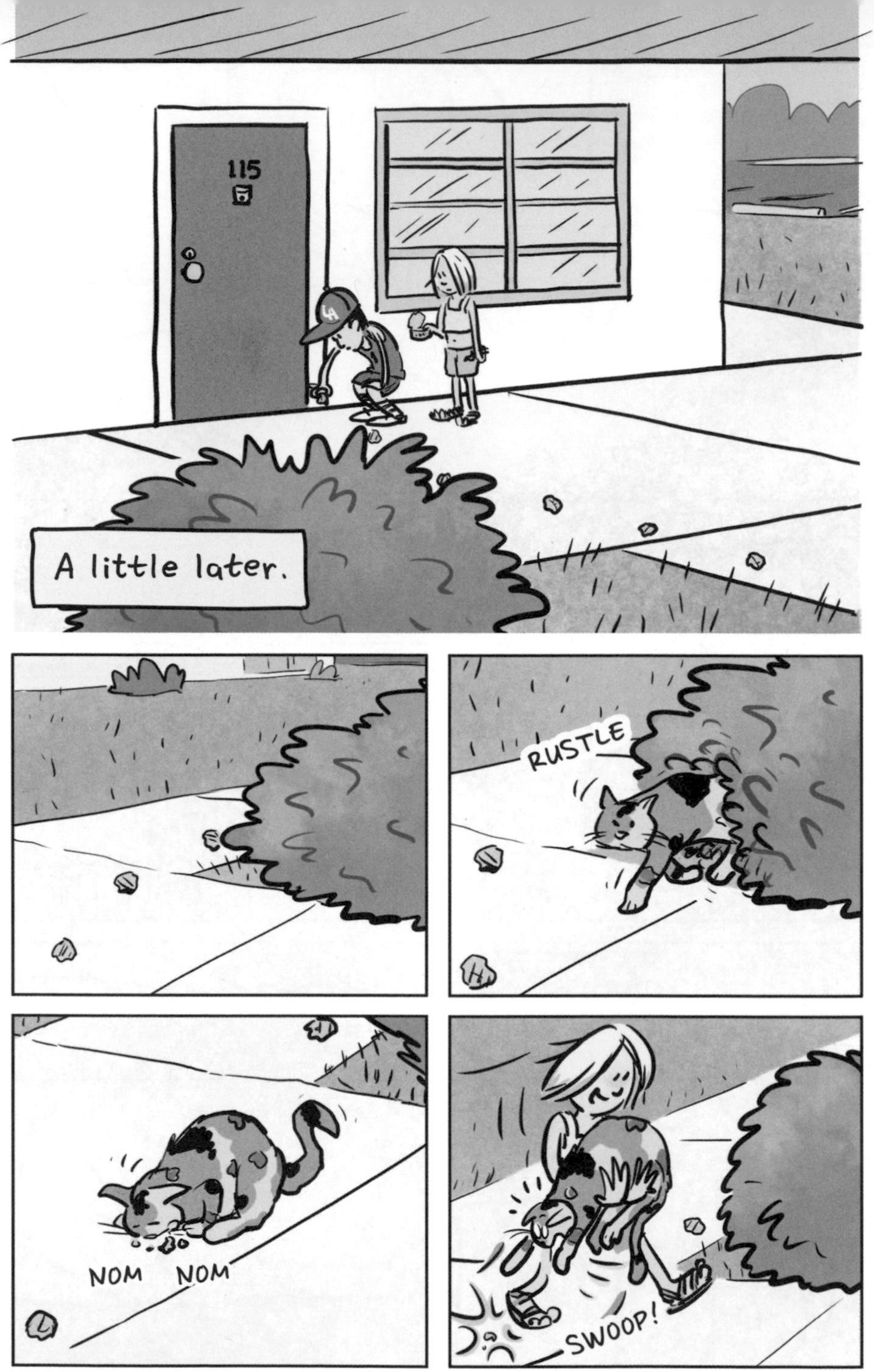
115
A little later.
RUSTLE
NOM NOM
SWOOP!

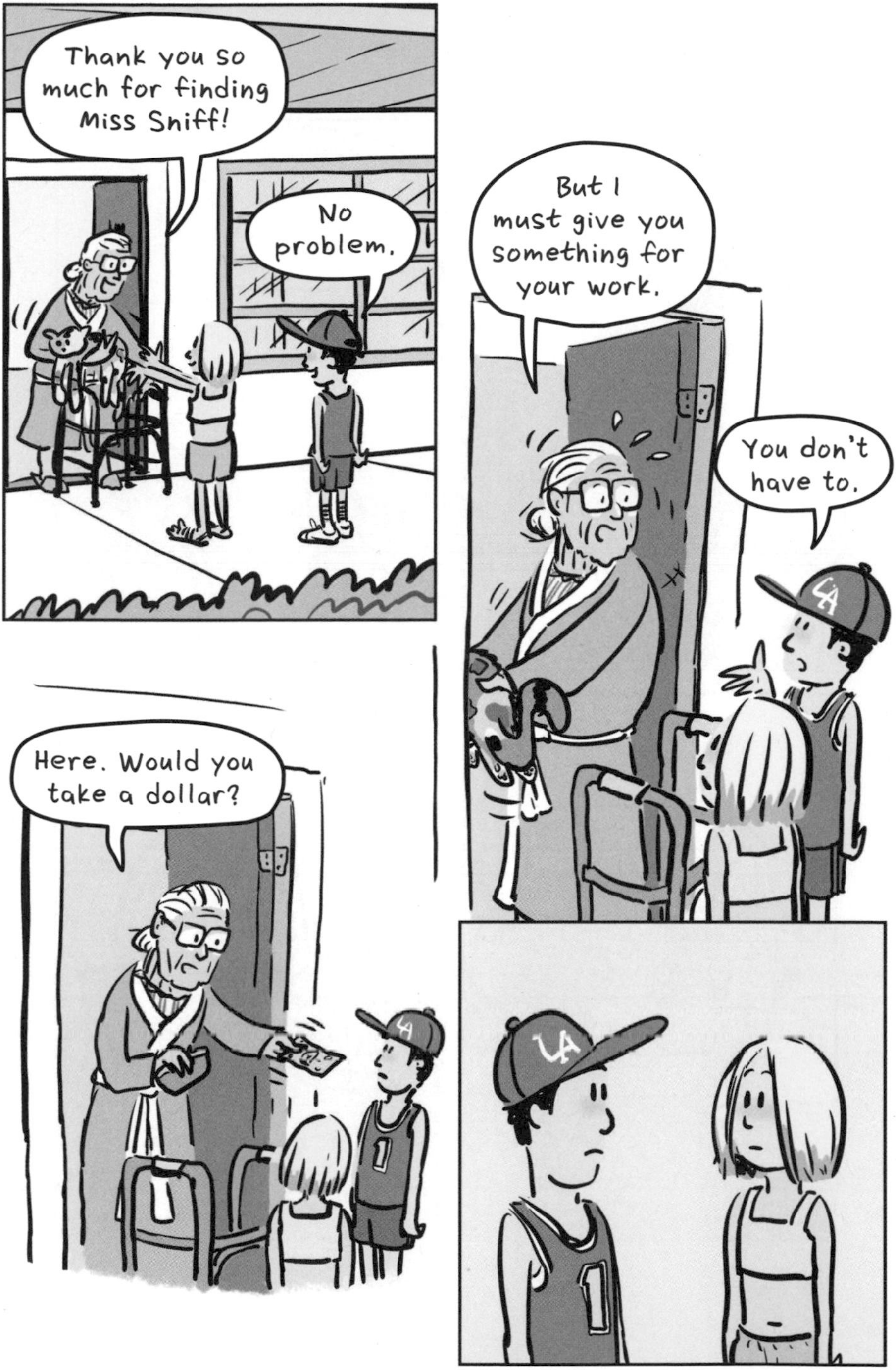
Thank you so much for finding Miss Sniff!
No problem.
But I must give you something for your work.
You don't have to.
Here. Would you take a dollar?
LA
1
LA
1

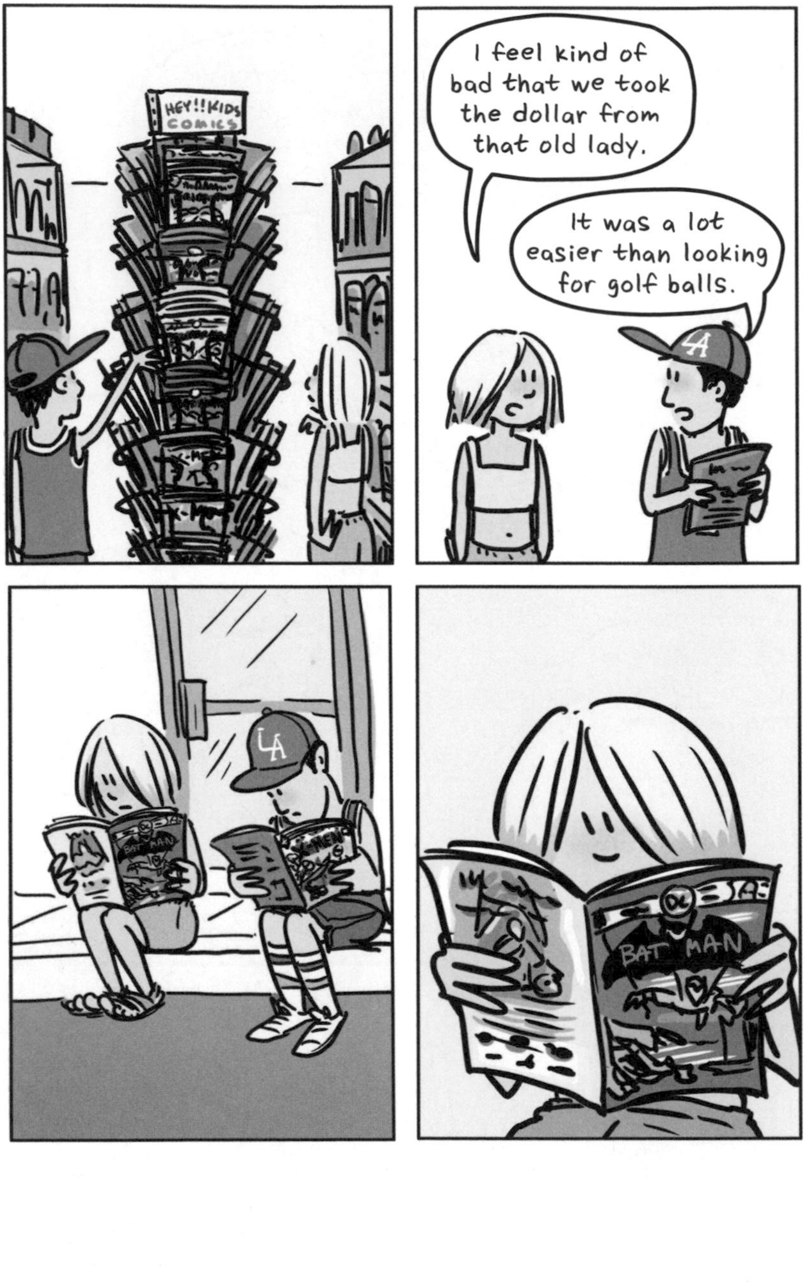
HEY!! KIDS COMICS
I feel kind of bad that we took the dollar from that old lady.
It was a lot easier than looking for golf balls.
BAT MAN

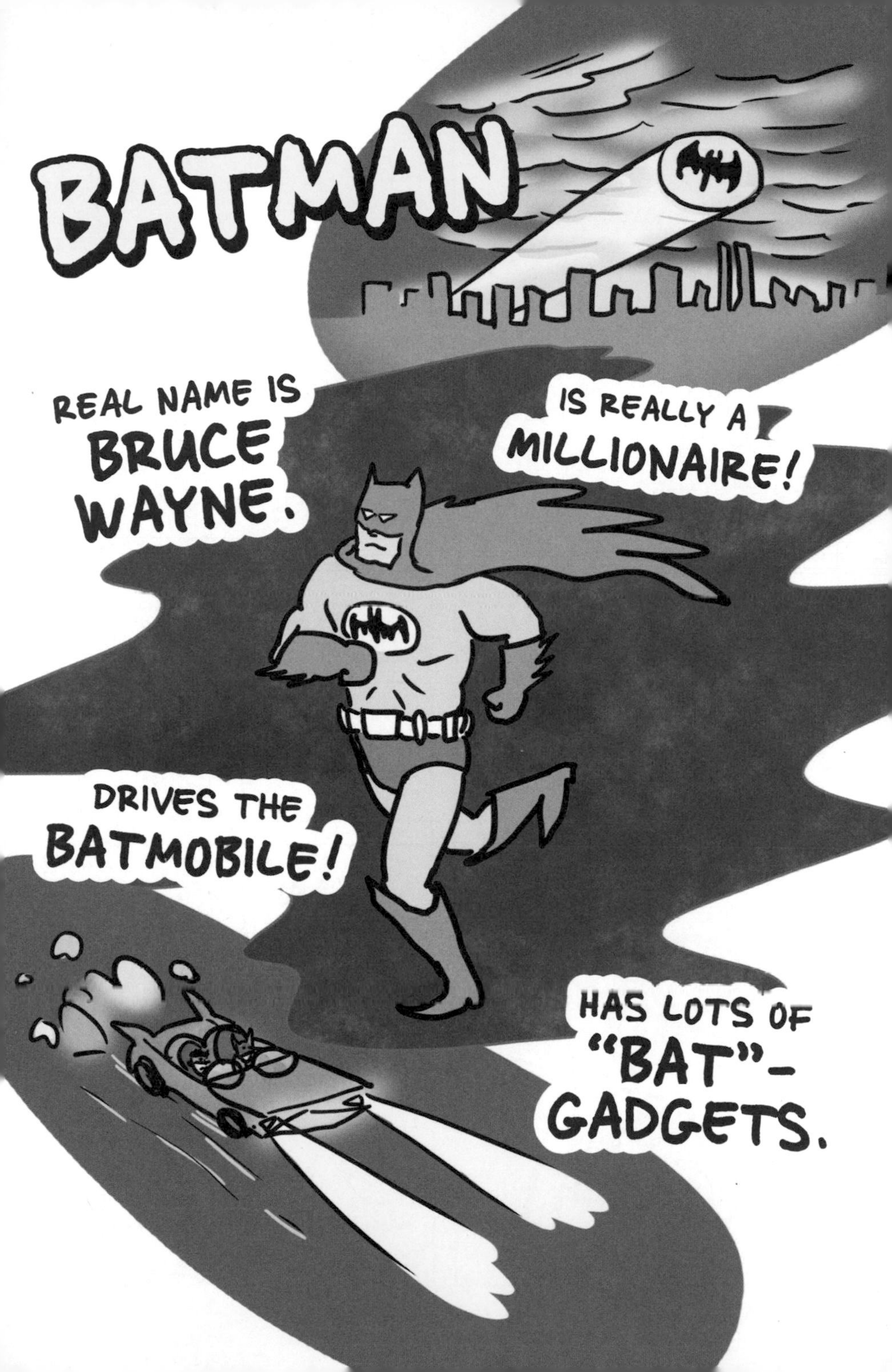
BATMAN
REAL NAME IS BRUCE WAYNE.
IS REALLY A MILLIONAIRE!
DRIVES THE BATMOBILE!
HAS LOTS OF "BAT"-GADGETS.

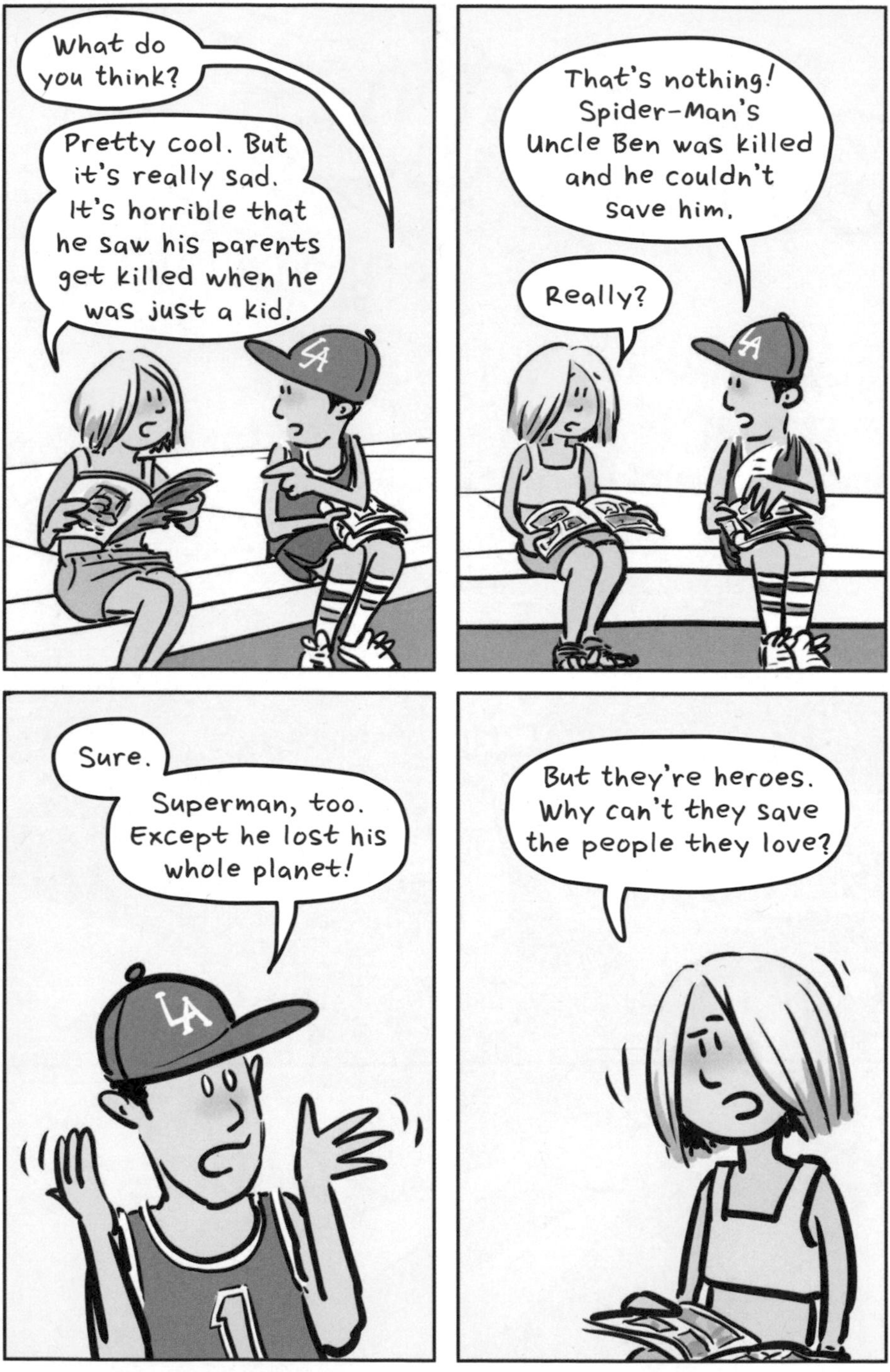
What do you think?
Pretty cool. But it's really sad. It's horrible that he saw his parents get killed when he was just a kid.
That's nothing! Spider-Man's Uncle Ben was killed and he couldn't save him.
Really?
Sure.
Superman, too. Except he lost his whole planet!
But they're heroes. Why can't they save the people they love?

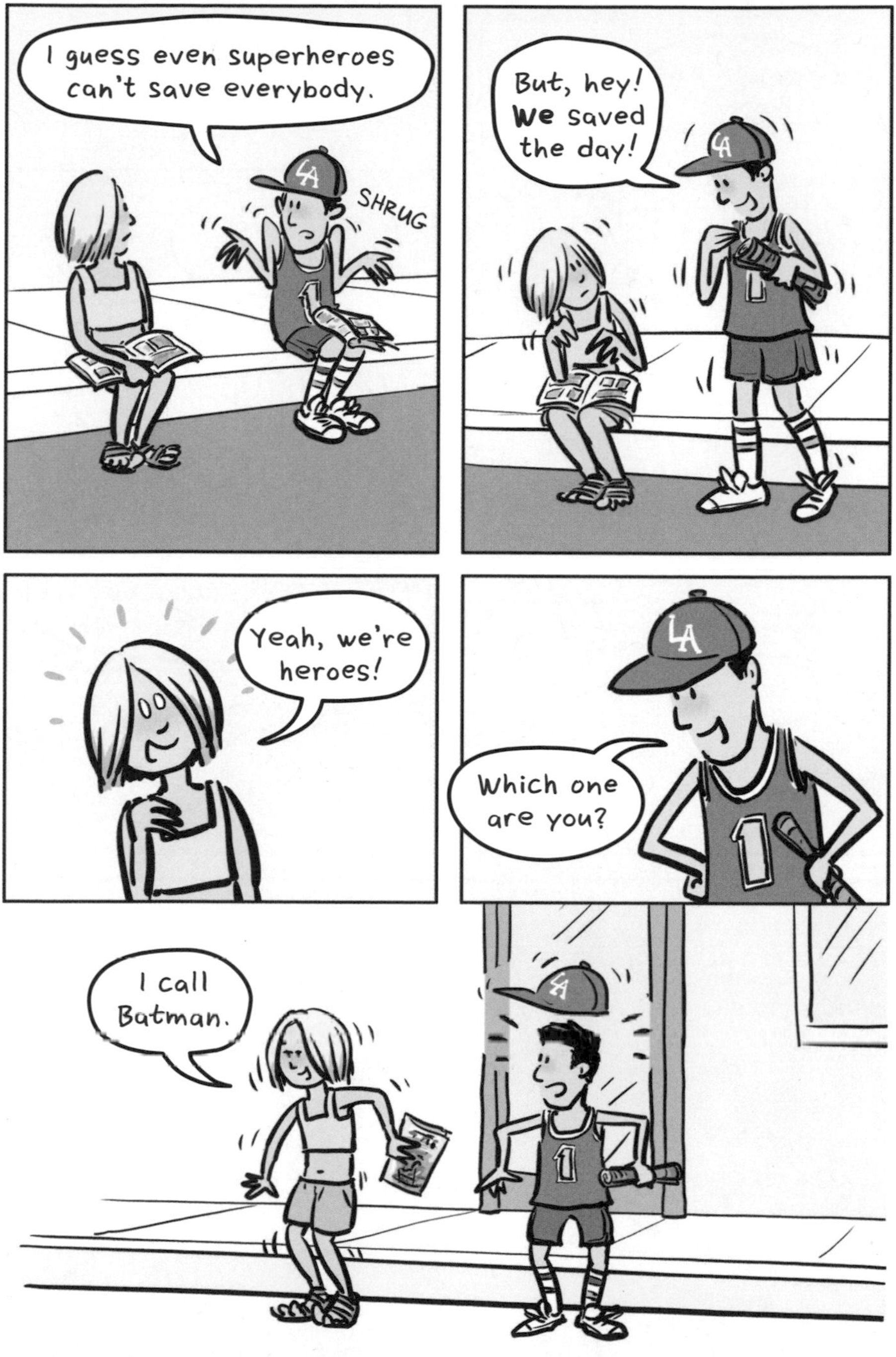
I guess even superheroes can't save everybody.
SHRUG
But, hey! **We** saved the day!
Yeah, we're heroes!
Which one are you?
I call Batman.

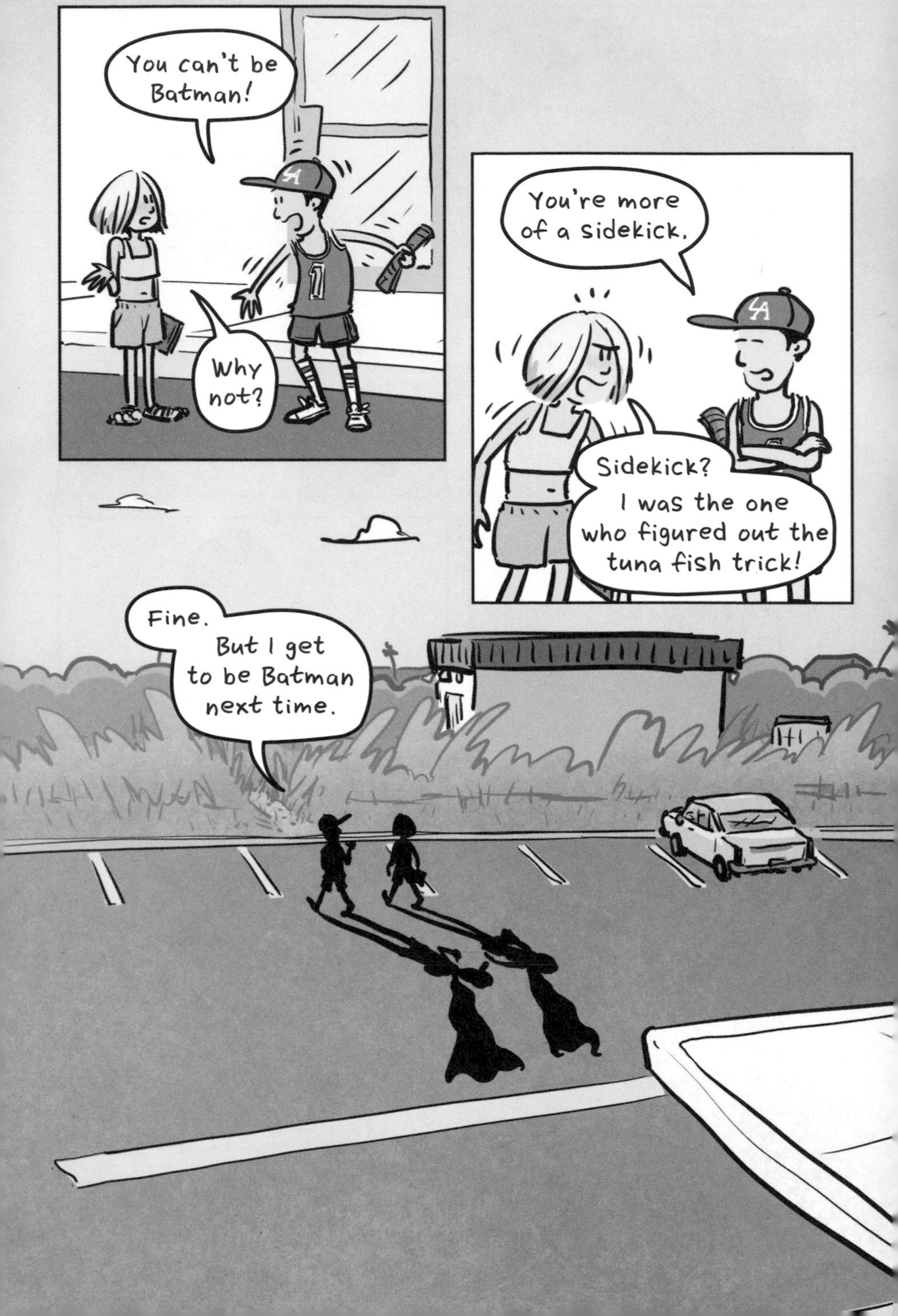
You can't be Batman!
Why not?
You're more of a sidekick.
Sidekick? I was the one who figured out the tuna fish trick!
Fine. But I get to be Batman next time.

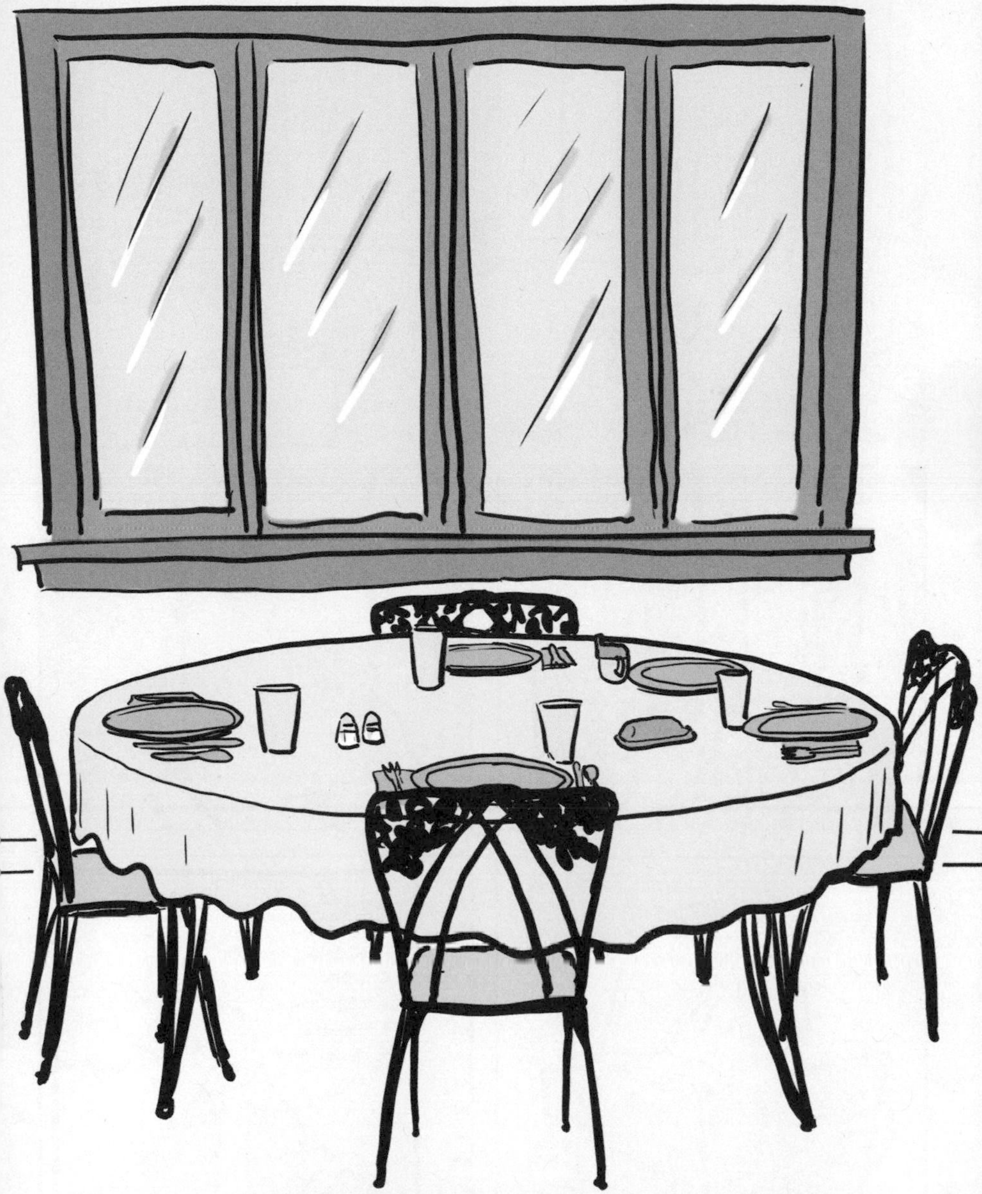

CHAPTER THIRTEEN: Pompeii

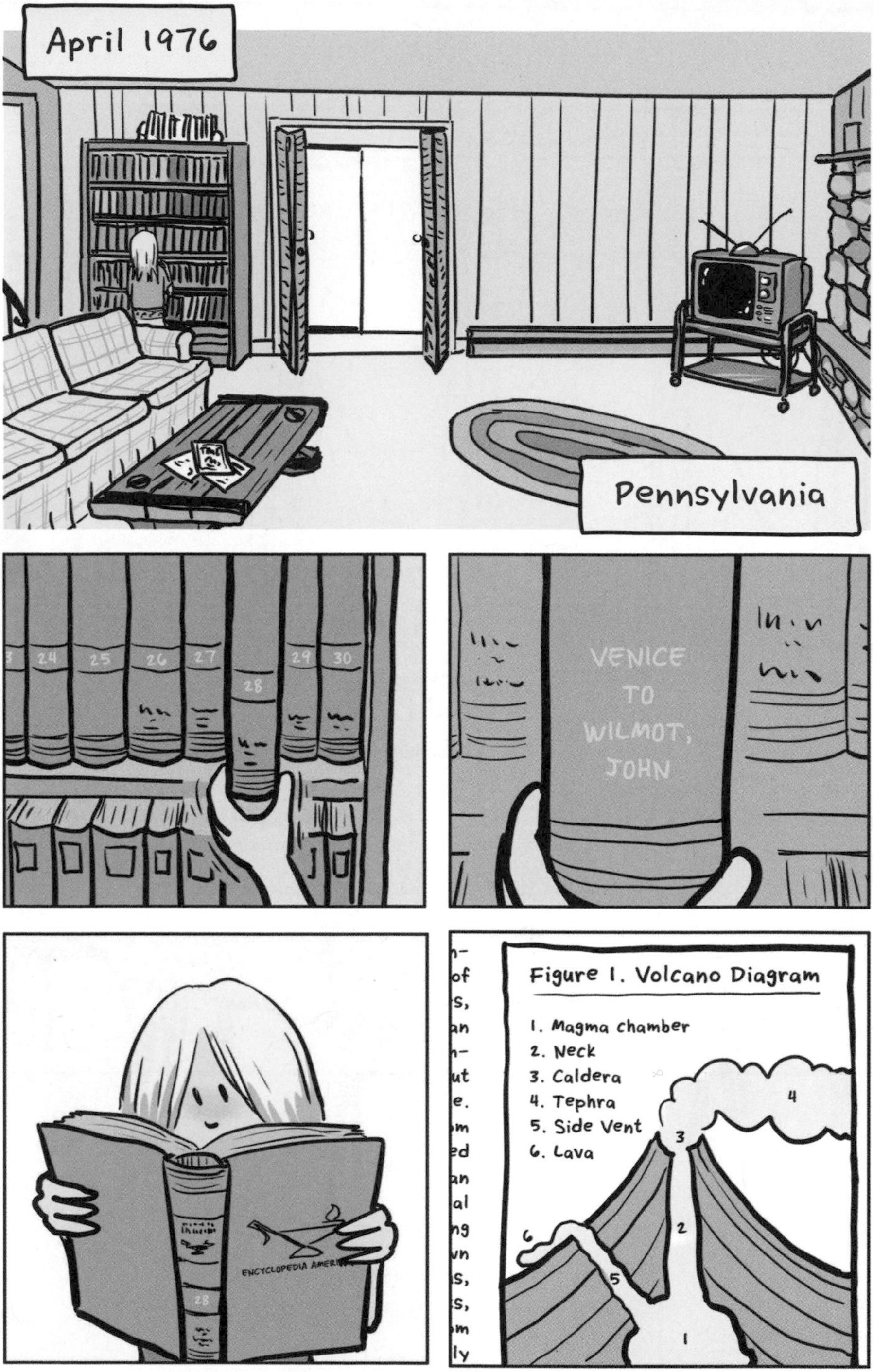
April 1976
Pennsylvania
24
25
26
27
28
29
30
VENICE TO WILMOT, JOHN
28
ENCYCLOPEDIA AMERI
Figure 1. Volcano Diagram
1. Magma chamber
2. Neck
3. Caldera
4. Tephra
5. Side Vent
6. Lava
1
2
3
4
5
6

NOTABLE VOLCANOES

Pompeii, Italy, AD 79. The ancient Roman city of POMPEII was destroyed by the eruption of the volcano VESUVIUS. Thousands were buried under a hail of ash, preserving them where they fell.

PLATES 1–3. Plaster casts of eruption victims

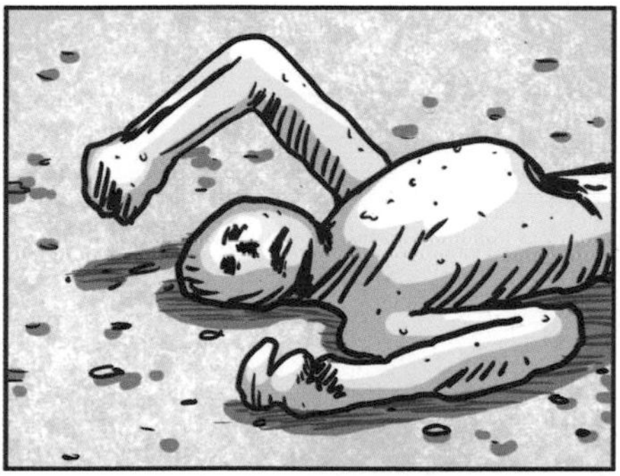

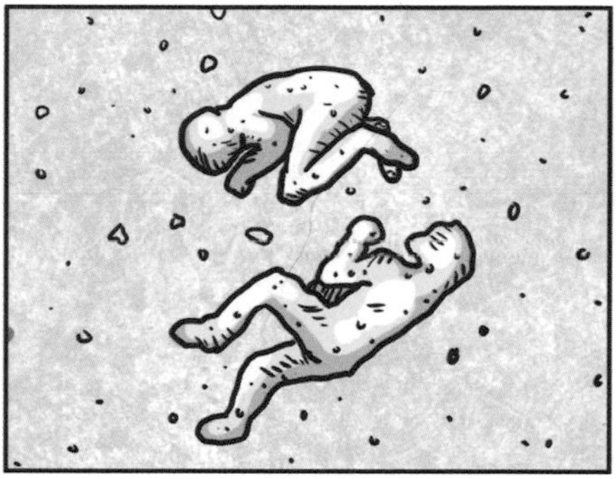

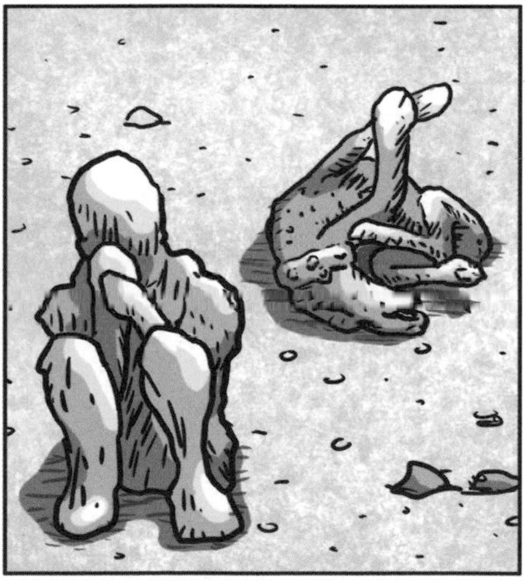

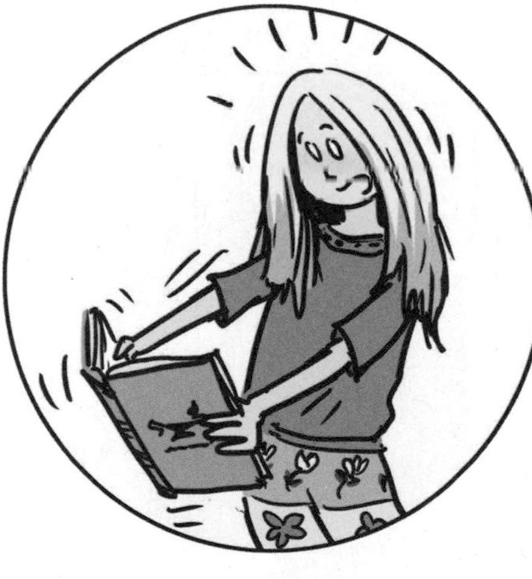

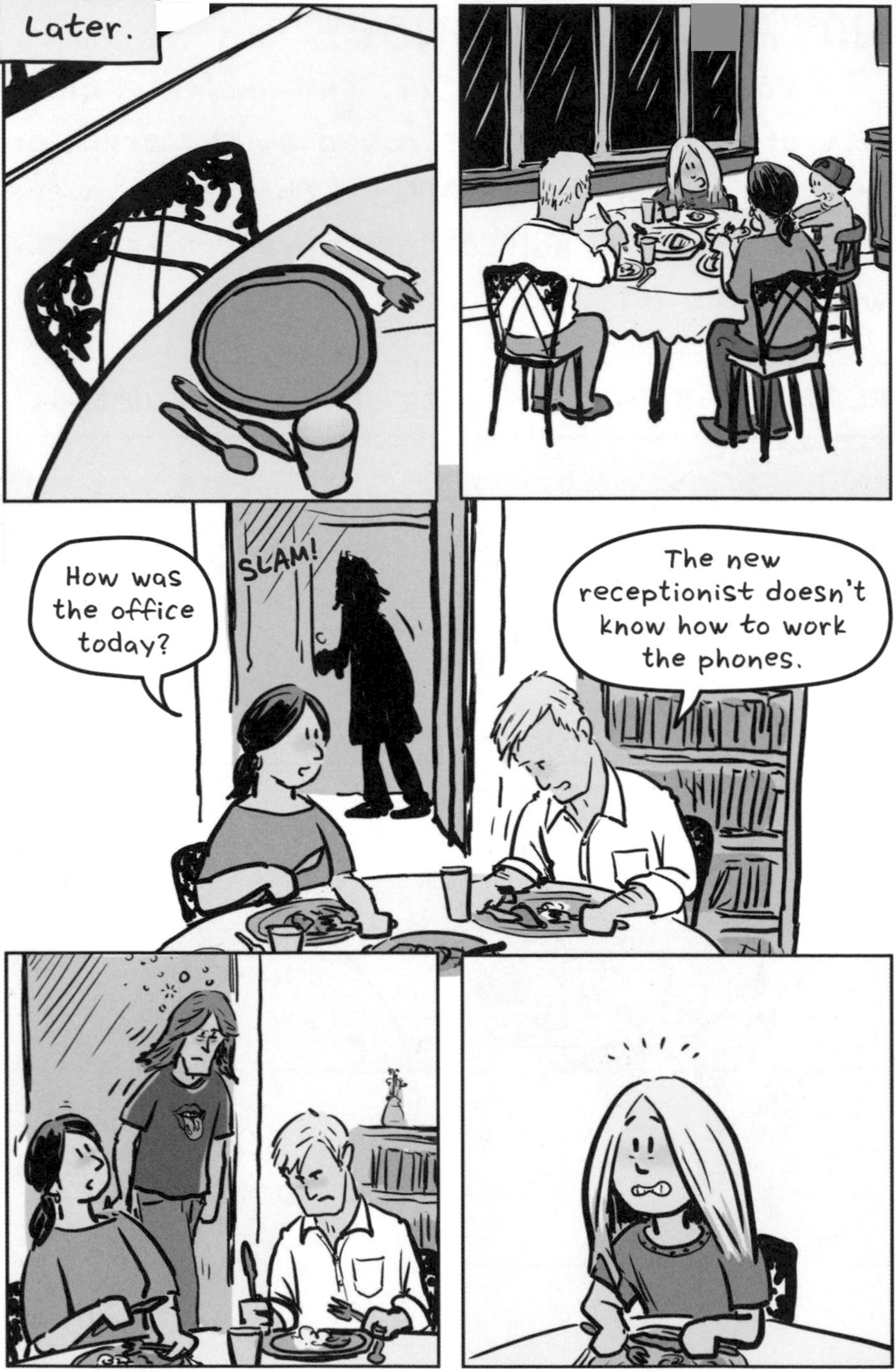
Later.
How was the office today?
SLAM!
The new receptionist doesn't know how to work the phones.

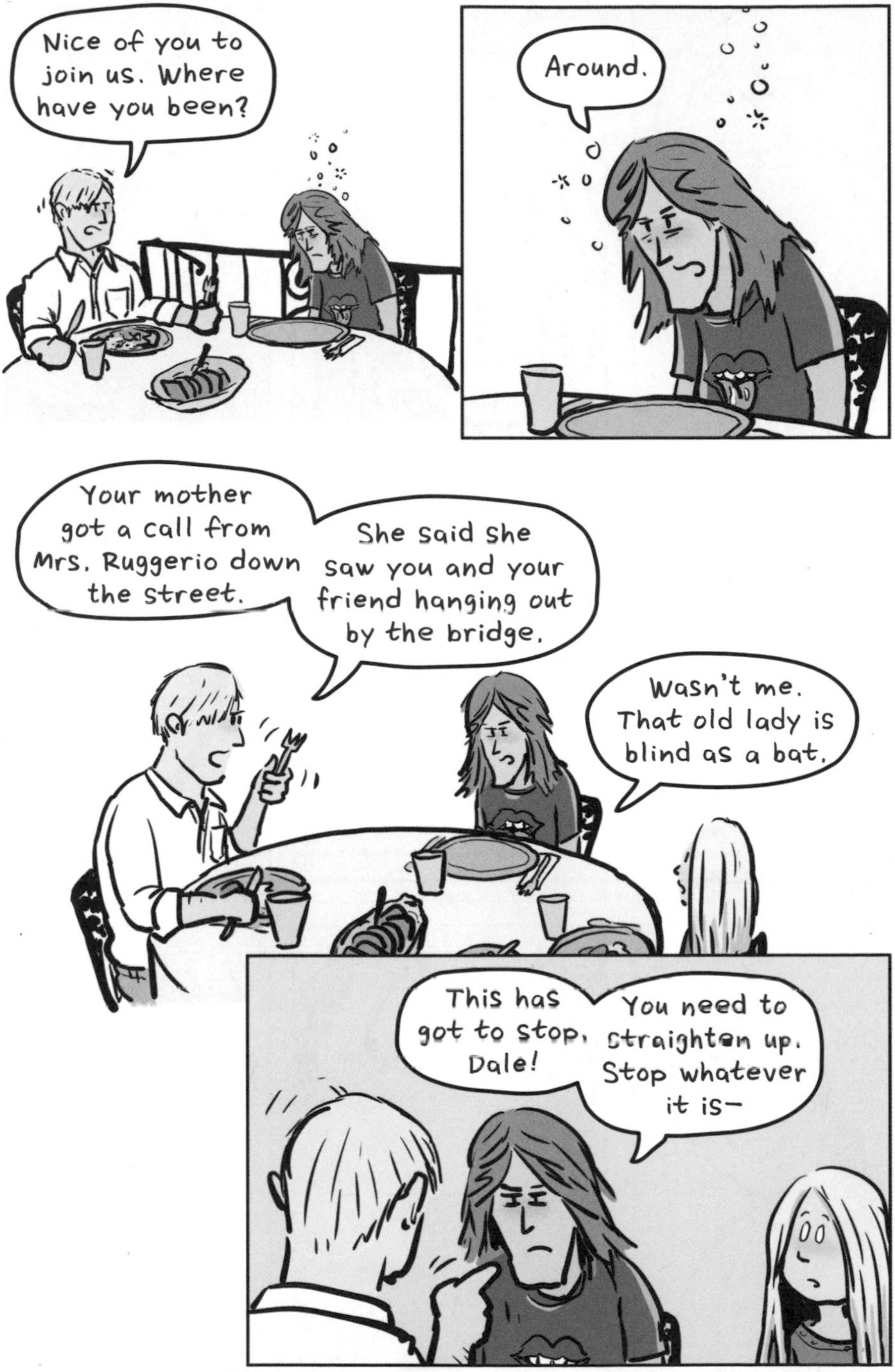
Nice of you to join us. Where have you been?
Around.
Your mother got a call from Mrs. Ruggerio down the street.
She said she saw you and your friend hanging out by the bridge.
Wasn't me. That old lady is blind as a bat.
This has got to stop, Dale!
You need to straighten up. Stop whatever it is—

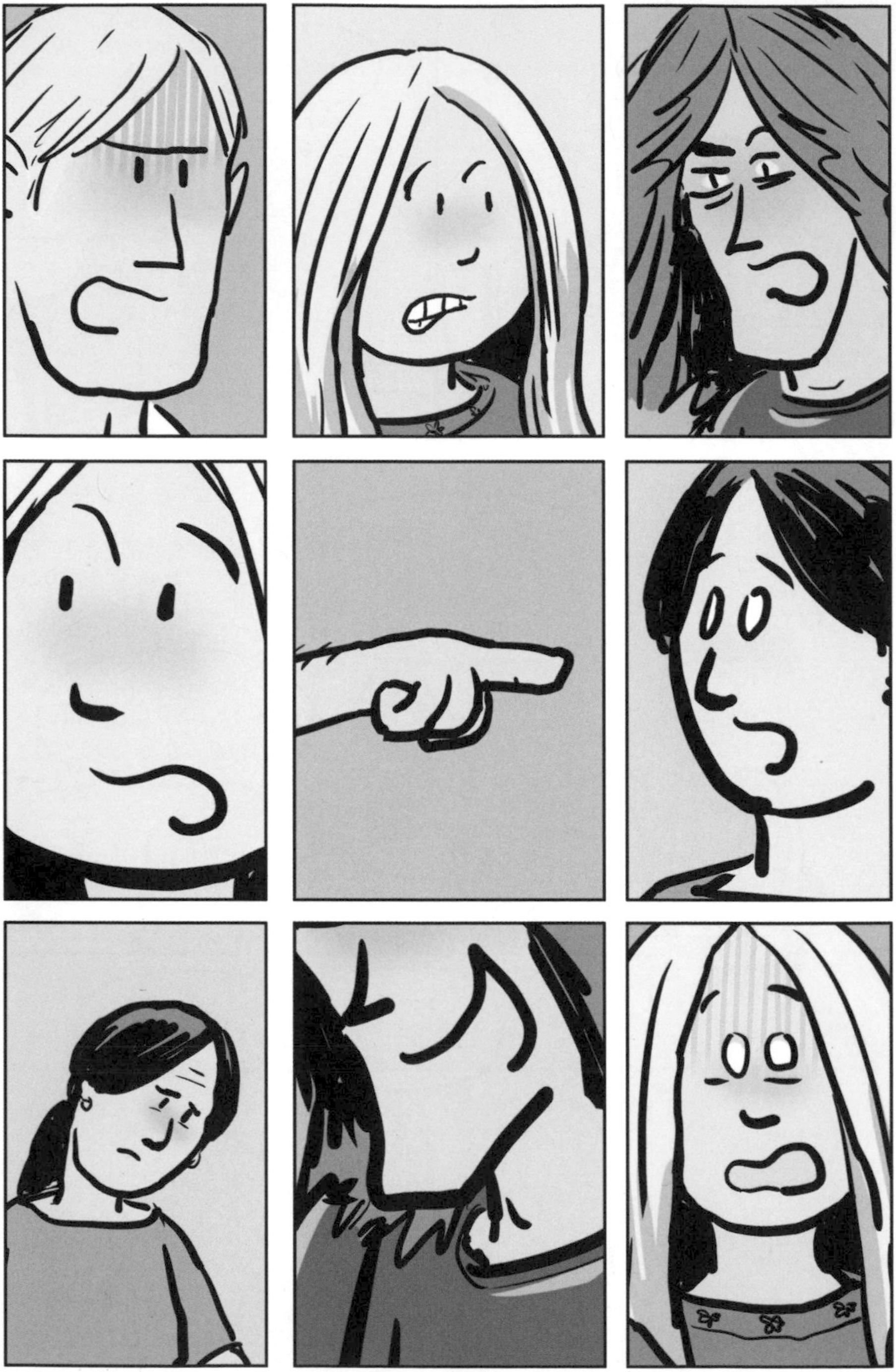

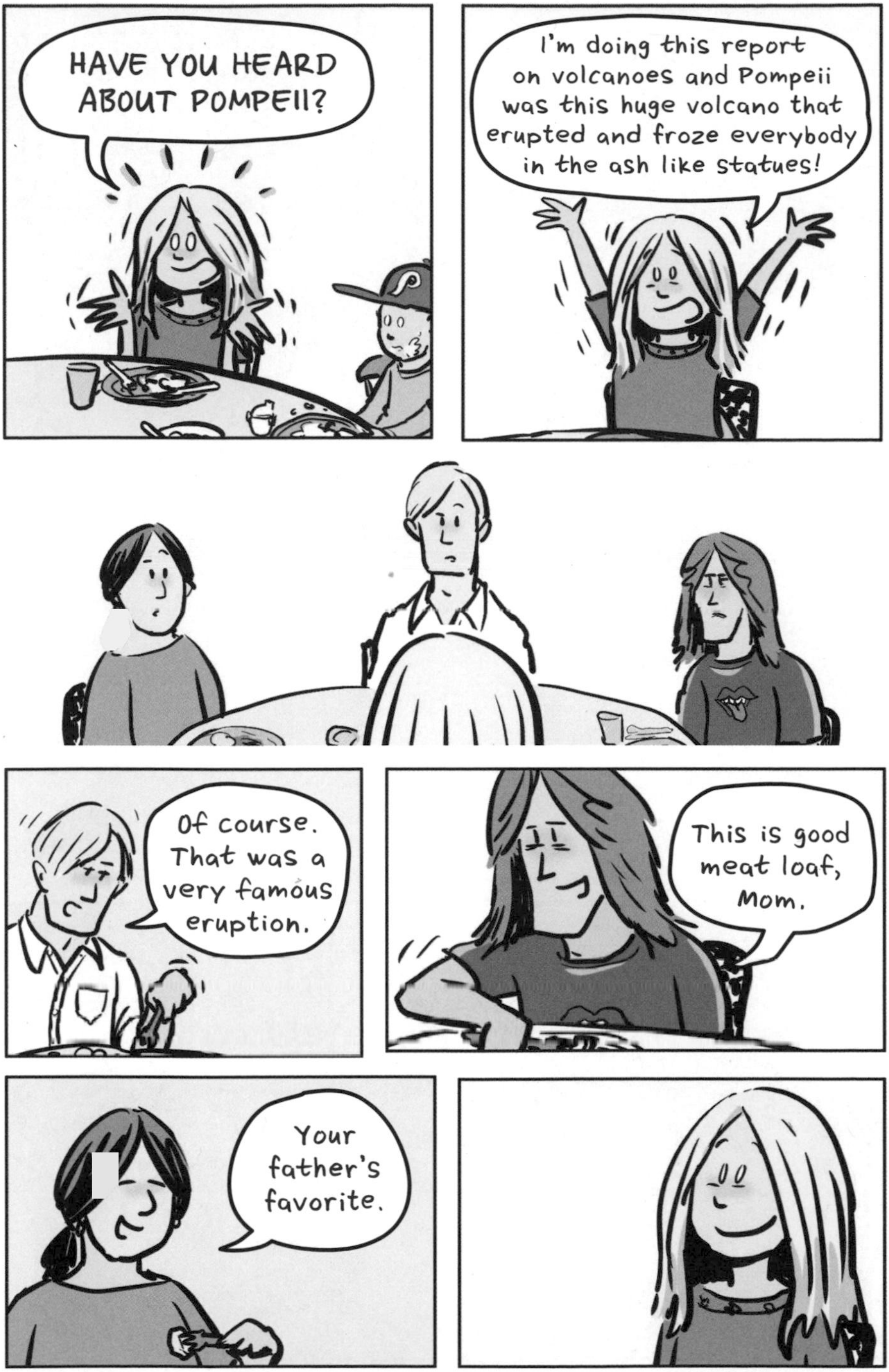
HAVE YOU HEARD ABOUT POMPEII?
I'm doing this report on volcanoes and Pompeii was this huge volcano that erupted and froze everybody in the ash like statues!
Of course. That was a very famous eruption.
This is good meat loaf, Mom.
Your father's favorite.

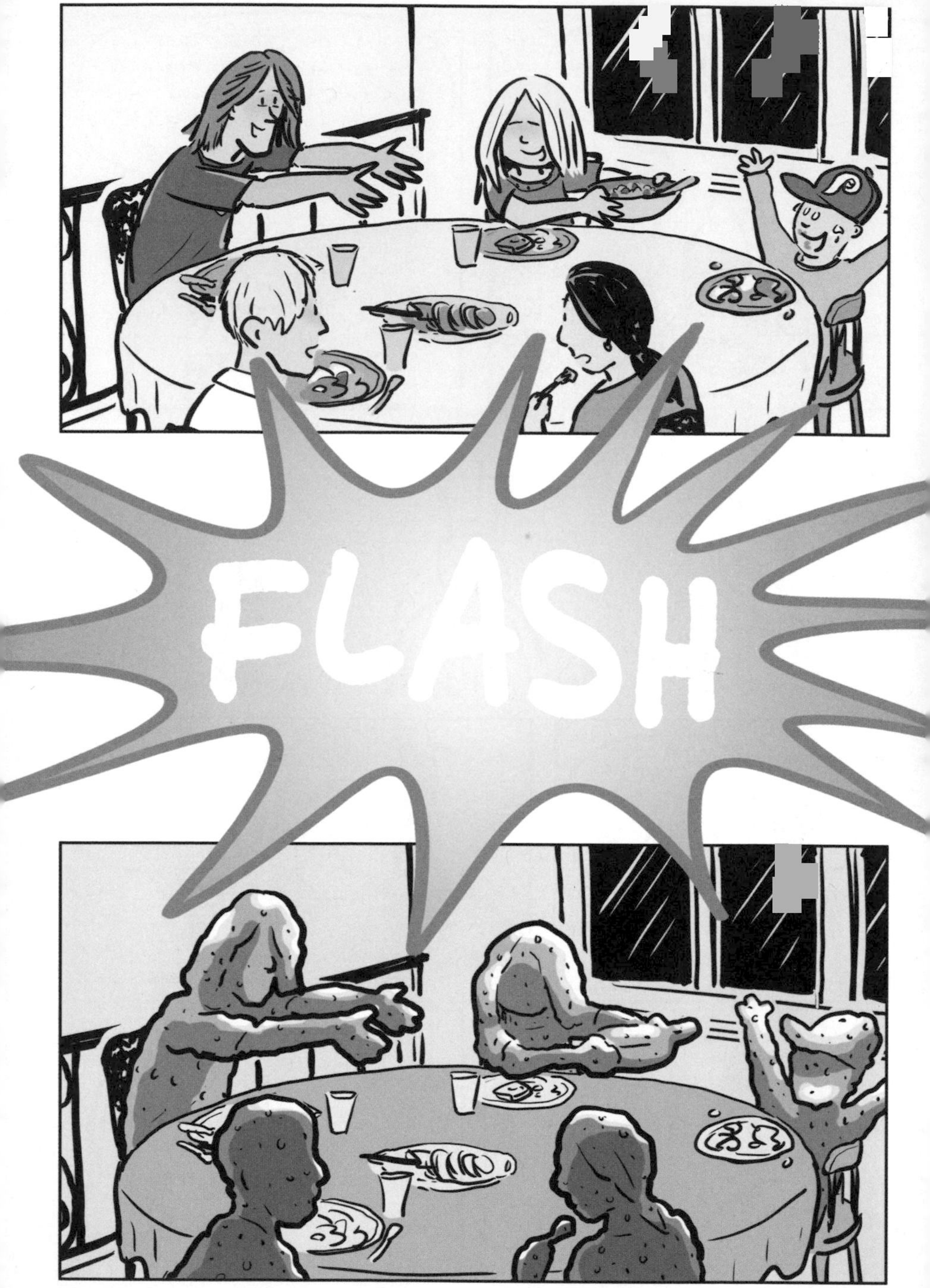
FLASH

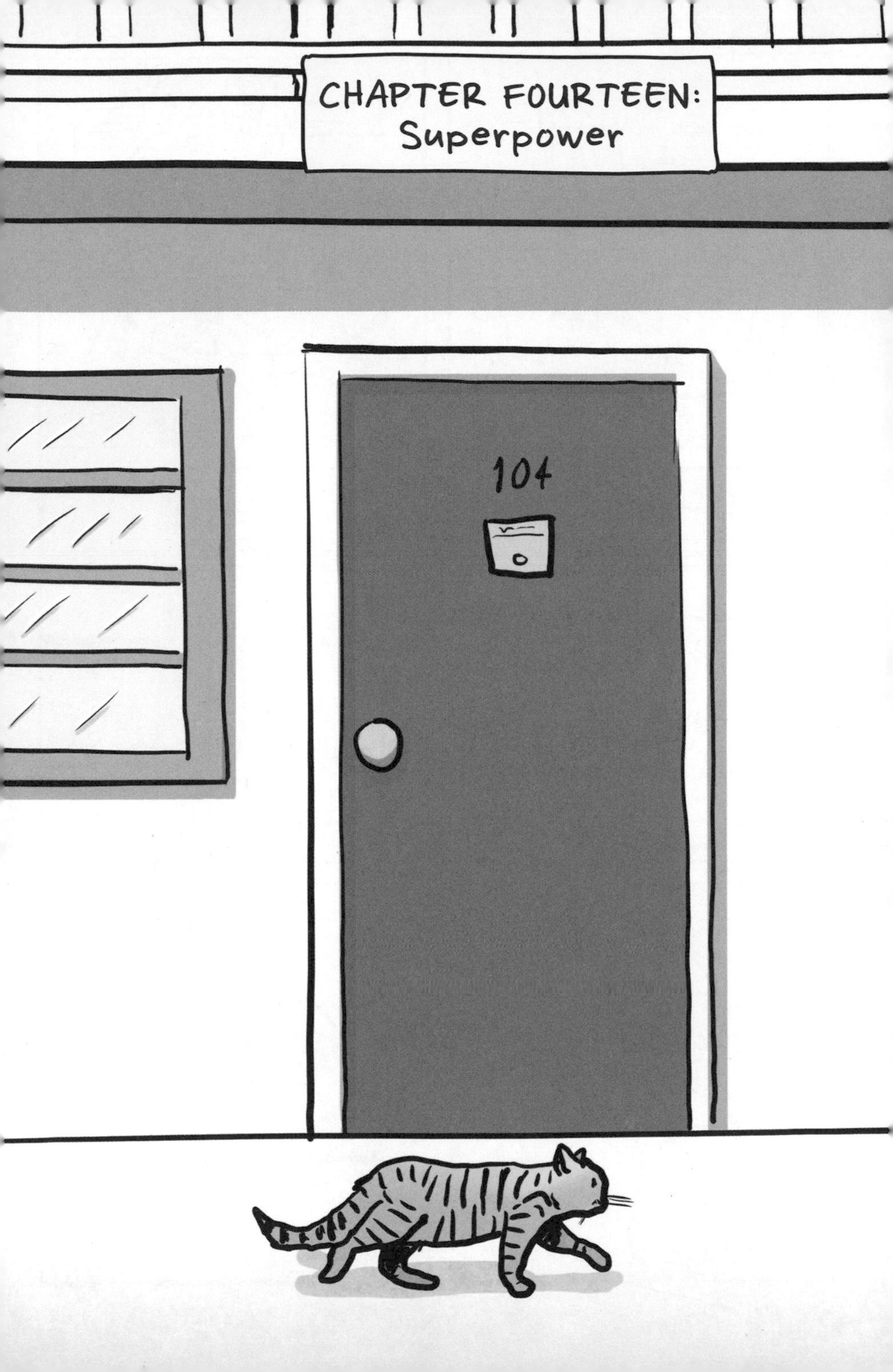
CHAPTER FOURTEEN:
Superpower
104

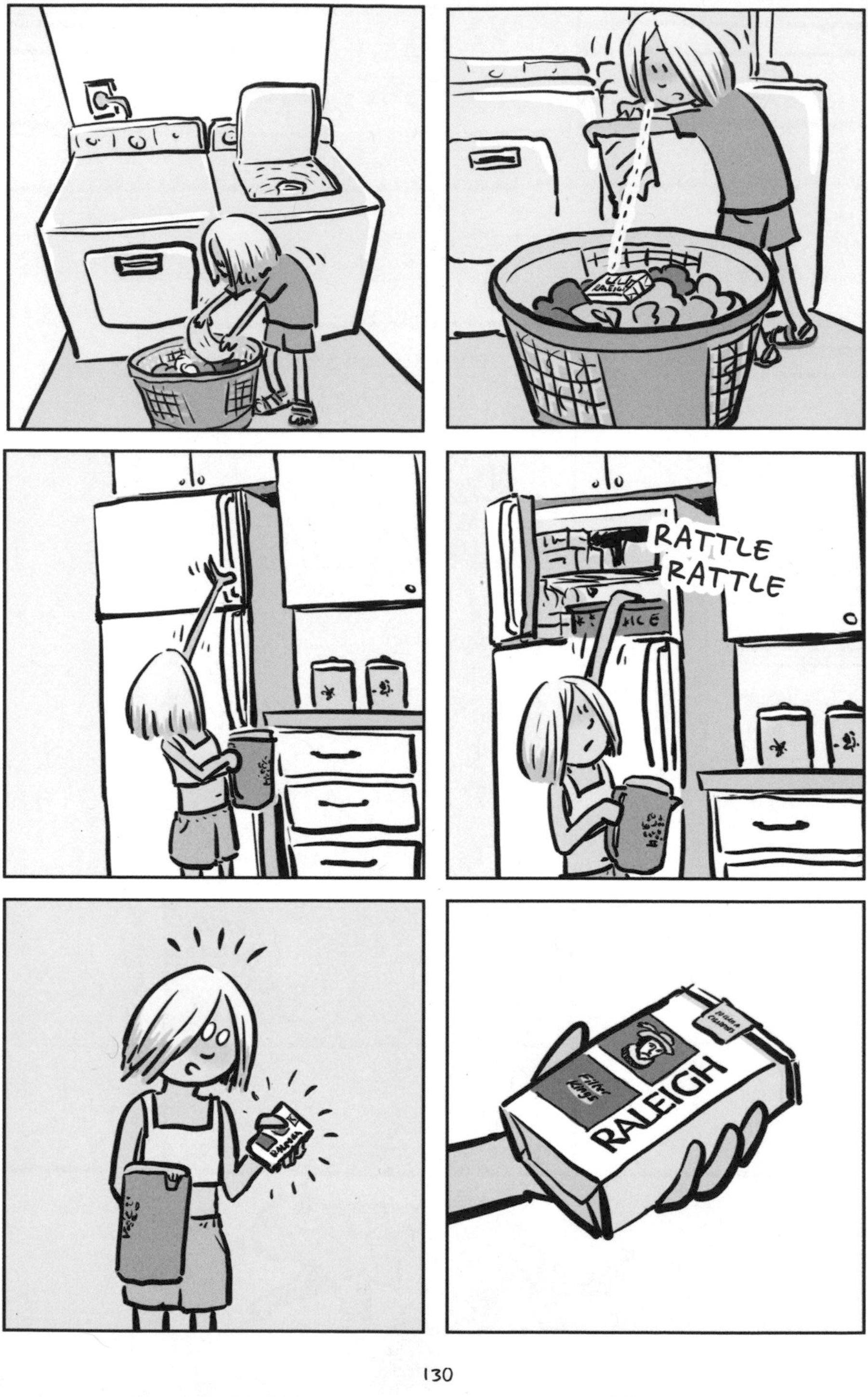
RATTLE
RATTLE
RALEIGH

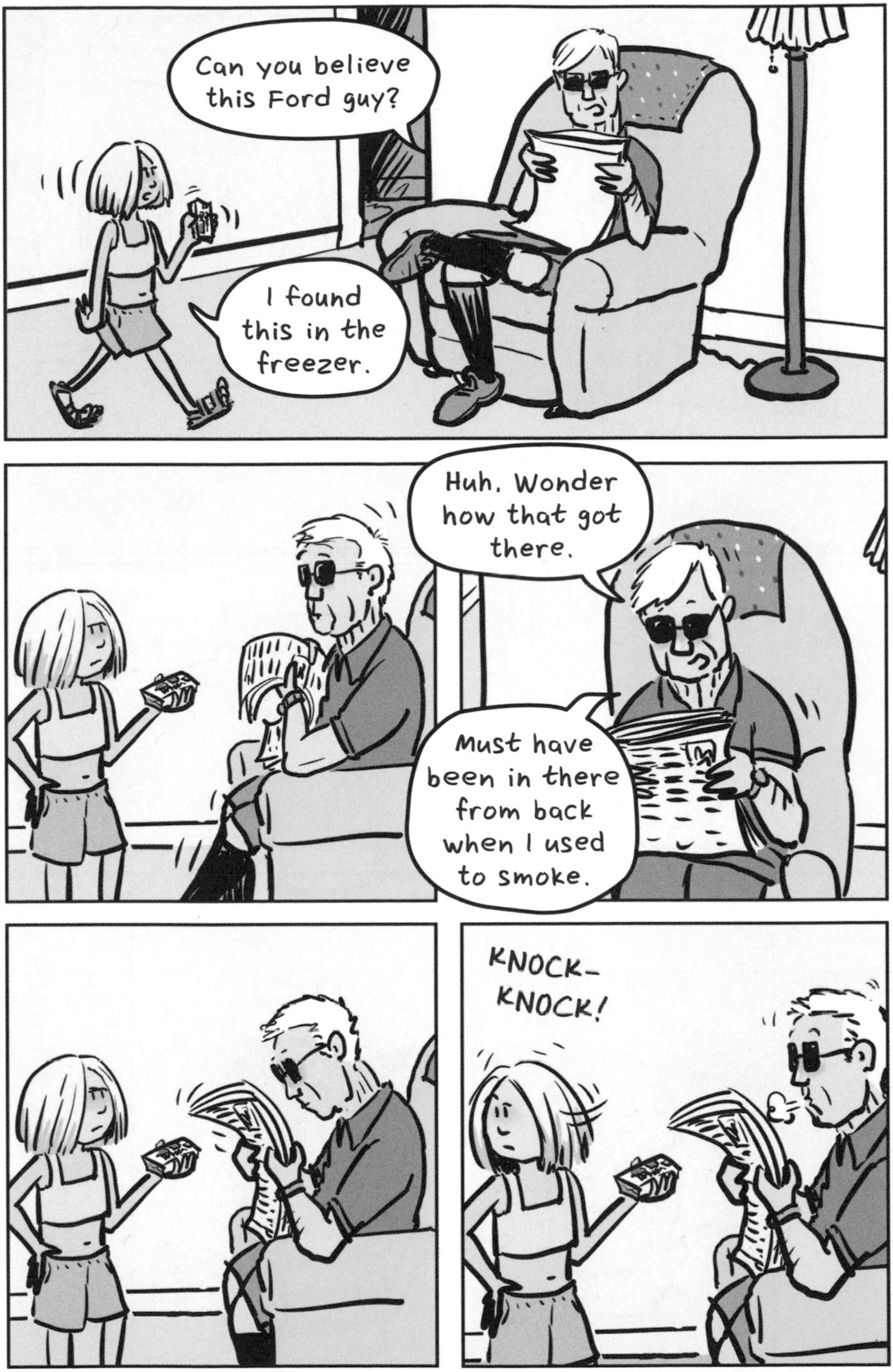
Can you believe this Ford guy?
I found this in the freezer.
Huh. Wonder how that got there.
Must have been in there from back when I used to smoke.
KNOCK-KNOCK!

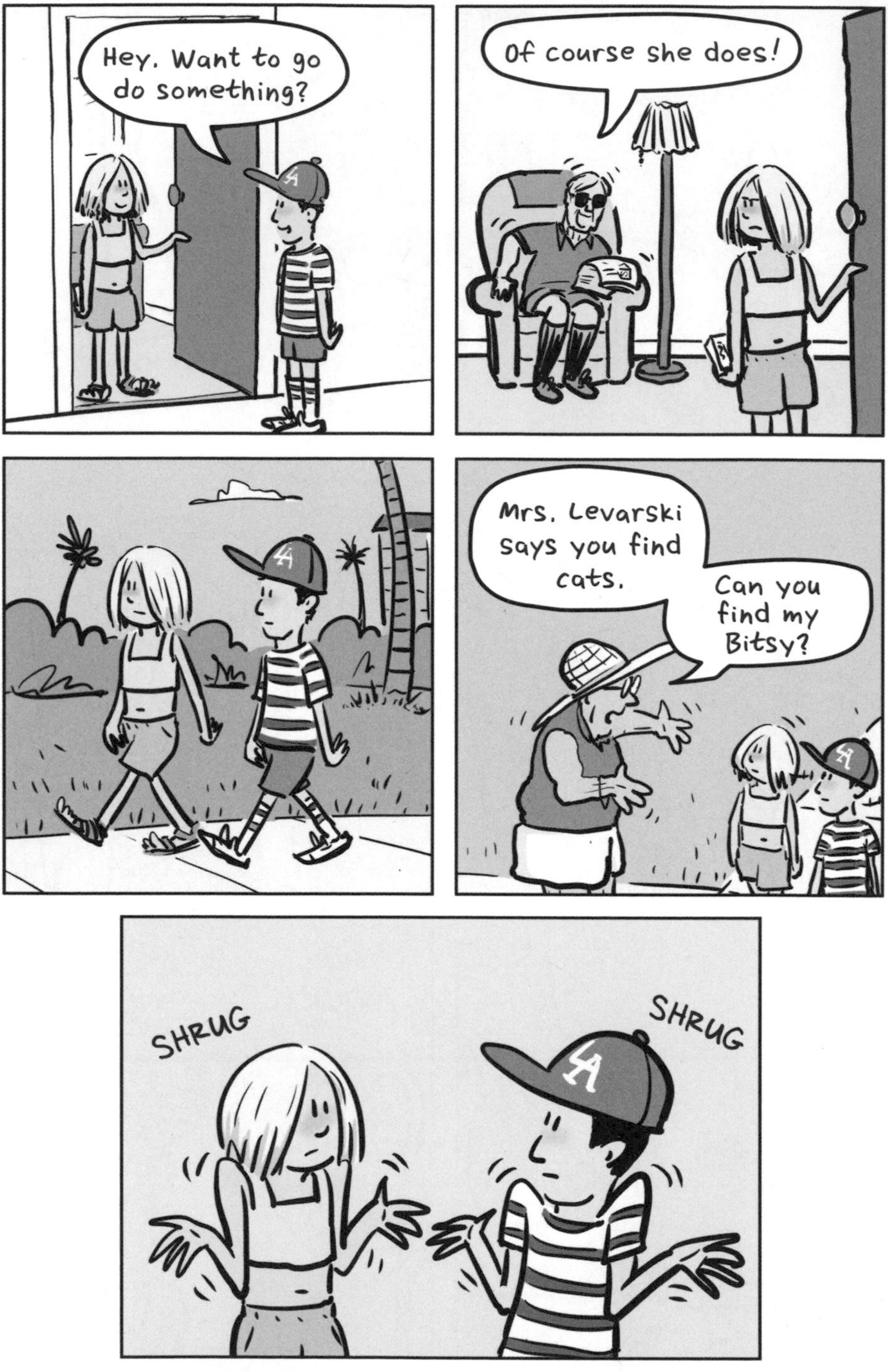
Hey. Want to go do something?
Of course she does!
Mrs. Levarski says you find cats.
Can you find my Bitsy?
SHRUG
SHRUG

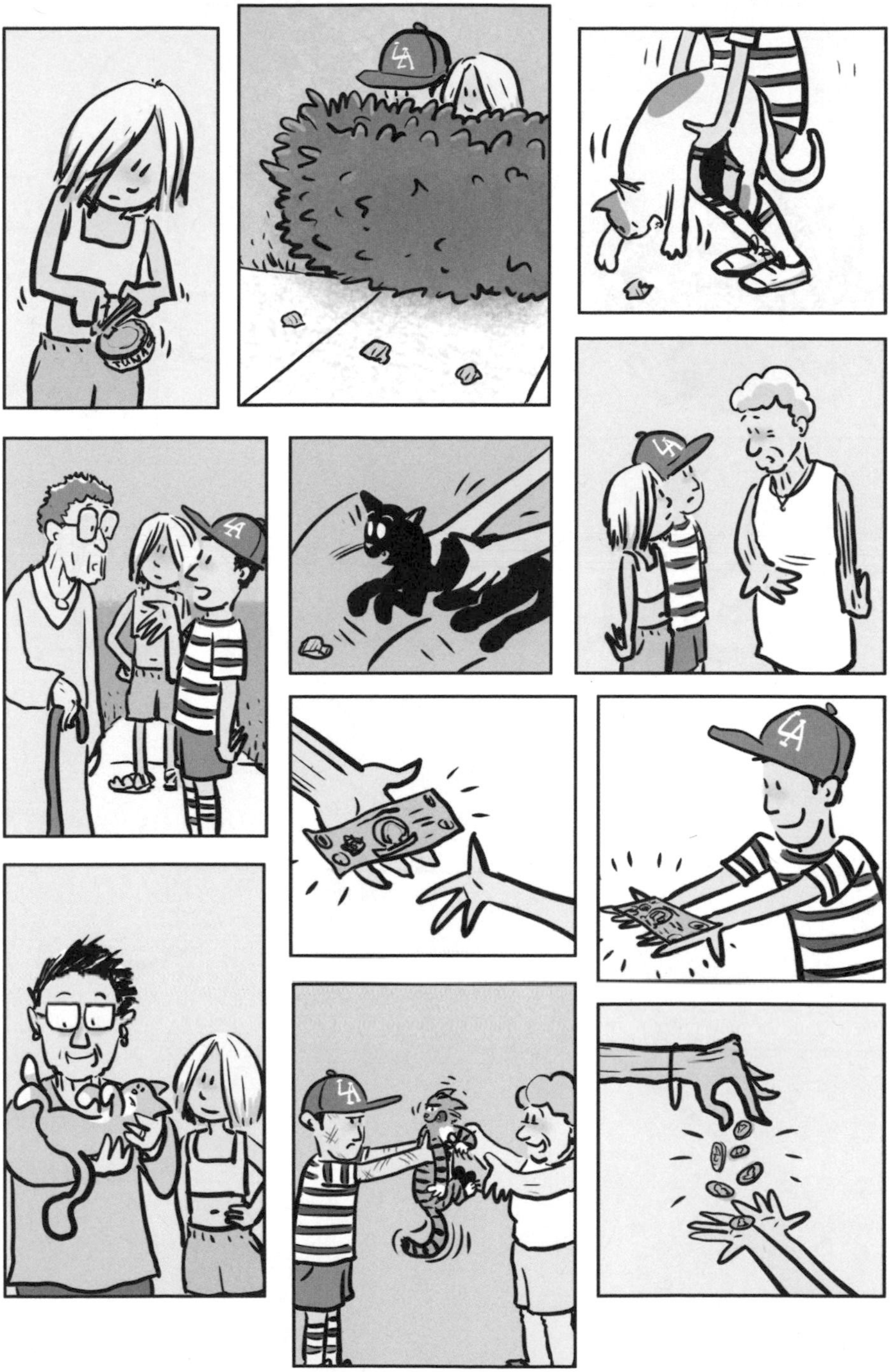
TUNA
LA

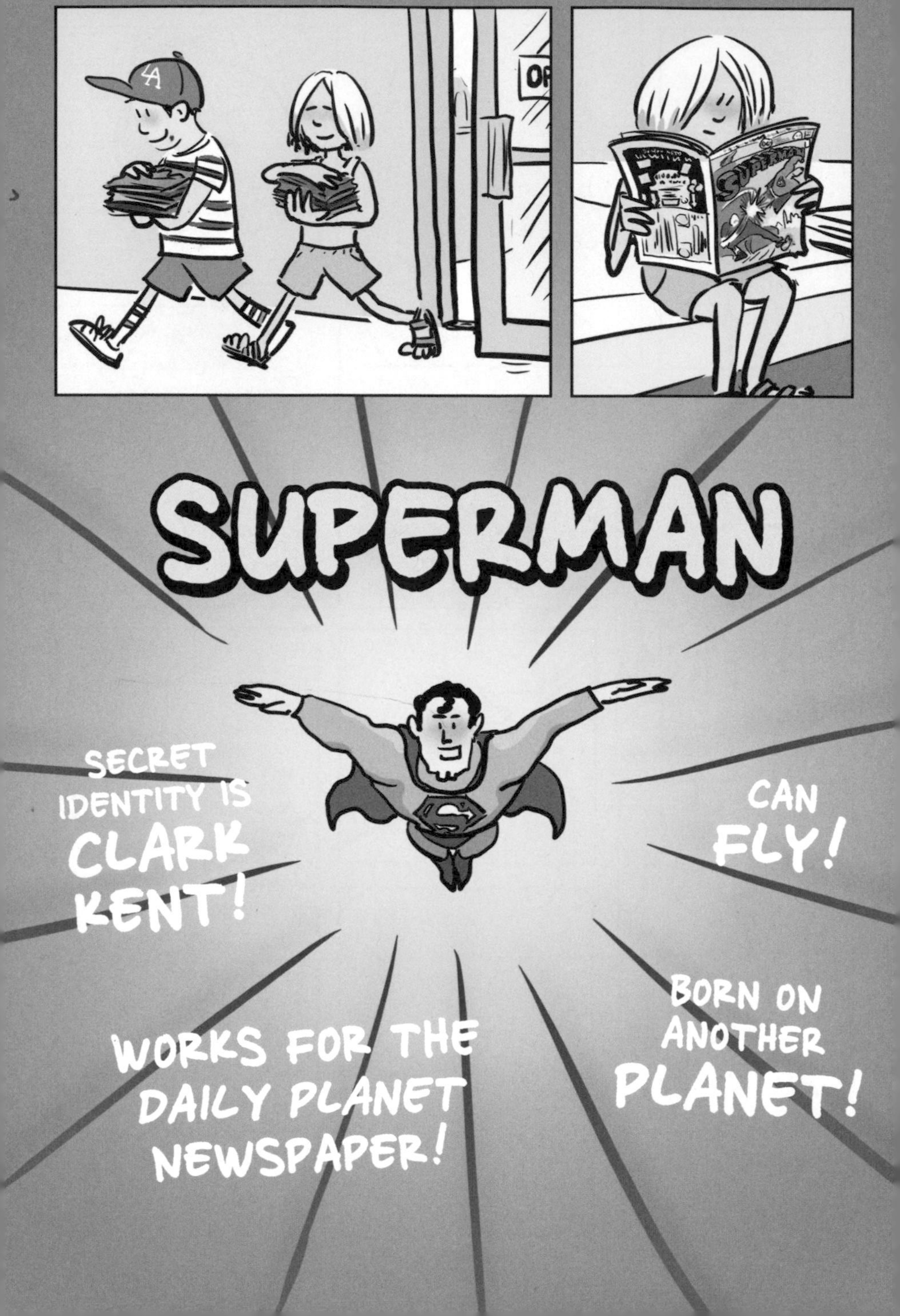
SUPERMAN
SECRET IDENTITY IS CLARK KENT!
CAN FLY!
WORKS FOR THE DAILY PLANET NEWSPAPER!
BORN ON ANOTHER PLANET!

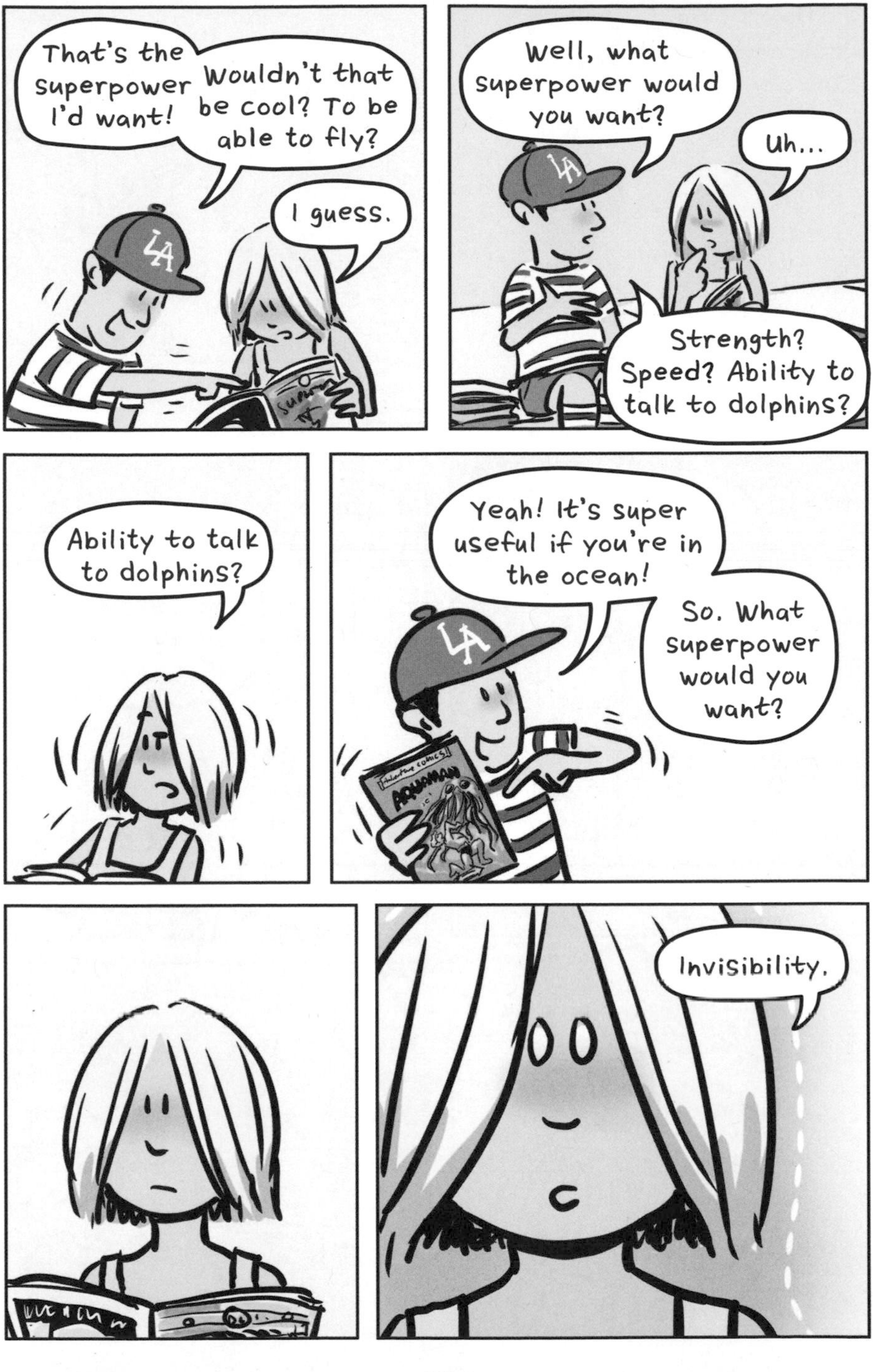
That's the superpower I'd want!
Wouldn't that be cool? To be able to fly?
I guess.
Well, what superpower would you want?
Uh...
Strength? Speed? Ability to talk to dolphins?
Ability to talk to dolphins?
Yeah! It's super useful if you're in the ocean!
So. What superpower would you want?
AQUAMAN
Invisibility.

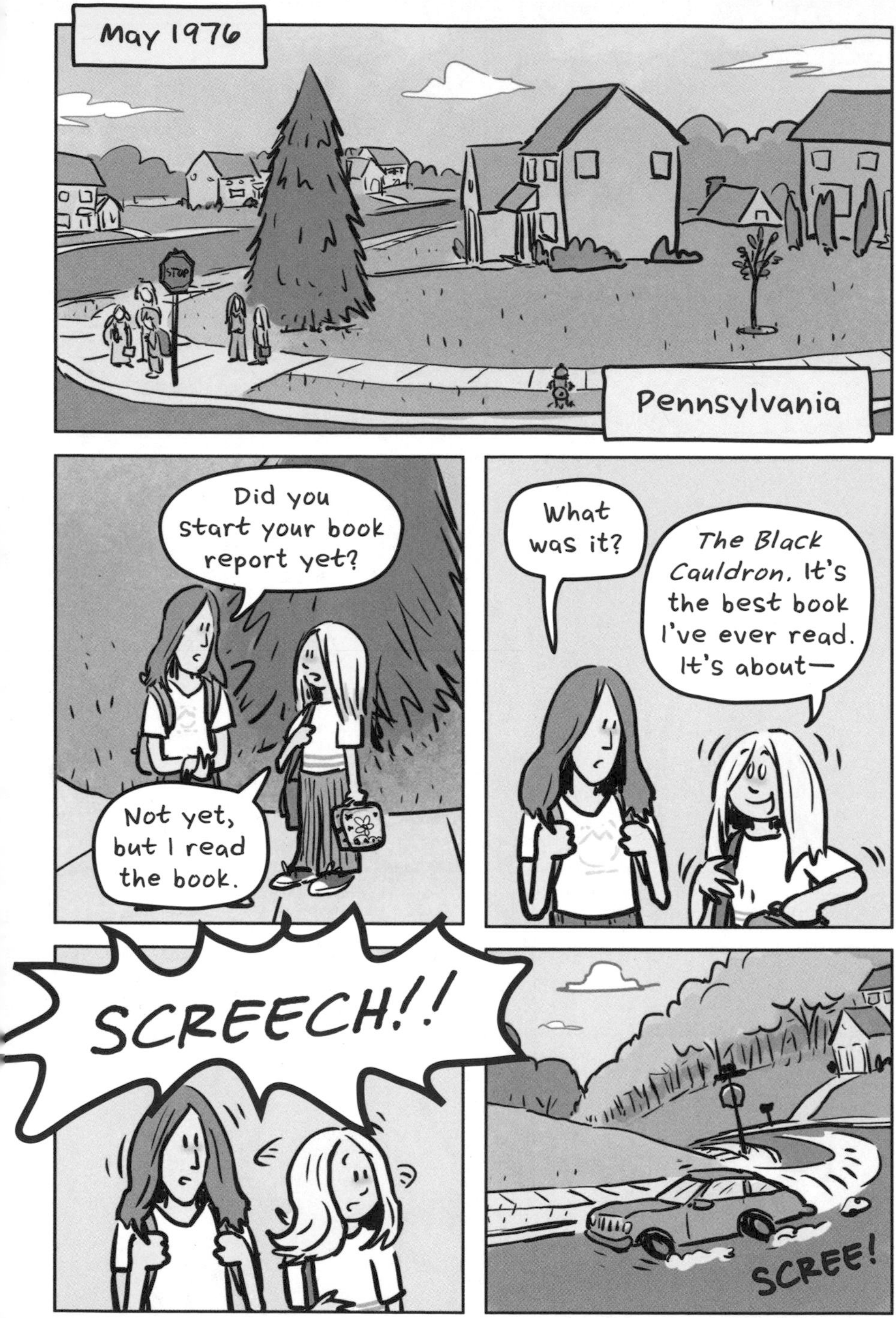
May 1976
Pennsylvania
Did you start your book report yet?
Not yet, but I read the book.
What was it?
The Black Cauldron. It's the best book I've ever read. It's about—
SCREECH!!
SCREE!

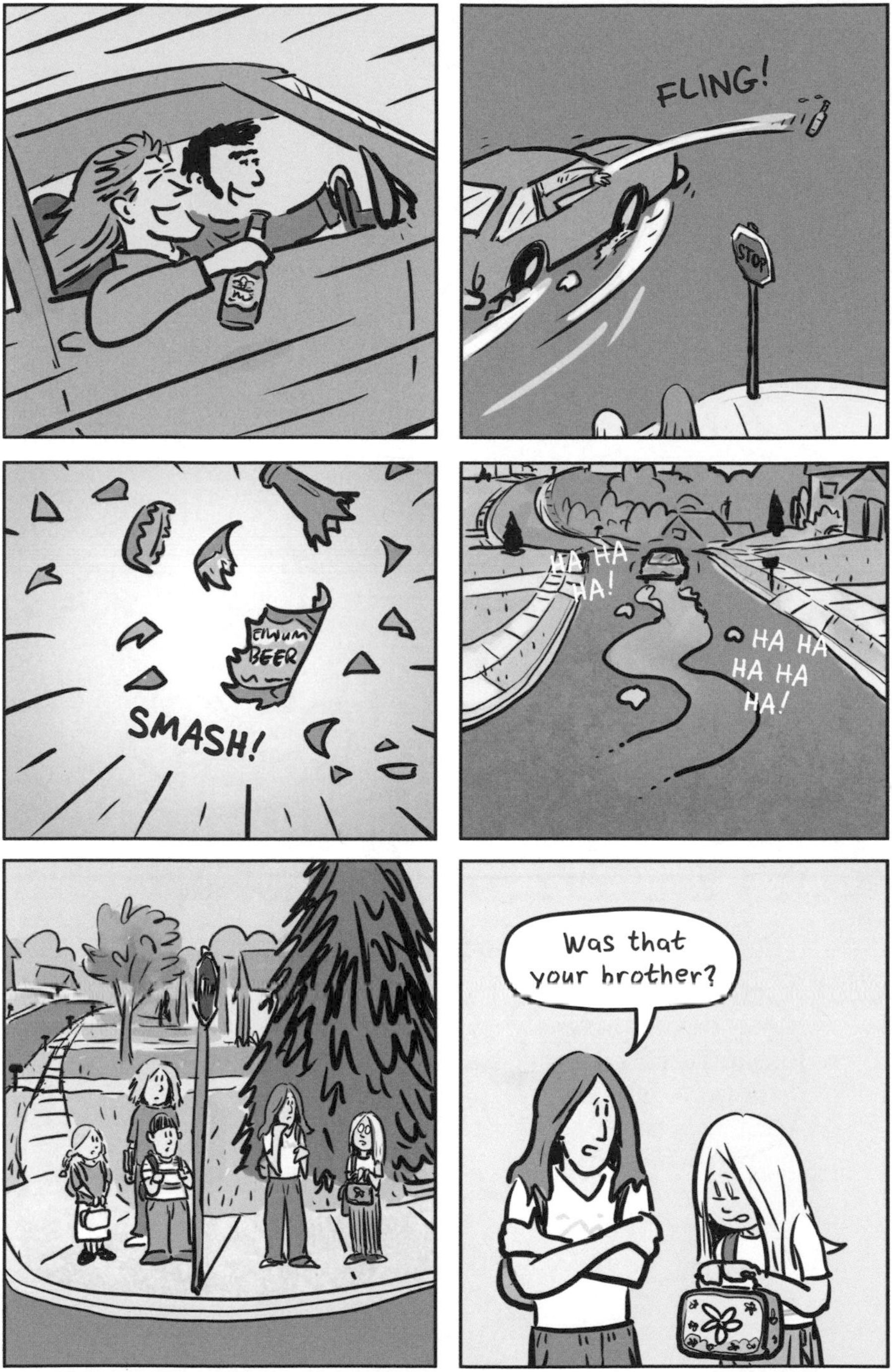
FLING!
STOP
BEER
SMASH!
HA HA HA!
HA HA HA HA HA!
Was that your brother?

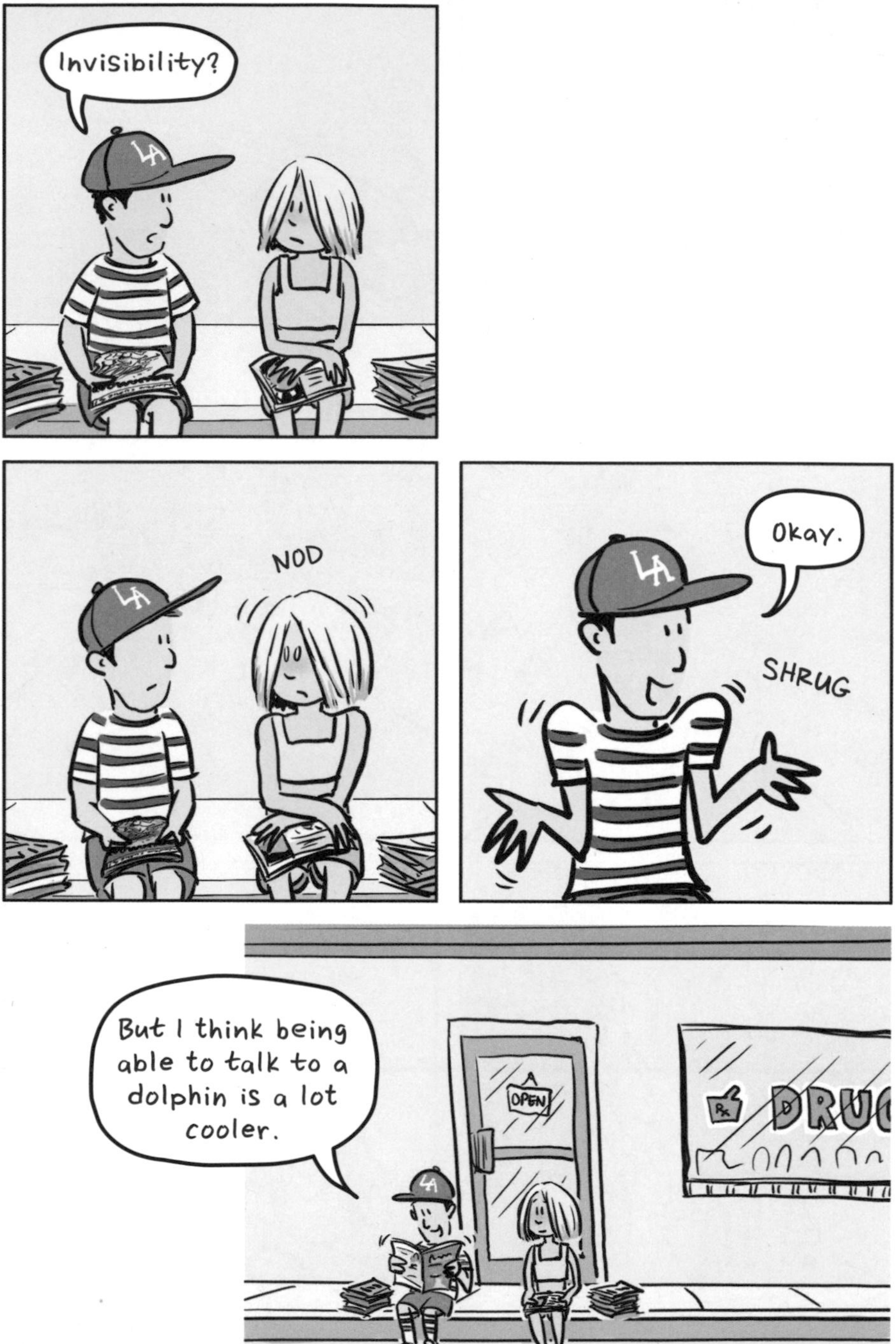
Invisibility?
NOD
Okay.
SHRUG
But I think being able to talk to a dolphin is a lot cooler.
OPEN
DRUG

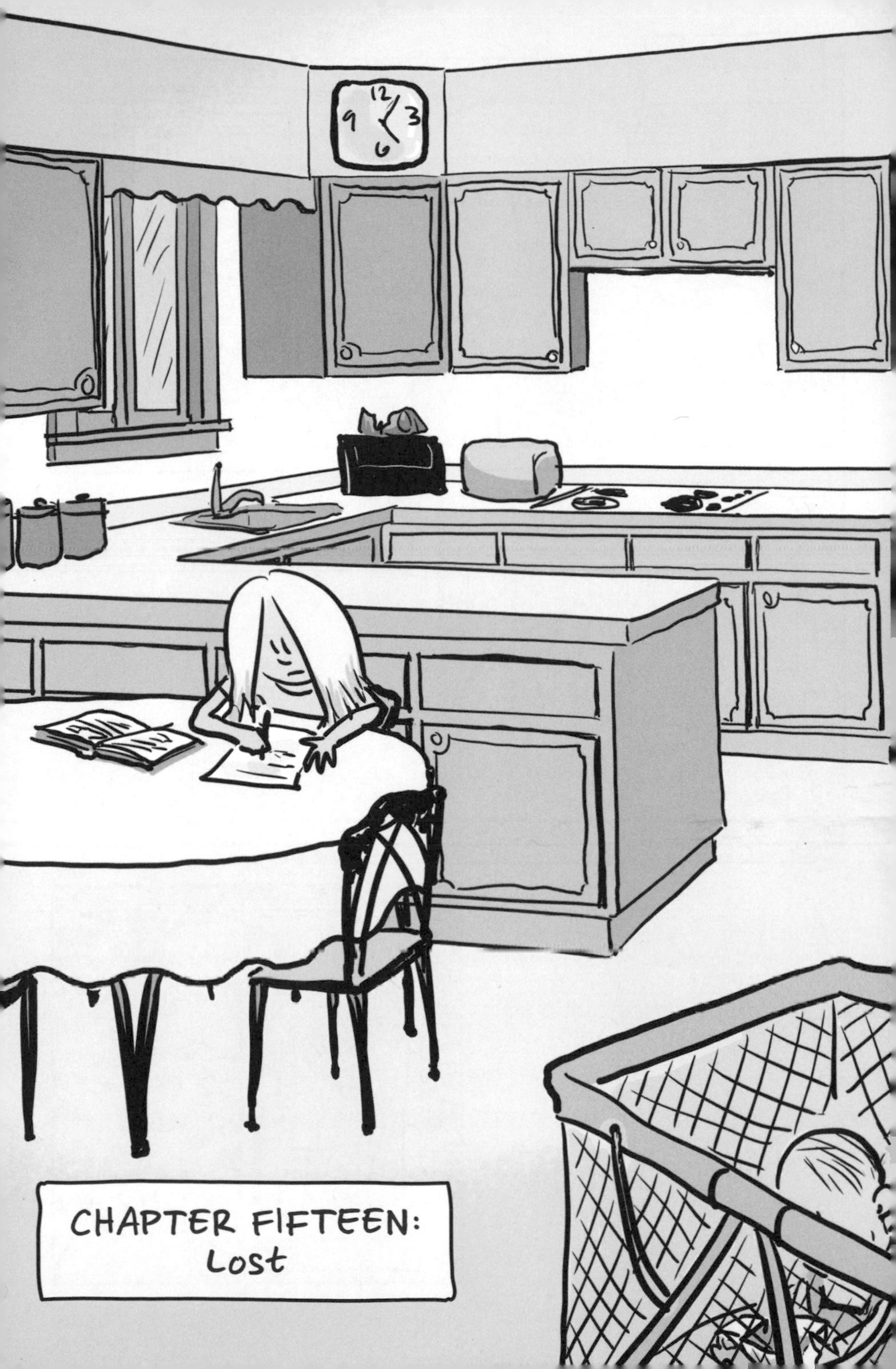
CHAPTER FIFTEEN:
Lost

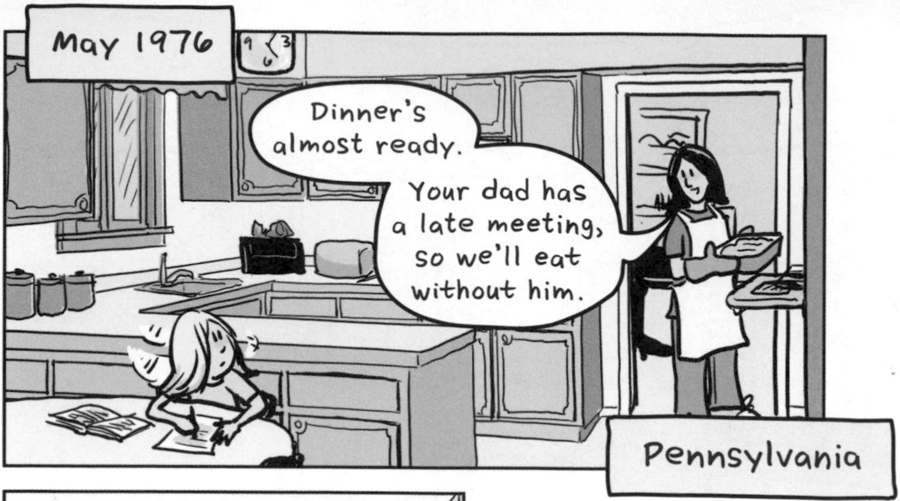
May 1976
Dinner's almost ready.
Your dad has a late meeting, so we'll eat without him.
Pennsylvania

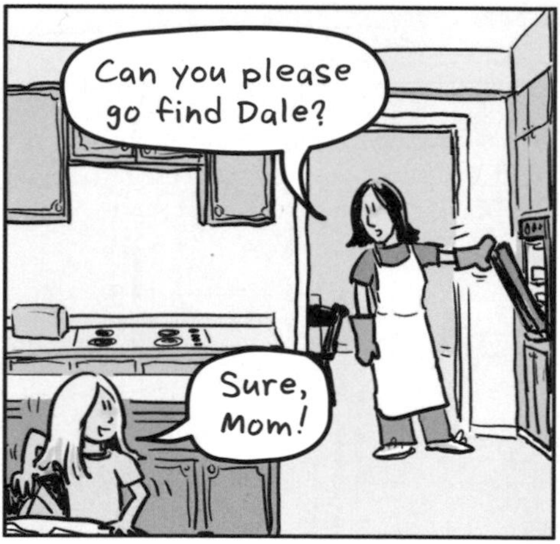
Can you please go find Dale?
Sure, Mom!

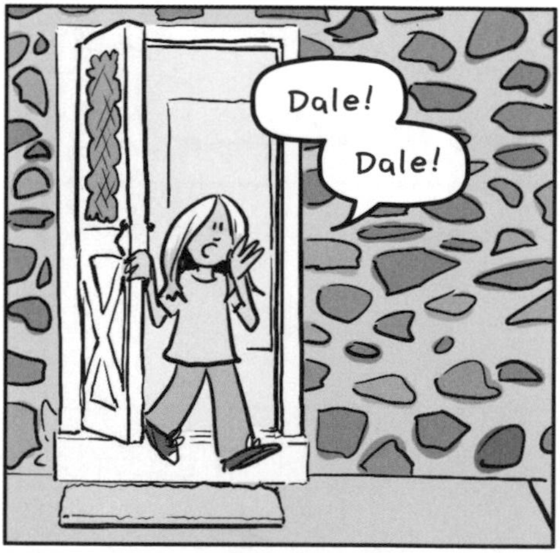
Dale!
Dale!

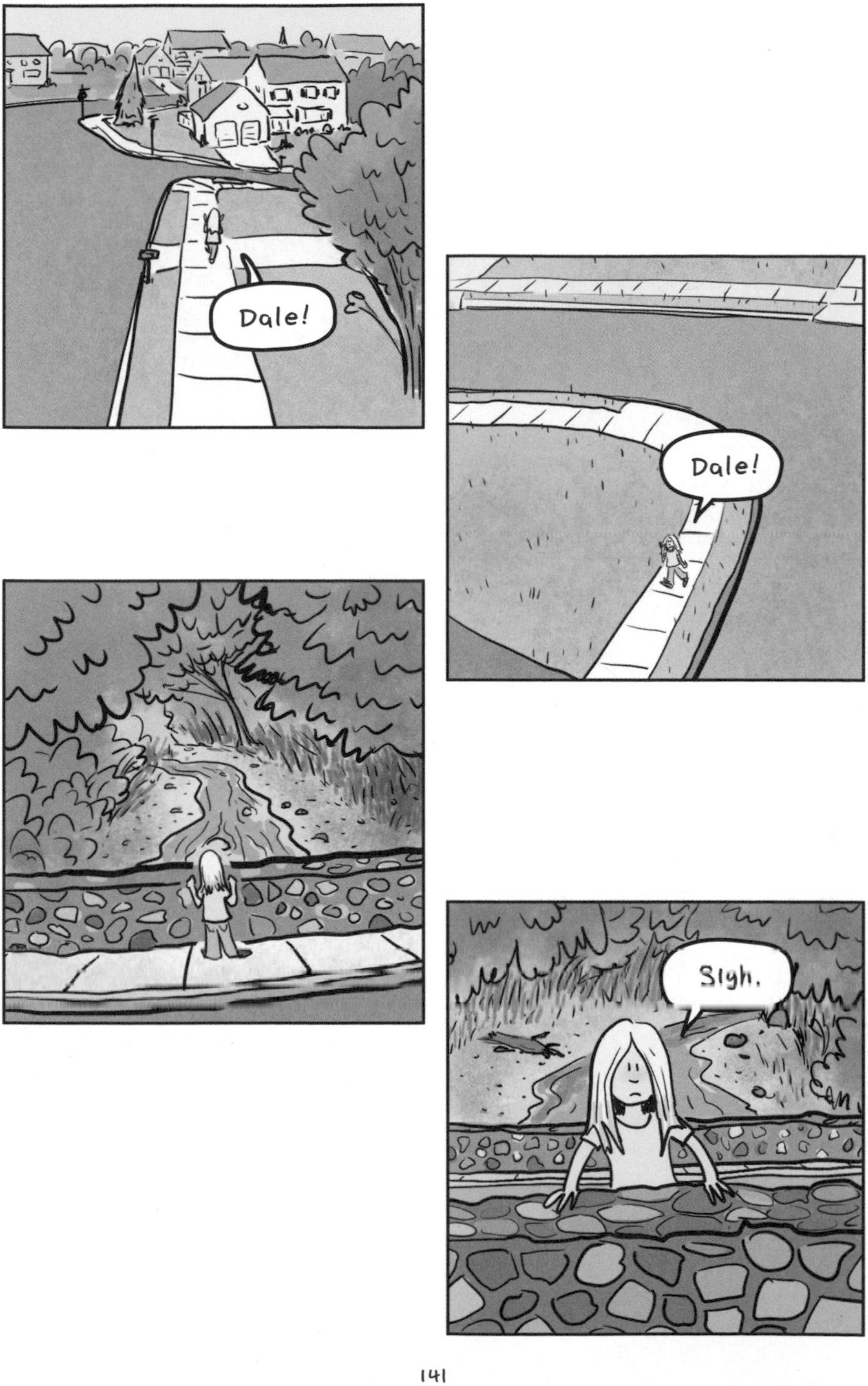

Dale!
Dale!
Sigh.

SNIFF
SNIFF
SLIDE

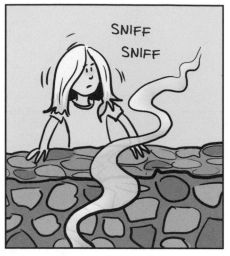

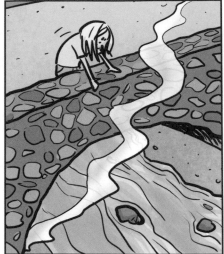

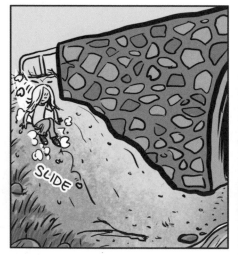

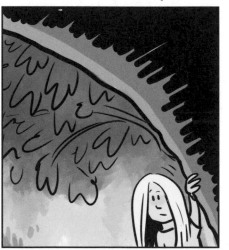

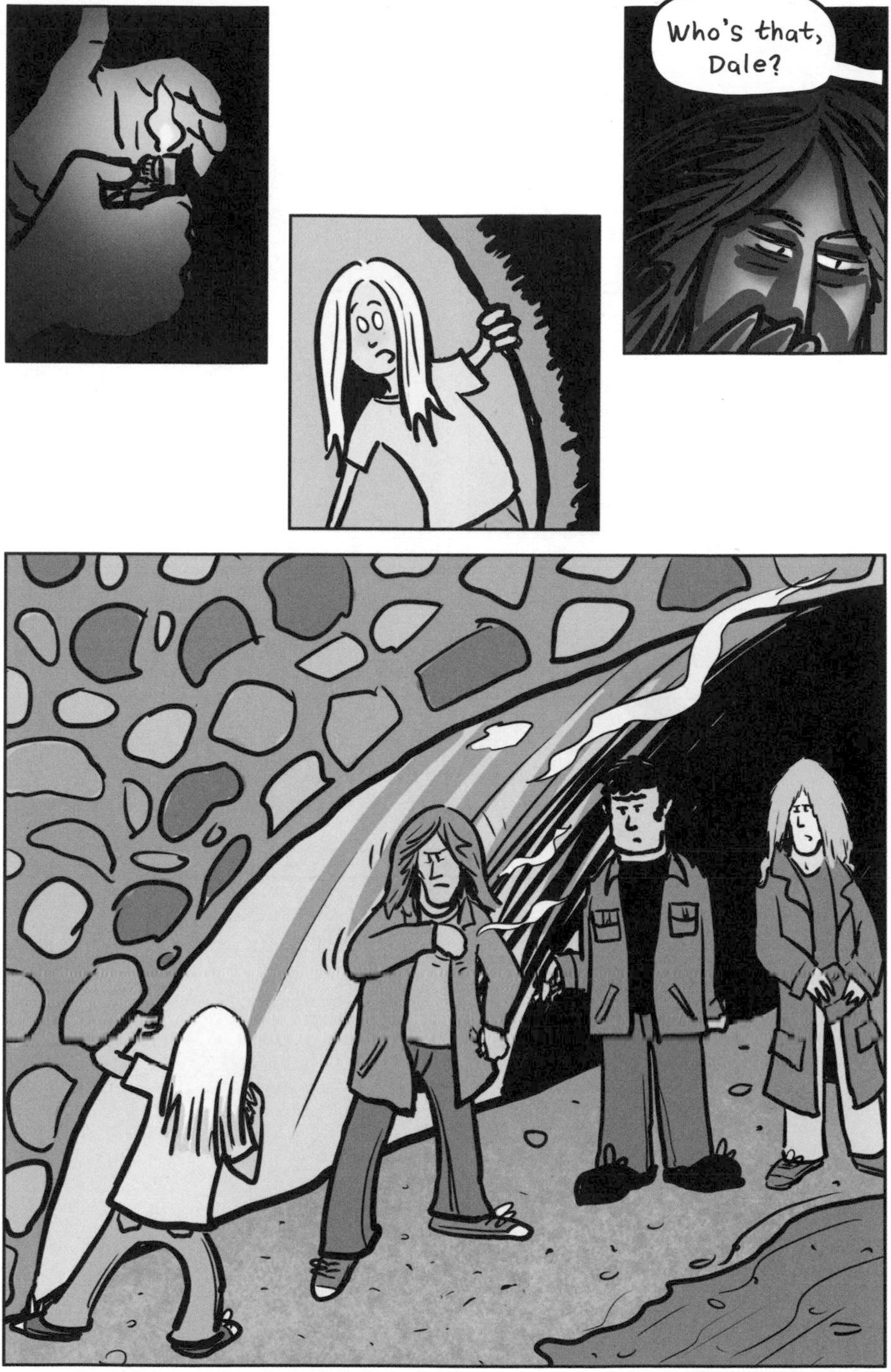
Who's that, Dale?

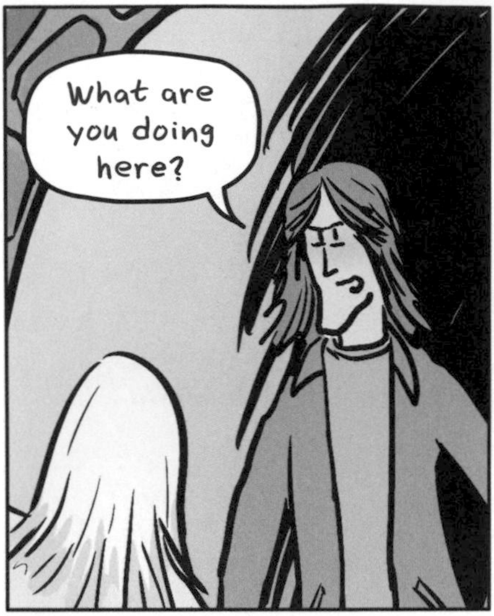
What are you doing here?

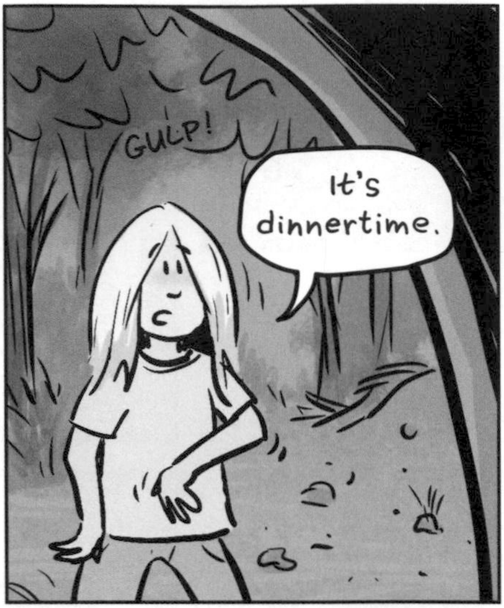
GULP!
It's dinnertime.

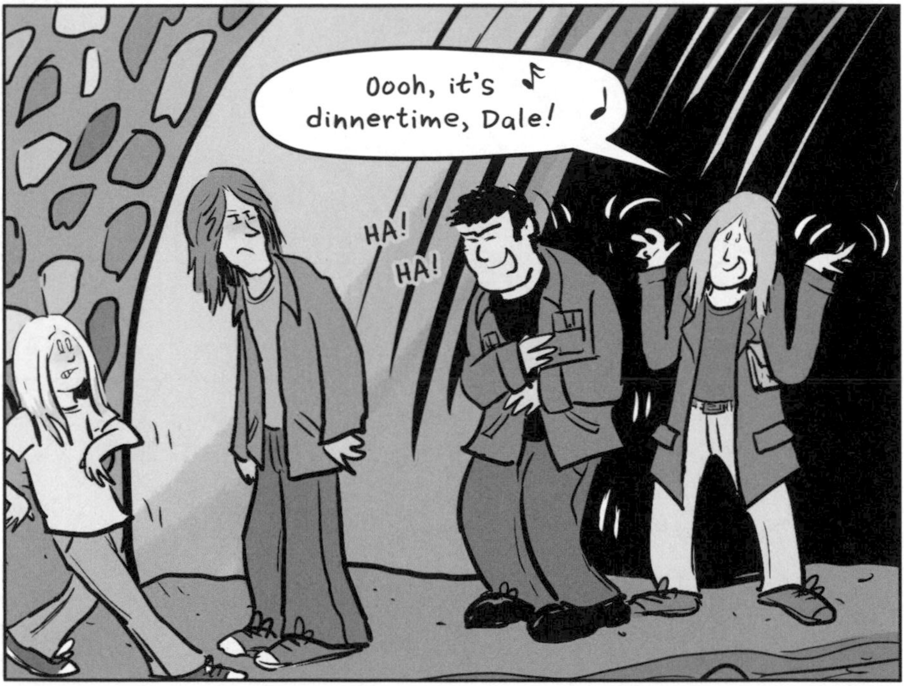
Oooh, it's dinnertime, Dale!
HA!
HA!

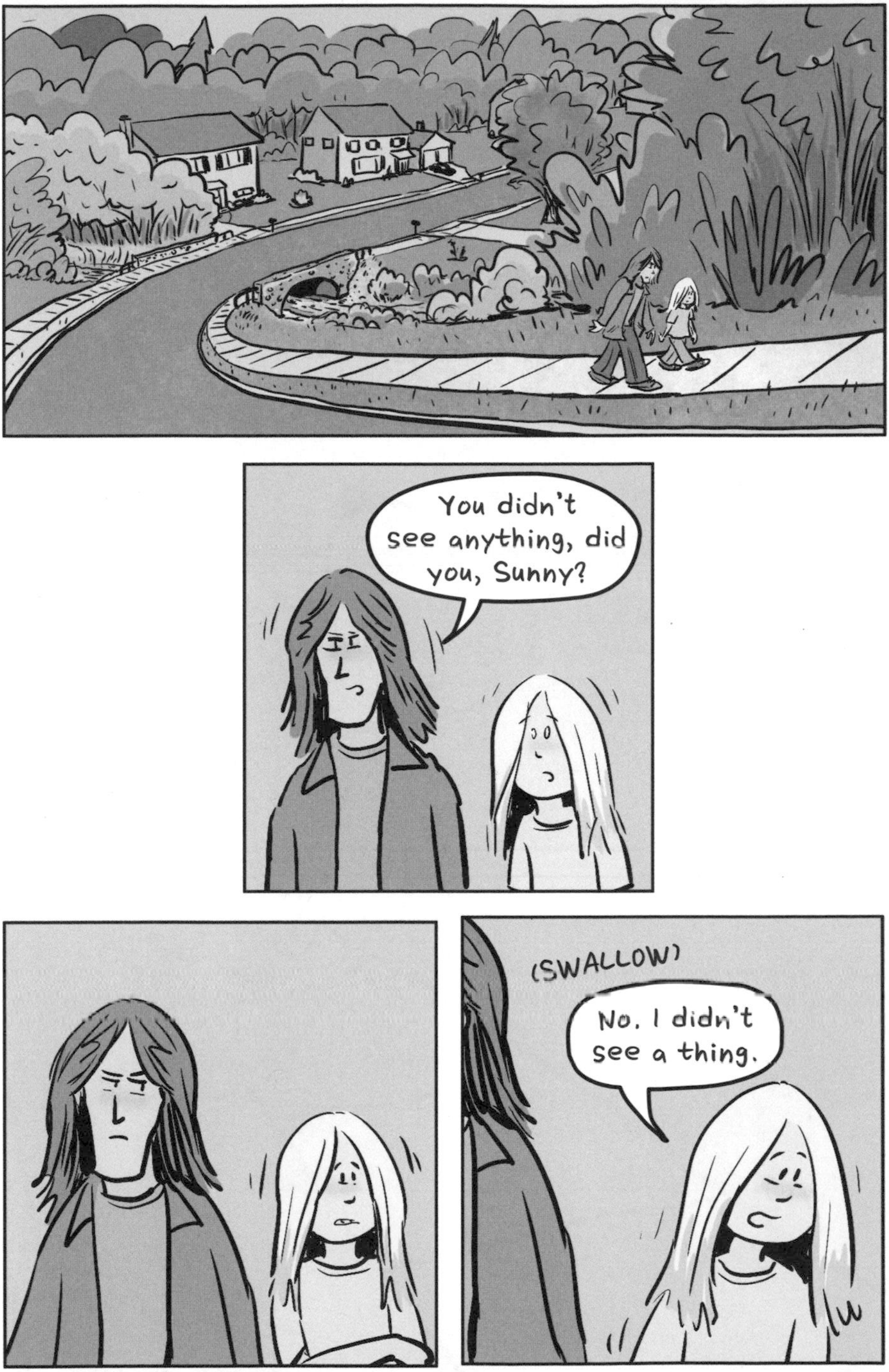
You didn't see anything, did you, Sunny?
(SWALLOW)
No. I didn't see a thing.

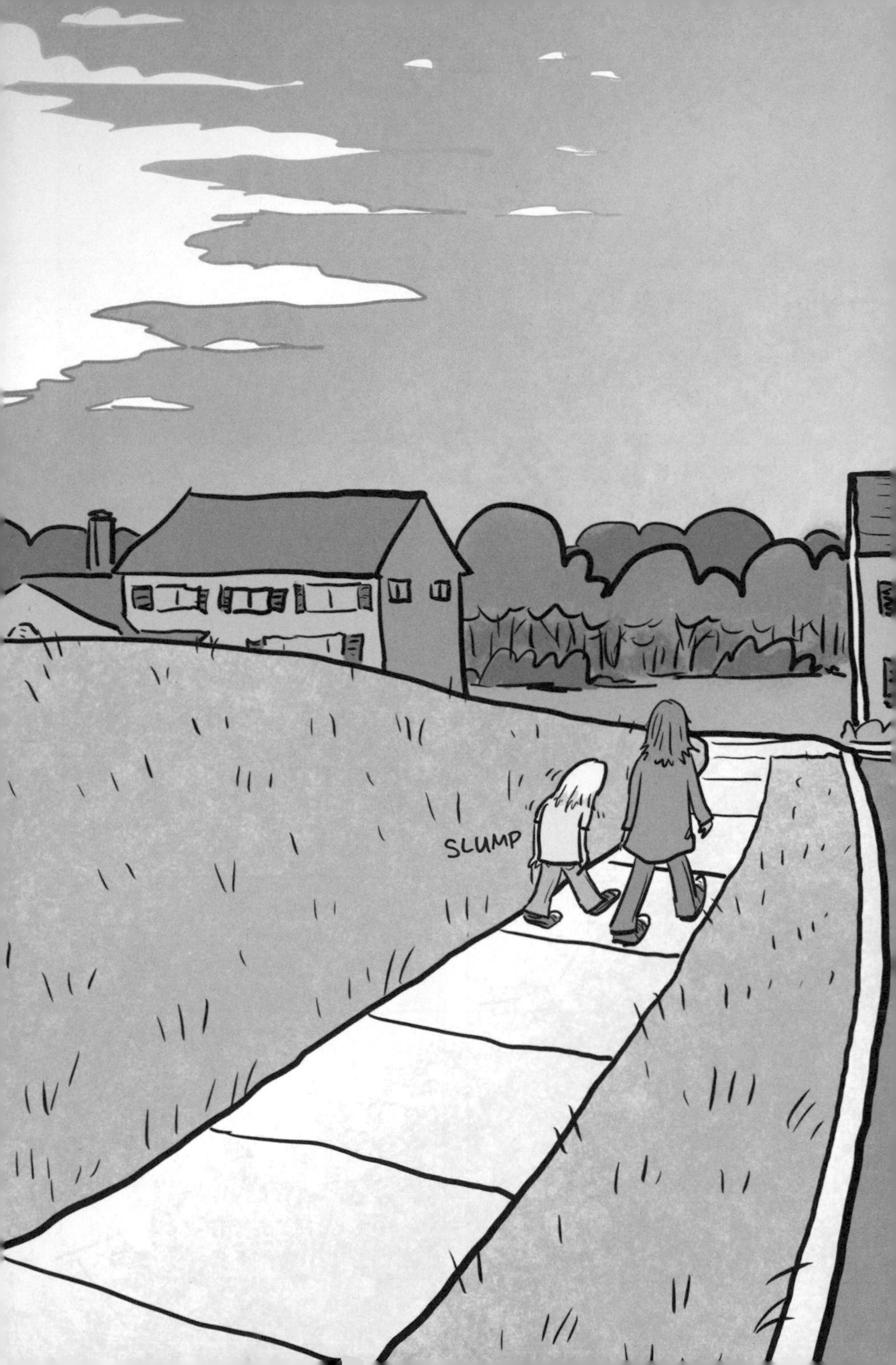
SLUMP

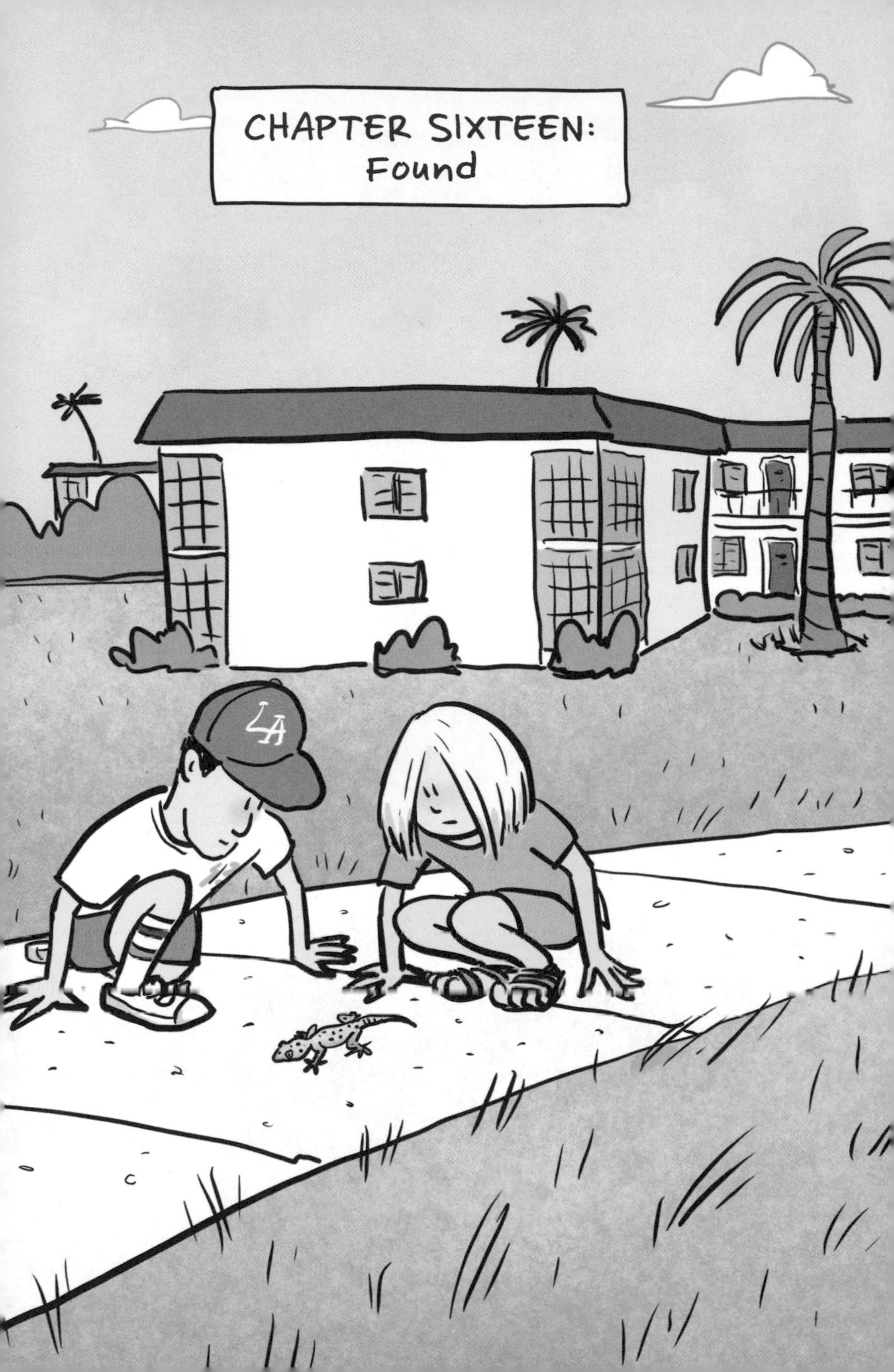
CHAPTER SIXTEEN:
Found
LA

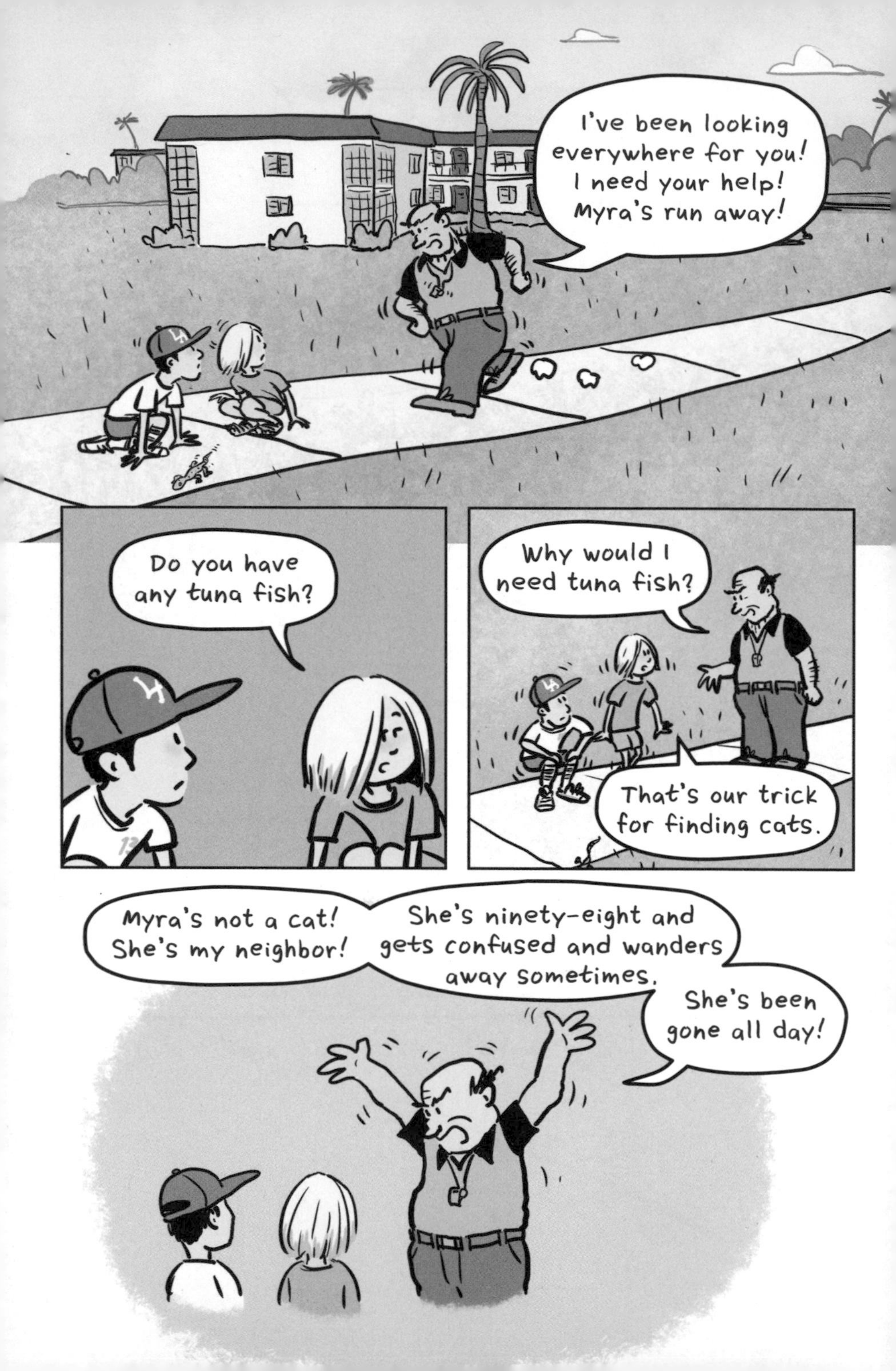
I've been looking everywhere for you! I need your help! Myra's run away!
Do you have any tuna fish?
Why would I need tuna fish?
That's our trick for finding cats.
Myra's not a cat! She's my neighbor!
She's ninety-eight and gets confused and wanders away sometimes.
She's been gone all day!

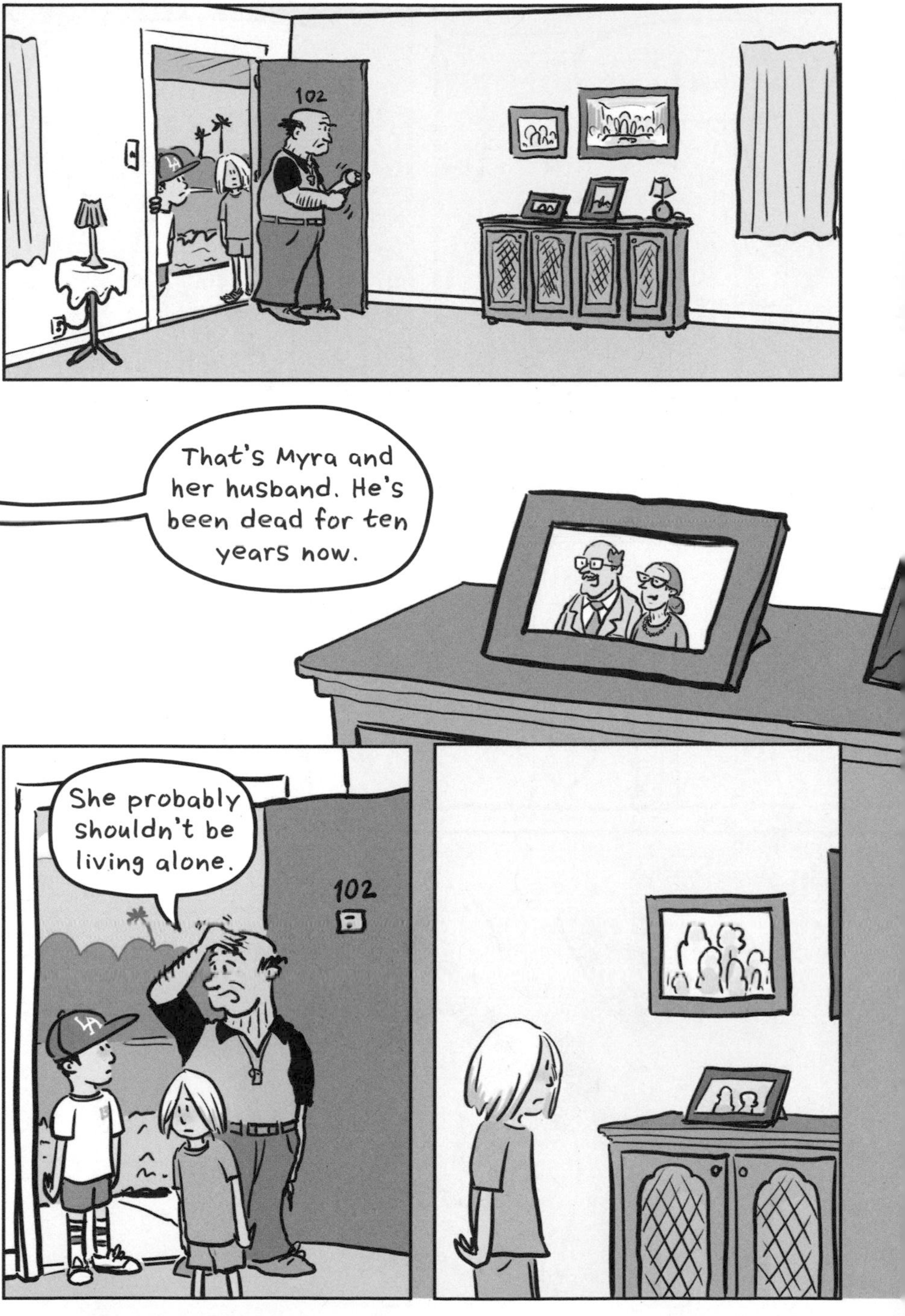
102
That's Myra and her husband. He's been dead for ten years now.
She probably shouldn't be living alone.
102

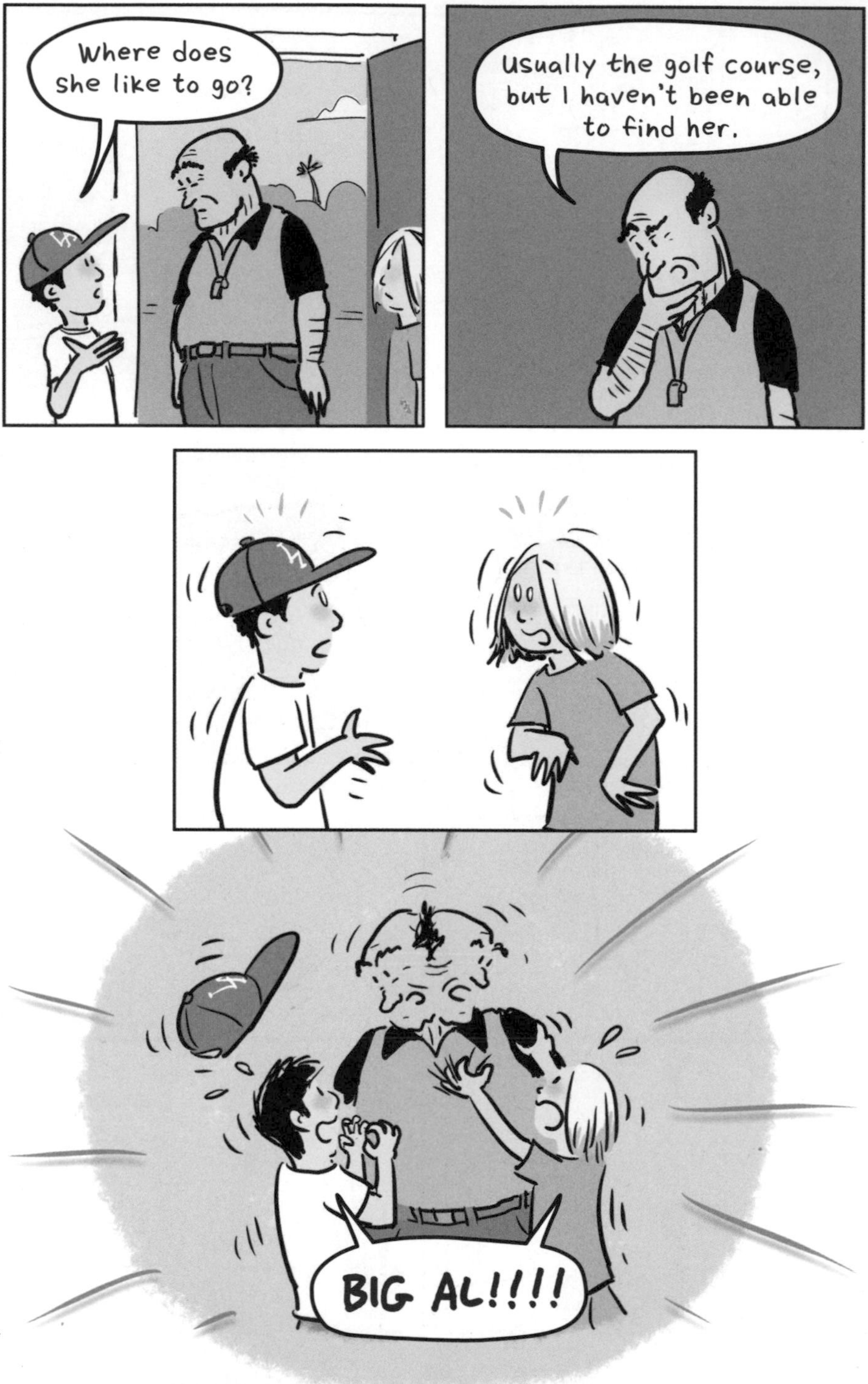
Where does she like to go?
Usually the golf course, but I haven't been able to find her.
BIG AL!!!!!

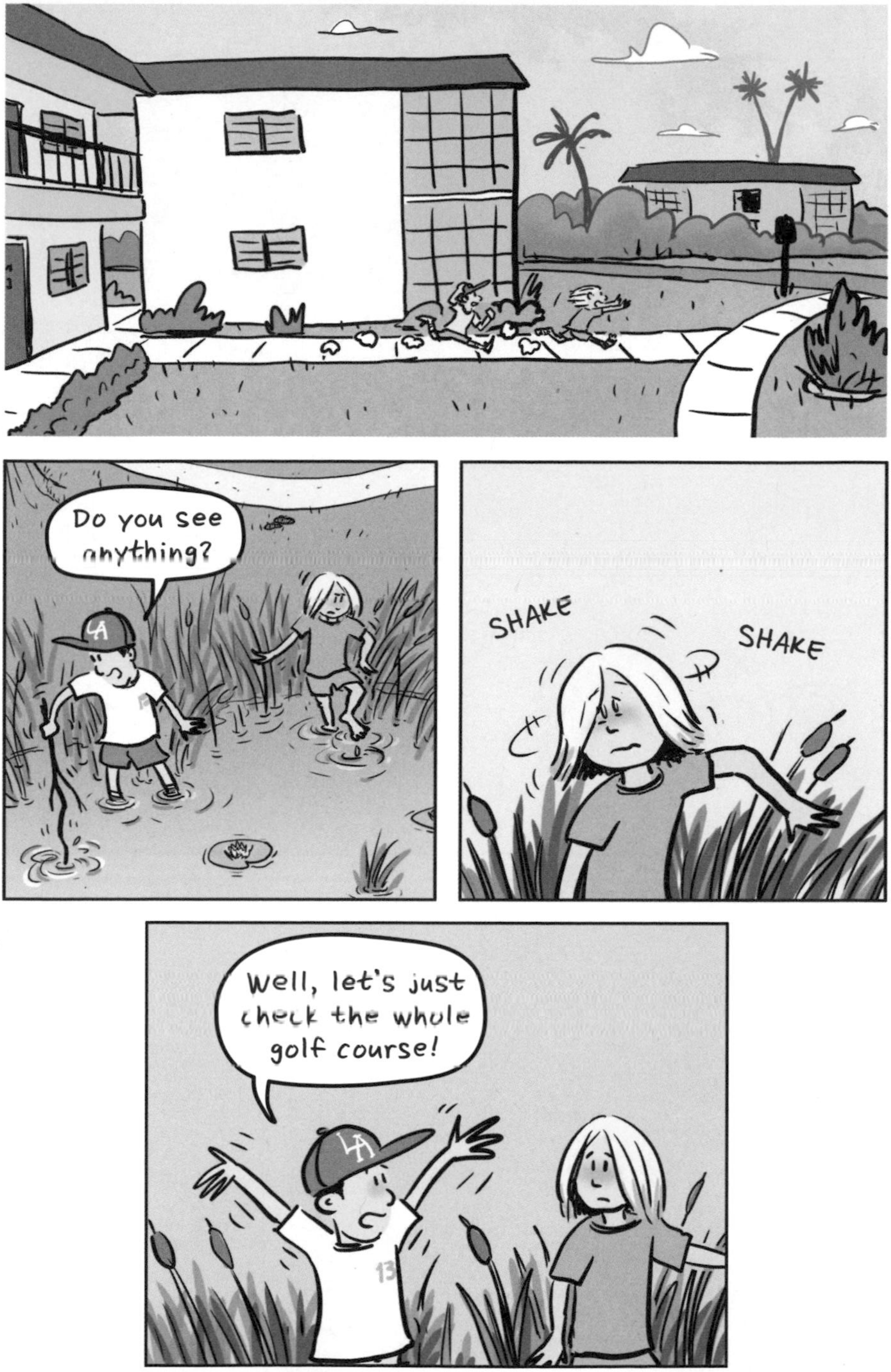
Do you see anything?
SHAKE
SHAKE
Well, let's just check the whole golf course!
13

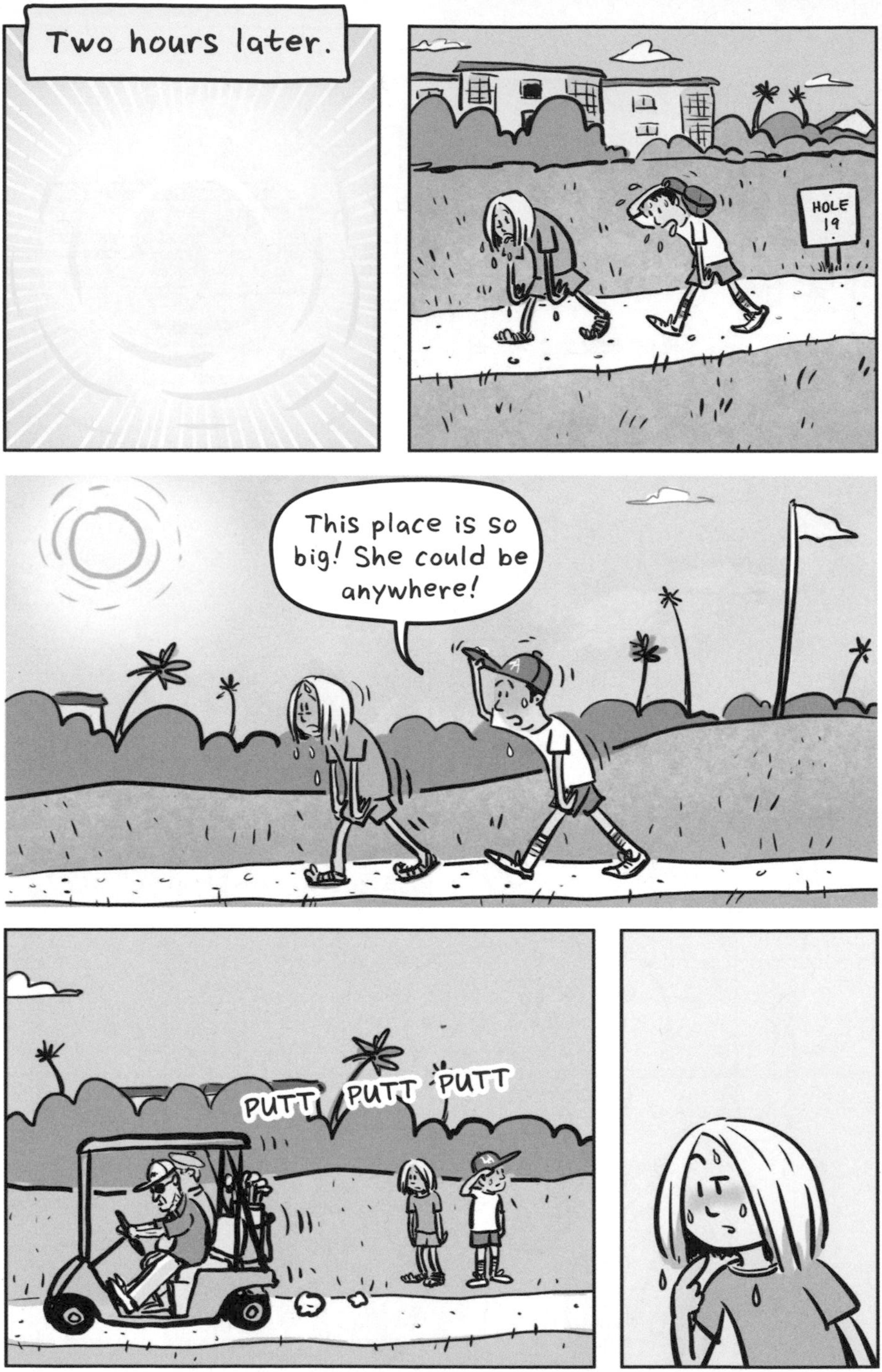
Two hours later.
HOLE 19
This place is so big! She could be anywhere!
PUTT PUTT PUTT

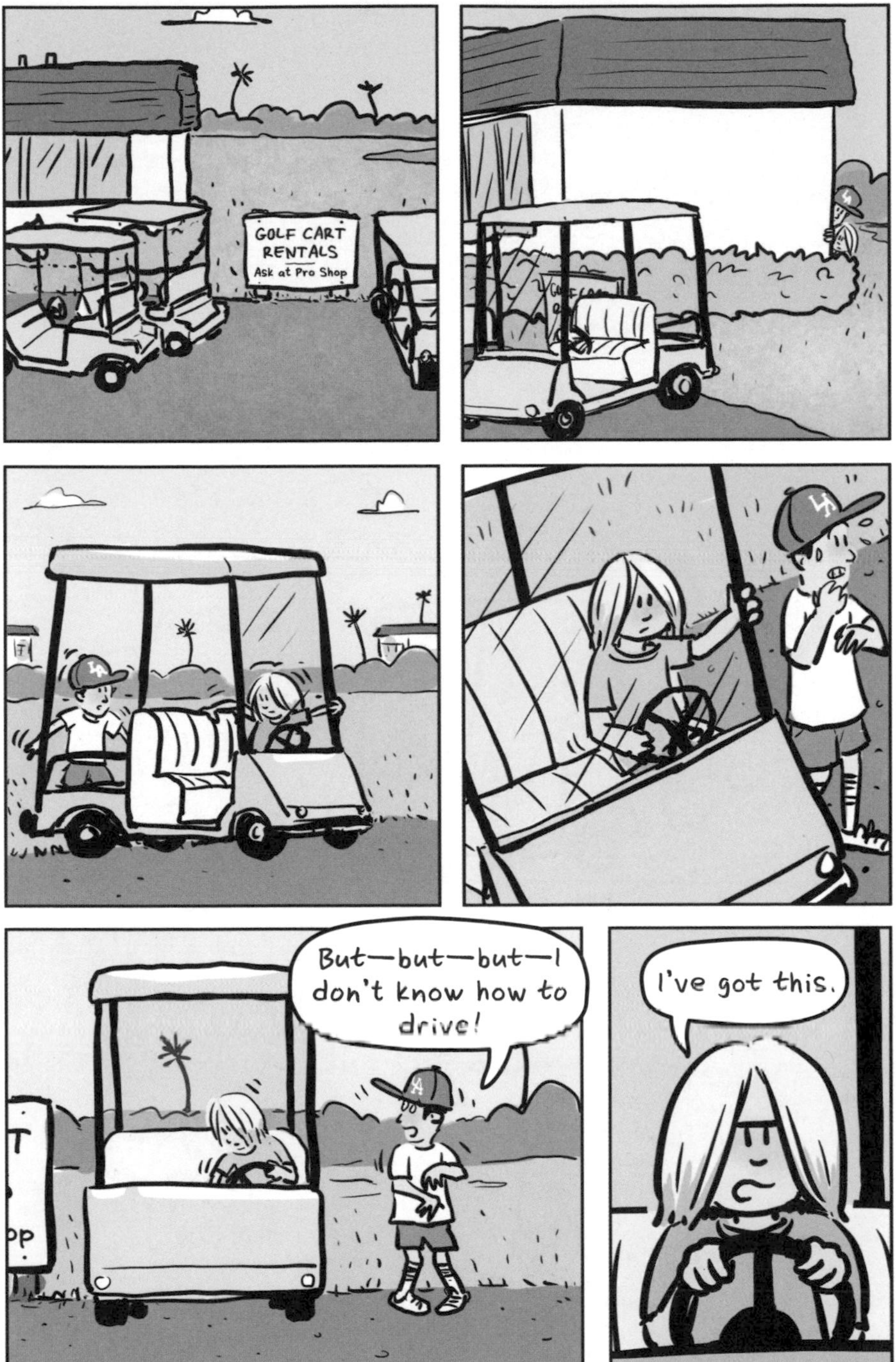
GOLF CART RENTALS
Ask at Pro Shop
But—but—but—I don't know how to drive!
I've got this.

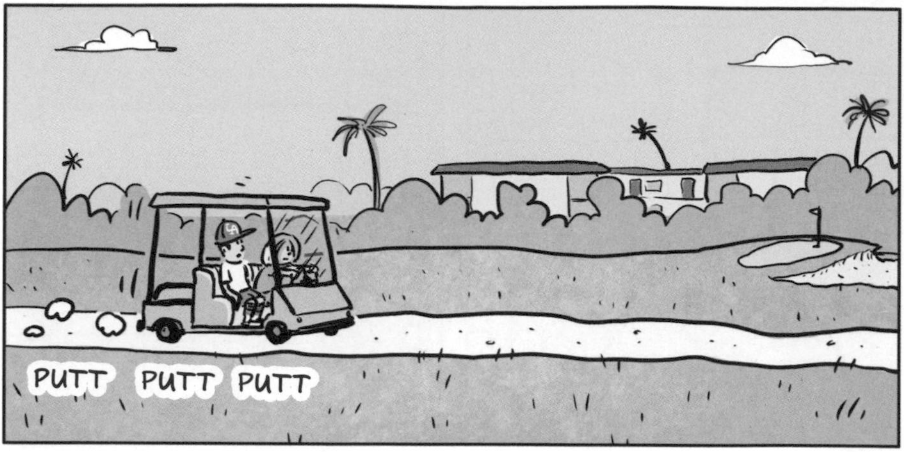
PUTT PUTT PUTT

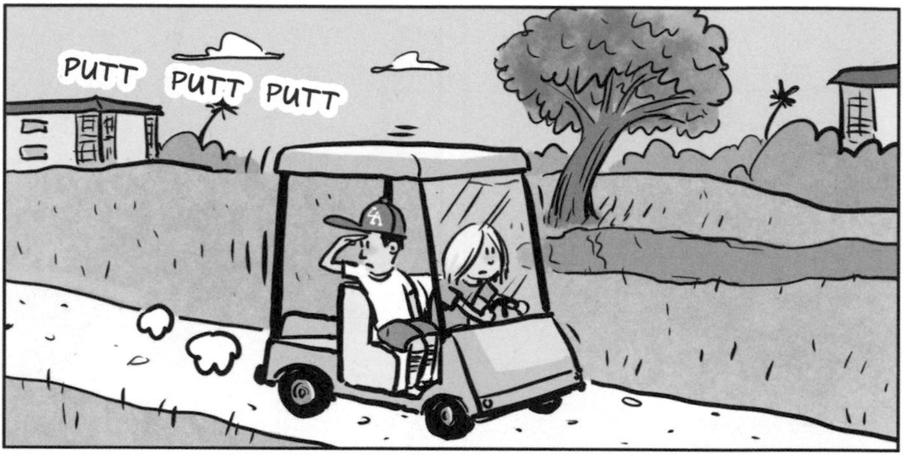
PUTT PUTT PUTT

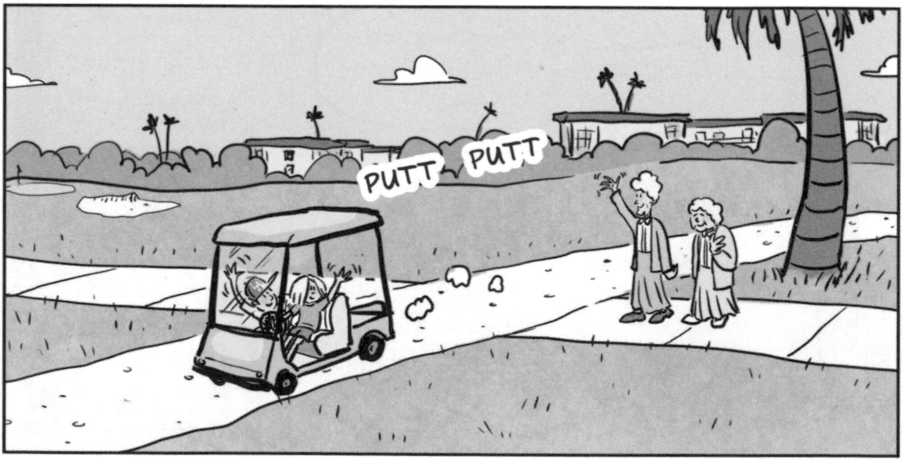
PUTT PUTT

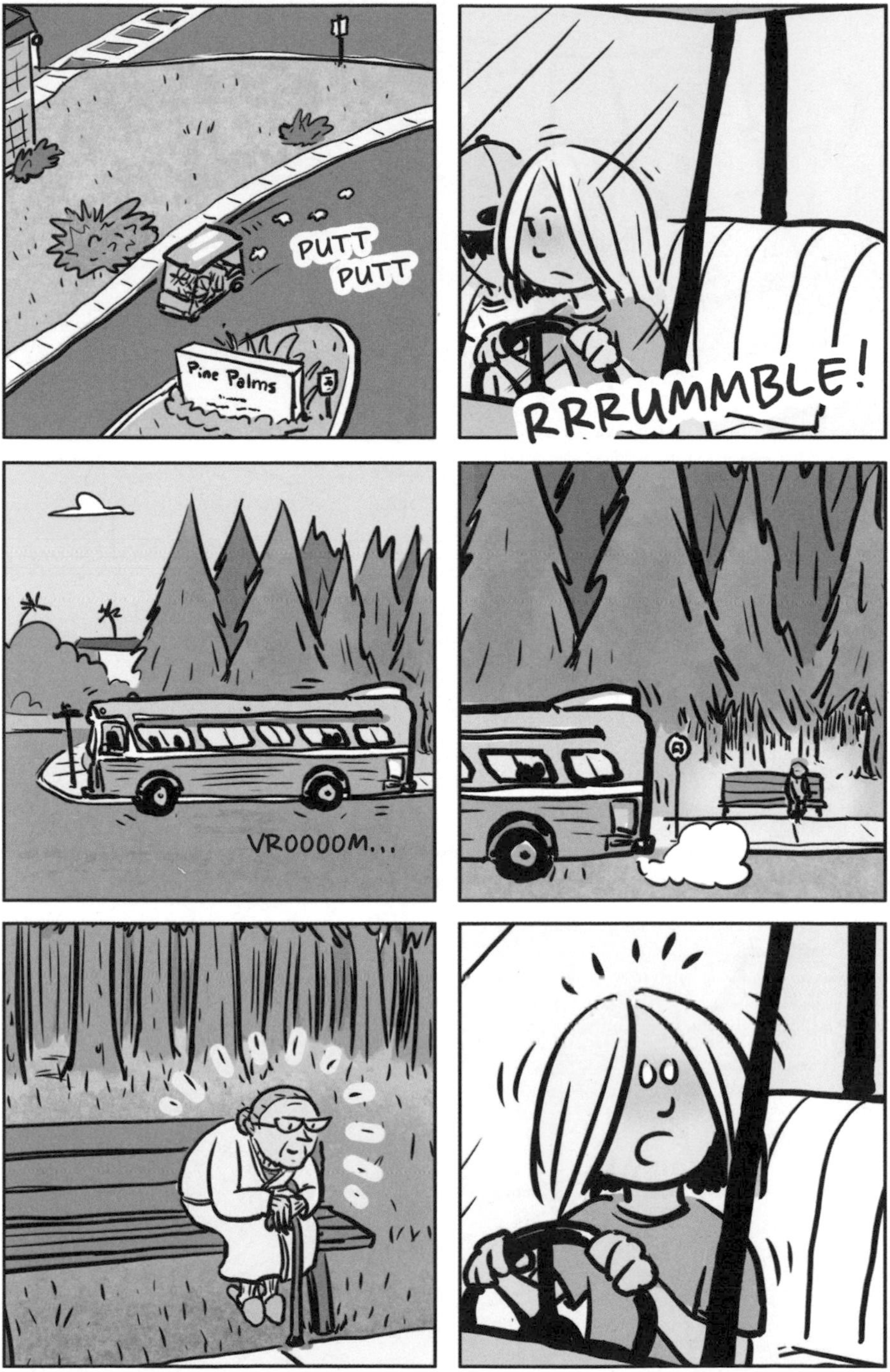
PUTT PUTT
Pine Palms
RRRUMMBLE!
VROOOOM...

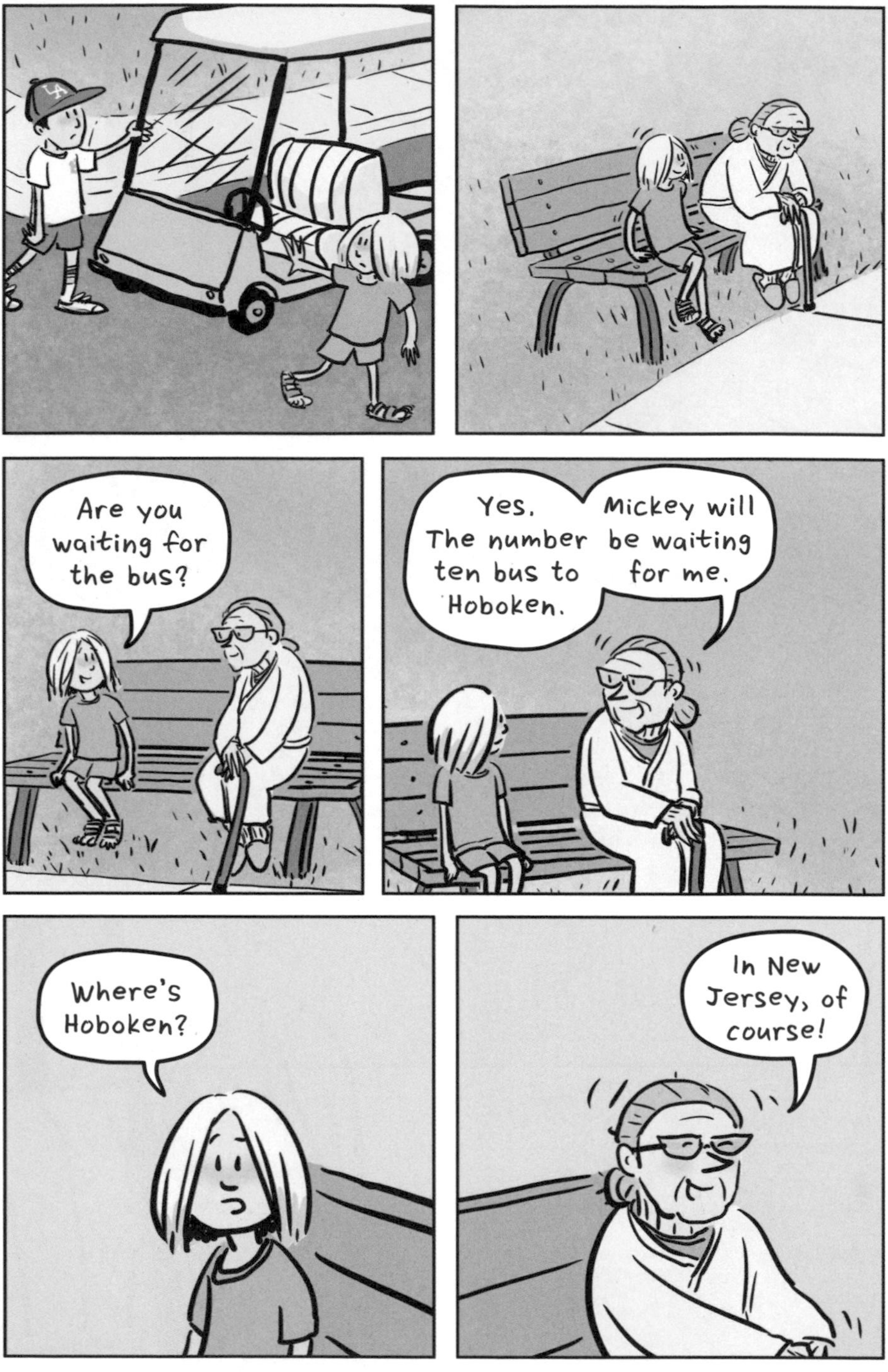
Are you waiting for the bus?
Yes. The number ten bus to Hoboken.
Mickey will be waiting for me.
Where's Hoboken?
In New Jersey, of course!

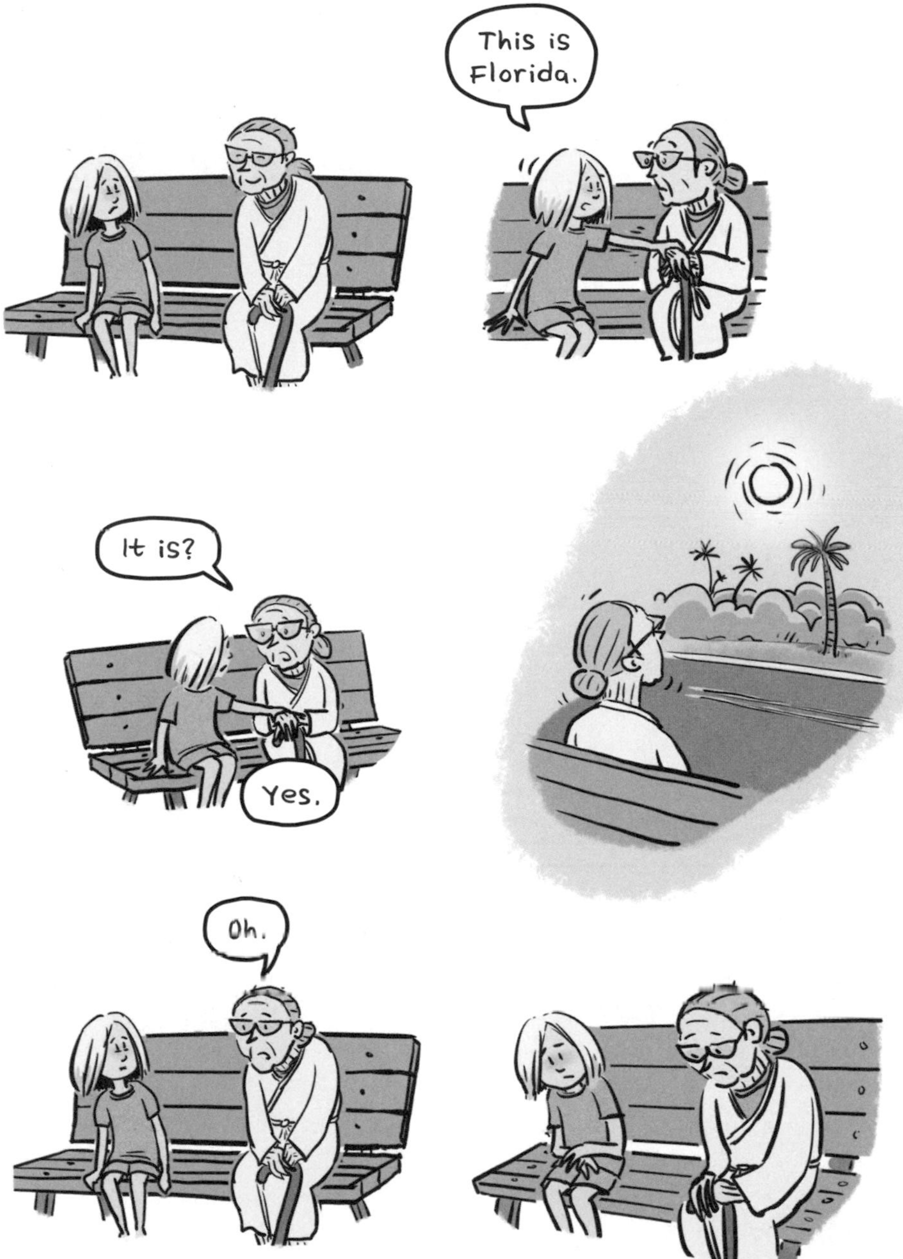
This is Florida.
It is?
Yes.
Oh.

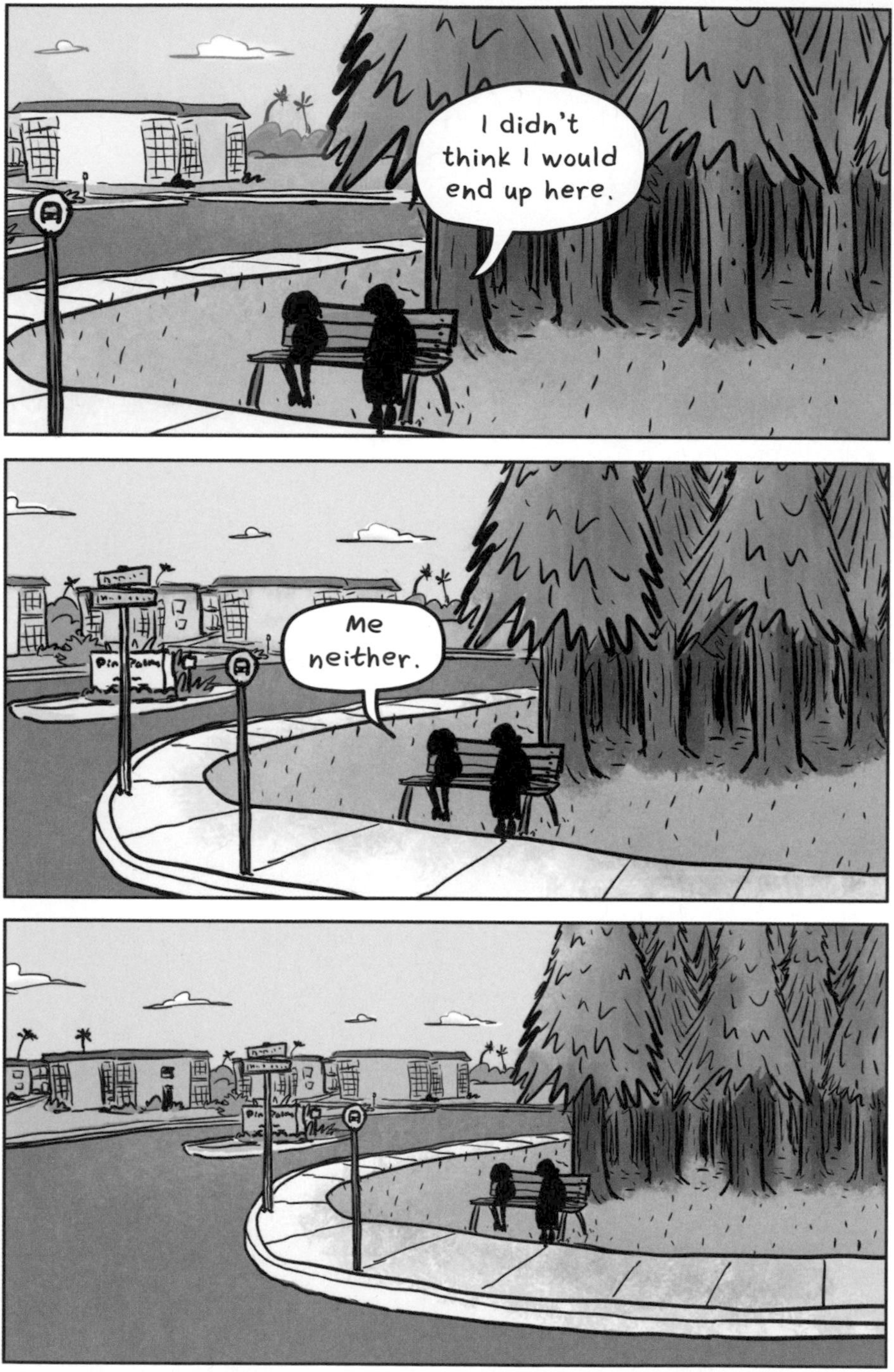
I didn't think I would end up here.
Me neither.

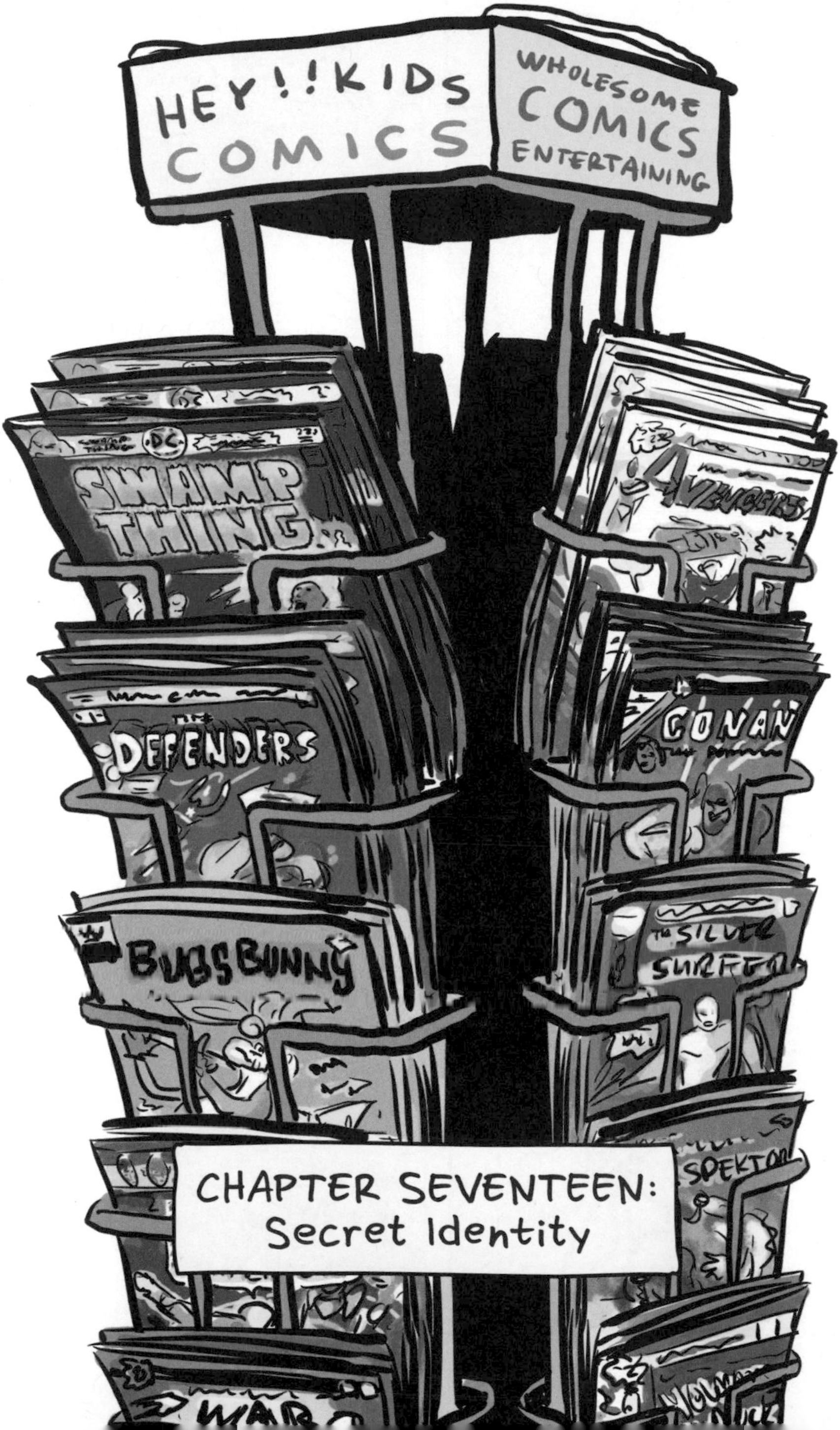
HEY!! KIDS COMICS
WHOLESOME COMICS ENTERTAINING
SWAMP THING
AVENGERS
DEFENDERS
CONAN
BUGS BUNNY
WAR

CHAPTER SEVENTEEN:
Secret Identity

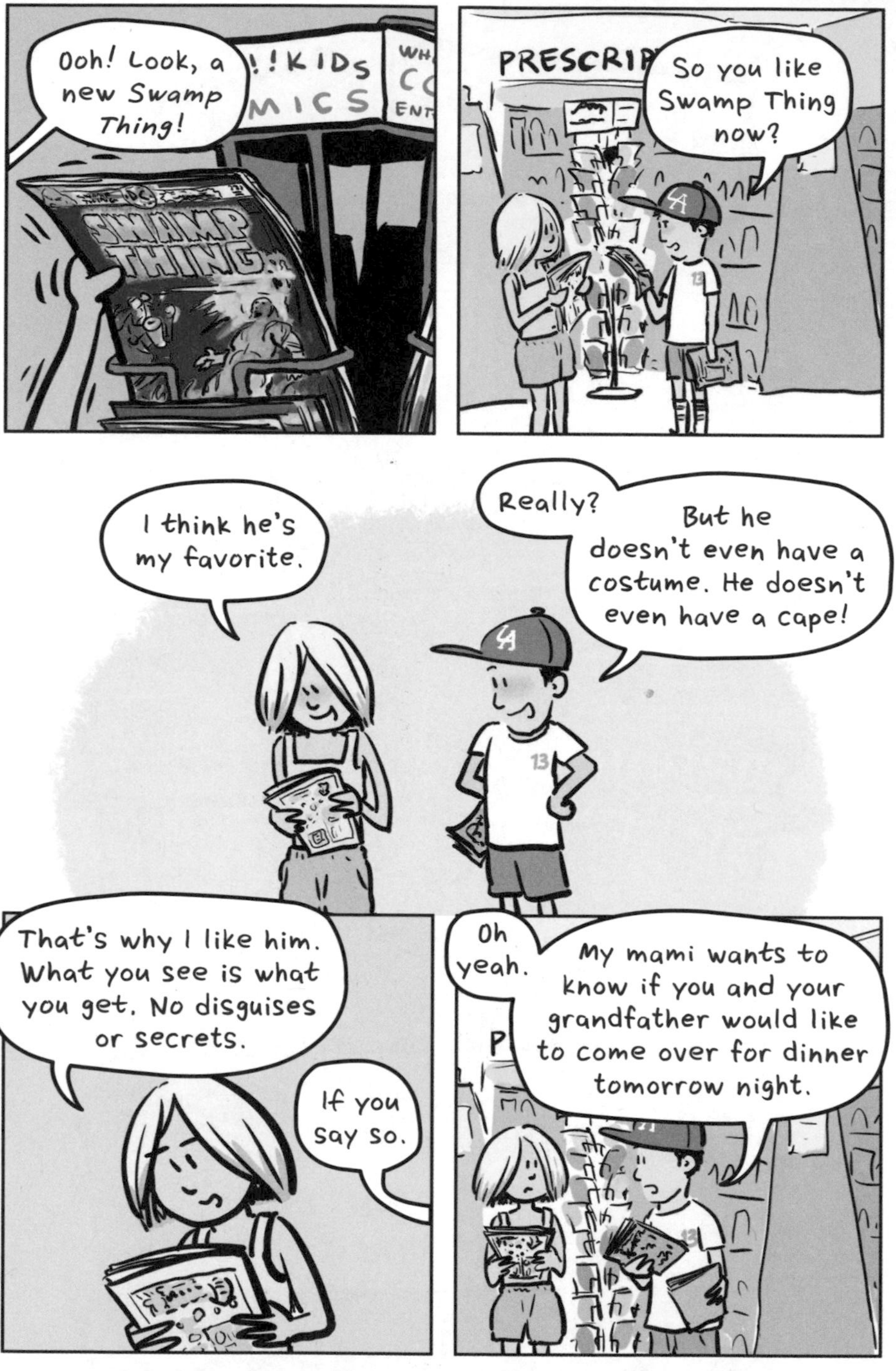
Ooh! Look, a new Swamp Thing!
SWAMP THING
So you like Swamp Thing now?
I think he's my favorite.
Really?
But he doesn't even have a costume. He doesn't even have a cape!
That's why I like him. What you see is what you get. No disguises or secrets.
If you say so.
Oh yeah.
My mami wants to know if you and your grandfather would like to come over for dinner tomorrow night.

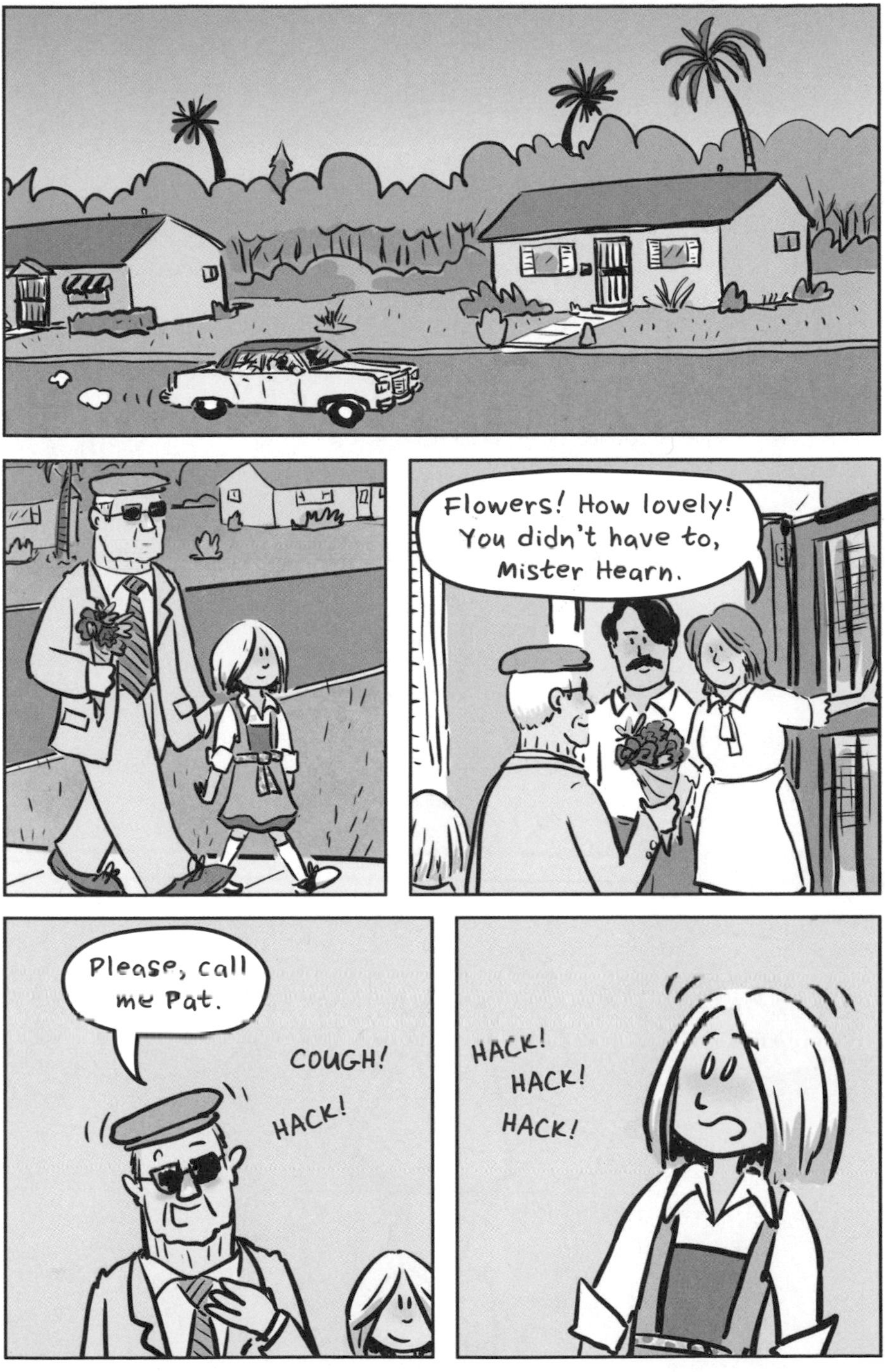
Flowers! How lovely! You didn't have to, Mister Hearn.
Please, call me Pat.
COUGH!
HACK!
HACK!
HACK!
HACK!

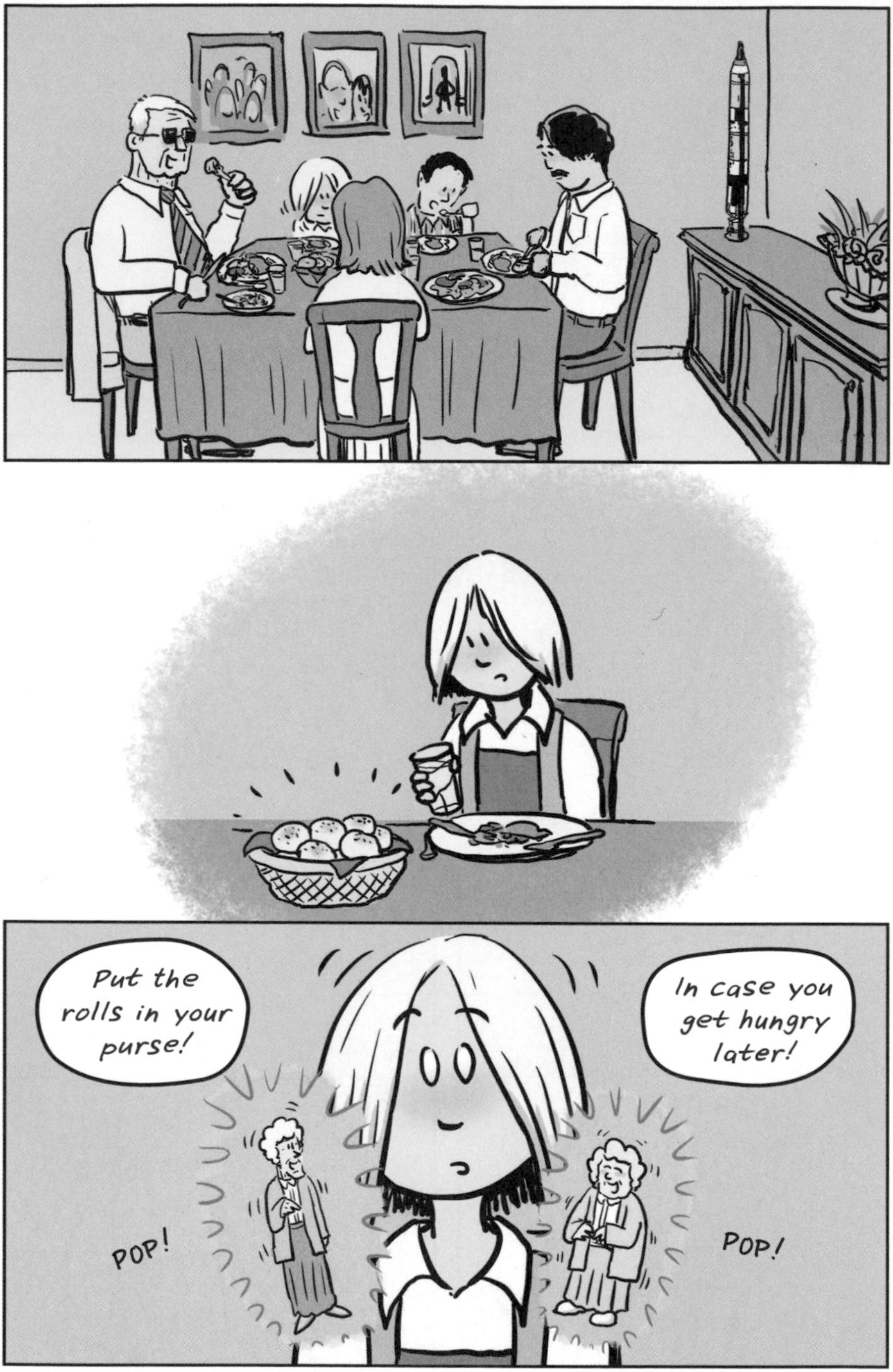
Put the rolls in your purse!
In case you get hungry later!
POP!
POP!

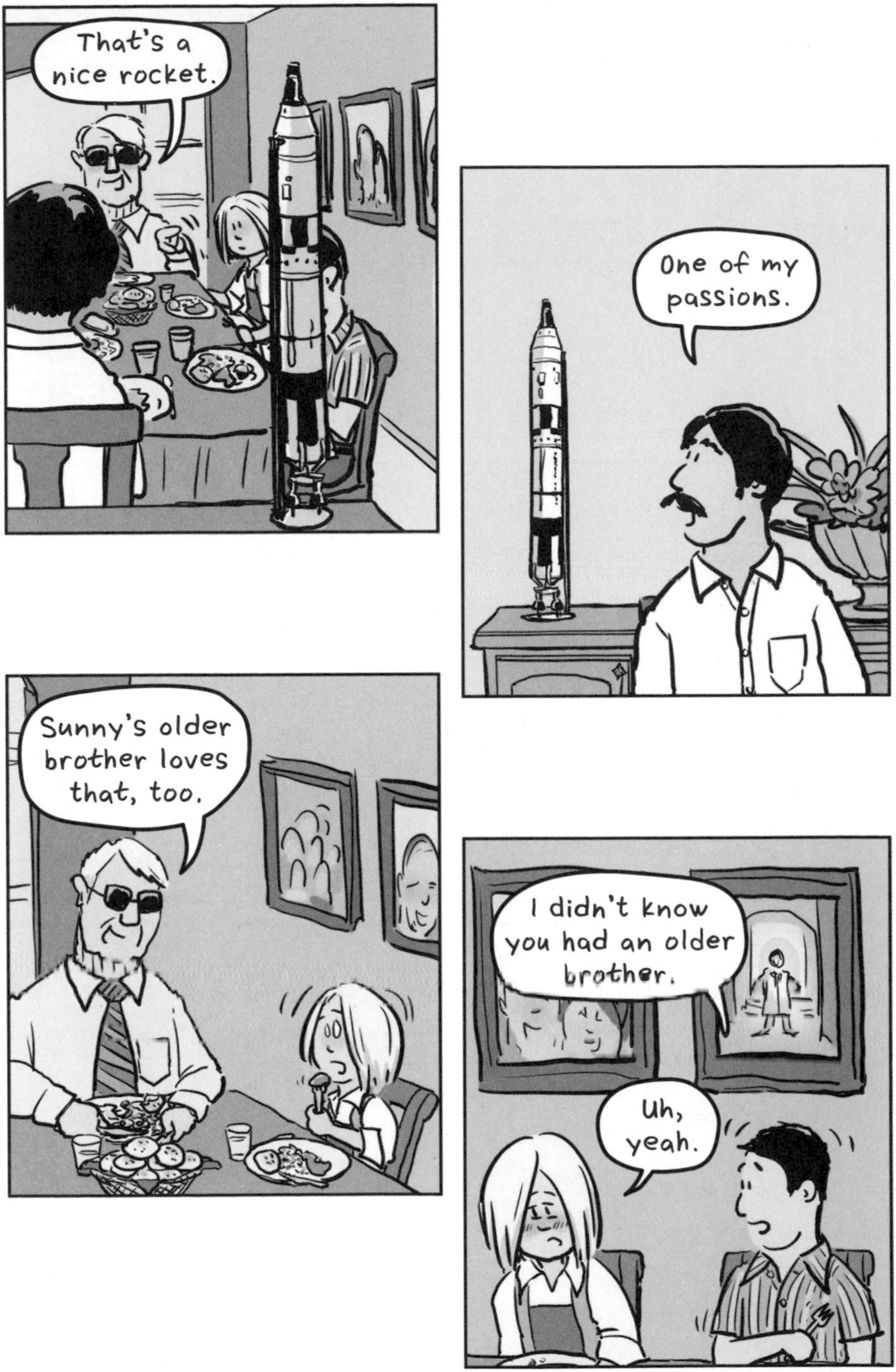
That's a nice rocket.
One of my passions.
Sunny's older brother loves that, too.
I didn't know you had an older brother.
Uh, yeah.

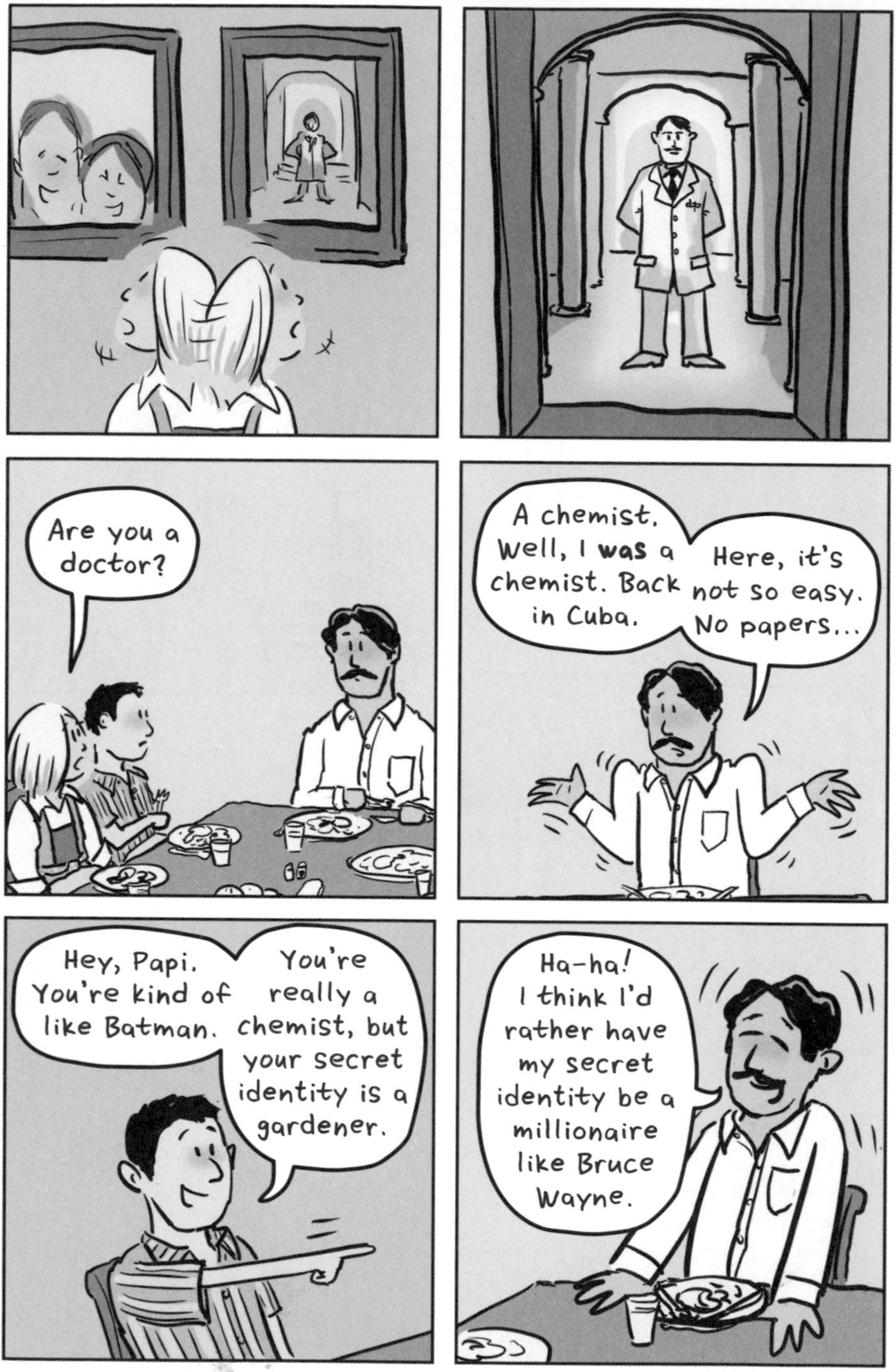
Are you a doctor?
A chemist. Well, I **was** a chemist. Back in Cuba.
Here, it's not so easy. No papers...
Hey, Papi. You're kind of like Batman.
You're really a chemist, but your secret identity is a gardener.
Ha-ha! I think I'd rather have my secret identity be a millionaire like Bruce Wayne.

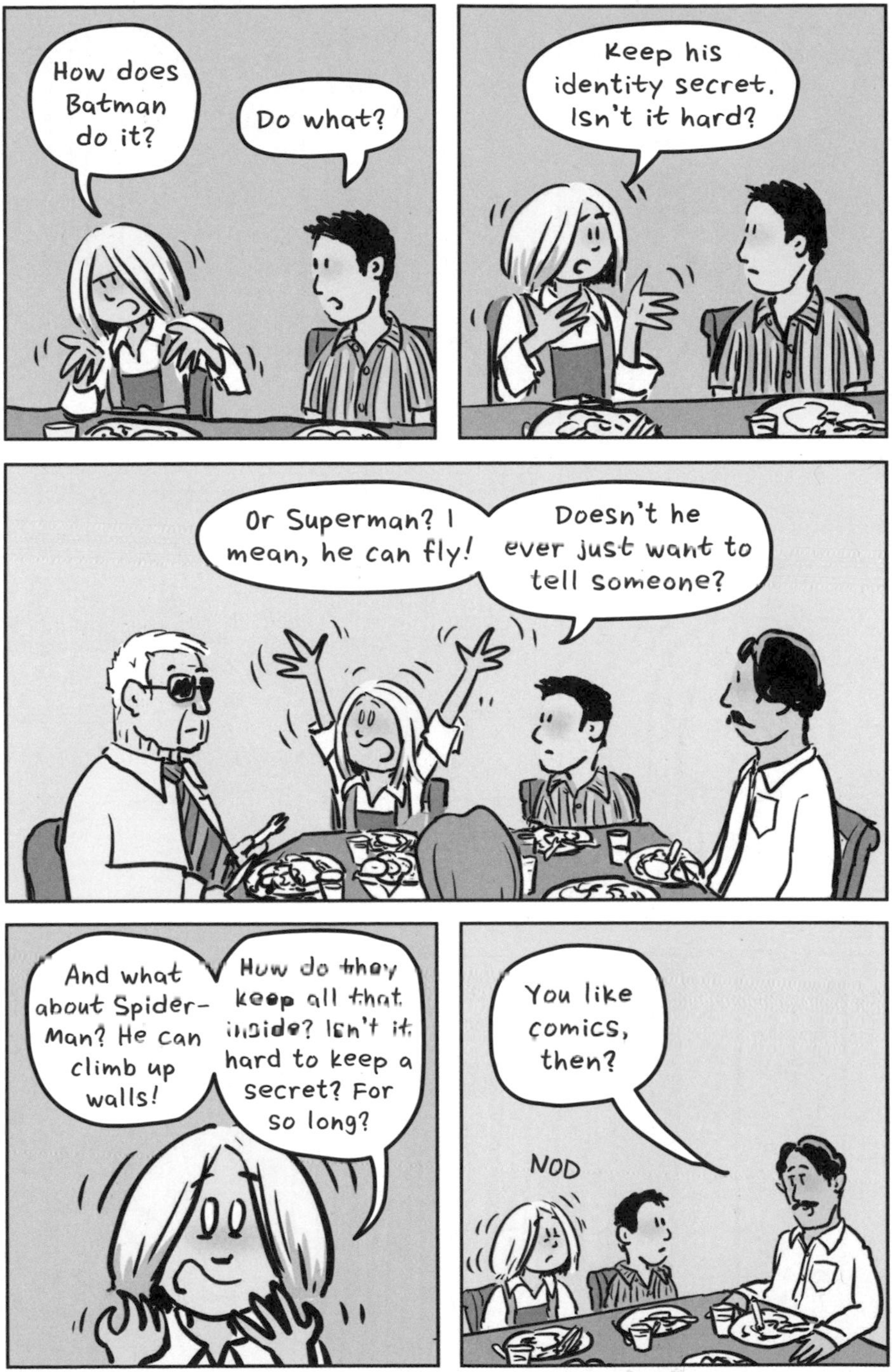
How does Batman do it?
Do what?
Keep his identity secret. Isn't it hard?
Or Superman? I mean, he can fly!
Doesn't he ever just want to tell someone?
And what about Spider-Man? He can climb up walls!
How do they keep all that inside? Isn't it hard to keep a secret? For so long?
You like comics, then?
NOD

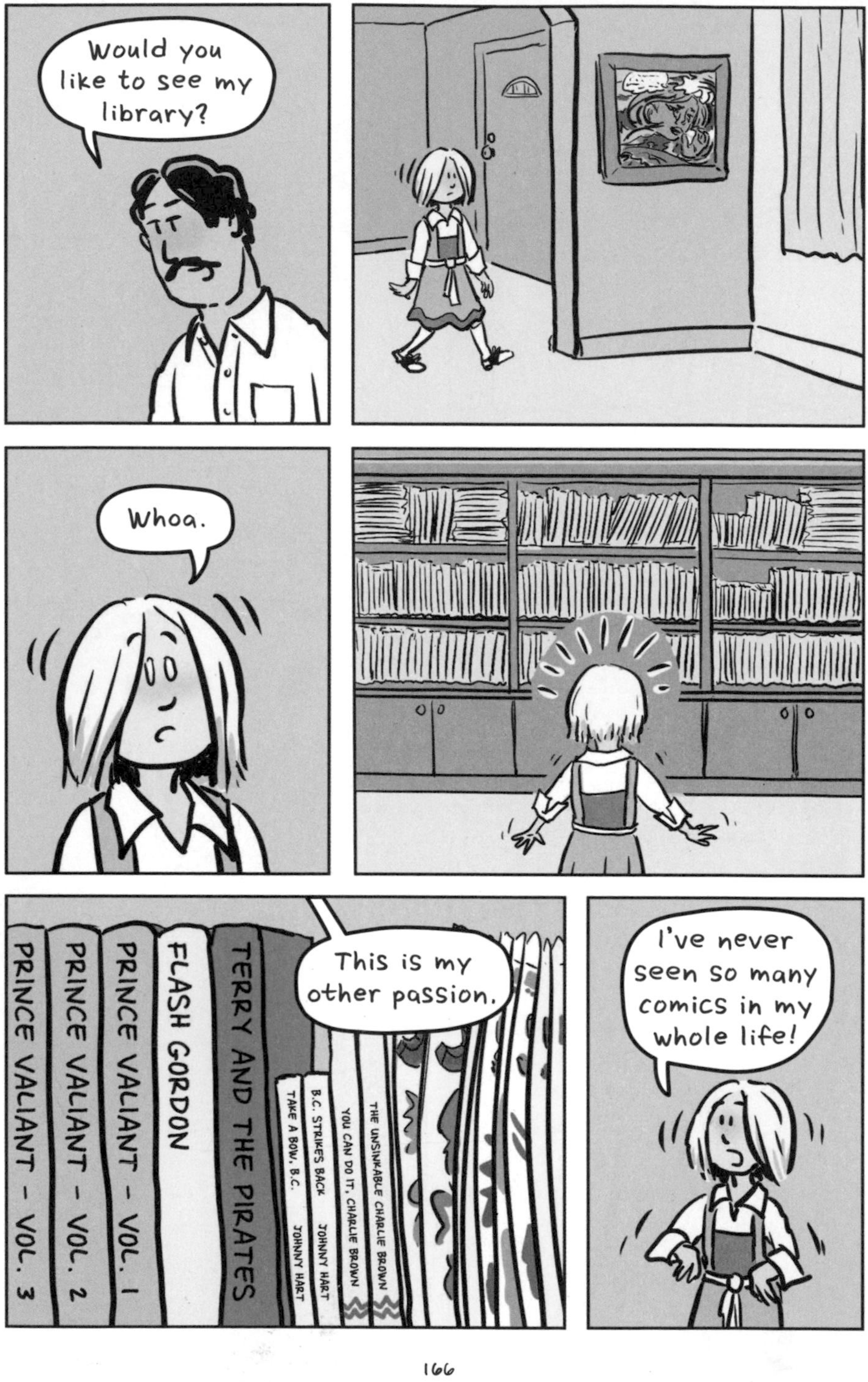
Would you like to see my library?
Whoa.
This is my other passion.
PRINCE VALIANT - VOL. 3
PRINCE VALIANT - VOL. 2
PRINCE VALIANT - VOL. 1
FLASH GORDON
TERRY AND THE PIRATES
TAKE A BOW, B.C. JOHNNY HART
B.C. STRIKES BACK JOHNNY HART
YOU CAN DO IT, CHARLIE BROWN
THE UNSINKABLE CHARLIE BROWN
I've never seen so many comics in my whole life!

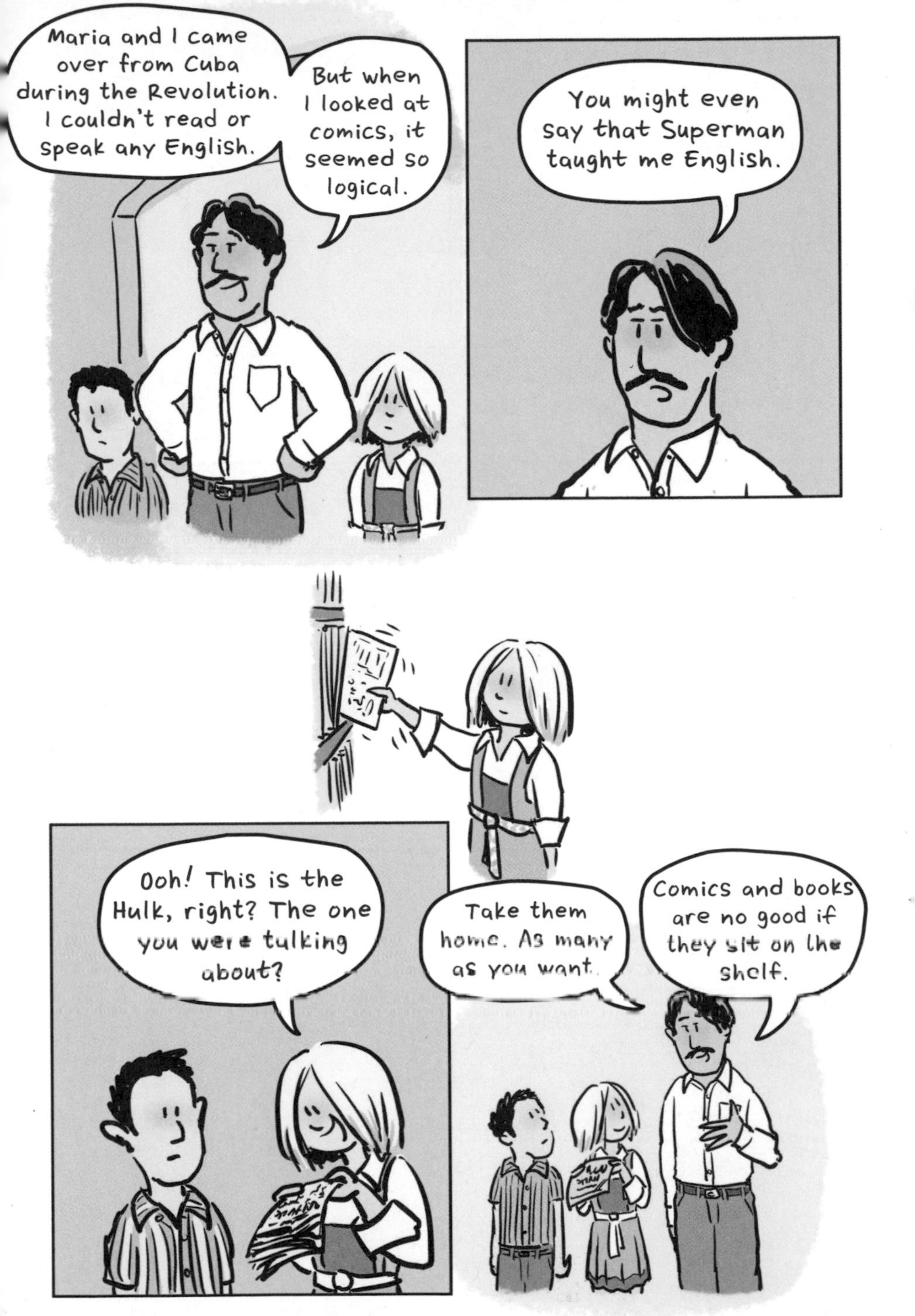

Maria and I came over from Cuba during the Revolution. I couldn't read or speak any English.
But when I looked at comics, it seemed so logical.
You might even say that Superman taught me English.
Ooh! This is the Hulk, right? The one you were talking about?
Take them home. As many as you want.
Comics and books are no good if they sit on the shelf.

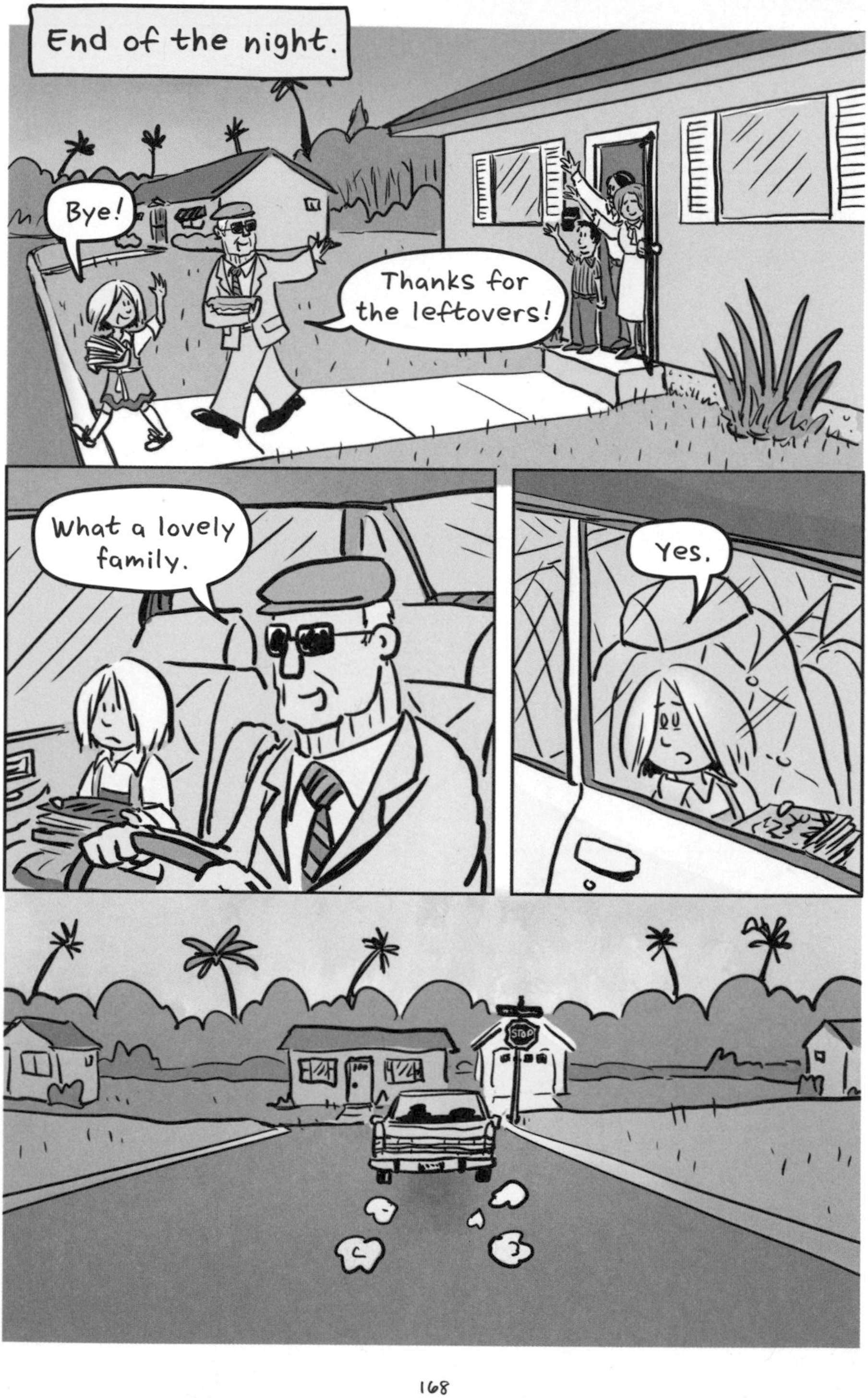
End of the night.
Bye!
Thanks for the leftovers!
What a lovely family.
Yes.
STOP

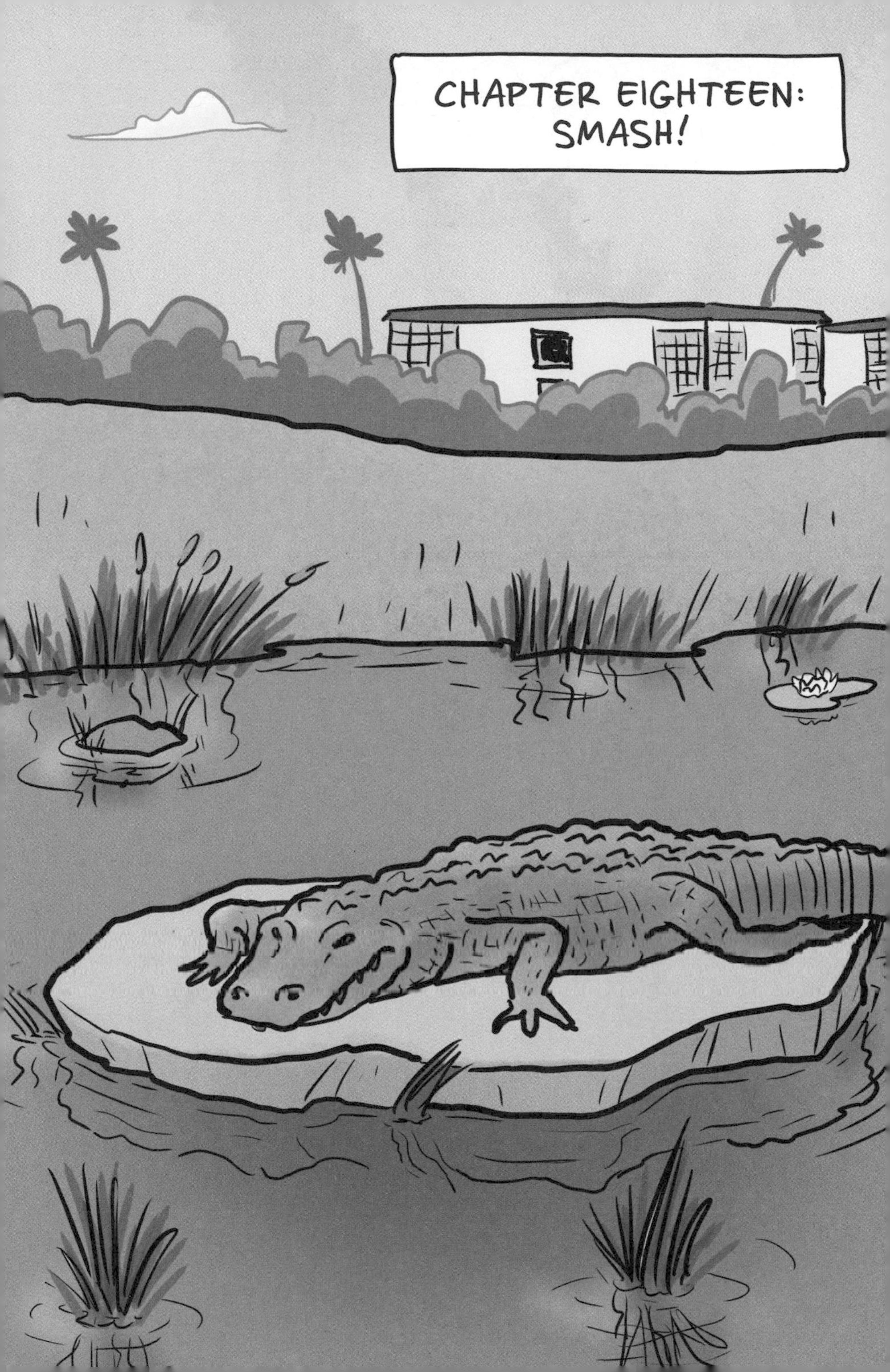
CHAPTER EIGHTEEN:
SMASH!

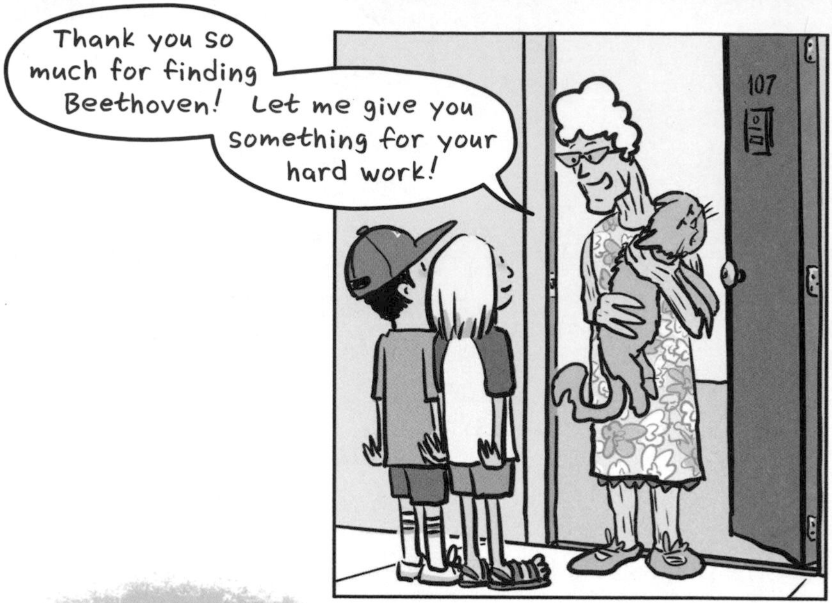
Thank you so much for finding Beethoven! Let me give you something for your hard work!
107

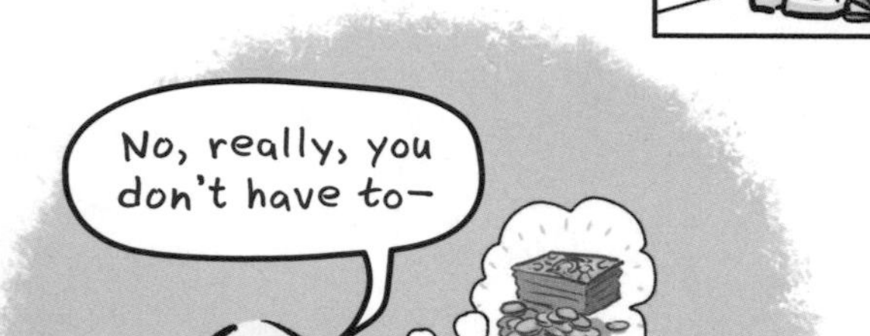
No, really, you don't have to–

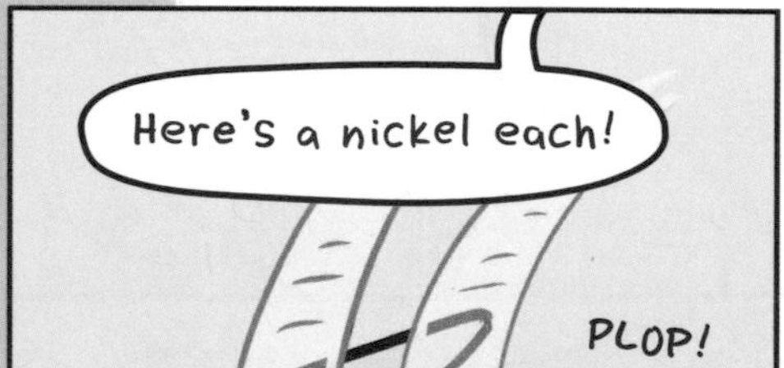
Here's a nickel each!
PLOP!
PLOINK!

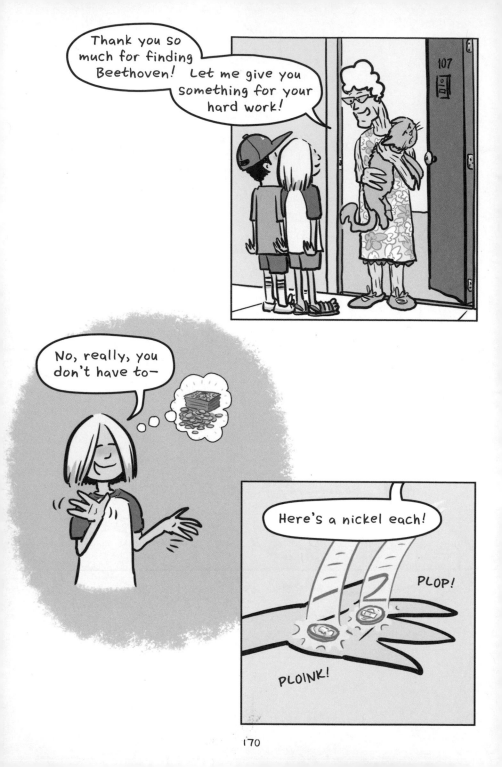

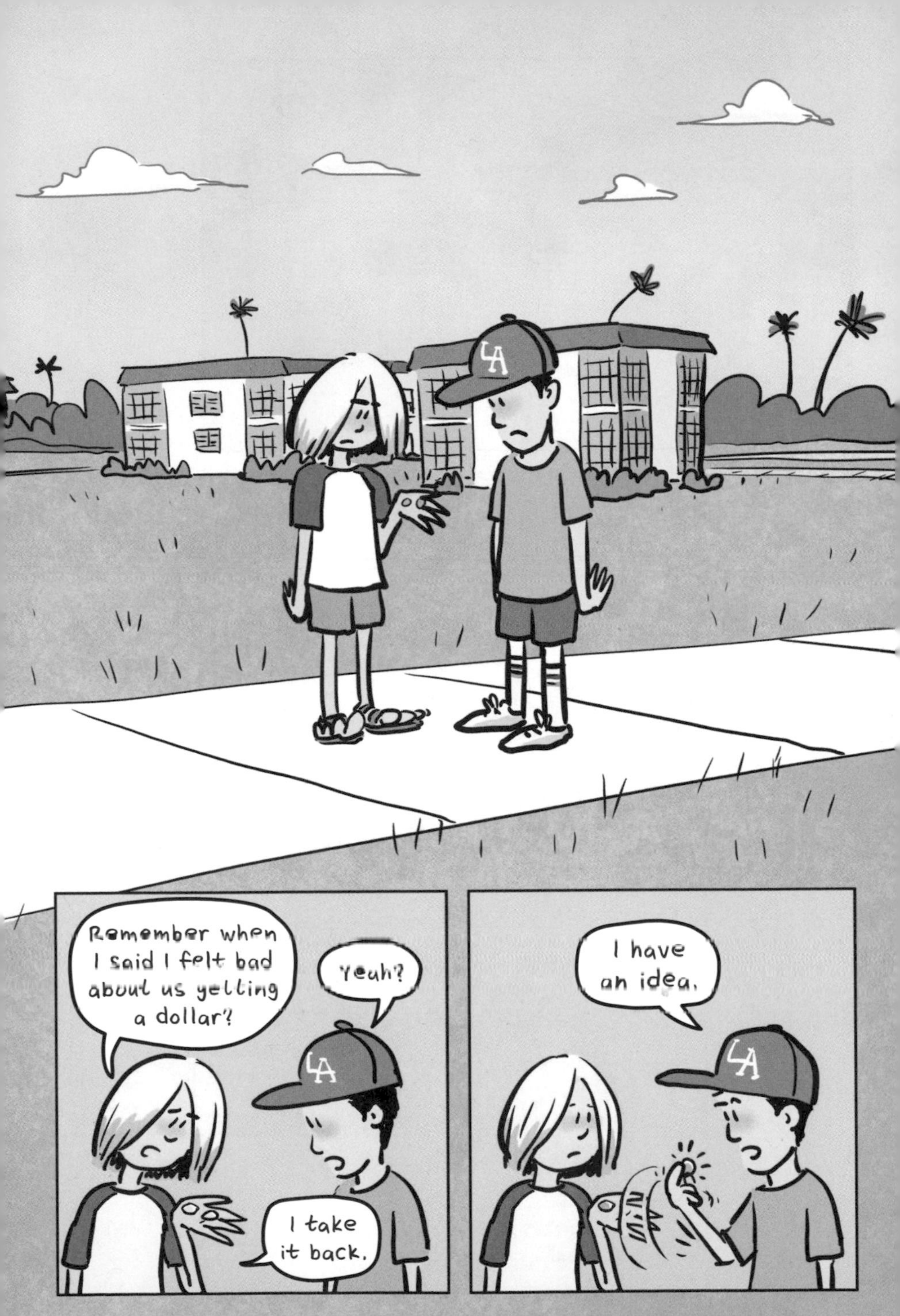
Remember when I said I felt bad about us getting a dollar?
Yeah?
I take it back.
I have an idea.

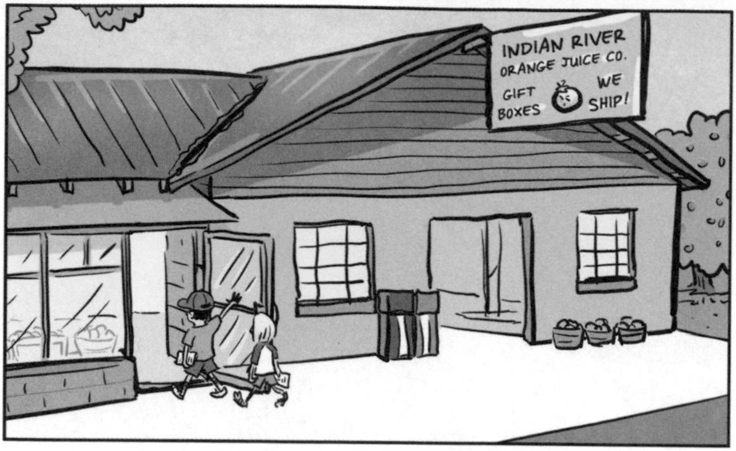
INDIAN RIVER
ORANGE JUICE CO.
GIFT BOXES
WE SHIP!

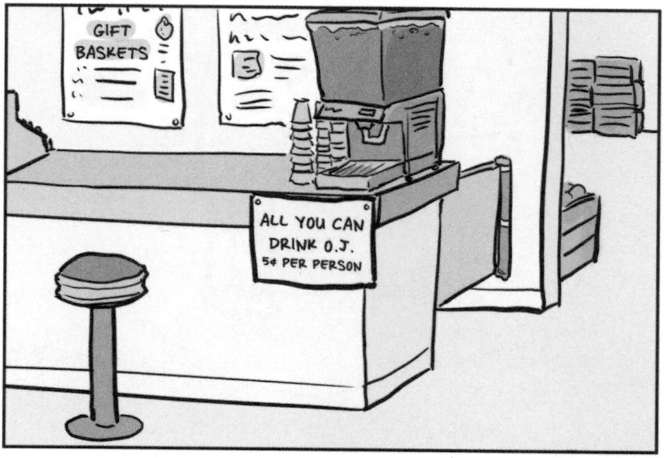
GIFT BASKETS
ALL YOU CAN DRINK O.J. 5¢ PER PERSON

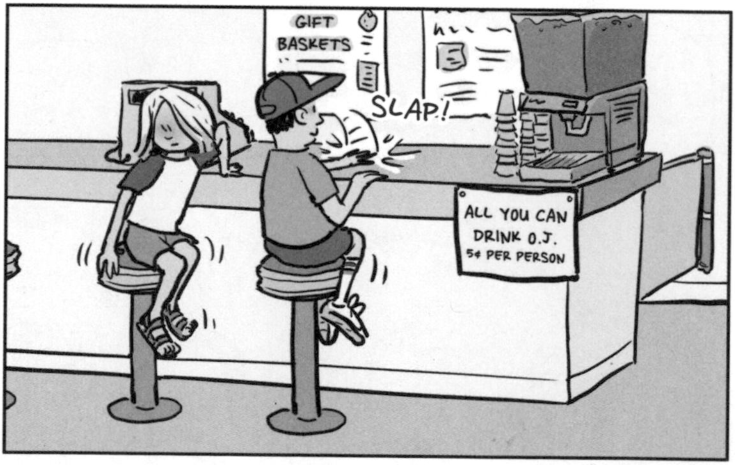
GIFT BASKETS
SLAP!
ALL YOU CAN DRINK O.J. 5¢ PER PERSON

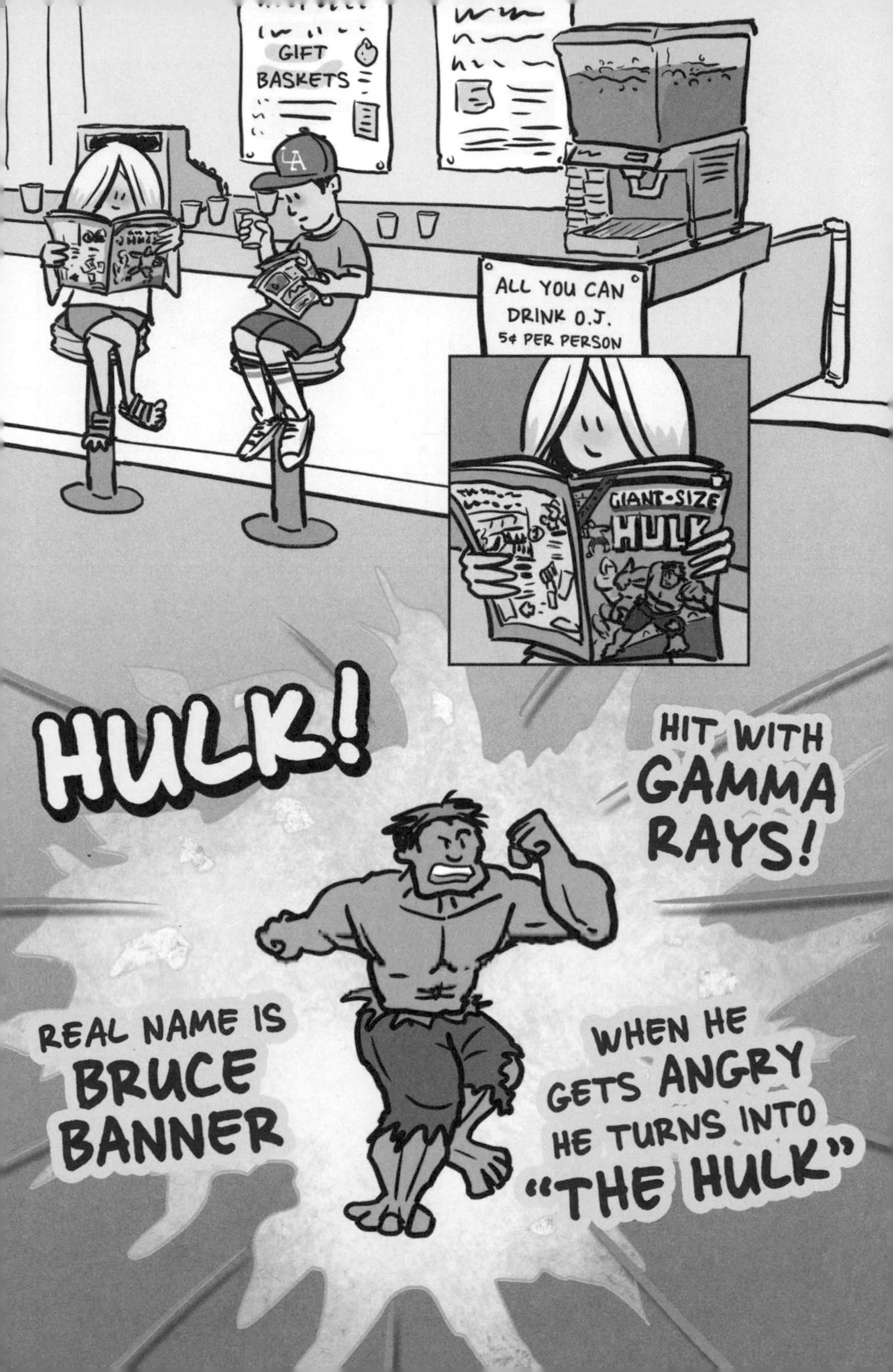
GIFT BASKETS
ALL YOU CAN DRINK O.J. 5¢ PER PERSON
GIANT-SIZE HULK
HULK!
HIT WITH GAMMA RAYS!
REAL NAME IS BRUCE BANNER
WHEN HE GETS ANGRY HE TURNS INTO "THE HULK"

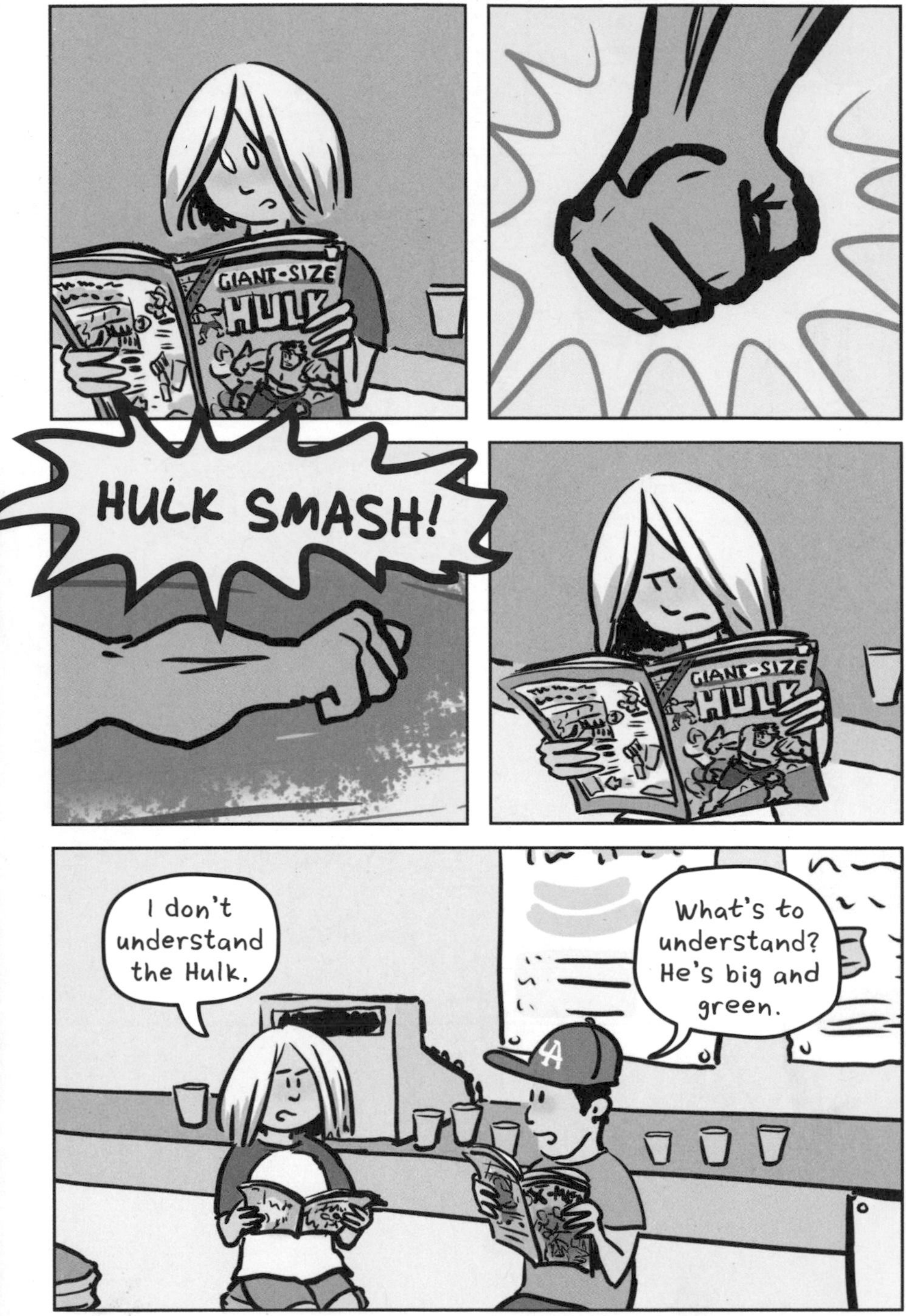
GIANT-SIZE
HULK
HULK SMASH!
GIANT-SIZE
HULK
I don't understand the Hulk.
What's to understand? He's big and green.

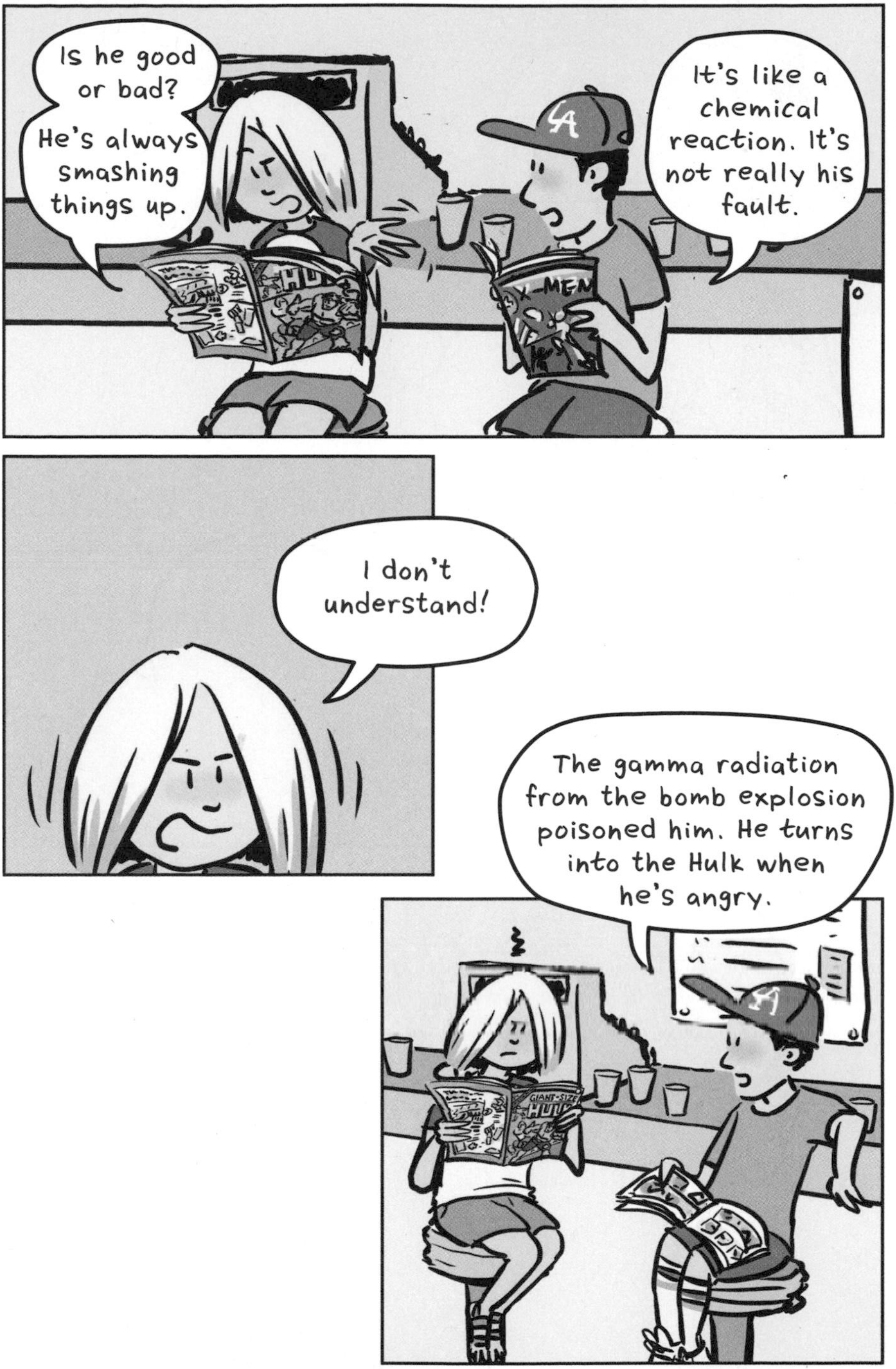
Is he good or bad?
He's always smashing things up.
It's like a chemical reaction. It's not really his fault.
I don't understand!
The gamma radiation from the bomb explosion poisoned him. He turns into the Hulk when he's angry.

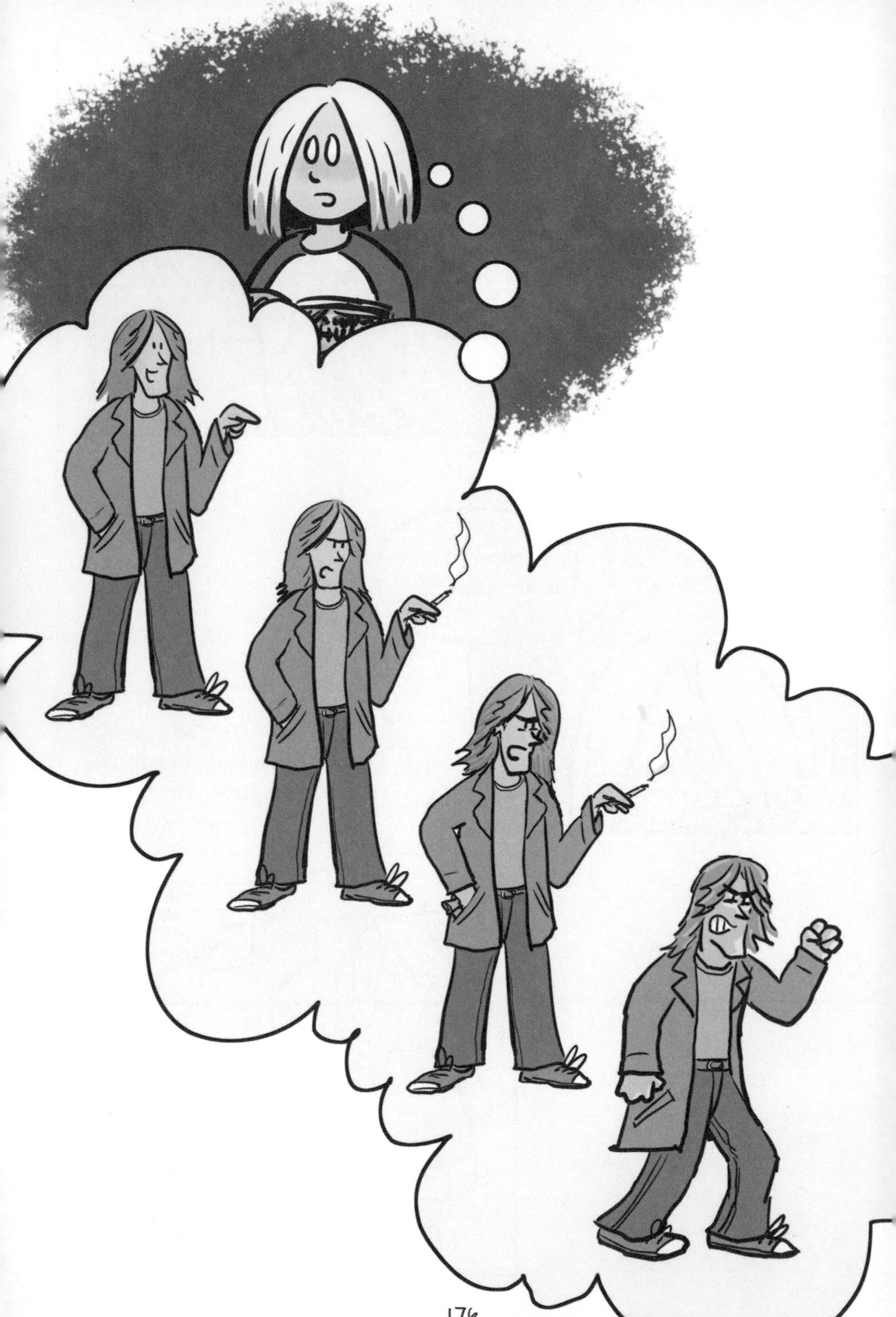

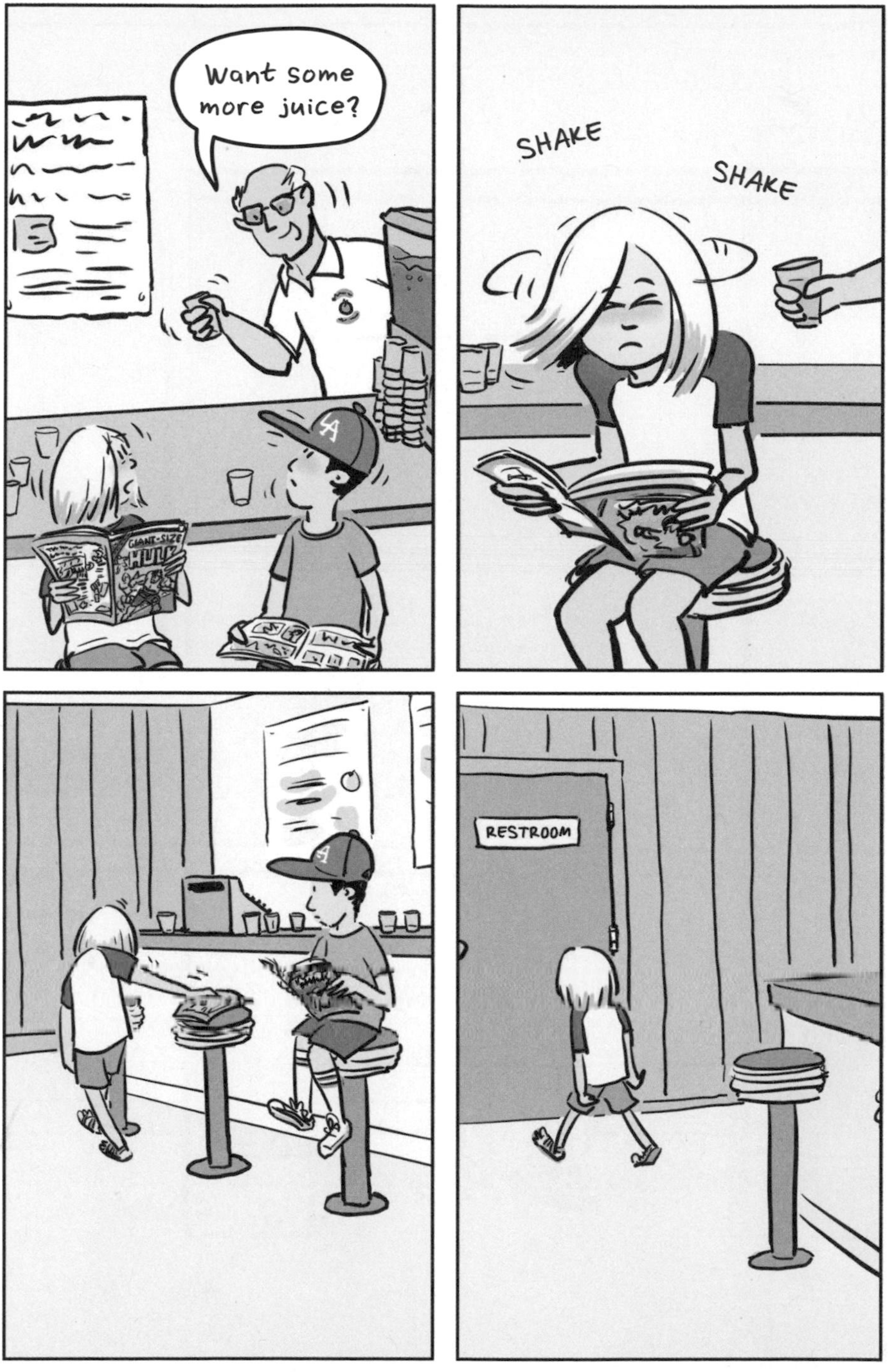
Want some more juice?
GIANT-SIZE HULK
SHAKE
SHAKE
RESTROOM

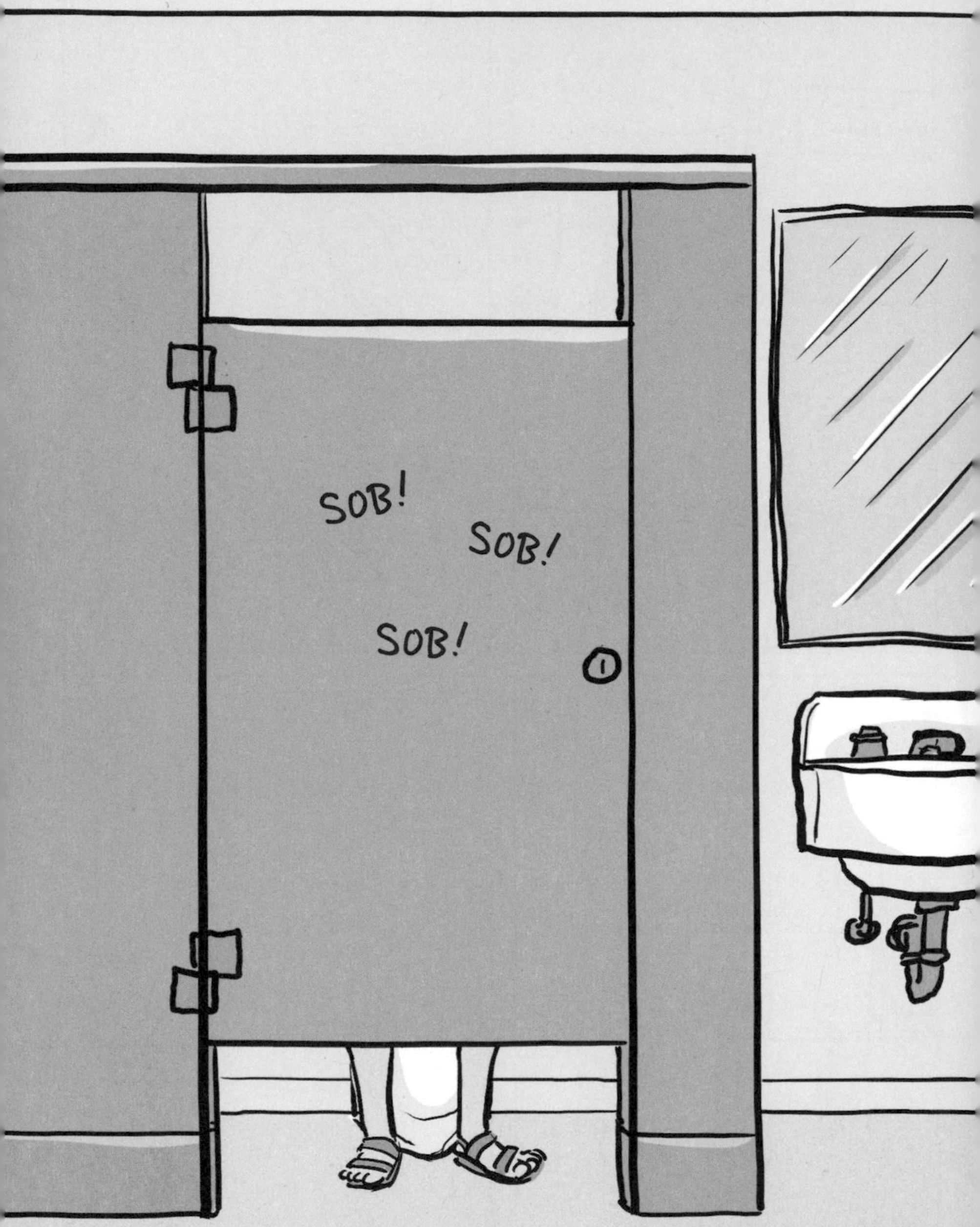
SOB!
SOB!
SOB!

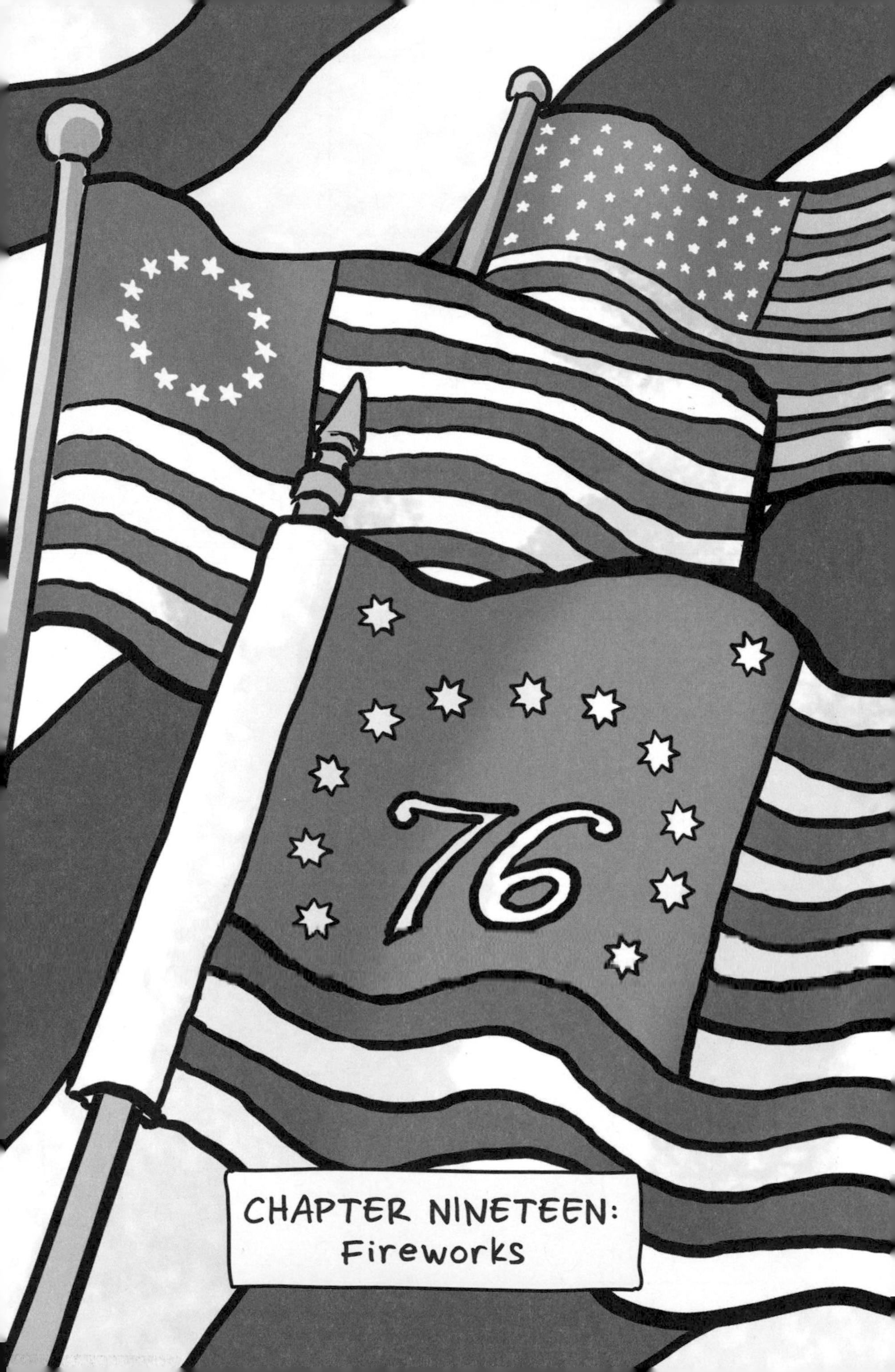

CHAPTER NINETEEN:
Fireworks

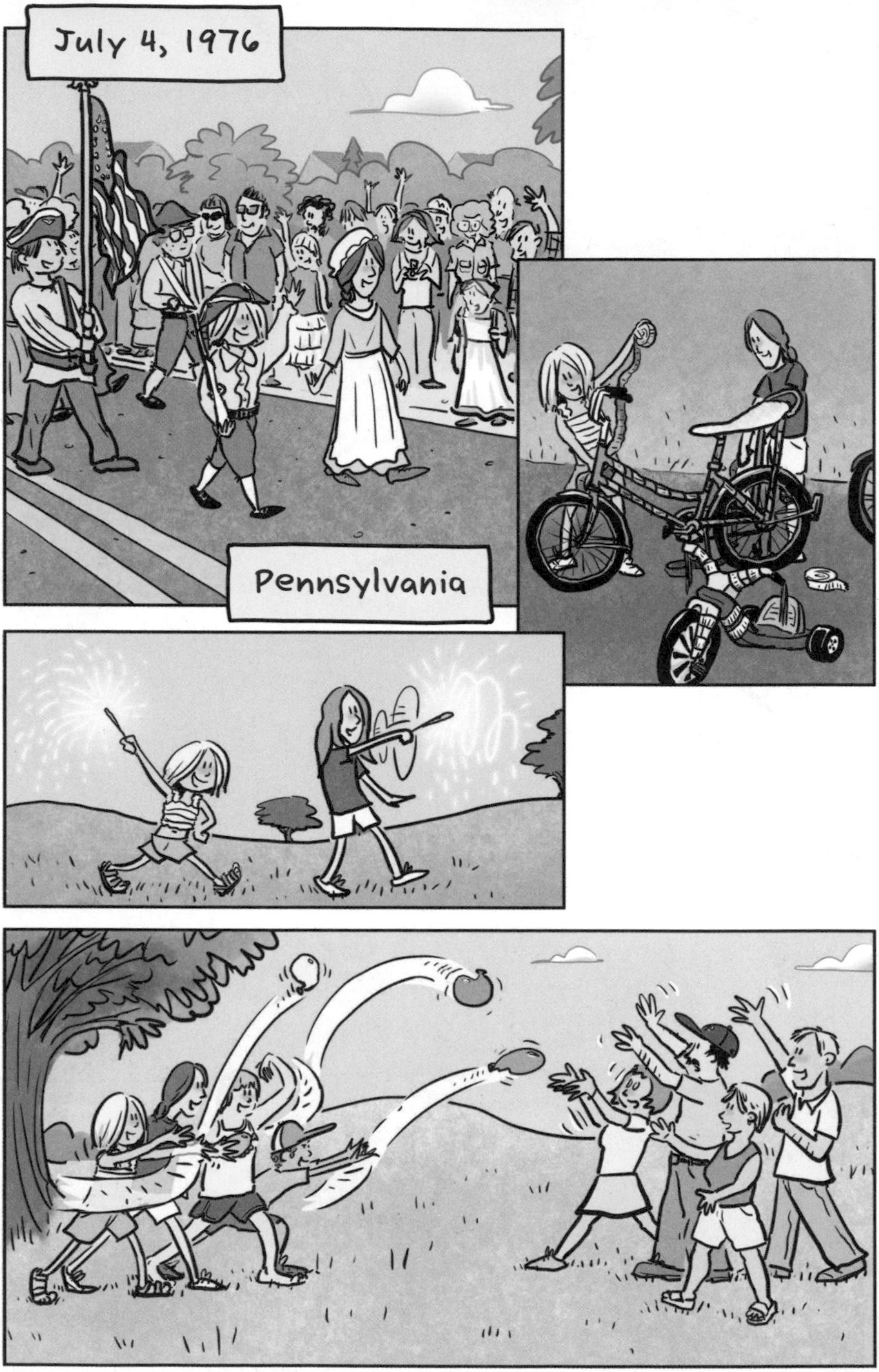
July 4, 1976
Pennsylvania

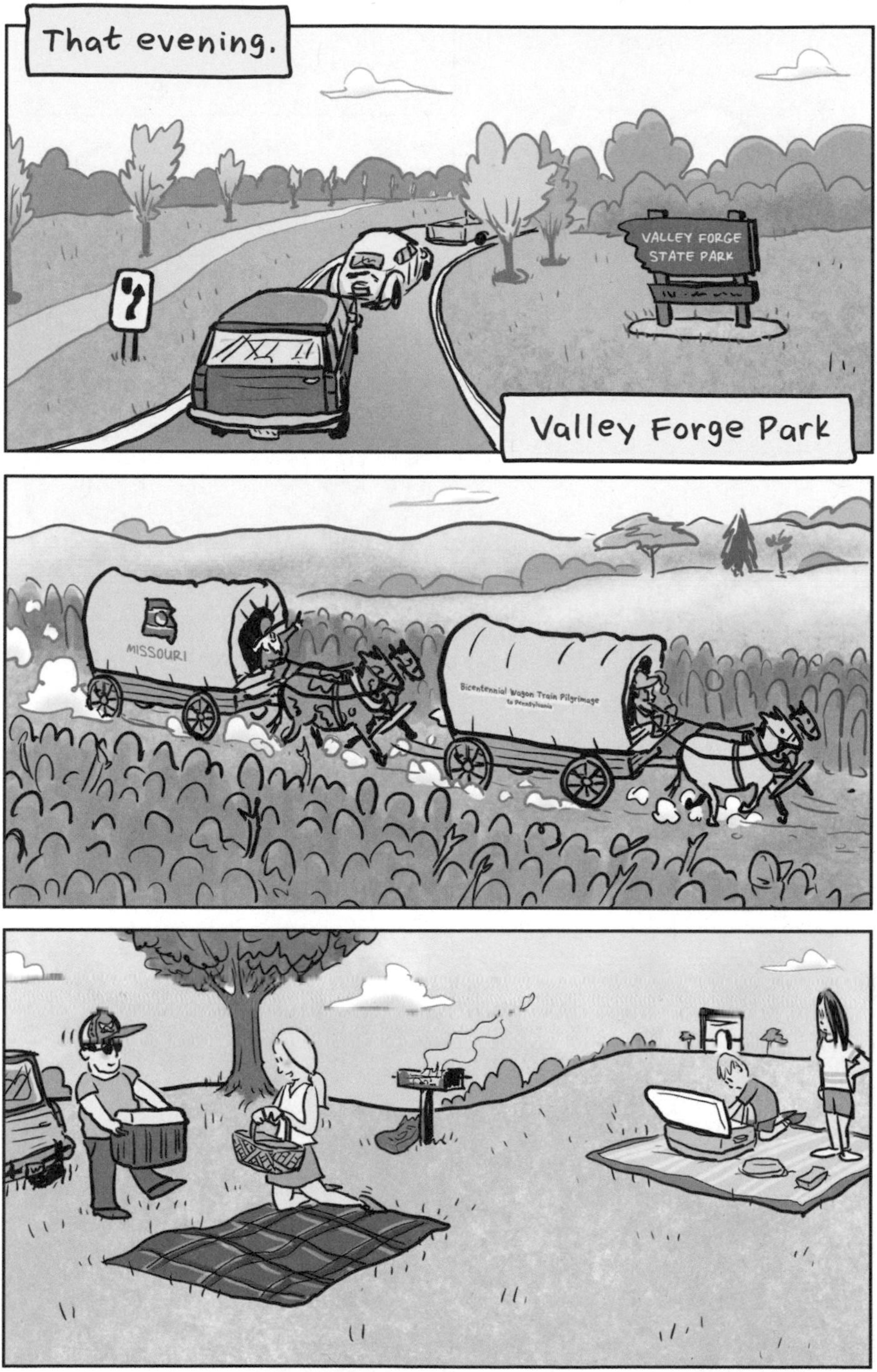
That evening.
VALLEY FORGE
STATE PARK
Valley Forge Park
MISSOURI
Bicentennial Wagon Train Pilgrimage
to Pennsylvania

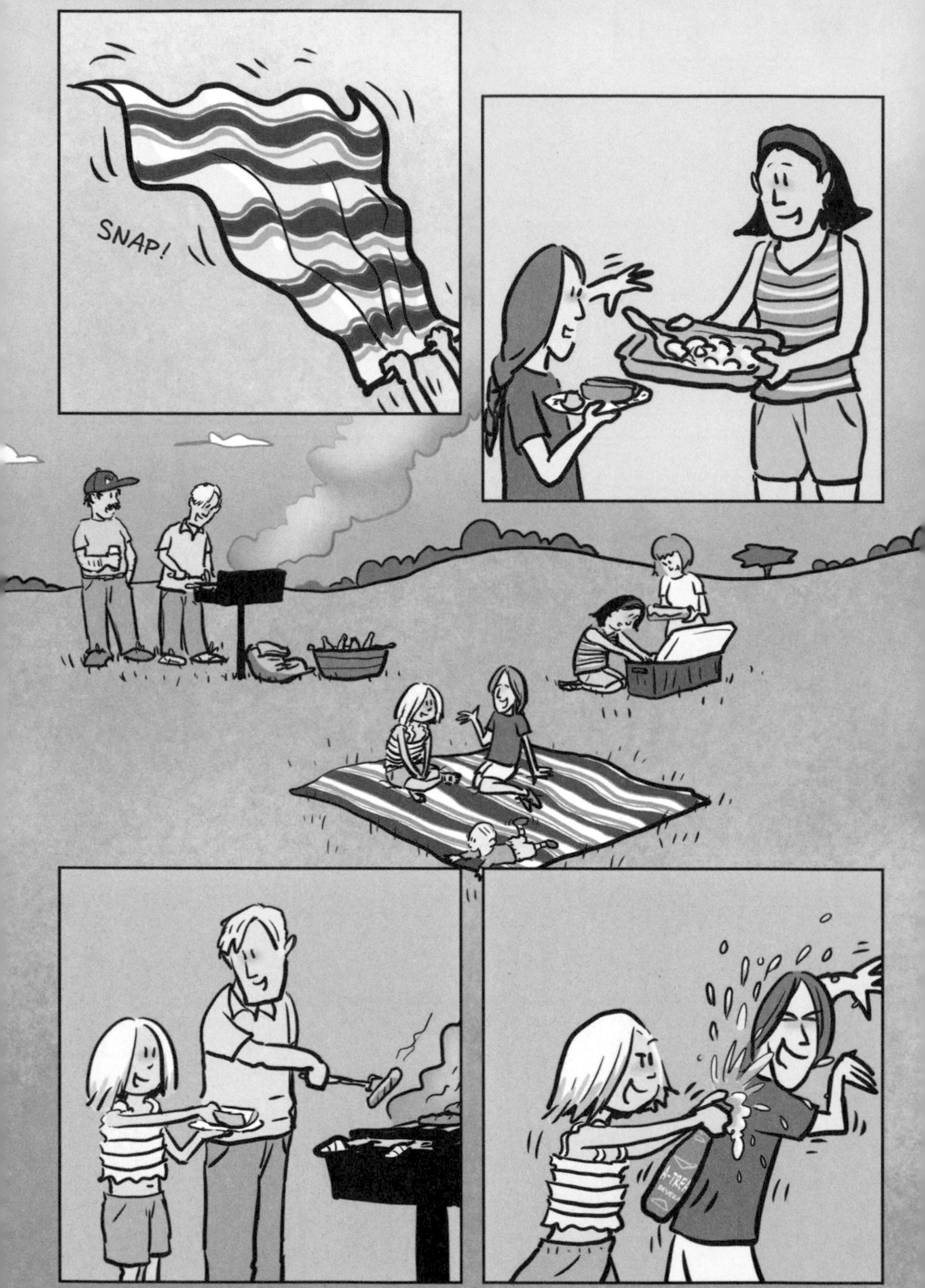
SNAP!

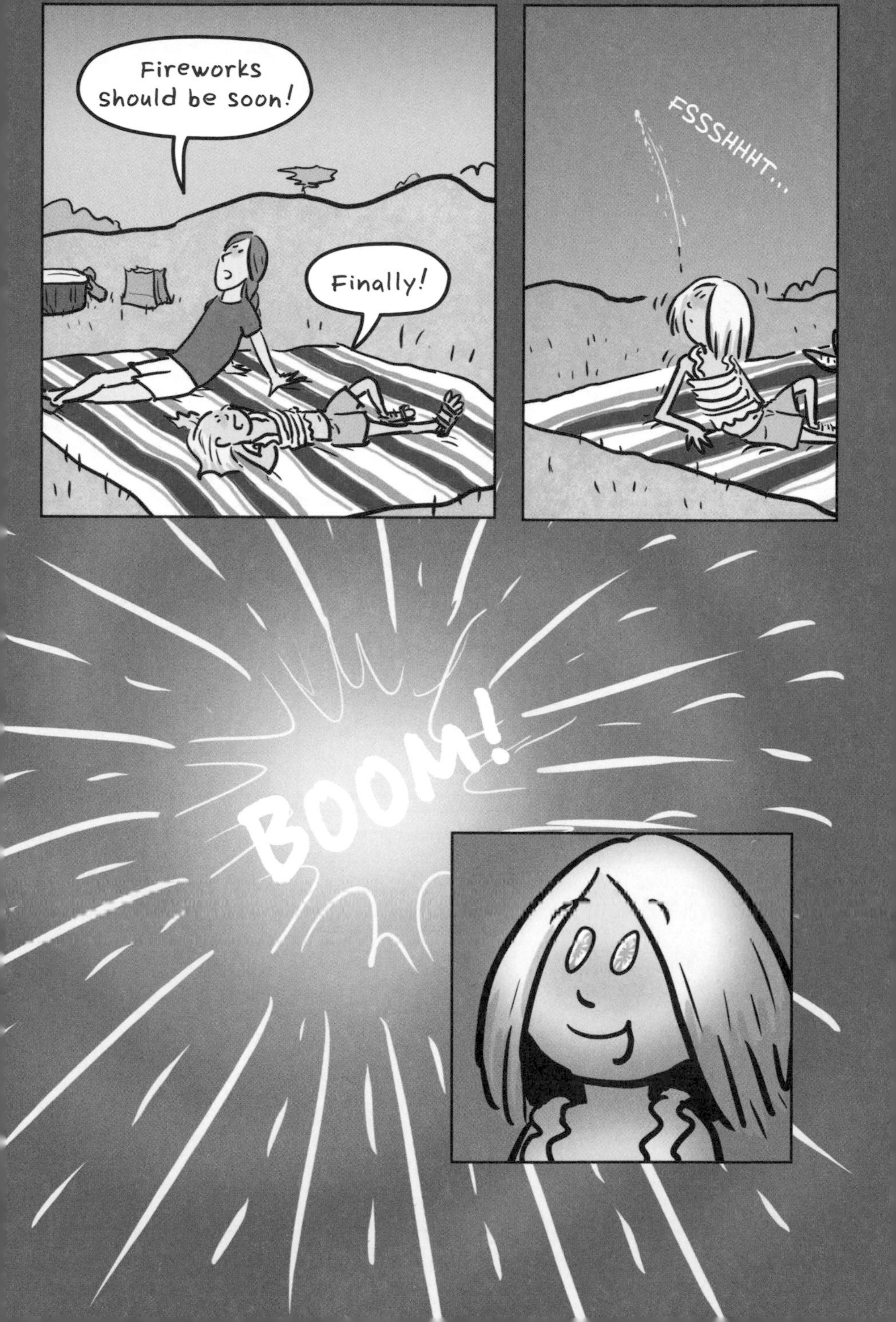

Fireworks should be soon!
Finally!
FSSSHHHT...
BOOM!

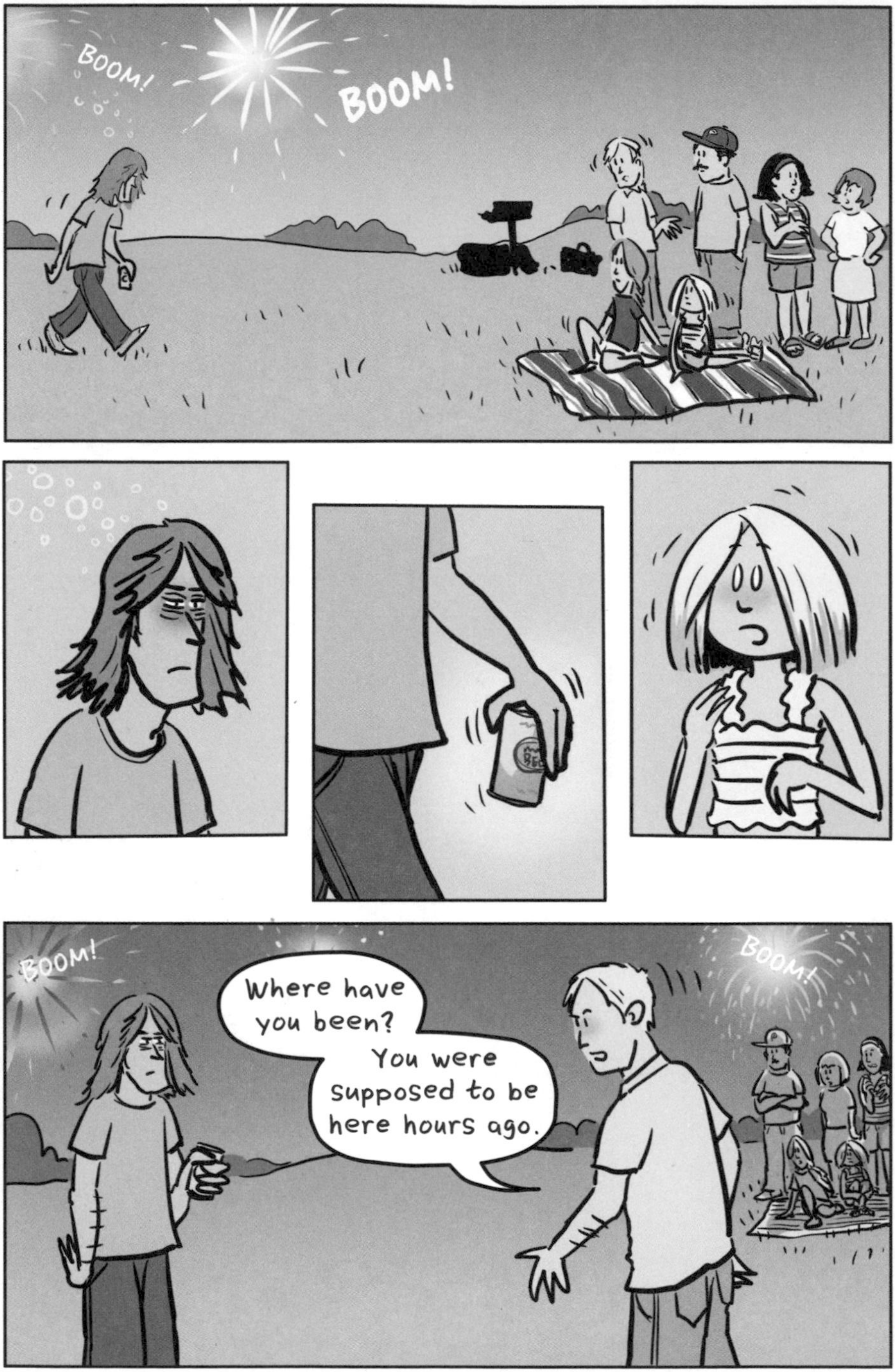
BOOM!
BOOM!
BOOM!
Where have you been?
You were supposed to be here hours ago.
BOOM!

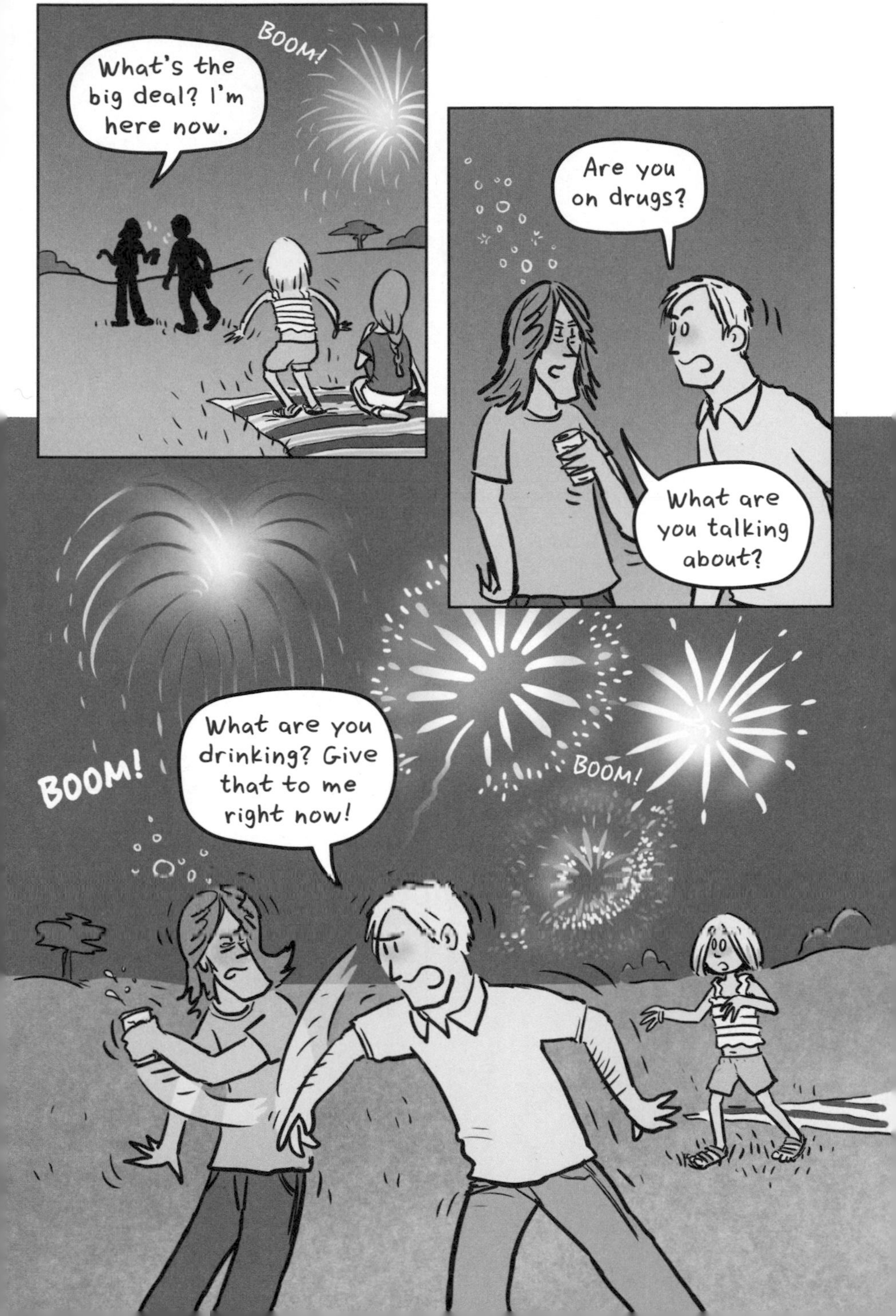
BOOM!
What's the big deal? I'm here now.
Are you on drugs?
What are you talking about?
BOOM!
What are you drinking? Give that to me right now!
BOOM!

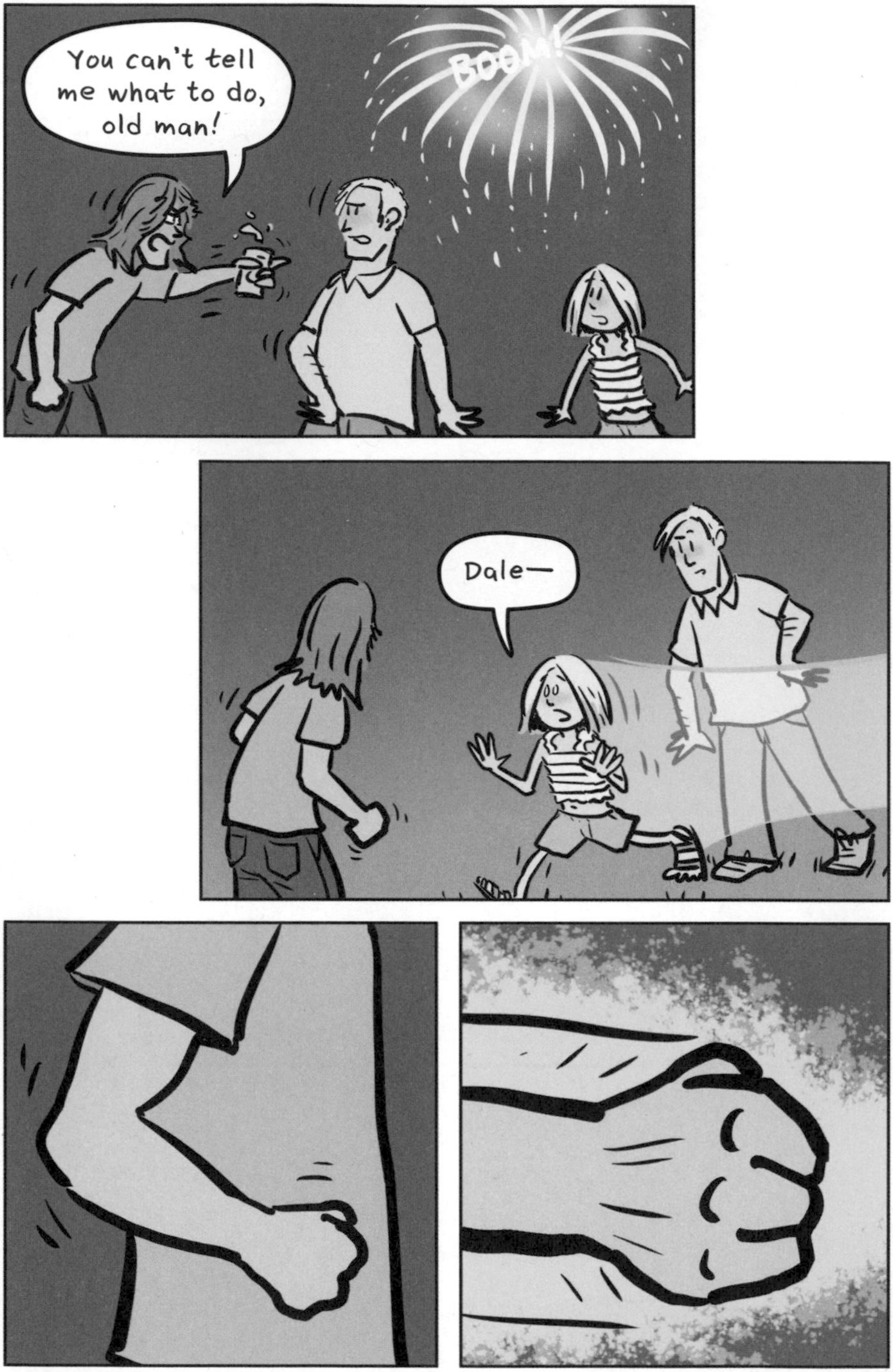
You can't tell me what to do, old man!
BOOM!
Dale—

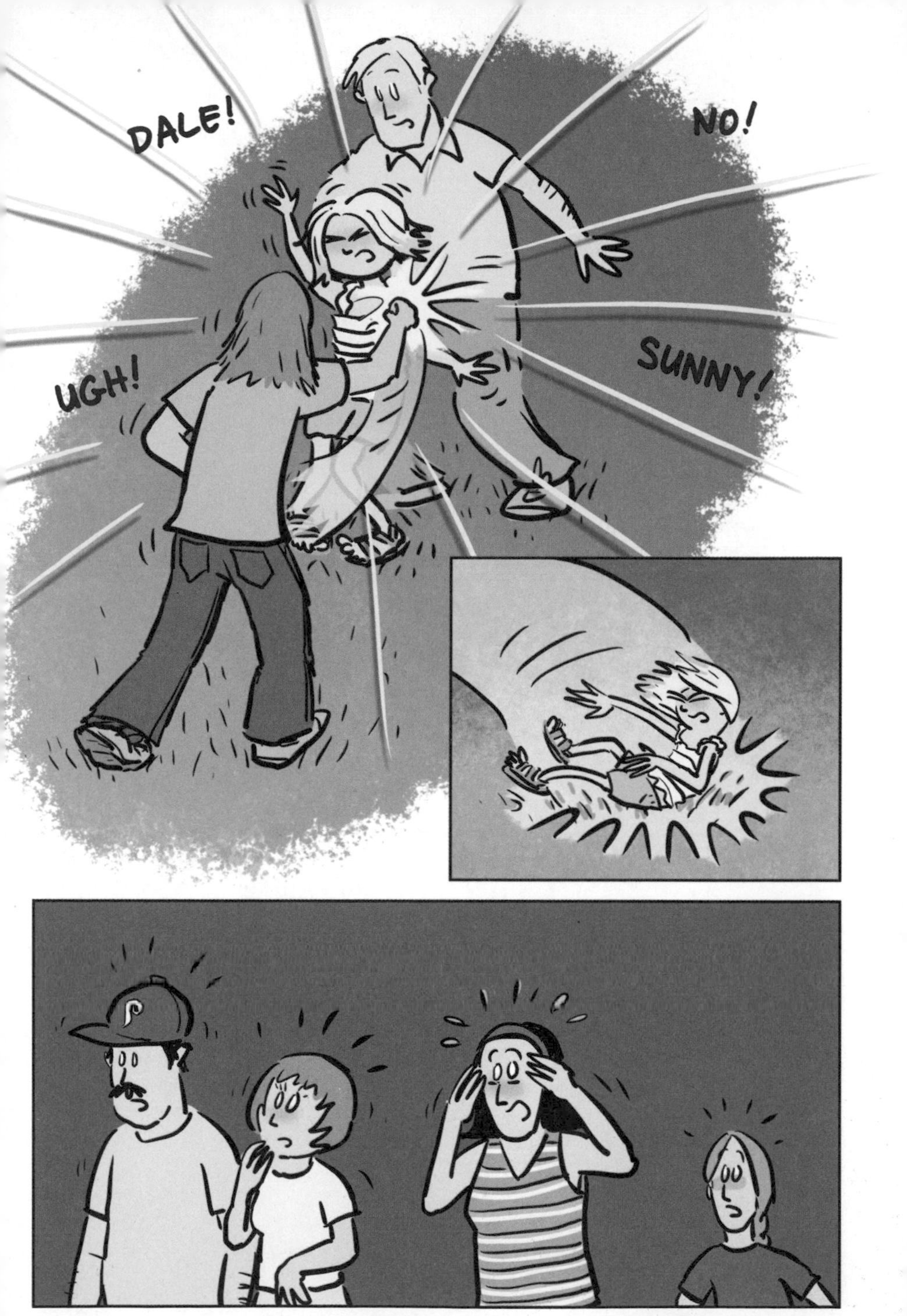
DALE!
NO!
UGH!
SUNNY!

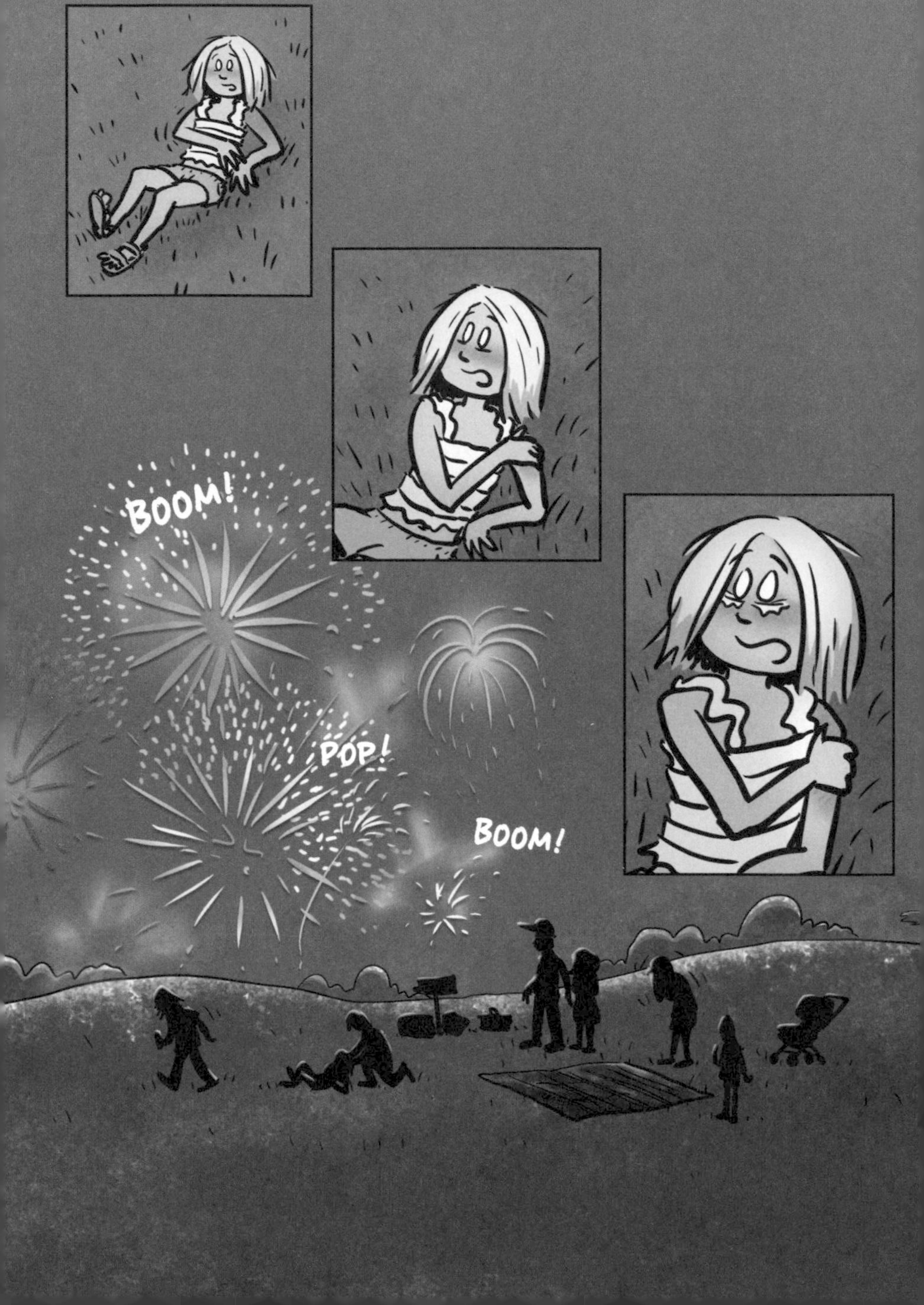
BOOM!
POP!
BOOM!

CHAPTER TWENTY: Volcano

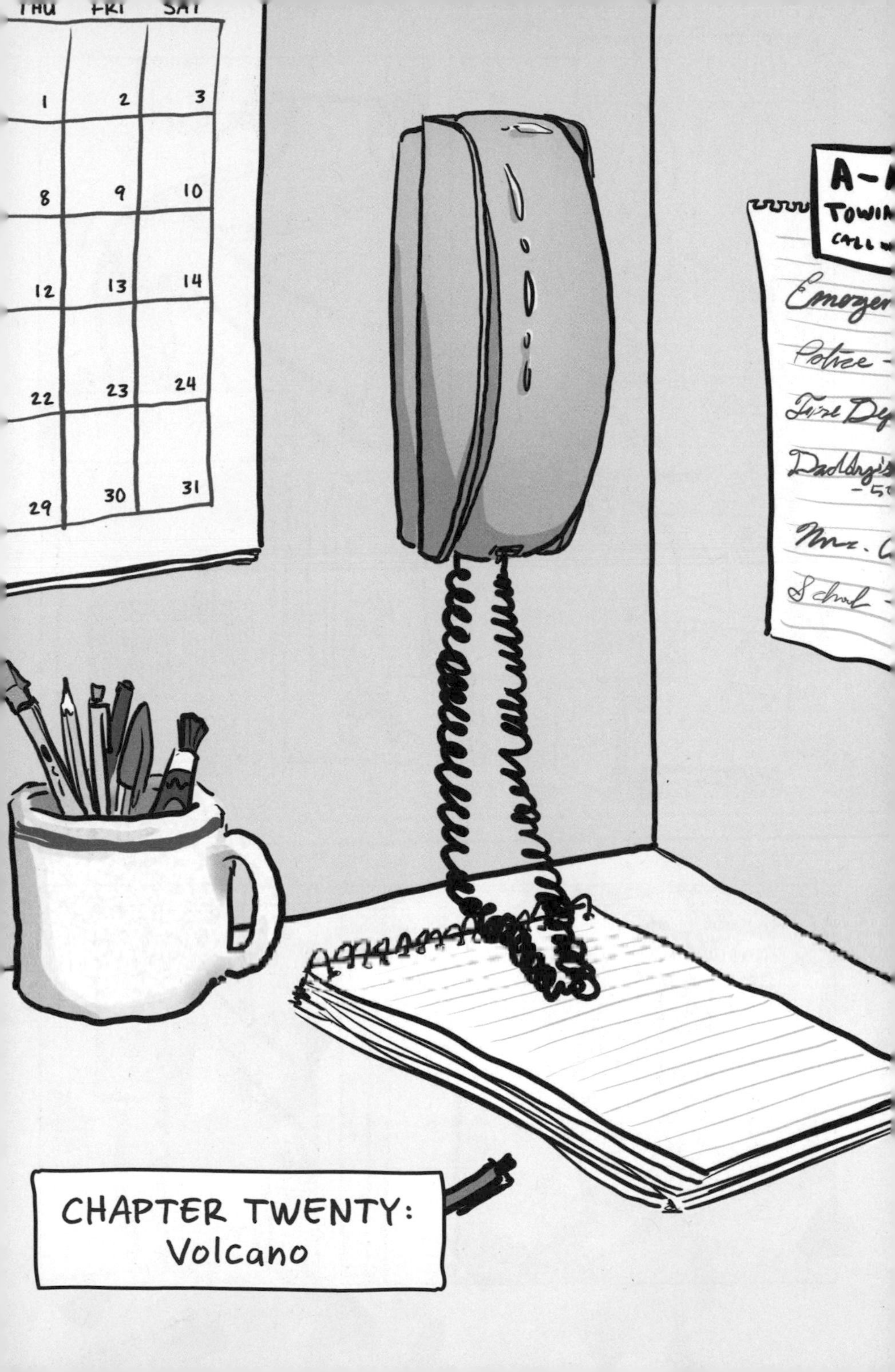
THU FRI SAT
1 2 3
8 9 10
12 13 14
22 23 24
29 30 31

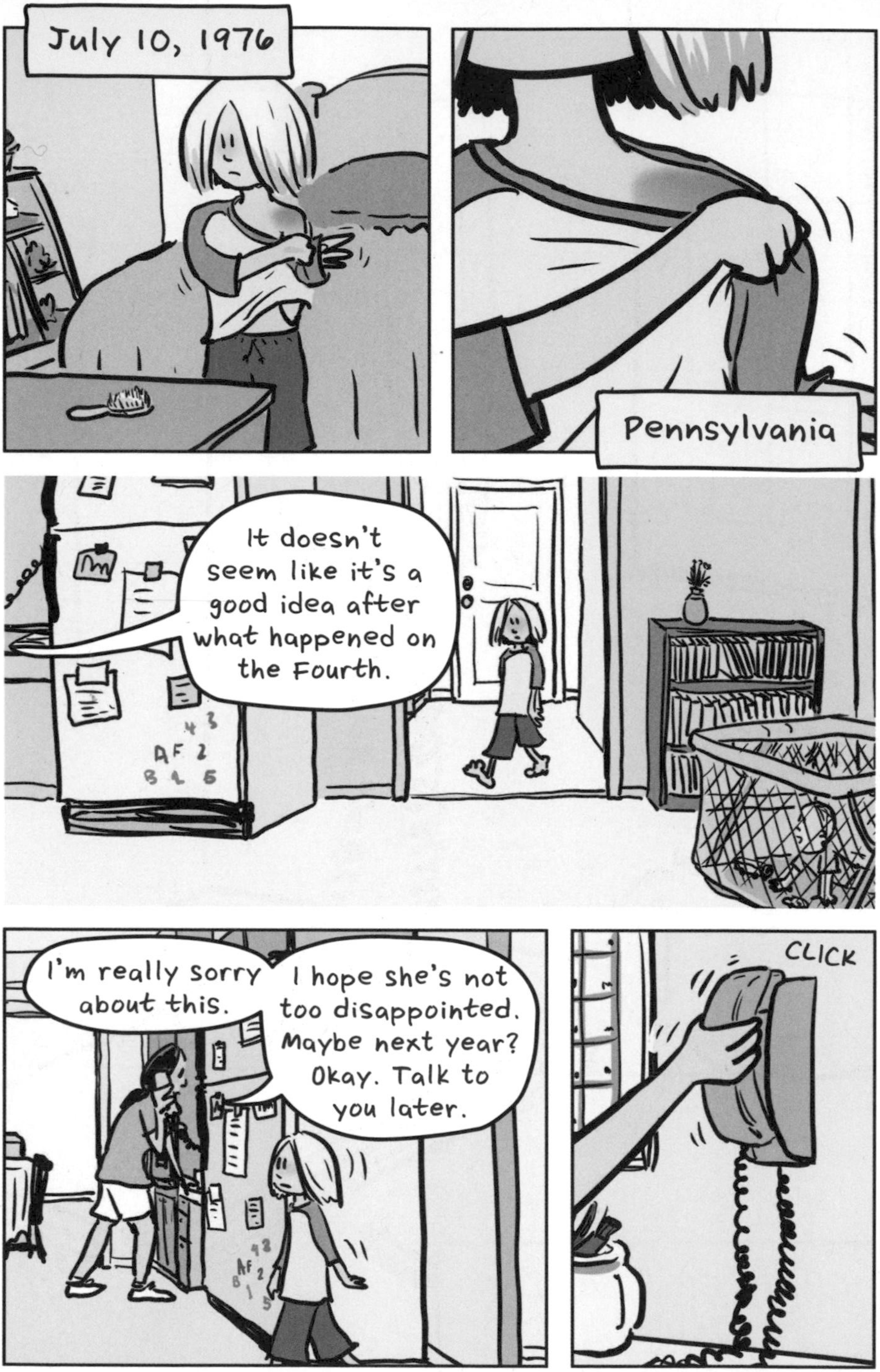
July 10, 1976
Pennsylvania
It doesn't seem like it's a good idea after what happened on the Fourth.
I'm really sorry about this.
I hope she's not too disappointed. Maybe next year? Okay. Talk to you later.
CLICK

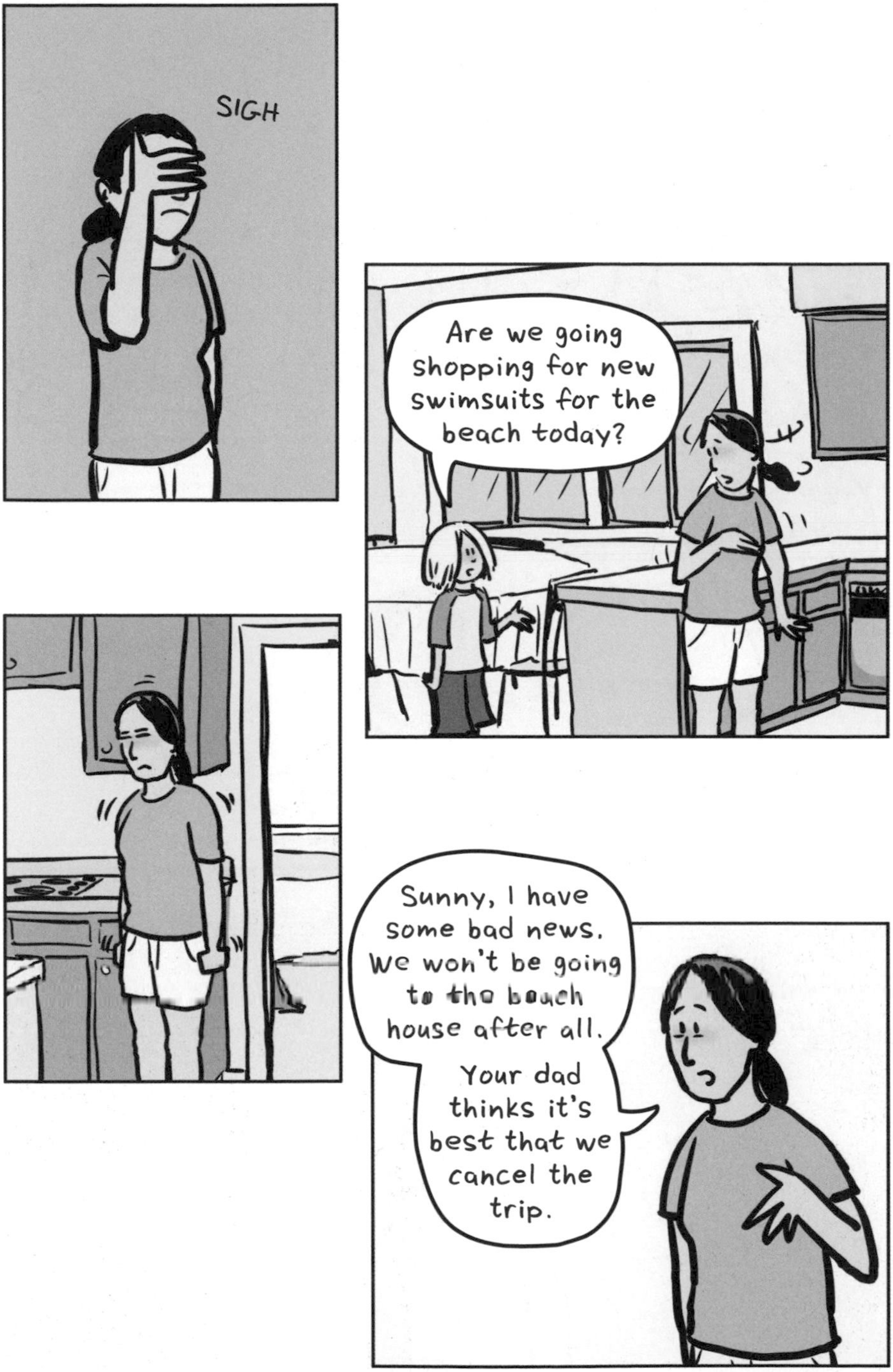
SIGH
Are we going shopping for new swimsuits for the beach today?
Sunny, I have some bad news. We won't be going to the beach house after all.
Your dad thinks it's best that we cancel the trip.

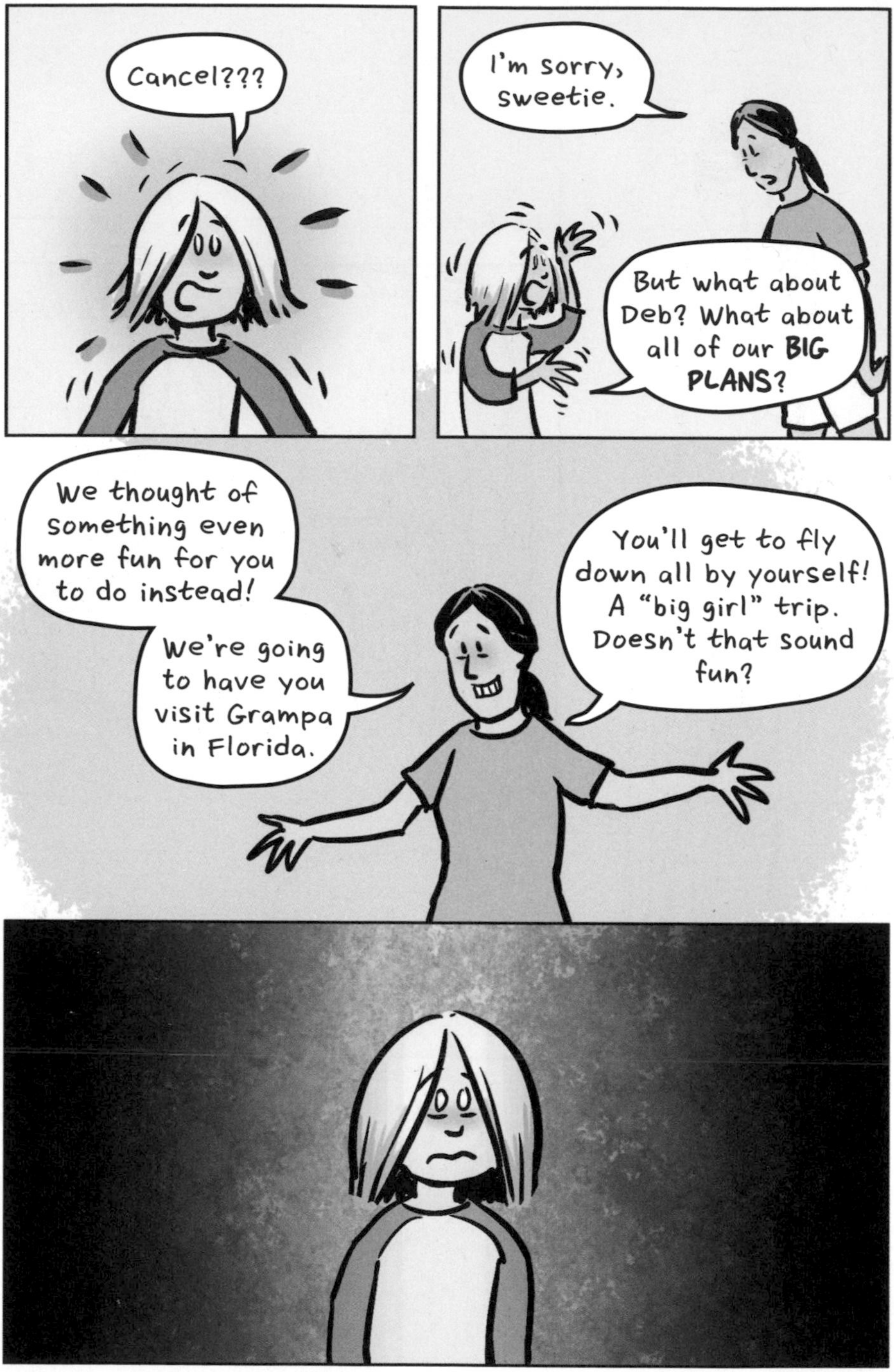
Cancel???
I'm sorry, sweetie.
But what about Deb? What about all of our **BIG PLANS**?
We thought of something even more fun for you to do instead!
We're going to have you visit Grampa in Florida.
You'll get to fly down all by yourself! A "big girl" trip. Doesn't that sound fun?

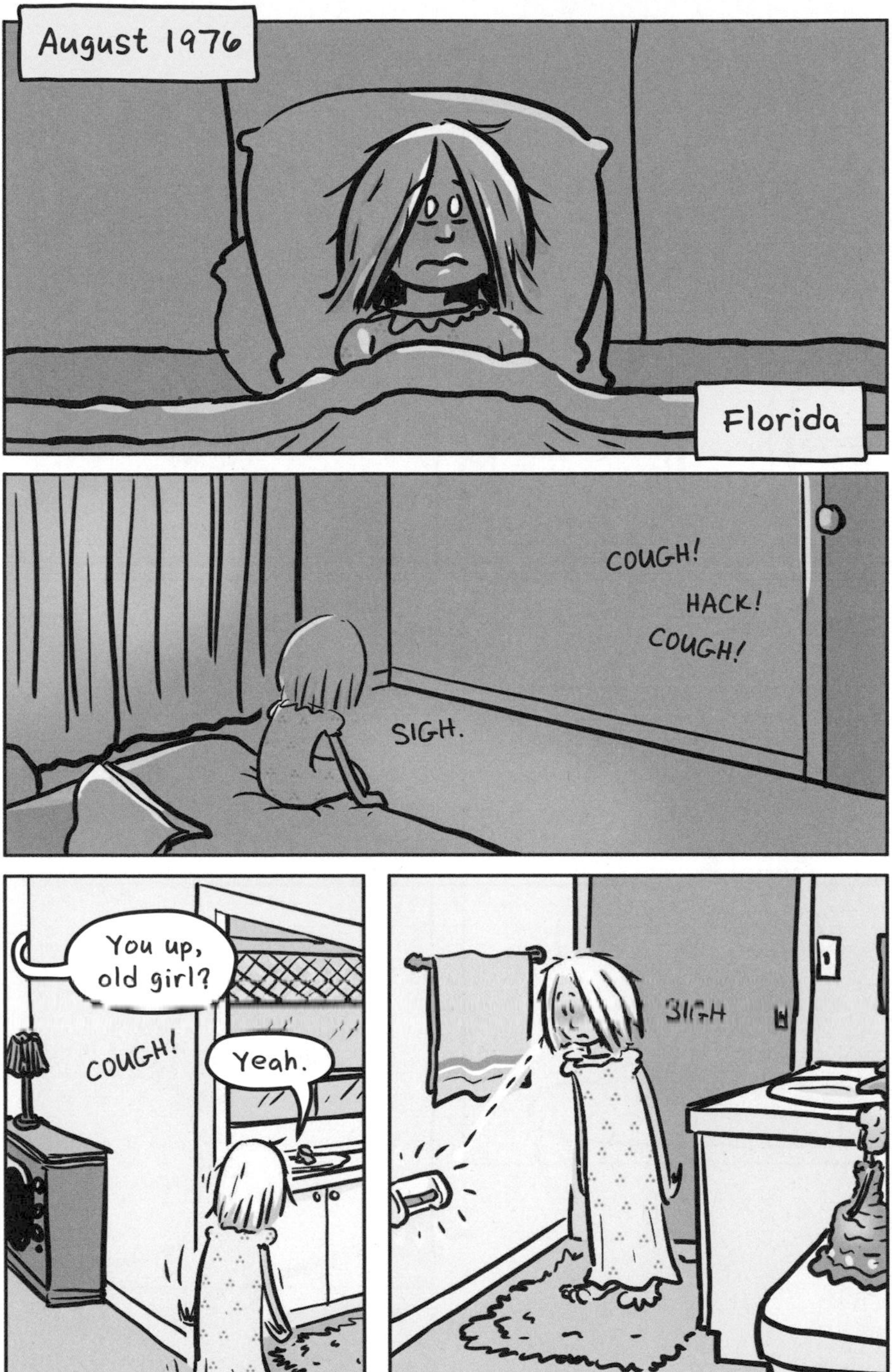
August 1976
Florida
COUGH!
HACK!
COUGH!
SIGH.
You up, old girl?
COUGH!
Yeah.
SIGH

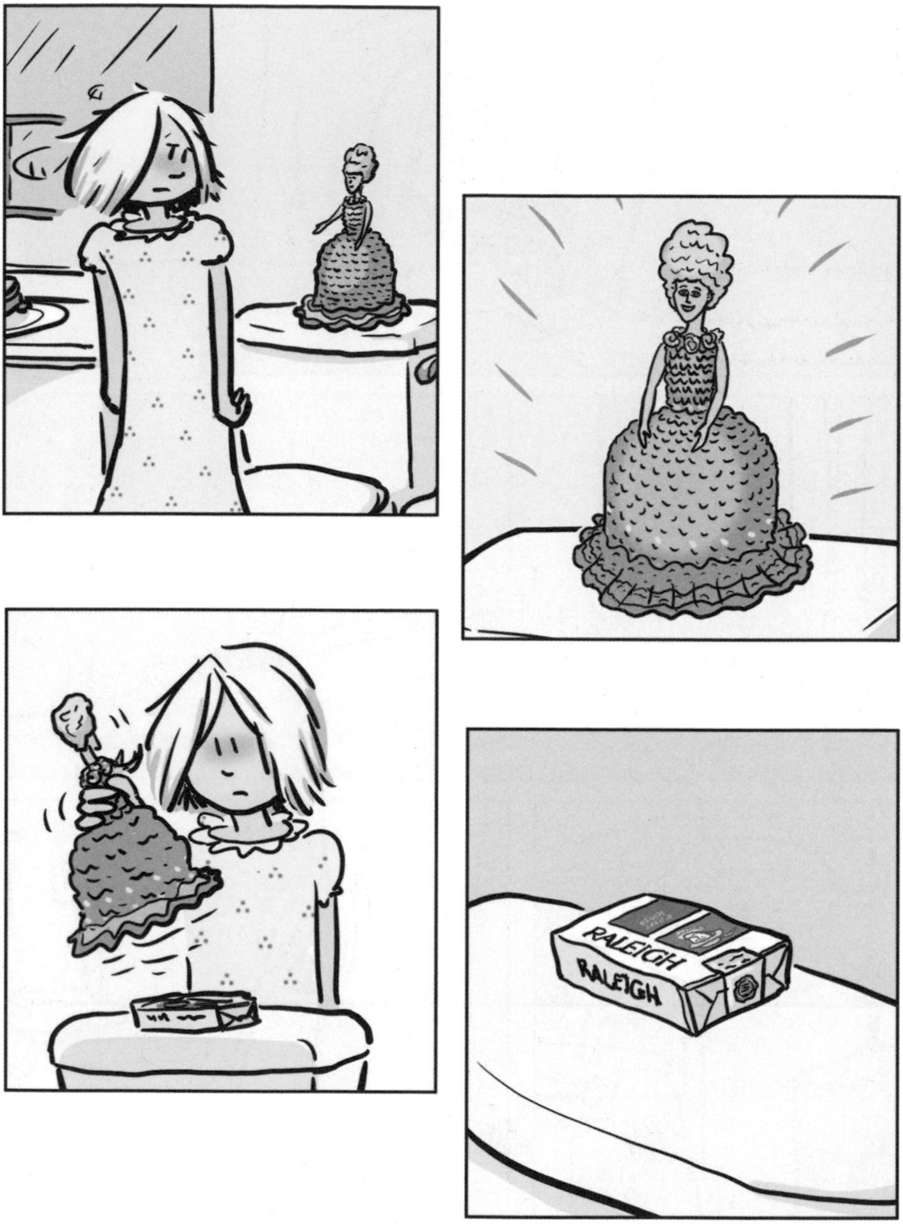
RALEIGH
RALEIGH

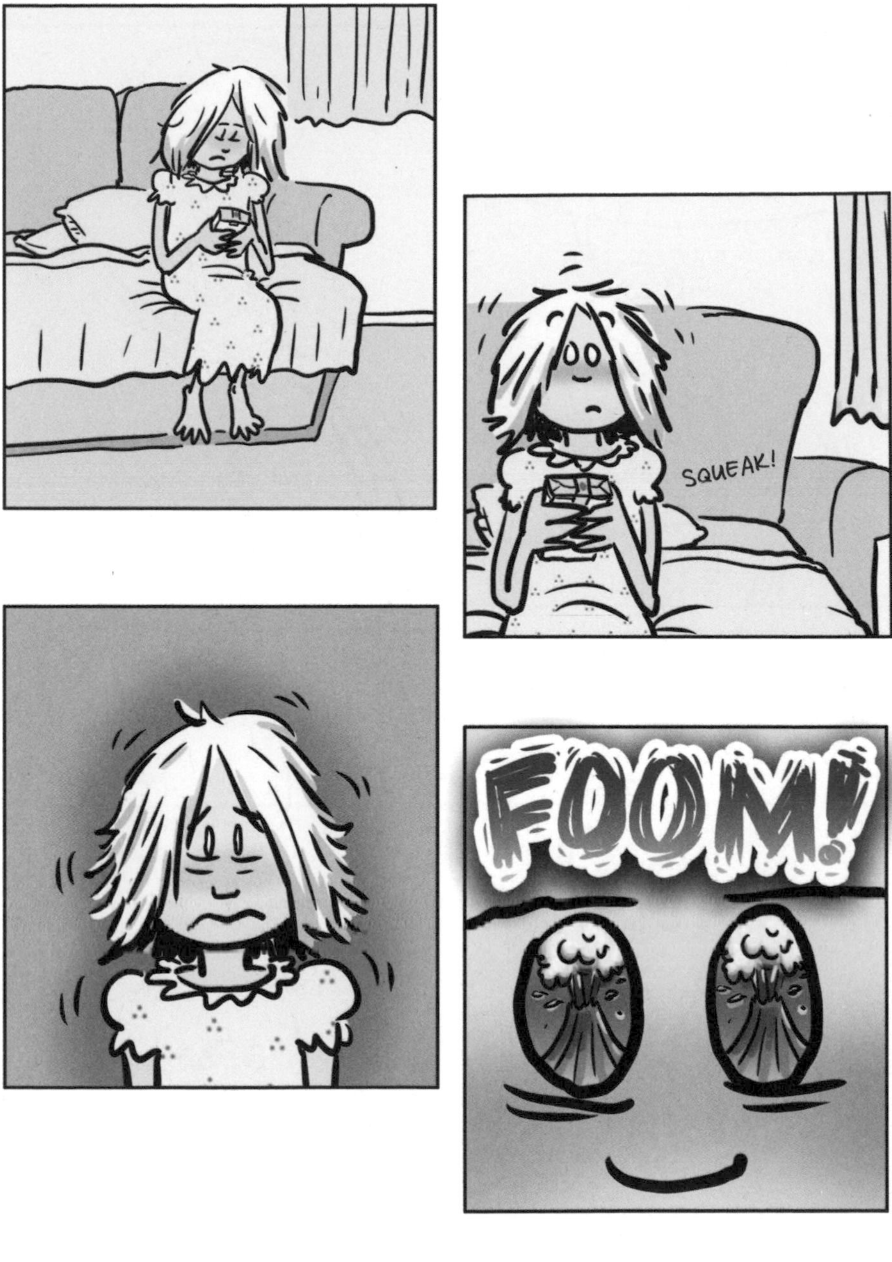
SQUEAK!
FOOM!

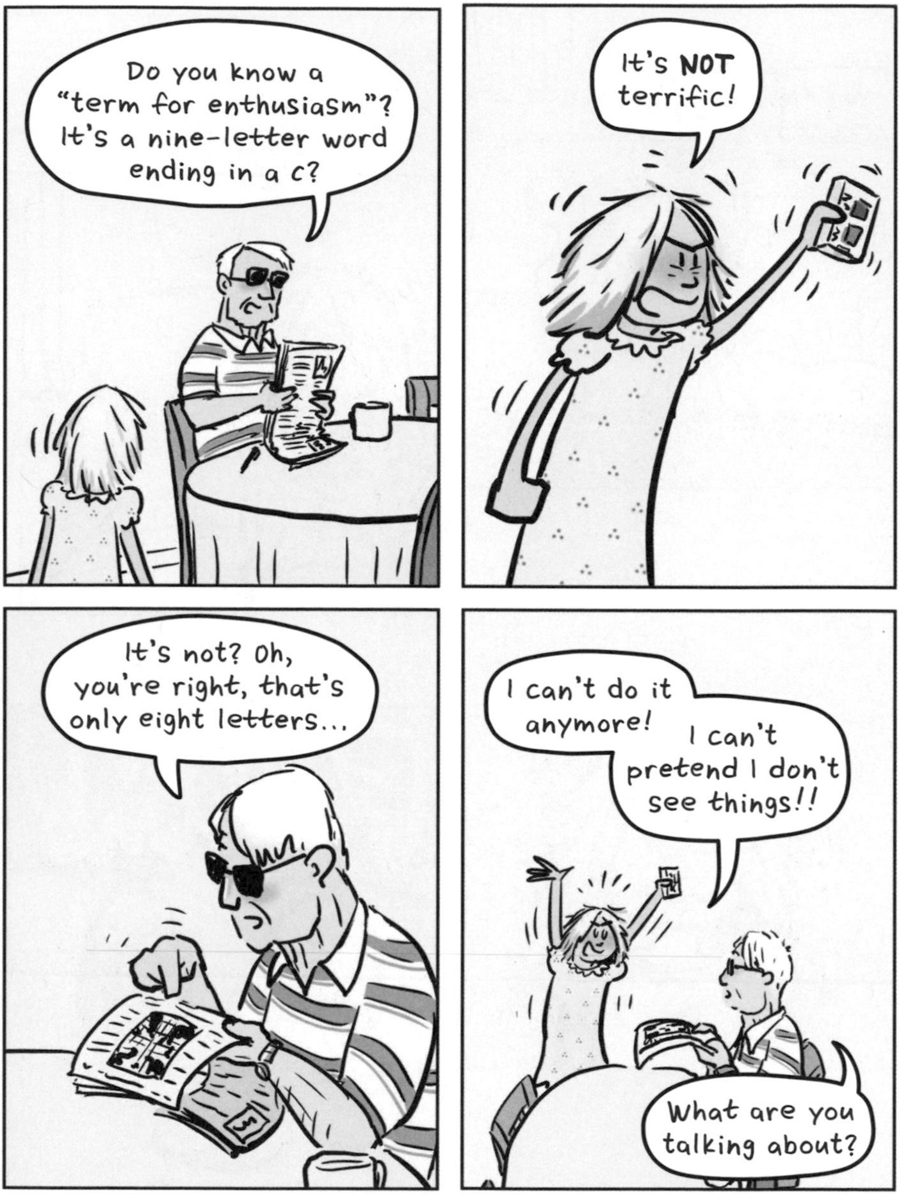
Do you know a "term for enthusiasm"? It's a nine-letter word ending in a c?
It's **NOT** terrific!
It's not? Oh, you're right, that's only eight letters...
I can't do it anymore!
I can't pretend I don't see things!!
What are you talking about?

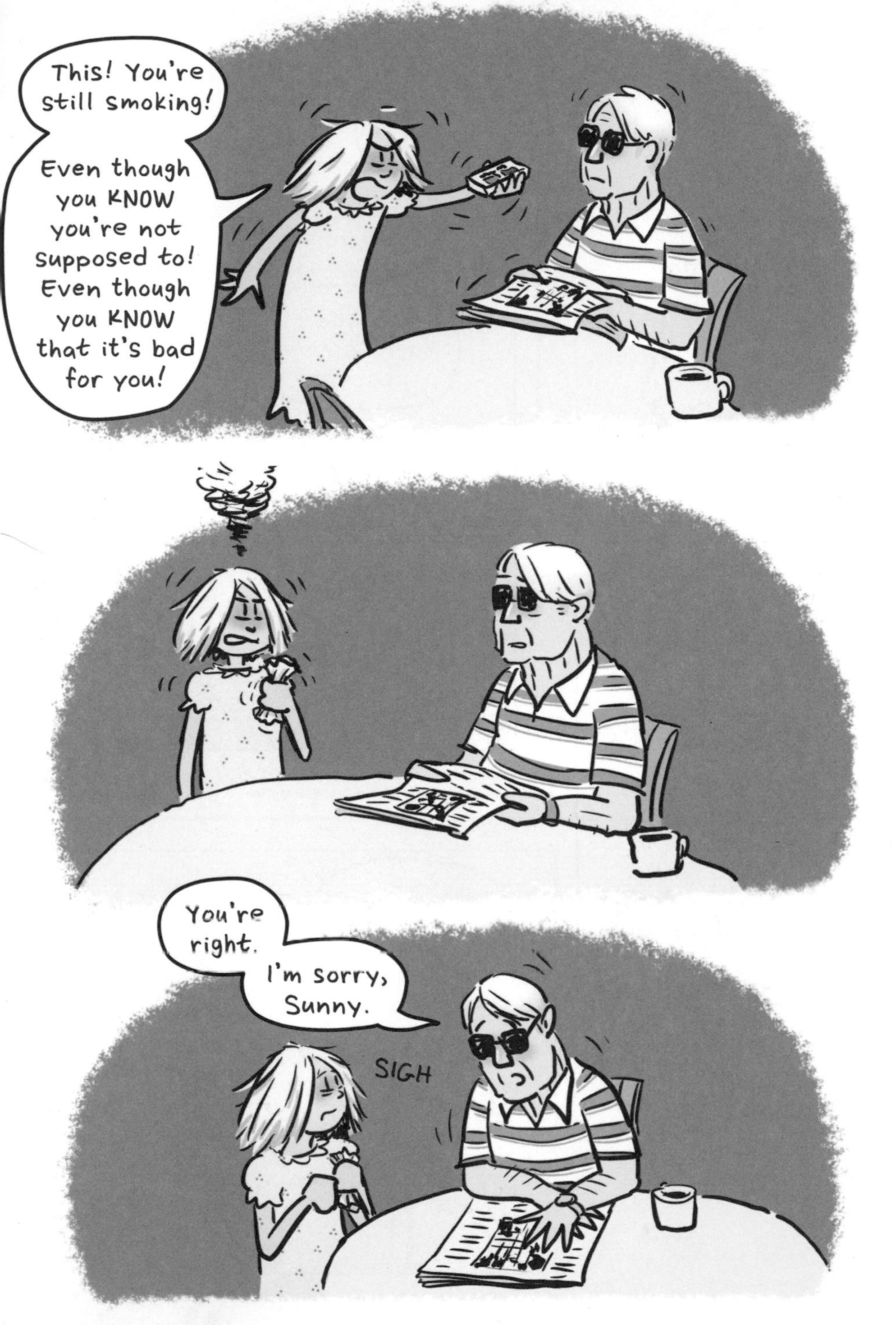
This! You're still smoking!
Even though you KNOW you're not supposed to! Even though you KNOW that it's bad for you!
You're right.
I'm sorry, Sunny.
SIGH

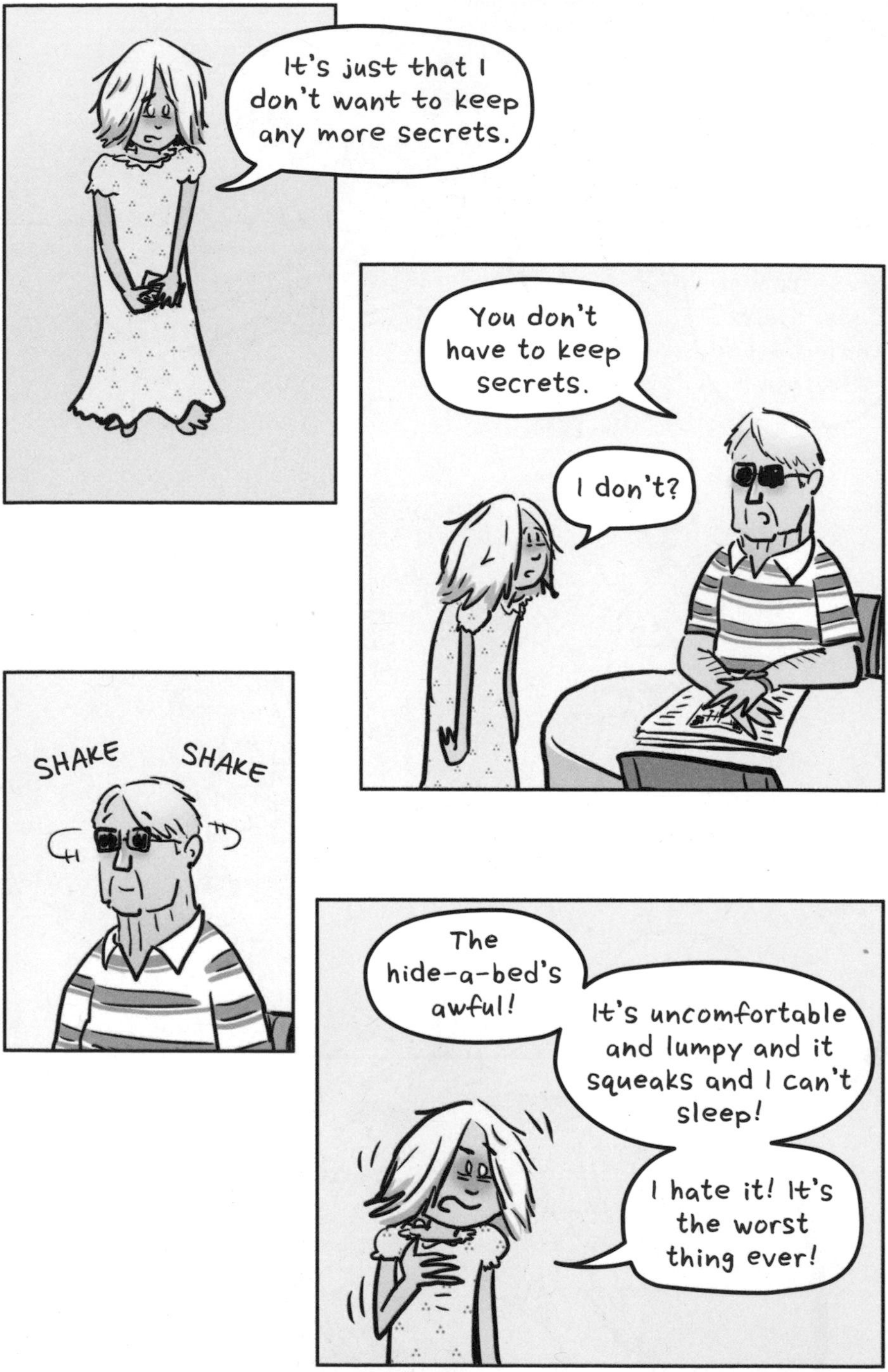
It's just that I don't want to keep any more secrets.
You don't have to keep secrets.
I don't?
SHAKE
SHAKE
The hide-a-bed's awful!
It's uncomfortable and lumpy and it squeaks and I can't sleep!
I hate it! It's the worst thing ever!

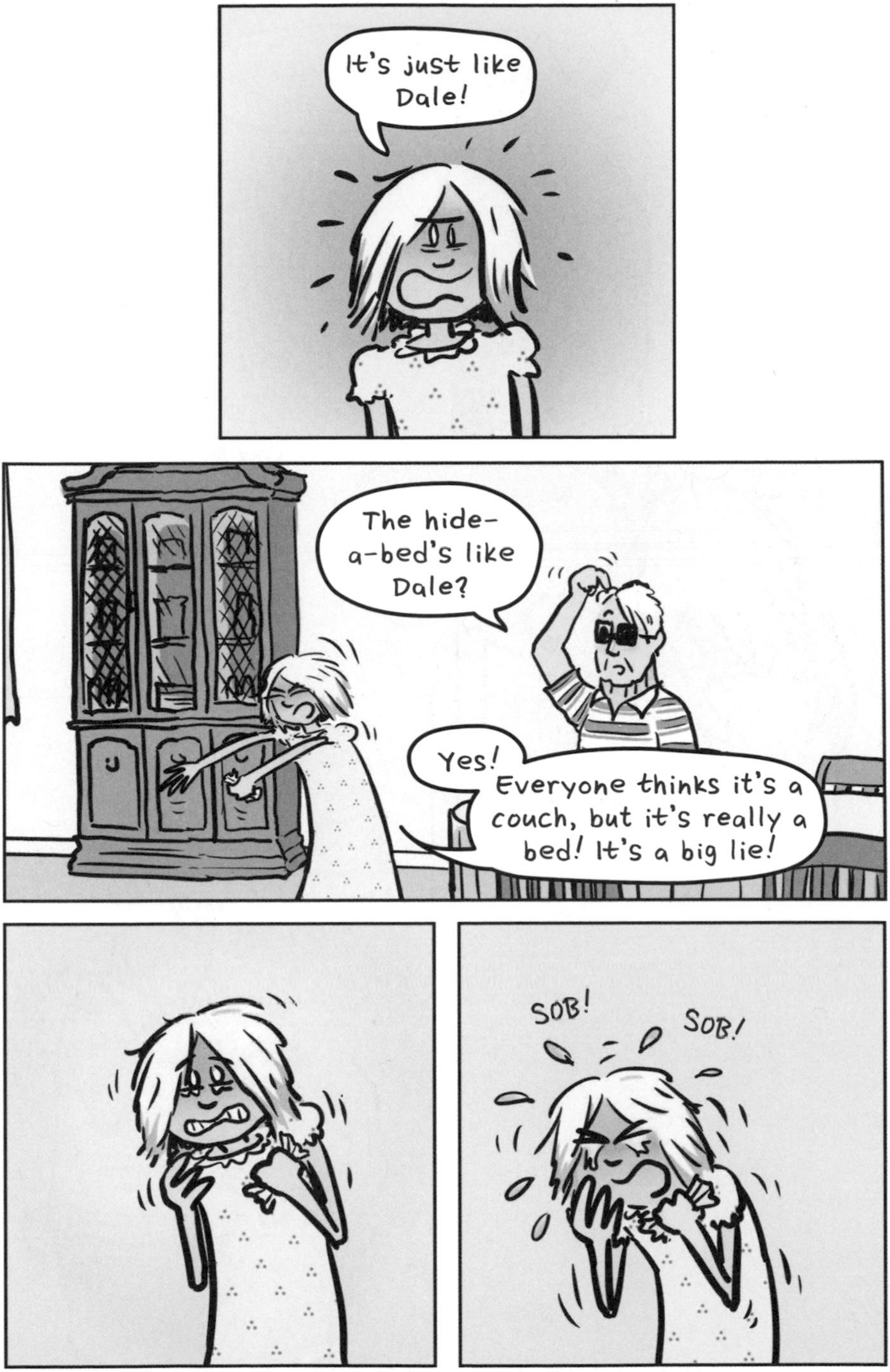
It's just like Dale!
The hide-a-bed's like Dale?
Yes! Everyone thinks it's a couch, but it's really a bed! It's a big lie!
SOB!
SOB!

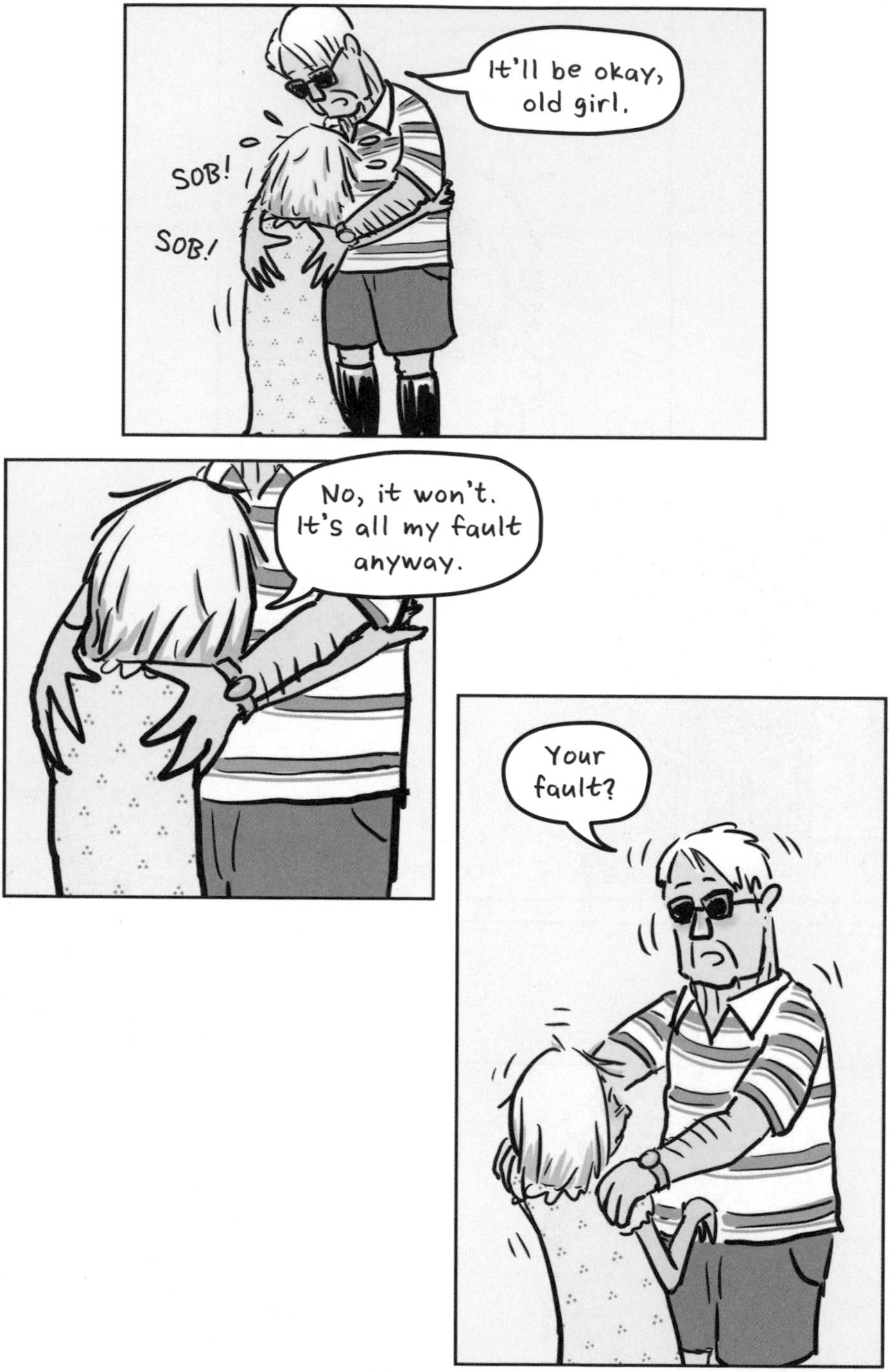
It'll be okay, old girl.
SOB!
SOB!
No, it won't. It's all my fault anyway.
Your fault?

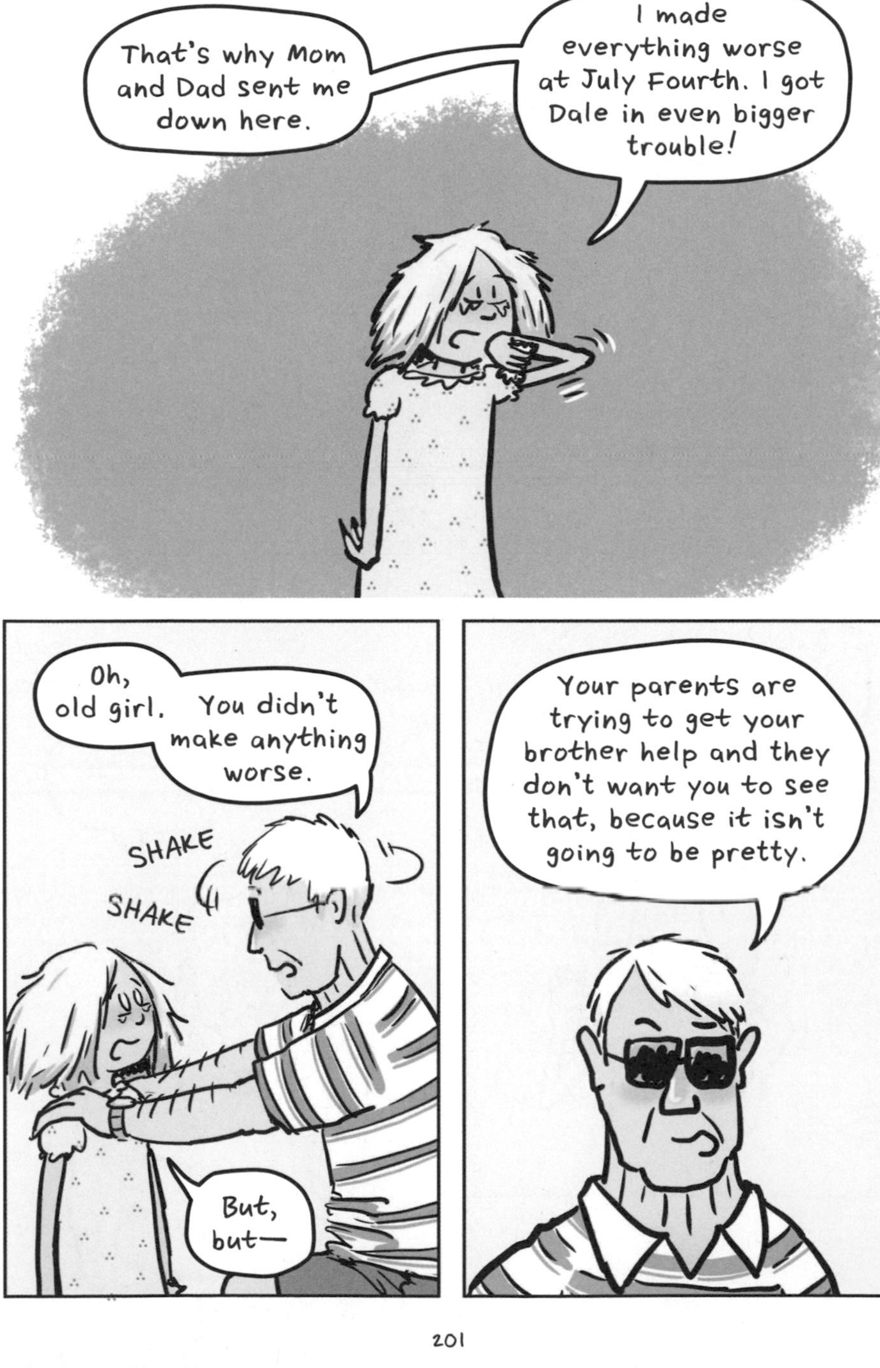
That's why Mom and Dad sent me down here.
I made everything worse at July Fourth. I got Dale in even bigger trouble!
Oh, old girl. You didn't make anything worse.
SHAKE
SHAKE
But, but—
Your parents are trying to get your brother help and they don't want you to see that, because it isn't going to be pretty.

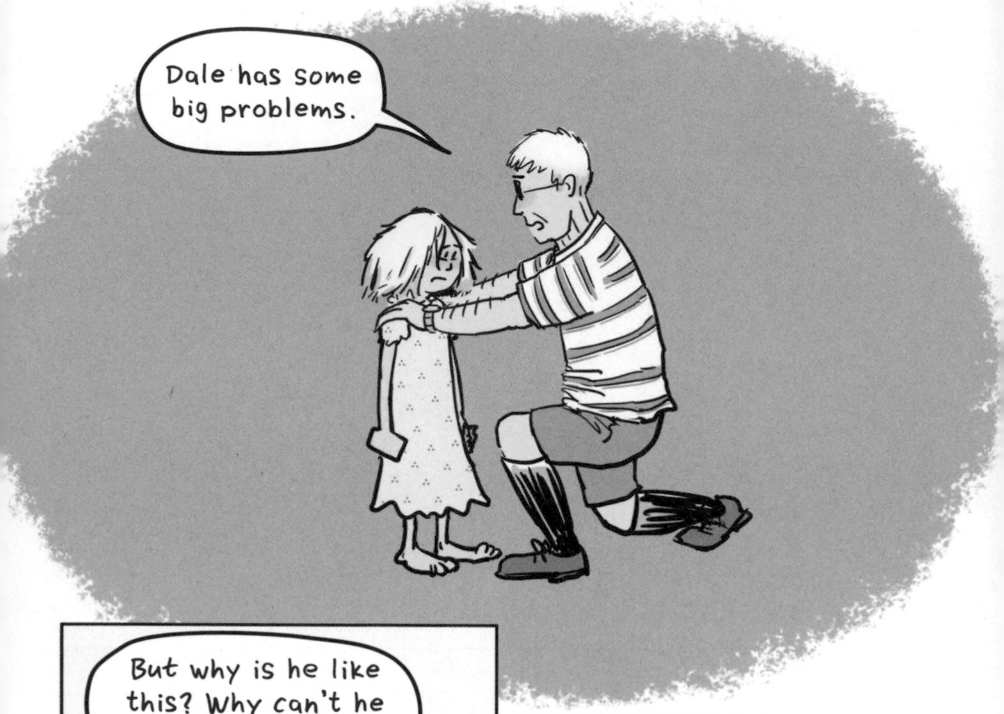
Dale has some big problems.

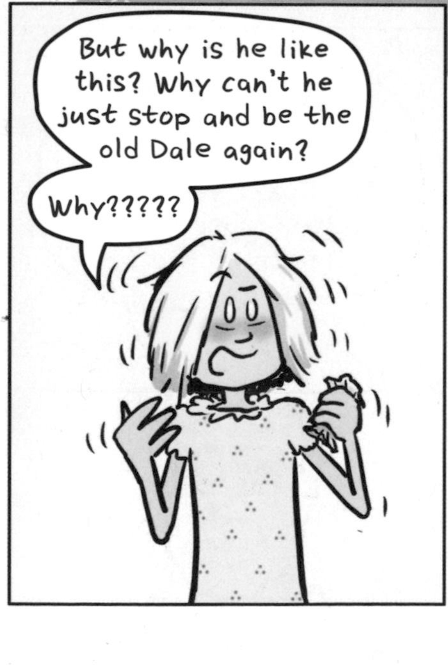
But why is he like this? Why can't he just stop and be the old Dale again?
Why?????

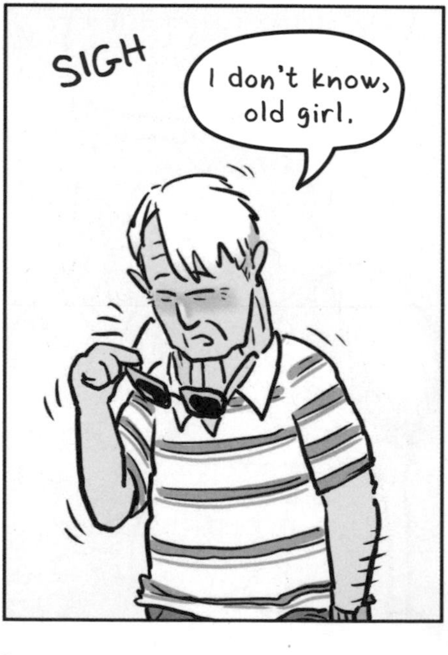
SIGH
I don't know, old girl.

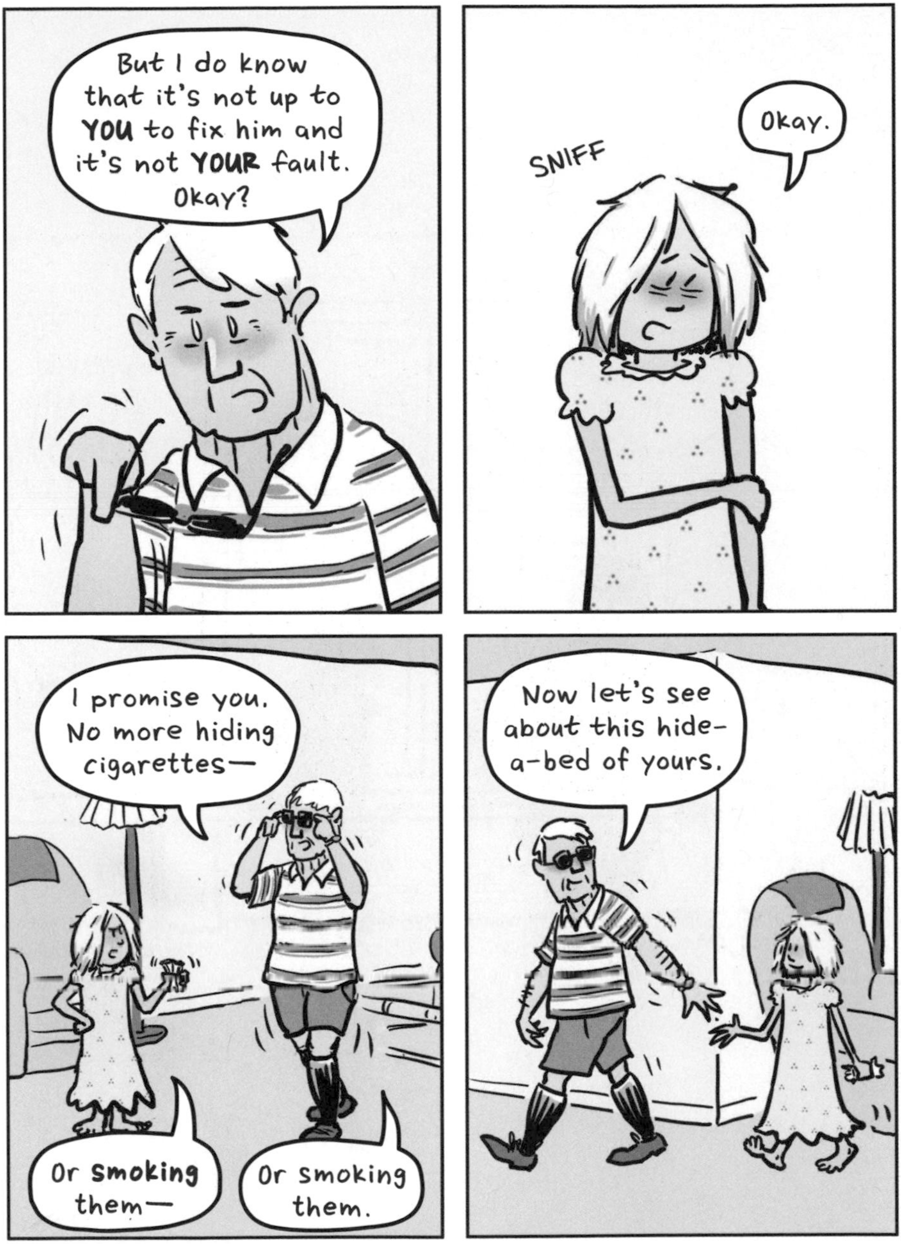
But I do know that it's not up to **YOU** to fix him and it's not **YOUR** fault. Okay?
SNIFF
Okay.
I promise you. No more hiding cigarettes—
Or **smoking** them—
Or smoking them.
Now let's see about this hide-a-bed of yours.

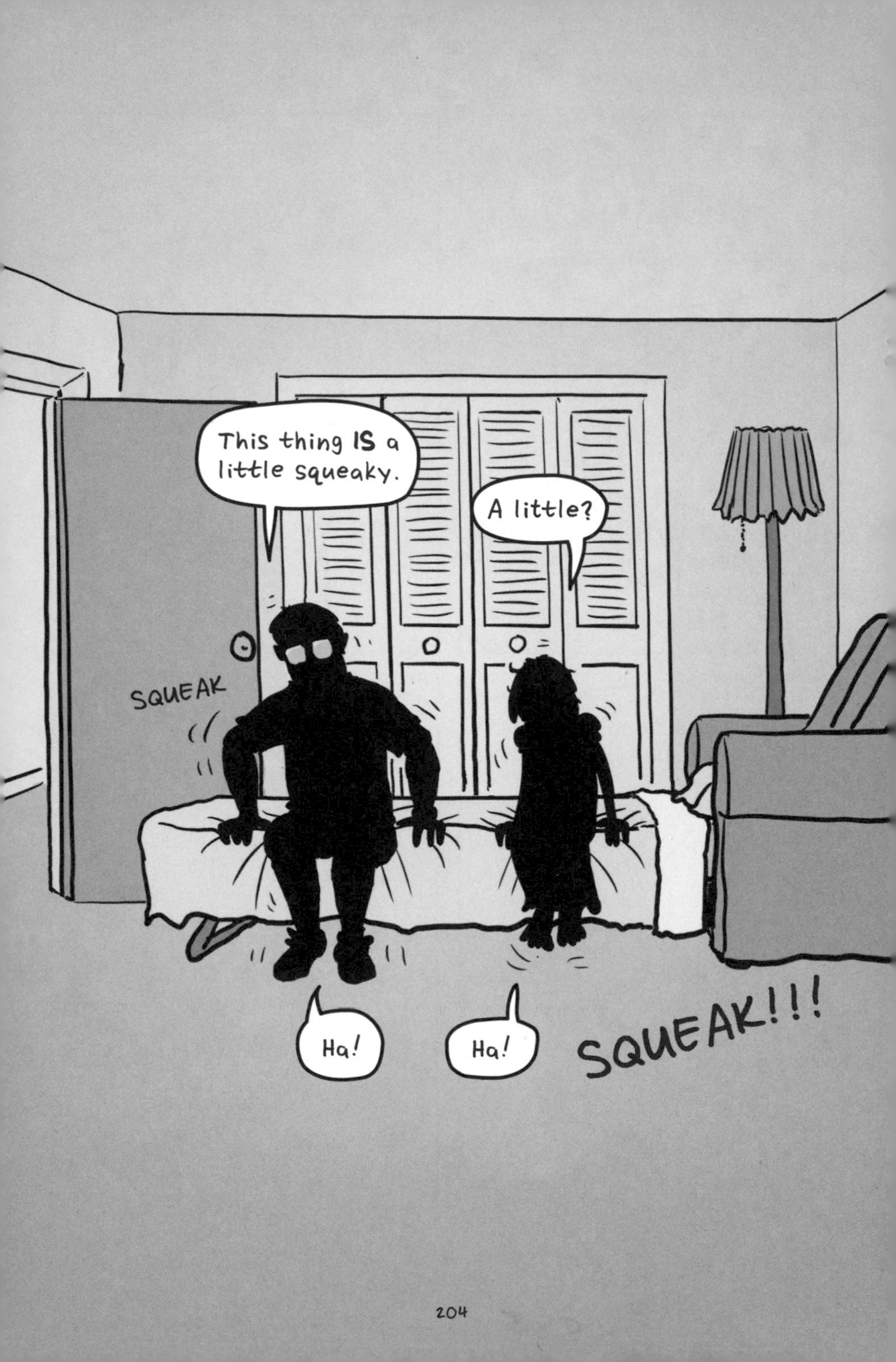
This thing IS a little squeaky.
A little?
SQUEAK
Ha!
Ha!
SQUEAK!!!

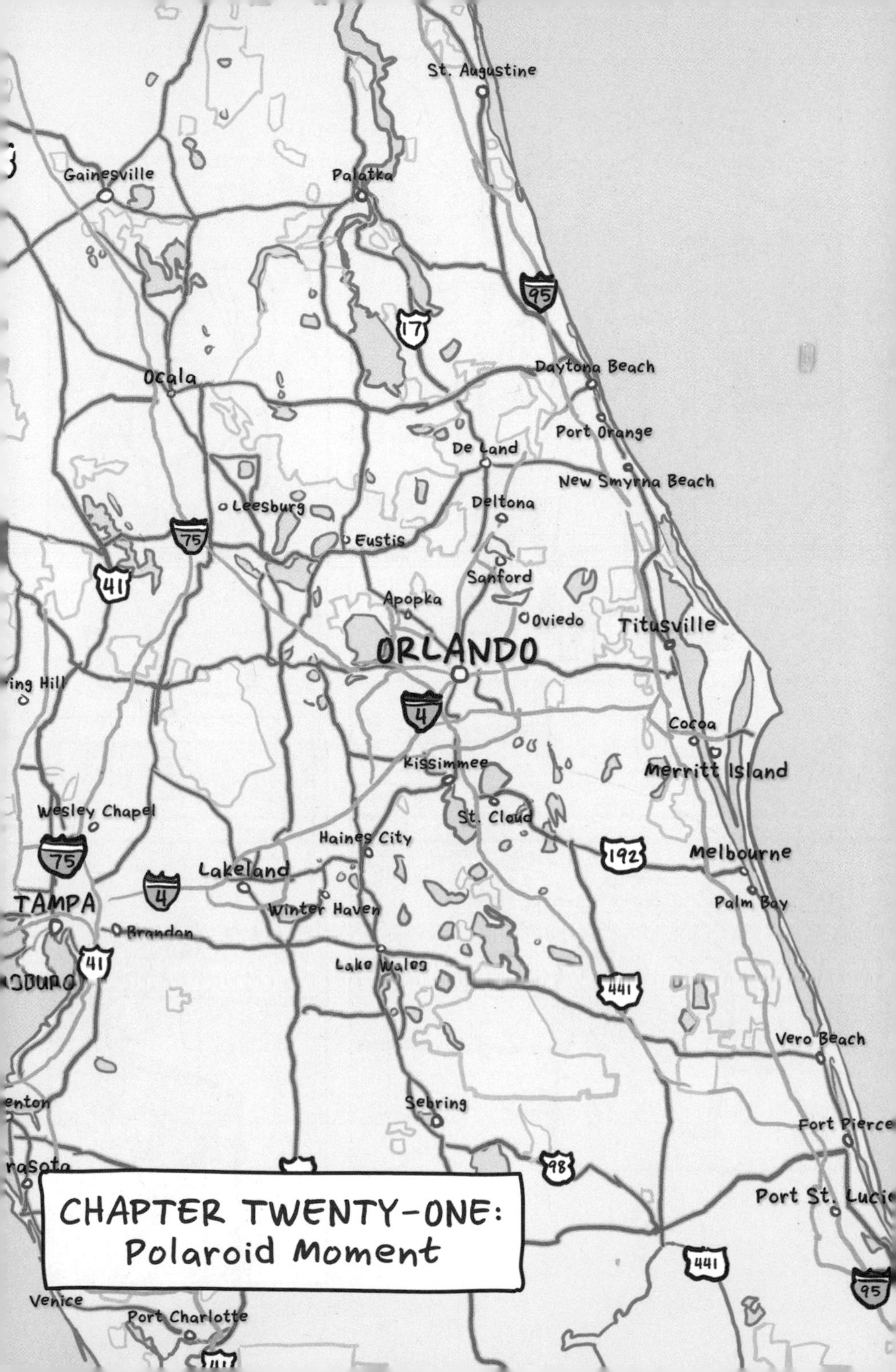
St. Augustine
Gainesville
Palatka
95
17
Ocala
Daytona Beach
Port Orange
De Land
New Smyrna Beach
Leesburg
Deltona
75
Eustis
41
Sanford
Apopka
Oviedo
Titusville
ORLANDO
ing Hill
4
Cocoa
Kissimmee
Merritt Island
Wesley Chapel
St. Cloud
Haines City
192
Melbourne
75
Lakeland
4
TAMPA
Winter Haven
Palm Bay
Brandon
41
Lake Wales
441
Vero Beach
Sebring
enton
Fort Pierce
rasota
98
Port St. Luci
441
95
Venice
Port Charlotte

CHAPTER TWENTY-ONE: Polaroid Moment

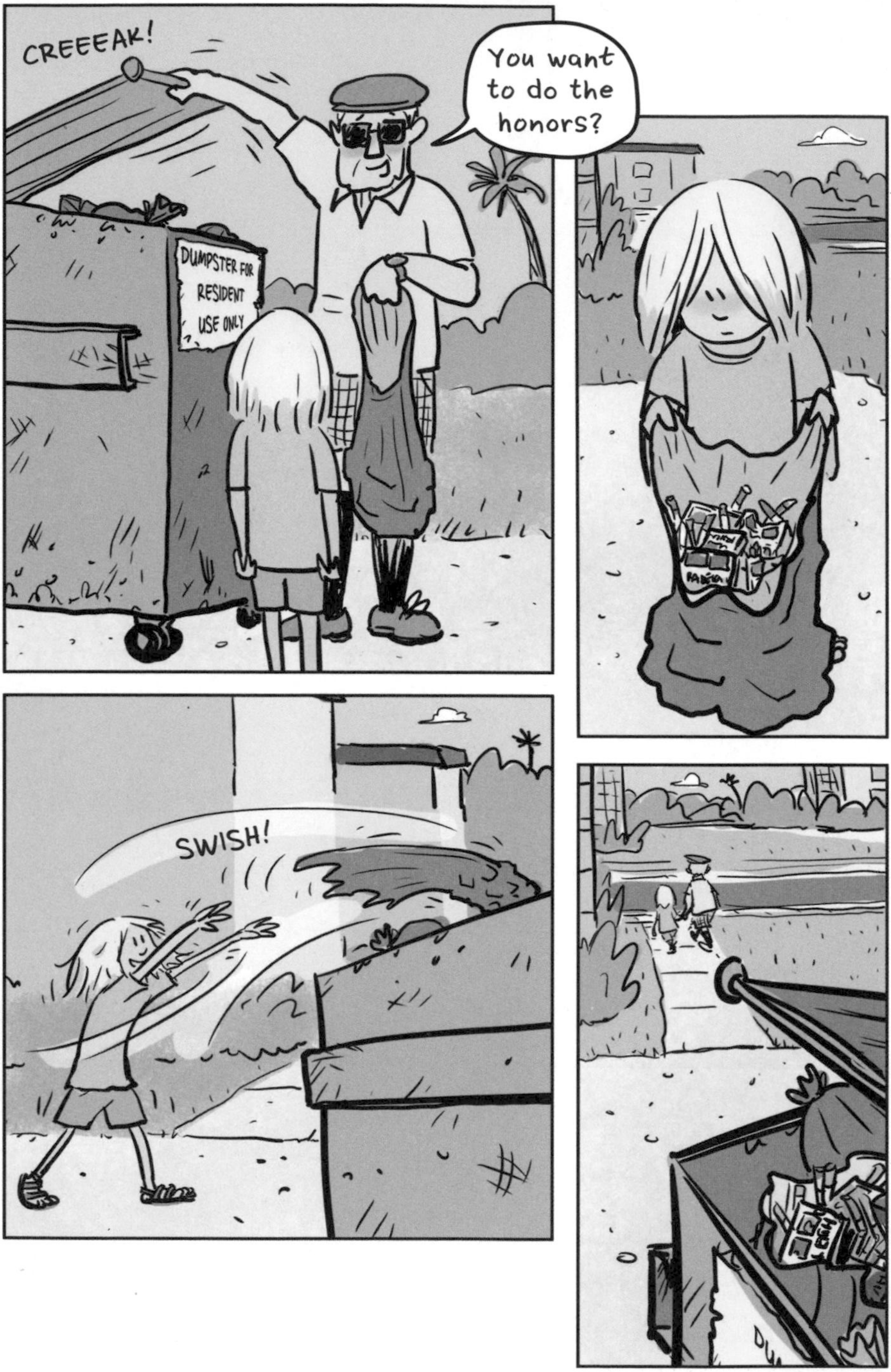
CREEEAK!
You want to do the honors?
DUMPSTER FOR RESIDENT USE ONLY
SWISH!

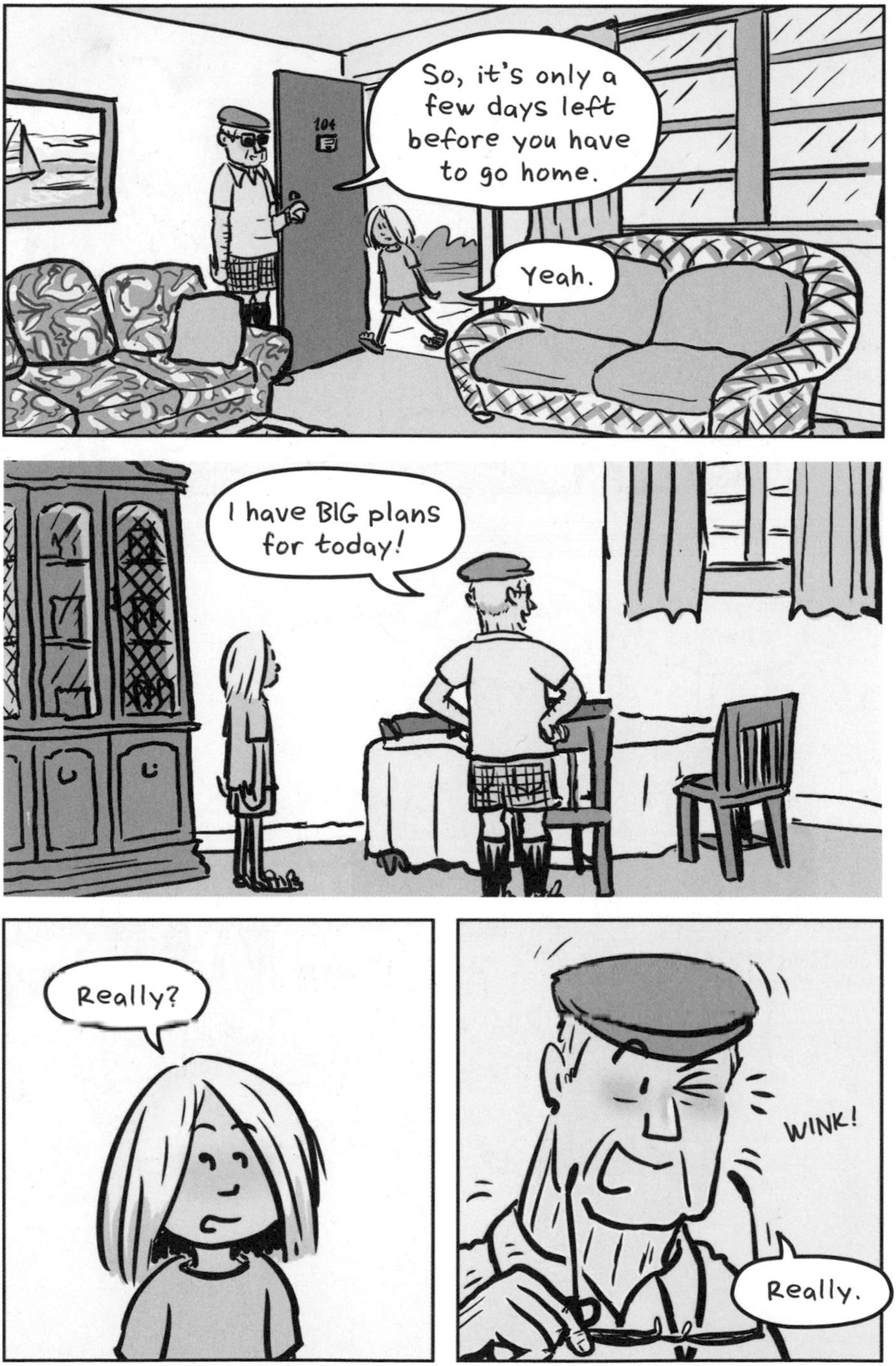
So, it's only a few days left before you have to go home.
Yeah.
104
I have BIG plans for today!
Really?
WINK!
Really.

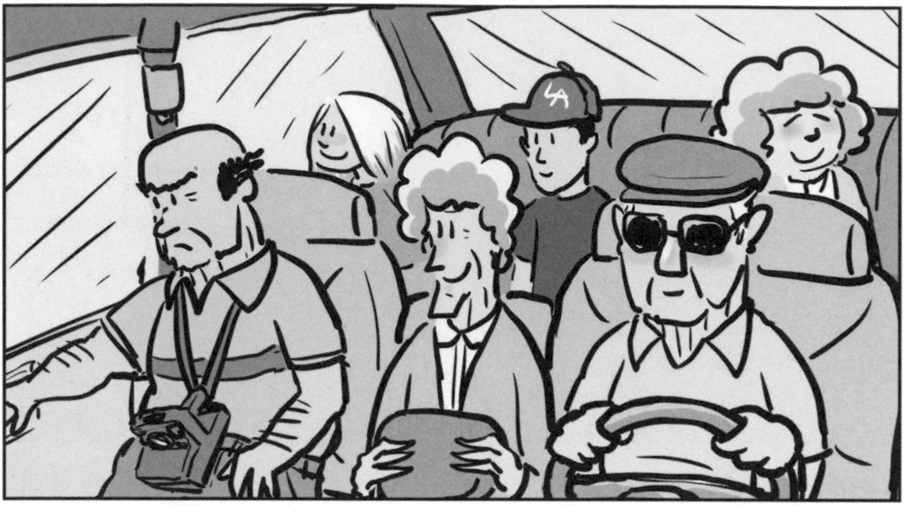

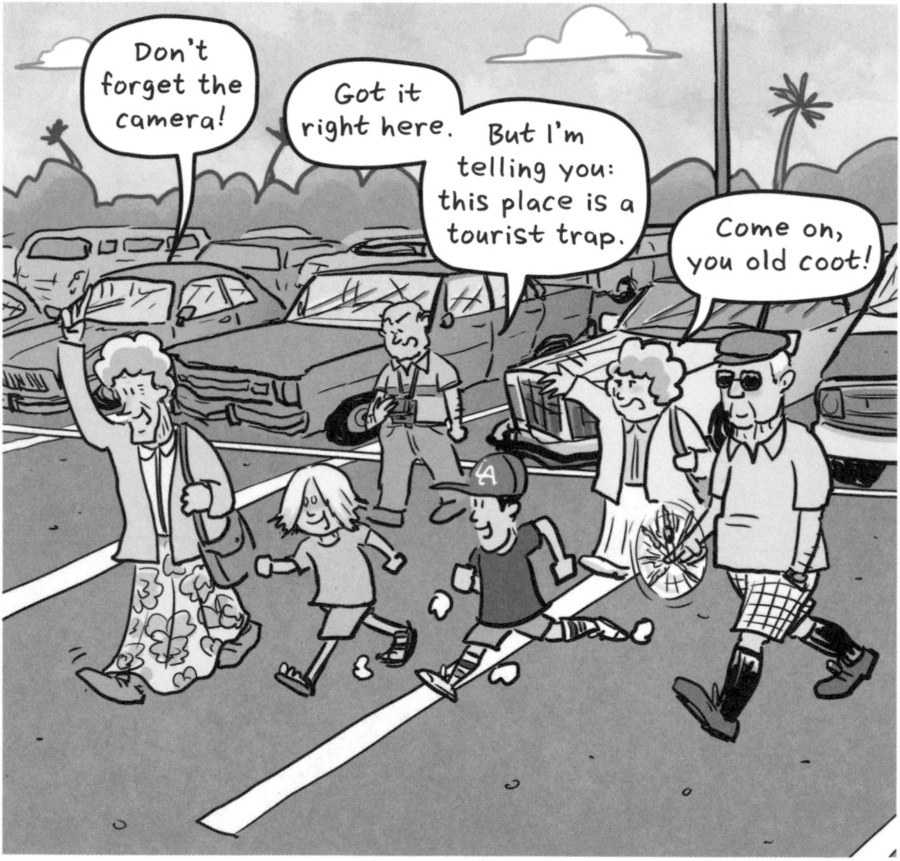
Don't forget the camera!
Got it right here.
But I'm telling you: this place is a tourist trap.
Come on, you old coot!

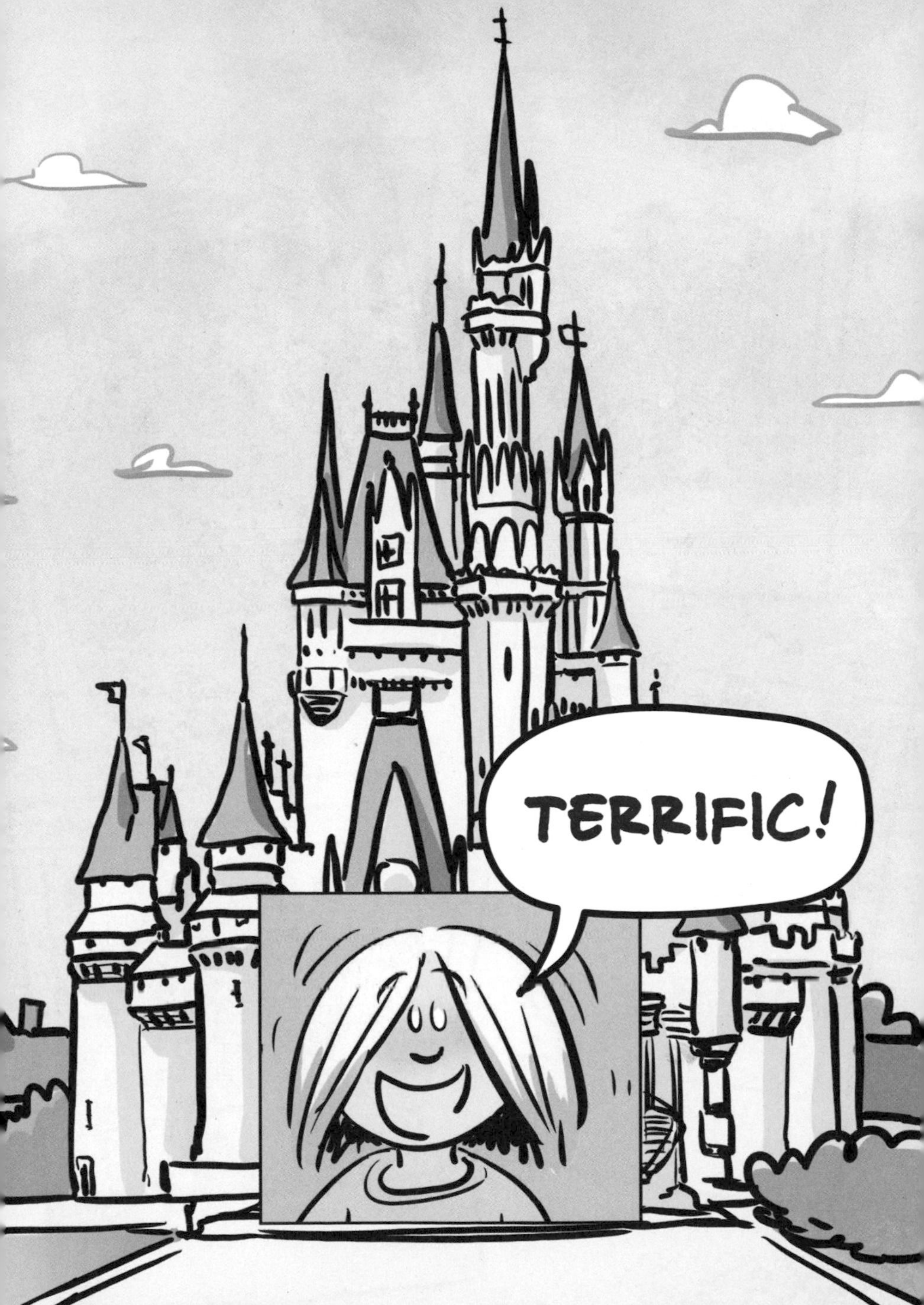
TERRIFIC!

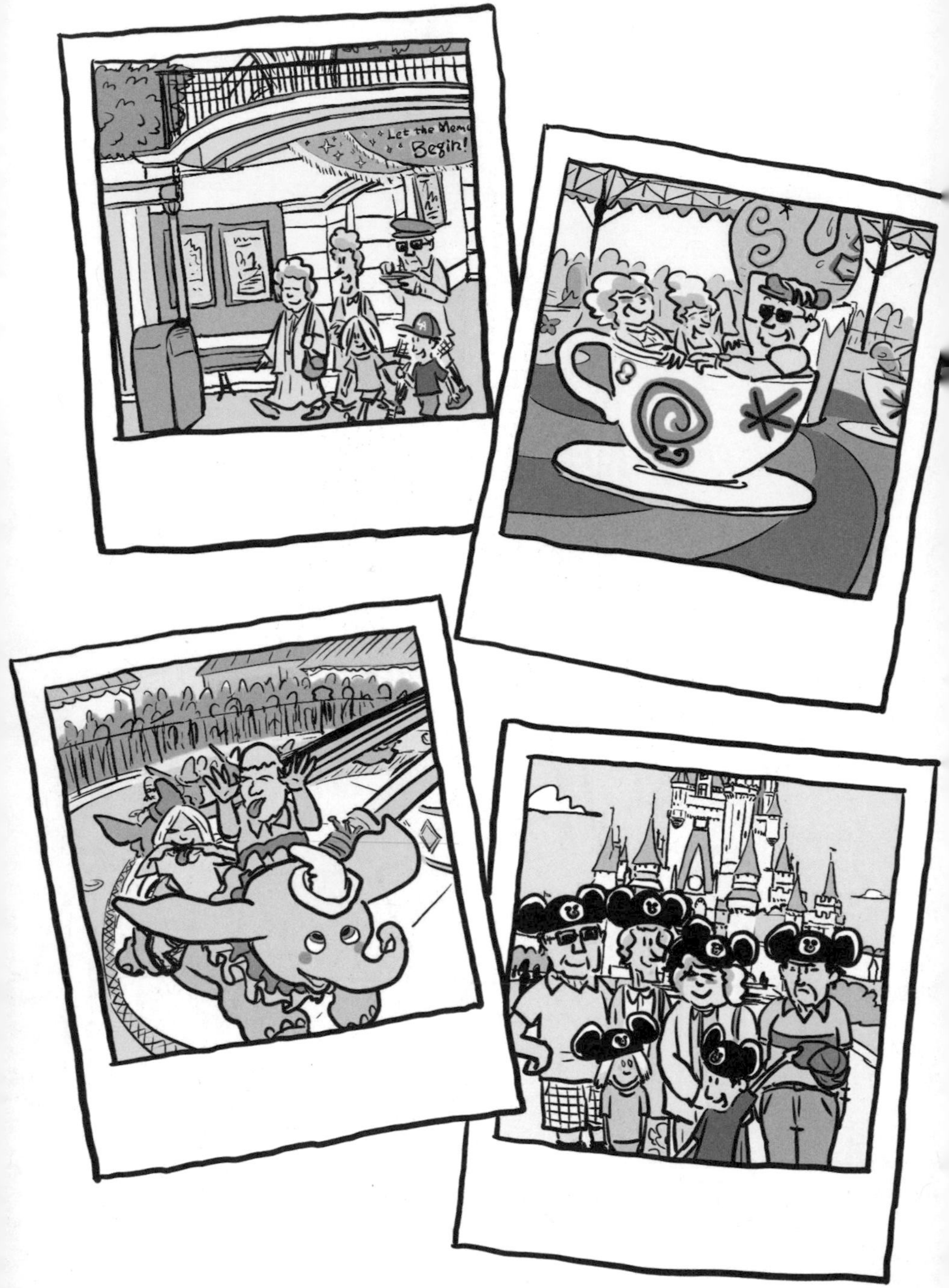
Let the
Begin!

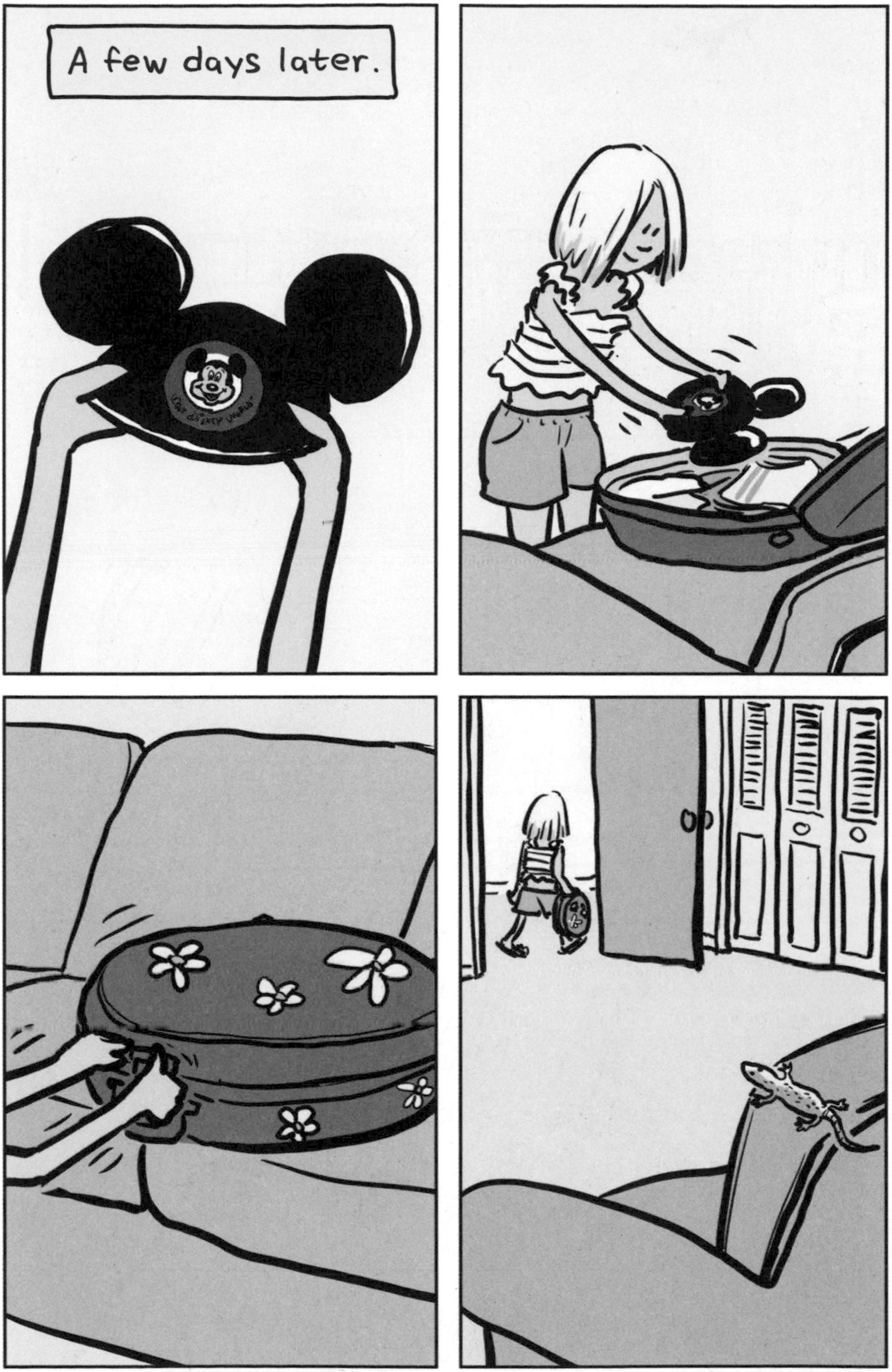
A few days later.

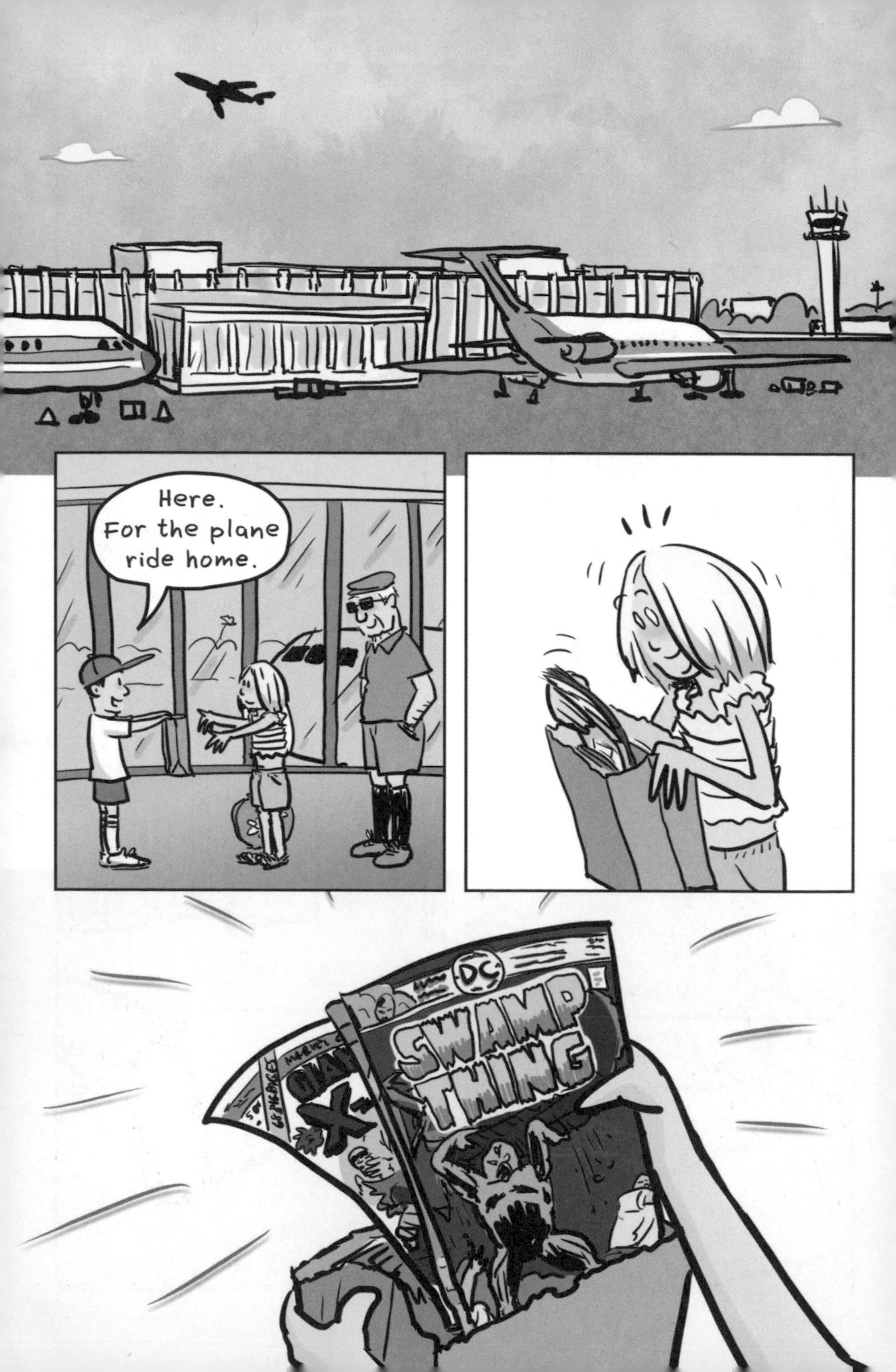
Here.
For the plane
ride home.
DC
SWAMP
THING

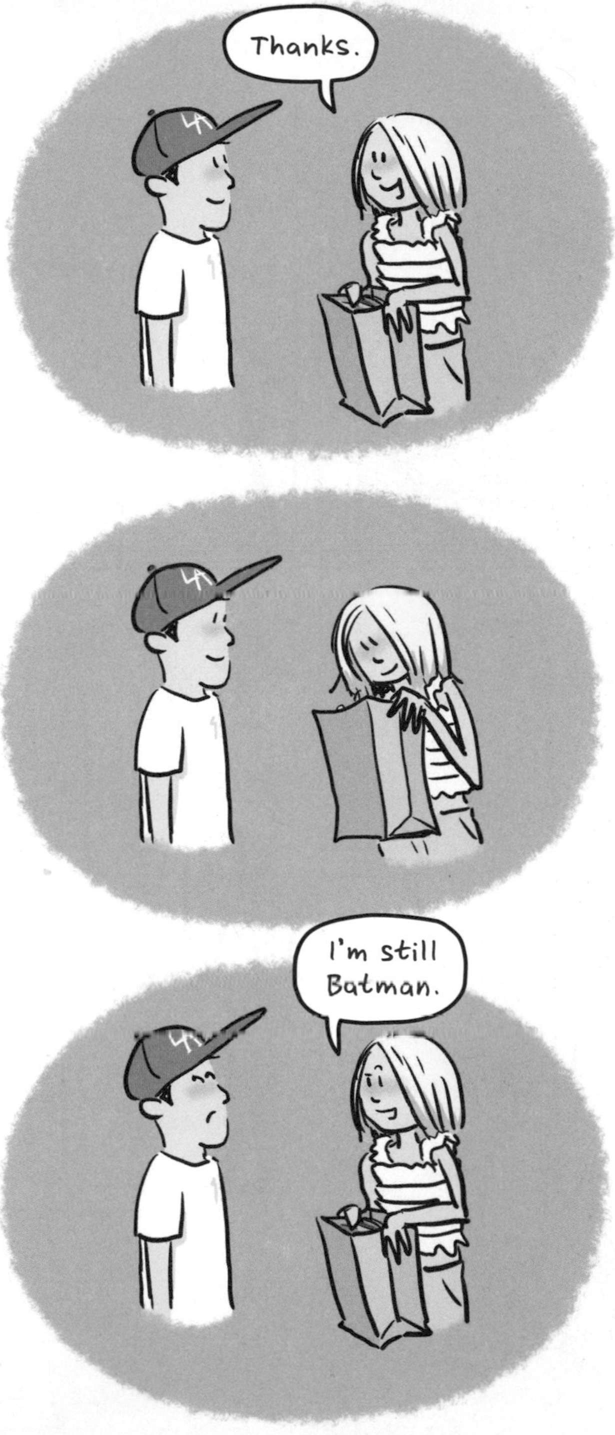
Thanks.
I'm still Batman.

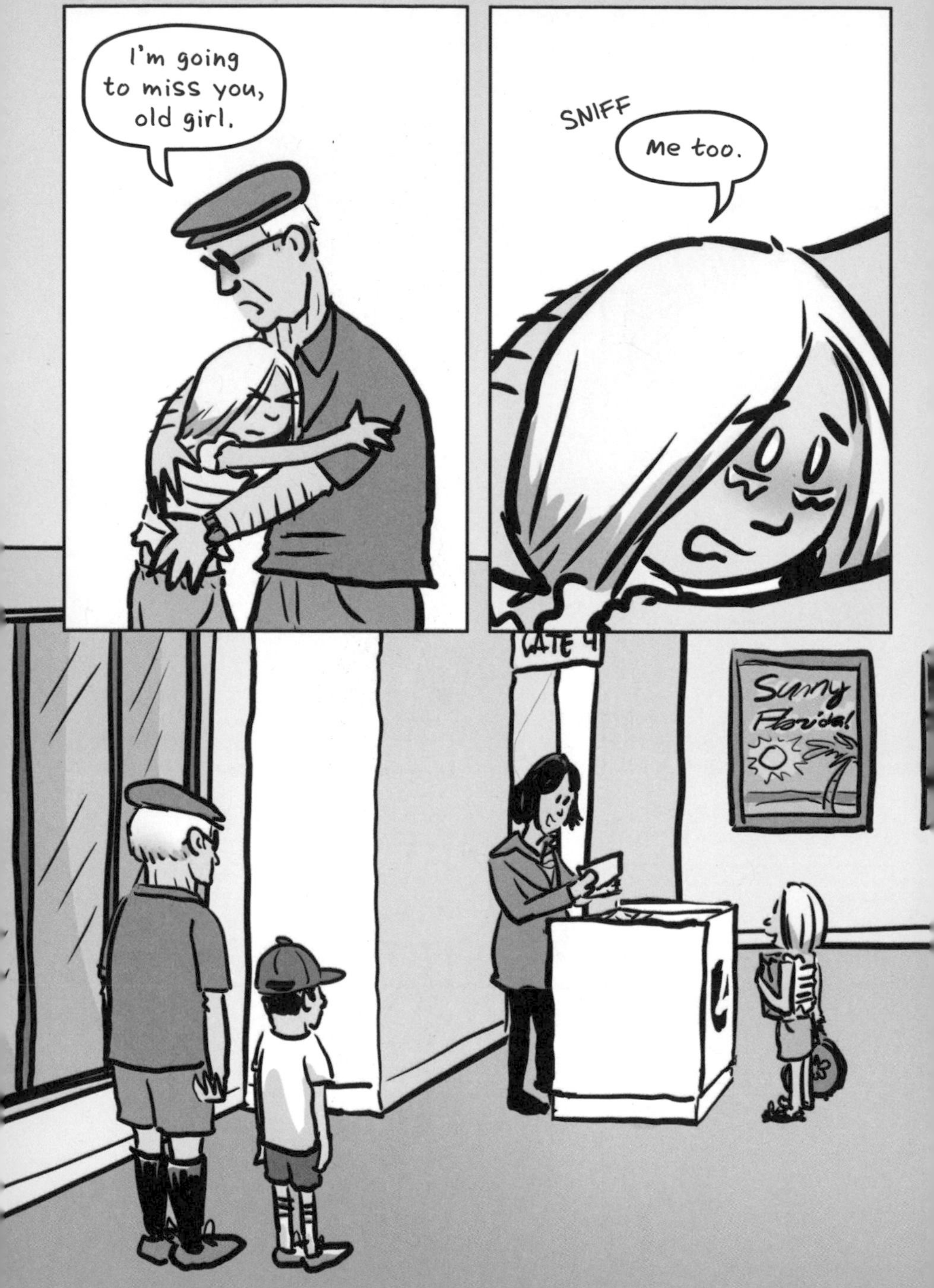
I'm going to miss you, old girl.
SNIFF
Me too.
GATE 4
Sunny Florida!

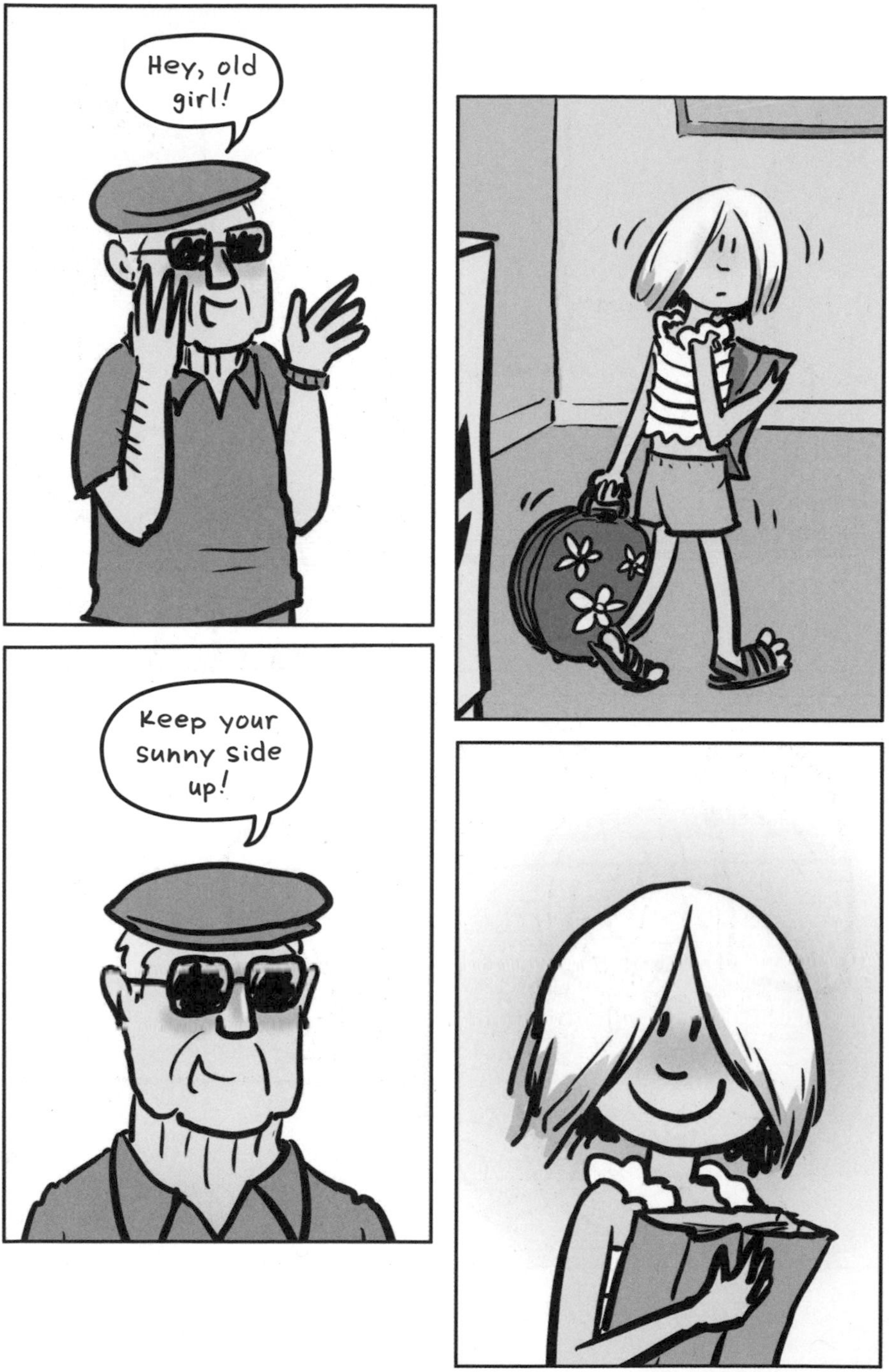
Hey, old girl!
Keep your sunny side up!

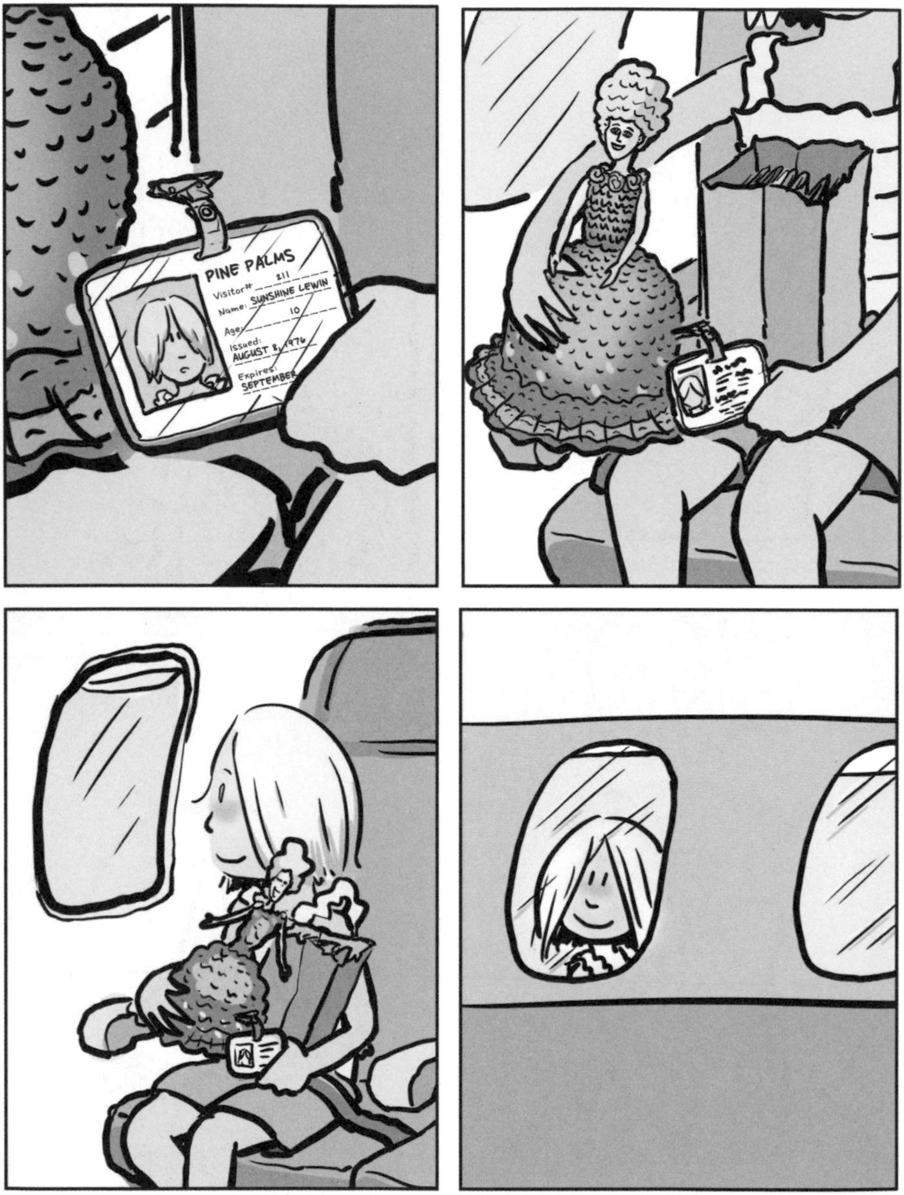
PINE PALMS
Visitor# 211
Name: SUNSHINE LEWIN
Age: 10
Issued: AUGUST 8, 1976
Expires: SEPTEMBER

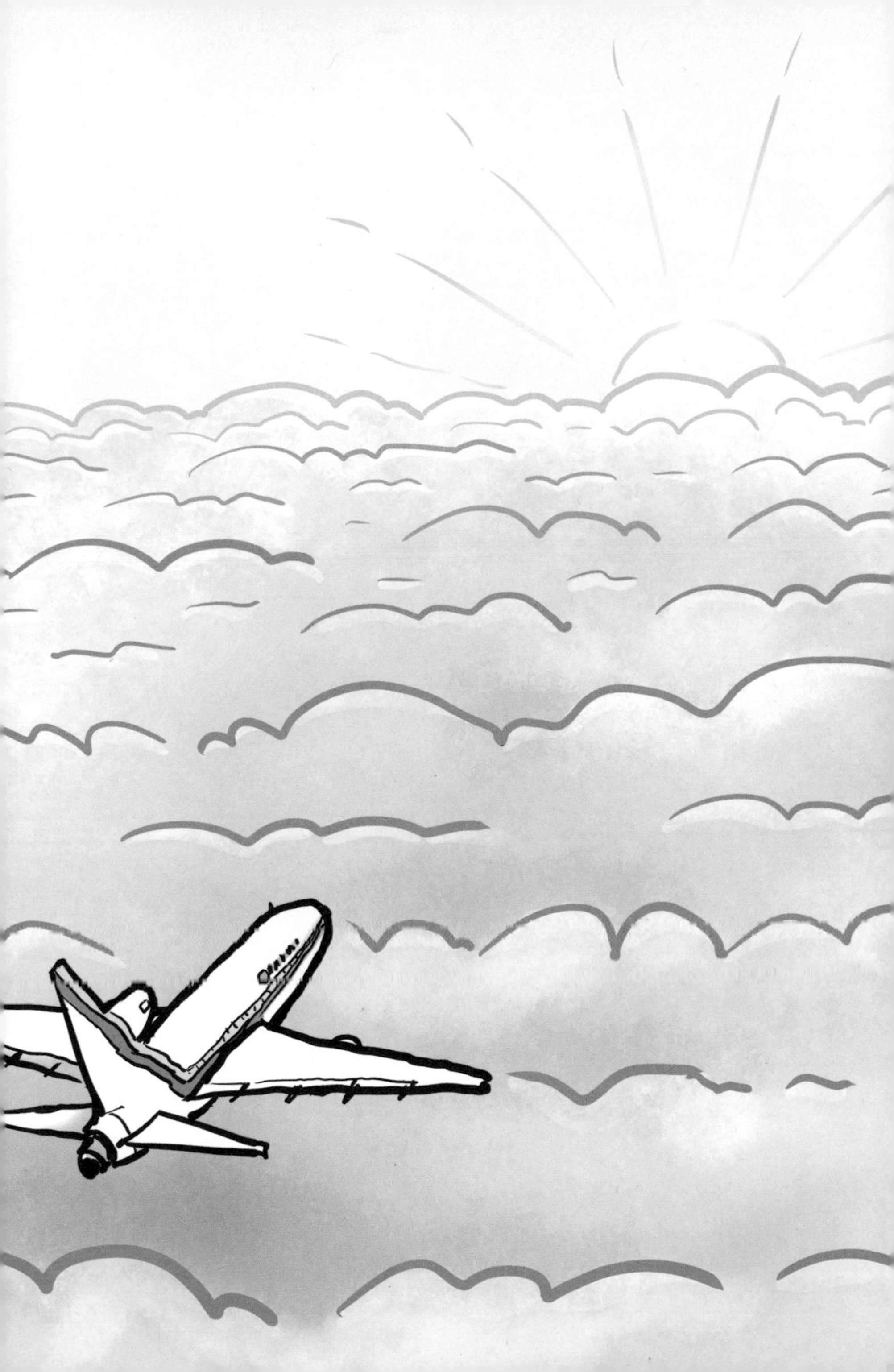

A NOTE FROM JENNIFER L. HOLM & MATTHEW HOLM

Sometimes it's hard to be a kid. It can be even harder when someone you love has a drug or alcohol abuse problem.

Like Sunny, we had a close relative who had serious issues with substance abuse. As children, we were bystanders to this behavior and yet it affected our whole world. It made us feel ashamed and embarrassed and scared and sad. Most of all, it was something that we felt we had to keep secret.

We wrote this book so that young readers who are facing these same problems today don't feel ashamed like we did. When someone in a family struggles with substance abuse, the whole family struggles. It's okay to feel sad and confused and to need some help. And it's definitely okay to talk about it.

If you find yourself in a situation like Sunny, don't be scared. Reach out to family members and teachers and school counselors. They'll be able to help you find the right resources so that you can keep your sunny side up.

ACKNOWLEDGMENTS

We would like to thank all the incredible people who helped Sunny find her way onto the page. With special thanks to David Levithan, Phil Falco, Lark Pien, Fawn Lau, Cyndi Koon, Ed Masessa, Sheila Marie Everett, Lizette Serrano, Elizabeth Krych, and Alexandria Terry. And for incredible encouragement, we are eternally grateful to Jill Grinberg, Shannon Rosa, Myly Posse, Larry Marder, and our readers everywhere.

JENNIFER L. HOLM & MATTHEW HOLM are the award-winning brother-sister team behind the Babymouse and Squish series. Jennifer is also the author of many acclaimed novels, including three Newbery Honor books and the NEW YORK TIMES bestseller THE FOURTEENTH GOLDFISH. SUNNY SIDE UP is a semi-autobiographical book inspired by their childhood.

LARK PIEN is an indie cartoonist from Oakland, California. She has published many comics and is the colorist for Printz Award winner AMERICAN BORN CHINESE, and BOXERS & SAINTS. Her characters Long Tail Kitty and Mr. Elephanter have been adapted into children's books. She holds the world's tiniest rainbow, which is way heavier than it looks. www.larkpien.blogspot.com